**The footsteps came closer,
halting perhaps six feet behind her. "I'm sorry."**

Well, that counted as something intelligent. "Sorry for what?" Lily asked, still not facing him. She brushed a portion of her horse's mane over to the other side of its neck.

"I'm sorry for making you upset or angry," he said. "How's that?"

Not precisely what she was looking for, but she'd take it. "All right." She twisted to face him, resting her elbow on the saddle.

"I think the problem has nothing to do with you—"

Finally.

"—but because Cecil doesn't regard me as true competition. Your grandfather would never accept my suit, even if it was real."

She should simply tell Mason that she had no interest in Cecil anymore. That there was no need for fake flirtation.

But when she opened her mouth, out came: "I'd say you're the best competition in camp." He went still.

She swallowed, then breathed, "Should we find out for certain?"

"How—" he started to say. But she bobbed up onto her toes, braced her hand on his shoulder, and pressed her mouth to his, shutting off any more words.

Sensation jolted through her. It was too much. She leaped back out of reach even as his arms started to come around her.

BADLANDS BRIDE

Adrianne Wood

POCKET BOOKS

New York   London   Toronto   Sydney   New Delhi

Pocket Books
A Division of Simon & Schuster, Inc.
1230 Avenue of the Americas
New York, NY 10020

This book is a work of fiction. Names, characters, places, and incidents either are products of the author's imagination or are used fictitiously. Any resemblance to actual events or locales or persons, living or dead, is entirely coincidental.

First Pocket Books paperback edition December 2012

POCKET and colophon are registered trademarks of Simon & Schuster, Inc.

For information about special discounts for bulk purchases, please contact Simon & Schuster Special Sales at 1-866-506-1949 or business@simonandschuster.com.

The Simon & Schuster Speakers Bureau can bring authors to your live event. For more information or to book an event, contact the Simon & Schuster Speakers Bureau at 1-866-248-3049 or visit our website at www.simonspeakers.com.

Designed by *Kyle Kabel*

Manufactured in the United States of America

10 9 8 7 6 5 4 3 2 1

ISBN 978-1-4516-9824-4
ISBN 978-1-4516-9826-8 (ebook)

To Kuo-Yu,
who's made so many of my dreams come true

Acknowledgments

Without the encouragement of friends and family, *Badlands Bride* never would have seen the light of day. Many thanks to Anthony Ziccardi, who took a chance on the book and helped it find a home at Pocket Books, to Abby Zidle for her enthusiasm and graceful editing, to Jenni Gaynor Smith for the initial edit and her insistence that I dive into the whole e-book "thing," and to Jose Trujillo for giving *Badlands Bride* it's first beautiful cover. Thanks also to Colleen Lindsay for her frank and spot-on advice on social media, and for always asking, "How's your writing going?" I'm so lucky to have parents who supported me every step of the way, even though I monopolized the family's only computer with my writing when I was a kid. I can only hope that I'll be as supportive of my daughter's crazy dreams as she grows up.

Chapter One

The scrap of red caught Mason Donnelly's eye again as his horse reached the base of the chalky Colorado hill.

Out here, where everything under the sky was the same uniform dusty olive color, the flash of scarlet would have grabbed the attention of a blind man.

Not that Mason was laying claim to any great amounts of perceptivity these days. *If I didn't know you better,* his editor had written about his last article, *I'd suspect you'd never been to that logging camp. There's an amazing lack of detail.*

Mason could have told him the real problem with the story: lack of interest. Instead, he'd asked for a few months off. With his editor's polite but thin assertion that he was still the best reporter in the West, his request had been granted with embarrassing speed.

Though the bone hunters' camp lay only fifty yards ahead, Mason heeled his horse into a trot. Maybe the jolting pace would knock these frustrating thoughts out of his head.

The bit of red disappeared again among the gray-green tents of the camp, but now he was close enough to this little oasis of civilization to pick out all kinds of colors, mostly from recently washed clothes hanging on lines strung between the tents. The colors were faded, of course. Nothing stayed bright very long out here in the relentless sun.

Maybe this visit wasn't the best idea in the world. Additional fading was the last thing he needed. He was only twenty-eight, but lately he felt twice that.

The tent town crouched by a squat ridge that looked like a line of stone vertebrae that had escaped from the spine of the Rockies. When he came within a dozen yards of the outermost tents, Mason turned his horse to circle the camp. The tent of Charles Bertrand Highfill, the expedition's financial backer, lay on the far side.

"Welcome back, Mr. Donnelly!" A bowlegged man appeared at Mason's knee, offering a hand.

Mason shook it. "Mr. Dickon." The other man's hand was as hard and weathered as a shovel blade. "It's good to see you again. Highfill been treating you well?"

"Never better. And we've been having a great season—the best one I've seen. We've been shipping box after box back east for the last three months. Good finds. No, I take that back: excellent finds. If you're looking for a good story, you've come to the right place."

The words would normally send his pulse into a gallop. Instead, interest percolated for an instant, then smoothed back out into apathy. "Maybe you can tell me about it later."

"I'd be happy to, if you stick around." Dickon cocked his head. "Highfill expecting you?"

"No. I was in the area, so . . ." Mason lifted one shoulder in a shrug. Hopefully Dickon wouldn't ask any more questions, because Mason really didn't have any more answers. Or any answers he wanted to give. The last thing he wanted to talk about was being on leave from the newspaper.

"Well, the old man will be glad to see you, invitation or no." Dickon picked up the speed of his stride, and Mason nudged his horse to match the man's pace.

Dickon's job was to catalogue and pack all the finds. He had worked in Highfill's Boston offices for two decades, but when his wife's death left him anchorless a few years earlier, Highfill had persuaded Dickon to go on his first fossil expedition out west. Dickon had been a mainstay of all the expeditions since then.

Mason said, "I wasn't sure I'd catch Mr. Highfill here, but I was hoping."

"Oh, the old man's always here," Dickon answered, chuckling. "If I didn't know better, I'd think he was hiding from a harpy of a wife back east."

Mason smiled. "If I had a harpy of a wife, I'd be hiding from her, too."

"How long are you planning on staying?"

"Not sure. No longer than a week." Assuming, of course, that Highfill let him stay. Mason believed the article he wrote last summer about Highfill's fossil hunters was fair, but the subjects of his articles often didn't see their portrayals the same way. He knew his story hadn't overflowed with flattery the way others about the wealthy businessman did. Heck, that was one reason why Mason had become so popular with readers. They knew he'd give the story to them straight. But stories like that also left him with a goodly number of people who, though not quite enemies, deliberately didn't remember him in their prayers at night.

He wasn't sure, then, why he'd come back here. Yet, he'd known he was coming back here as soon as he'd gotten off the train in Denver, his satchel in one hand, his hat in the other, and a million possibilities spread out before him.

"You remember where Mr. Highfill's tent is?" Dickon asked. "It's the big one right on the southern edge of town."

"Sure."

"I'd come with you, but I have a lazy assistant I have to keep a tough eye on." Dickon winked.

Mason nodded, though he wasn't sure what the joke was. "I'll stop by later. Maybe watch your assistant for you so that you can have a break."

Dickon chortled. "I hope you do. It's a painful job, that's for sure." Still laughing, the man gave Mason a little slap on the knee and disappeared into the maze of gray canvas tents.

When Mason had first visited the previous summer, he'd assumed all the tents housed people, and the size of this practically unknown excavation amazed him. It had taken him three days to realize that he was in the middle of a ghost town: Most of the tents held merely the bones of long-ago inhabitants.

Both embarrassed and annoyed—for the diggers

had considered Mason's assumption of a larger population quite a good gag—he had quickly come up with a way to tell the rubble-filled tents from the human-filled ones. Live humans dried their laundry on their tent ropes; dead prehistoric creatures did not.

Highfill's tent, the largest in the camp, had no laundry flapping from its guy lines. A very civilized clothesline set between two posts and sagging with shirts and pants was just one of the signs that Mason had reached the tent of the man who ran the expedition. The small hitching post out front and the corner of a woven rug sneaking out from underneath one of the tent walls were others.

Mason swung down from his horse and looped its reins over the hitching post. Two of the tent's sides had been rolled up to invite in any passing breeze, but etiquette dictated that Mason go to the "door" rather than saunter in through one of the open sides.

"Mr. Highfill," Mason called through the half-open door flap. "It's Mason Donnelly, just stopping by on my way through."

"On your way through to where, boy? Hell?" a loud voice demanded from the depths of the tent. "As far as I know, that's the only thing on the other side of that dang ridge." A big gnarled hand swept the flap open all the way, and Highfill beckoned Mason inside. "Come in, come in. Tell me what's going on in the world. We get the papers, of course, but Dickon is always stealing them away to wrap my bones in before I get a chance to read them."

A much more enthusiastic welcome than he'd dared

to hope for. Shoulders loosening with relief, Mason ducked into the tent.

Over six feet tall, Highfill looked like a snow-topped plinth. A very wealthy snow-topped plinth. His blue eyes focused with youthful intensity, denying the sixty years that his white hair and knobby knuckles signaled. Shaking his hand was like shaking hands with a boulder.

"Sit down." Highfill gestured toward a folding chair next to a table strewn with so many papers, a stray puff of air would create a small blizzard. Mason sat, careful not to disturb the precariously balanced piles, and stretched out his legs, wincing at the tenderness in his knees. He'd set his saddle's stirrup leathers too high and had been too lazy to fix them. His knees were now paying the price.

"I read the article you wrote about this operation," Highfill said, leaning back in his own chair. "My granddaughter clipped it from your paper and mailed it to me, along with a few choice words about you. I didn't appreciate being called a 'hands-off financier.'"

"You aren't out there digging, sir."

"True, but I'm here, aren't I? Better than those other fellows at their museums who simply have the bones shipped back to them. I'm *here*." He thumped the table with his fist.

One of the paper mountains shivered, spasmed, then avalanched. Mason grabbed at the pile, ending with half the stack clutched to his chest. The other half settled over the top of the desk in a gentle layer of white. Wonderful. Now there wasn't any spot where he could put the papers he held without launching another disaster. Maybe he could put the papers on another desk or table. He glanced around, but every flat surface in the tent was piled high with books, other papers, or chunks of rocks.

Apparently oblivious to Mason's predicament, the gentleman said, "Still, I thought it was a fair article. And great publicity, which I always appreciate."

"Thank you, sir."

"Here to write another one?"

"No, sir. Looking for a few days of relaxation, actually."

"Hmm. You're welcome to stay, of course."

"Thank you. I'd like that."

"It won't be relaxing, though. We're going to get mighty busy soon, as the season's coming to an end in a few weeks and we still have a lot of territory to excavate. I may even put you to work." Highfill chuckled. "Not that you'll stay until the end of the season. What did you tell me last time? Something about never stopping in one place for more than a handful of days?"

The swish of footsteps on carpet sounded behind him. Either someone didn't understand tent etiquette or felt himself at home enough to ignore it. "I hear this is the reporter fellow," a male voice said, a Boston accent smoothing the final *r*'s on his words into *ah*'s.

Moving quickly without appearing hasty, Mason got to his feet and turned to face the visitor. Too many travels through rough places and one nasty knife fight had left him with a six-inch-long scar on his shoulder blade and the habit of never turning his back on a stranger.

The lean, smartly dressed newcomer fixed Mason with light brown eyes. "Mick Donnelly, correct?"

"*Mason* Donnelly."

Highfill said, "Donnelly, this is Cecil St. John. He's helping Richter oversee everything."

His arms still full of papers, Mason nodded. "Good to meet you."

"You, too." St. John didn't bother to hold eye contact long enough to look sincere.

Settling into another chair without asking, St. John said, "Work went well today. We won't know what we've got until we sift through the piles, but I'm hopeful that something will turn up."

"A game of patience, this dig is," Highfill grunted. "Mason, why are you still standing up? And why are you hugging those drawings?"

Mason looked down. Yes, they were drawings. Drawings of bones. "Who did these? They're quite detailed." And far better than those he'd seen when he was here last year.

"Oh, those must be mine," St. John said, a modest smile touching his mouth. A shock of gingery hair fell across his eye, and he artfully flicked it away with one long finger.

Well, if they were his, then he could have them. Mason stepped forward, ready to dump the drawings into the younger man's lap, when Highfill said, "No, those are Lily's."

Mason stopped. "Lily?"

Highfill jumped to his feet. "Speak of the devil."

Still clutching the drawings to his heart like they were love letters, Mason turned.

A young woman stood in the tent entrance, the bright sunlight edging her silhouette in copper and making the fitted red jacket and matching scarf she wore wrapped around her hair look as bright as flames.

Aha. Mystery solved.

She stepped deeper into the tent and tugged off the scarf. No longer squinting against the sunlight, Mason could now see her more clearly. In her early twenties, perhaps, she walked toward Highfill with the confidence of a person who knew she'd be welcome. When she tossed a hank of honey-brown hair over her shoulder, she did it with a carelessness that contrasted with St. John's self-conscious deliberation.

"We've found something that Dickon thinks you should look at," she said to Highfill.

St. John sat up quickly. "What—" He cut himself off, glancing at Mason.

The girl gave Mason an uncertain look, but when no one explained who he was, she continued. "It was in a box of rubble we'd decided to sort through one more time."

Ah, so this was Dickon's lazy assistant. She wasn't a raving beauty, but with her big brown eyes and delicious figure, she was well worth a long look. Mason now understood Dickon's joke about the painful job of watching her. The sight of her would make any man's day a little bit brighter.

Whose wife was she? Single young ladies didn't

usually scrabble around for fossils lodged in cliff faces, and Mason doubted Highfill would allow such a pretty distraction on his expedition. Perhaps she was St. John's wife. Mason frowned. If so, hopefully her natural ease would rub off on him.

"Grandfather . . ." the girl said impatiently, propping one hand on her nicely shaped hip.

Good God, Highfill was her grandfather? She must be rich as a princess. Heck, as rich as four princesses.

A story idea began to form. *Boston Heiress Labors in Search for Prehistorical—*

"My drawings!" she cried.

Mason shook his head and brought his focus back to the present. The princess was staring at him in horror.

No, not at him. At the papers he held smashed to his chest.

Delicately plucking the drawings from his arms like a farm girl plucking eggs from beneath hens, she made little distressed noises under her breath.

Mason tried to explain. "They were falling off the table—"

"Don't worry," St. John cut in. He strode over, nudged her aside, grabbed the papers out of Mason's arms, and then threw them in a clump onto the table. The mass of drawings already residing on the table trembled but held firm.

At Mason's elbow, Highfill's granddaughter sighed with relief.

Then she looked up at him.

She had the roundest eyes he'd ever seen, making

her look perpetually astonished. Or perhaps she was simply astonished now at finding him so close.

"Hello," Mason said.

The princess turned her big eyes on her grandfather.

Ah, the rules of upper-crust society. She was waiting for Mason to be introduced to her. God forbid she actually say hello without knowing exactly who he was, despite the fact that he was standing in her grandfather's house. Or tent.

A familiar impatience began to simmer. This was why he stayed out of cities—especially eastern cities—as much as possible.

Highfill said, "Mason Donnelly, meet my granddaughter Lily Highfill. My eldest son's eldest daughter."

Eldest son's eldest daughter. Jesus, perhaps she was as wealthy as nine princesses. Though now that he could see her jacket up close, the collar and sleeves looked a little worn.

"Mason Donnelly, the journalist?" she asked.

He nodded.

"Pleased to meet you," she said, after a slight pause. She didn't sound pleased, though. Not a surprise, considering that she seemed to think he'd been mauling her drawings when she'd arrived. She narrowed her eyes at him.

He tried to assert his innocence again. "Your drawings were falling off the table, so I grabbed them—somewhat hastily, I admit—and tried to—"

"Lily, never mind about the silly drawings," St. John interrupted.

Lily stopped giving Mason a suspicious look and arched her eyebrows at St. John. "I beg your pardon?"

"Sorry, darling." He took her hand and started to lift it to his lips. Then he rubbed his thumb over her fingertips and frowned. "Your hands are getting rough. You're too delicate to be picking through rocks all day."

Delicate? As delicate as a bowie knife, he'd bet. Mason had to suppress a smile when she shifted her shoulders as if to pull away.

But then Lily looked at her hands clasped in St. John's. She lifted her gaze to the Bostonian's, and her indignant expression softened like butter at noontime. "I'll wear gloves next time."

Finally kissing her hand, Cecil St. John bestowed a smile on her.

Mason managed to turn away before he rolled his eyes. The mating dance of the wealthy. Few activities were more repulsive.

"Perhaps we should see what this fragile flower of womanhood has come to tell us about, eh?" Highfill suggested to St. John, his voice containing the barest hint of mockery. "Lily, sweetheart, while we're talking to Dickon, would you show Mr. Donnelly around and find him a spare tent?"

Her face fell, though whether at the chore of attending to him, at being excluded from examination of the discovery, or at being banished from the side of her precious St. John, Mason couldn't tell.

"I can find an empty tent for myself," Mason said.

"No, no," St. John said. "Lily should be acting like a hostess instead of a rock picker."

For the barest moment, Mason thought she was going to object. She didn't, but she didn't agree with St. John's statement, either, instead turning to the drawings on the table and shuffling them into some sort of order.

"Supper's an hour before dusk," Highfill said to Mason, then slapped his hat on his head and exited.

St. John began to follow, but paused. "Lily has never been west of the Rockies," he told Mason with a smugness that proclaimed that he himself had. "Perhaps you can tell her of the wild sights you've seen. Lily adores stories of adventure."

"Sure," Mason drawled. "I'll show her a good time."

Mistrust flickered over the Bostonian's face. He nodded once, then ducked through the tent opening.

Mason watched as the girl's gaze tracked St. John until he was out of sight. Lovesickness had obviously turned her brain if she found St. John's condescension attractive.

Finally she turned her big dark eyes on him. "Shall we go?" she asked. Without her grandfather or St. John talking over her, Mason could hear how her voice sometimes rose into a squeak. It was strangely endearing. He suddenly had the urge to pat her on the head, as if she were a kitten.

"Lead the way," he said, sweeping his arm out.

She pivoted and headed for the tent flap.

Mason's mouth went dry. Without a doubt, she possessed the finest rear end he had ever had the luck to lay eyes on. Somehow both luscious and pert, it made his pulse hammer in his ears.

Disquiet crept through him as he forced his feet to move. The next few days were going to be awkward if he couldn't avoid swiveling his head to follow her every movement. Highfill was apparently happy to have him stay, but his hospitality would not stretch to ignoring Mason ogling his granddaughter's backside.

He might do it when only St. John was around, though. It was obvious the man considered Lily his personal property. And St. John's smooth feathers could use a good ruffling.

Speeding his steps, Mason caught up to Lily outside the tent. If he wanted to conduct any sort of coherent conversation, it would be better to walk beside her instead of behind her.

"Since you're going to be here overnight, we should turn your horse into the corral," Lily said, undoing his horse's reins from the hitching post. She kept hold of them as they walked to the corral, leaving Mason with nothing to do and feeling rather useless.

Well, he could tell her stories, as St. John had suggested. He used to be rather good at it. "What sort of stories do you want to hear?" he asked. "Railroad towns, Indian raids, deadly blizzards, gold strikes—"

"I'm twenty-two years old, Mr. Donnelly, not twelve. I've lived in Denver for the past eight years, so I've heard plenty of stories of that sort and lived through my share of blizzards. What I *would* like to hear about is why you've come back here after writing such an article about my grandfather."

So the big-eyed kitten knew how to use her pretty white teeth. Good—this was going to be more interesting than telling blizzard stories. "What do you mean, 'such an article'?" Hopefully she wouldn't notice that he hadn't answered her question about why he was there.

She turned her head to look at him fully, and her red scarf fluttered with the movement. She frowned. "You made him sound selfish."

"I did?" Mason cast his thoughts back. He'd written the article nearly a year ago, and perhaps twenty others since, so his recollection of his exact words was unclear. "Before you arrived, your grandfather told me that he thought the story fair."

The girl let out a very unprincess-like snort. "I love him dearly, but Grandfather can be overly generous."

They entered the corral, and Mason didn't have to answer for the next several minutes. He unsaddled the beast and removed his blanket roll and saddlebags. Swinging the saddlebags over his shoulder, he ushered Lily through the corral gate and got another eyeful of her backside. God, just lovely. He rolled his tongue back up into his mouth and resumed his position at her side as they weaved their way into the tent settlement.

"Do you have a copy of the article?" he asked. "I'd like to see it again, refresh my memory."

"It's in my room," she replied.

"In your tent?"

"No, in Milton, the town a few miles to the west."

Mason stared at her. "You stay in town, not here?"

She nodded.

For a moment, her feisty defense of her grandfather had sparked admiration in him. But this new revelation squashed that admiration pretty fast. "The accommodations are better there?" he asked, careful to keep his voice expressionless.

She nodded again. "Hot water whenever I want it and a lovely breakfast. Grandfather—and St. John—prefer that I stay at the hotel. Some nights I stay here, though."

At St. John's preference as well? Mason wanted to ask. But he bit down on the caustic question. Her infatuation with the man was none of his concern. That was her grandfather's headache to deal with.

Still, he couldn't resist seeing how much Highfill and St. John coddled her. "Do you ride back and forth alone, or does someone escort you?" A seasoned woman would not give a thought to riding a few miles alone.

"I have an escort."

She must have caught something revealing in his expression, for her big eyes narrowed. "Do you consider me ridiculous as well, Mr. Donnelly?"

Mason met her gaze directly. "I don't consider your grandfather ridiculous, Miss Highfill. I respect him, in fact, and what he's doing here. I hope tomorrow you and I will have the chance to look at the article I wrote, and I hope that I conveyed that respect in the article, not an opinion of ridiculousness." He rubbed his hand over his chin. "As for you . . ."

He paused, savoring the sudden uncertainty in her eyes.

"I haven't made up my mind," he concluded abruptly. "First impressions are never the whole story."

Not only was that true, but if she actually thought about it, it might leave her wondering exactly what his first impressions of her were.

The princess pressed her lips together. "I see."

And she probably did, too. She wasn't an idiot— even if she allowed Cecil St. John to treat her like one.

A stray breeze caught the tail of her red scarf, sending it streaming toward him, tickling his cheek with a silken kiss. She swept it back into place with an impatient hand just as he reached up to flick the material away. Their knuckles collided.

She yelped. Instinctively Mason cupped her assaulted hand in his own. Lifting her hand closer to his face, he tried to examine it for any damage.

"Mr. Donnelly," she said in a dangerous voice, "if you attempt to kiss my hand, I will likely punch you in the nose."

Mason dropped her hand. She wasn't a princess; she was a porcupine. "The thought never crossed my mind. I wanted to see how rough your delicate hands really are."

"My hands are still smooth," she said, but she hid them behind her back.

He wanted to laugh. If he were here to write an article, he'd be sure to include her in it: the Highfill heiress with rough hands who threatened to brawl with him like a miner.

She halted abruptly. "This tent is empty. Good evening, Mr. Donnelly."

"You aren't coming to supper tonight?"

"You'll be there?" She smiled sweetly. "Suddenly my appetite is off."

This time he did laugh. The smug St. John was going to have his hands full with this one. "Good night, Miss Highfill."

As she turned away, sunlight spotlighted her red jacket and scarf again. He'd seen all sorts of reds during his travels crisscrossing this sprawling country: the dusky red of rocks in Utah Territory; the bright red that Chinese immigrants living in San Francisco considered lucky; the lurid purplish red of a sunset after a summer thunderstorm had strode across the wide Wyoming sky, leaving tattered clouds crumpled in its wake . . .

Yes, he'd seen plenty of reds. But this one was a color that he couldn't quite define or compare to anything else.

A little bit like the girl who wore it, maybe.

Her chin high and her back straight as a railroad tie, she marched away, the picture of righteous indignation. Then a breeze off the hills smoothed her skirt against her lovely backside.

Mason's smile widened. She didn't like him. Ah, well. At least that would leave him with the frequent pleasure of watching her stalk off.

Chapter Two

Ladies never stomp, Lily imagined her mother admonishing her as she stomped away. Wrapped up in her fuming, she caught her toe on one of the many tent lines that crisscrossed the ground like a loom. She stumbled, but luckily no wild arm windmilling was needed to regain her balance. She didn't need additional reasons to look ridiculous today. Catching her breath, she continued, this time being more careful about where she stomped. She refused to look back to see if Mason Donnelly was watching her. Or laughing at her.

Ladies stomp, she silently replied to her mother, *when the situation demands it.* And this situation certainly demanded it. She privately thought that this situation demanded that she stomp on Donnelly's foot rather than stomp away, but she knew for certain that that action went beyond the pale.

Though what did it matter? She already had little hope of measuring up to her mother's expectations of ladylike behavior.

As soon as she had swept imperiously around a corner and out of Donnelly's sight, she let her shoulders curve and her footsteps drag.

Cecil's words echoed in her mind: "Lily should be acting like a hostess instead of a rock picker." Clearly Cecil St. John and her mother had similar thoughts about the importance of ladylike behavior. Perhaps that explained why they had gotten along so well when her mother had met Cecil in Boston before he and her grandfather had traveled out to Colorado this summer.

Lily touched her pocket, and the letter there made a crinkling noise. Pulling the letter free, she read the gorgeously loopy script again.

Darling Lily,

We're awaiting your return home with great anticipation. Mr. Grant already has spoken about you in glowing terms to several young men, who are now just as eager as we for your arrival.

But of course you know that we have high hopes for Cecil St. John. We've known his family forever, and he's such a nice gentleman! He's written several letters to me already, praising you in each one.

Remember your manners, darling.

Love,
Mama

A loving note, as all her mother's weekly letters were. She didn't know quite why it made her heart hurt to read it, but it might have had something to do with the final line, which her mother always used as her closing. Her mother considered anything west of the Mississippi the wilderness, full of savages who undoubtedly didn't know anything about such important matters as when the proper time was to wear gloves (always) and how to correctly ask a lady to dance. It was Lily's duty to remember her gentle upbringing and to bring manners to an uncivilized world.

And she'd tried. Upon being shipped out to Denver eight years ago to stay with Aunt Evaline, her father's sister, Lily had done her very best to mind her manners, guided by weekly missives from her mother on what to do and what not to do. Stomping had been a subject thoroughly covered early on. After her mother had doffed her black mourning attire and begun smiling at other gentlemen, Lily had made her displeasure known by stomping about (and lying and throwing tantrums). That conduct had led to her temporary exile to Colorado, so her mother's concentration on that aspect of her bratty behavior made a great deal of sense.

Armed with her mother's instructions and desperate to be returned to her family, Lily reread her mother's letters like they were scripture and had obeyed the strict rules of ladylike behavior. For one year.

After one year, her aunt shook her head, told Lily to stop being so starchy-spined and hoity-toity, and insisted that she have fun and make friends.

Since then, she had lost her manners bit by bit.

Lily folded the letter back up and placed it in her pocket.

She had returned only once to Boston, when she was seventeen, for her mother's wedding to William Silas Grant. She'd almost—*almost*—stopped hoping for another invitation to return to her family when one had arrived at the beginning of the summer. Her mother hadn't made clear whether she expected Lily to stay in Boston for good or to return to Denver at some undetermined time, but her none-too-subtle hints about young men and about Cecil's eligibility in particular showed that she was retaking the reins of motherhood with a vengeance, her eye bent on Lily marrying well.

Lily slowed as she turned the final corner before Dickon's large tent. Two sides of the tent were rolled up to invite in breezes, and she saw Dickon, her grandfather, and Cecil gathered around the large worktable in the front. Cecil looked like a golden jaguar next to two old tomcats.

Cecil: clearly her mother's favorite. And he'd been Lily's favorite, too . . . until he'd commented on her rough hands in front of a stranger today. She ground her teeth together. When she'd first arrived at camp, Cecil had been as charming and witty and cultured as she had imagined the young bluebloods of Boston should be. And he'd paid her particular attention, escorting her back to Milton at night and giving her kisses and sweet words at the foot of the boarding-house stairs. But his attention had begun to flag recently. Undoubtedly her rough hands weren't helping her keep his interest.

With a sigh, Lily looked at her palms. Despite her

words to Mason Donnelly, they weren't as smooth as a true lady's would be. She hardly ever wore gloves, even when she and Dickon were pawing through piles of rocks, looking for fossil fragments the diggers had missed. And ink stains, which ruined her hands even more, weren't an uncommon side effect of sketching fossils.

Gloves. She must remember to wear gloves tomorrow.

"You're a marvel, my girl," her grandfather declared when she stepped into the tent. "A great find—a great find!"

Surely the ability to find fossils in rubble was more important than having smooth hands? Lily glanced at Cecil to see how impressed he was, but he wasn't even looking at her.

"It's some kind of horn, isn't it?" she said, moving to her grandfather's elbow to gaze at the fossil he cradled in his hand. She reached out and touched the horn with a fingertip. Then she snatched her hand back before Cecil could again comment on its callused state.

"Ah, but from what?" Cecil asked. His fingers, clutching a charcoal stick, were flying over a sheet of paper as he dashed off a quick sketch. A sketch that didn't approach her worst efforts, she decided. If Dickon let her, she'd take the horn back to Milton with her tonight and do a proper one.

"Well, a dinosaur, I thought."

"See?" her grandfather said, slapping Cecil on the shoulder, making him scratch a heavy black line across the paper. "Exactly what I said."

"Too soon to know," Cecil said repressively. "Far too soon. An expert needs to look at it more closely. It could be from an old bison."

"Well, son, that's what you're here for, isn't it?" her grandfather said. "Look away. Look at it all night, if you like."

If Cecil studied the horn all night, she wouldn't get a chance to sketch it—and wouldn't be escorted back to Milton by Cecil. She cleared her throat. "Can it wait an hour or so? Cecil, I'd hoped you might take me back to Milton tonight."

"Someone else will have to. This is more important."

Lily flushed and shuffled a half step back. He must not realize how dismissive he sounded. Though of course this find was important. Perhaps even the most important find of the season, if it was indeed from a dinosaur no one had found before.

Cecil had taken the horn from her grandfather and was turning it over in his hands. He looked up at her again. "I would like you to ride with me tomorrow to the dig."

Her heart began pitter-pattering like a silly little thing.

"You obviously have the devil's own luck," Cecil continued. "Perhaps we'll uncover something worthwhile if you are about."

Did he expect her to simply sit on a horse and direct lucky thoughts at the cliff face the diggers were currently searching? Her heart resumed its natural rhythm, though it gave a half-dejected, half-angry *bump-bump-bump* every so often.

"Lily has a good eye," Dickon said to Cecil, "so as soon as you're done with her, I'd like her back."

Lily sent Dickon a smile.

"You're right, of course," Cecil said briskly. "I almost forgot that credit for the find goes to you, Lily. Good girl. I'll make a note of it."

"And I'll take you home," Dickon said to her.

"I had hoped to go now, if that's all right," she said.

"Why doesn't Donnelly take you back to town?" her grandfather asked.

"No, unfortunately that won't work," Lily said, hearing tension creep into her voice. If she had to face Mason Donnelly's sneer again today, she'd either expire with anger or outright kill him. And since she didn't enjoy the thought of dying young, and ladies never killed, she thought it best that she stay out of his presence. "I just left him and he, uh, said he was going to rest," she lied.

Mason Donnelly entered the tent and surveyed the crowd. "Is this a private party?"

Lily's stomach curled like a dying snail.

Perhaps he sneered only when they were alone, for the expression on his face now was of clean curiosity. He nodded to her as he approached. Then his gaze slid to a spot close behind her for a moment before he fastened it on the object in Cecil's hand. "What's that?"

Lily surreptitiously swiped her hand across her bottom. Maybe she had dust or dirt clinging to her. Or a large blotch of ink. Just one more hideous embarrassment to try to live through today.

"We're not sure yet," her grandfather replied. "What do you think it looks like?"

Mason cocked his head and studied the fossil. "Like a rock," he said. He shrugged. "I could never get the hang of seeing what you see."

"Since you're little help here," Highfill said, chuckling, "make yourself useful and take my granddaughter home, will you? Won't take more than an hour."

Lily thought fast. If she changed her mind and stayed for supper, maybe she could shake Mason from her skirts and find another escort. Maybe Cecil would reconsider by then. "I wouldn't want to put you out," she told Mason, staring at his left cheekbone so she wouldn't have to look him in the eye. He could sneer with just those Prussian blue eyes of his, she knew. "I'm reconsidering remaining for supper."

"Pshaw," her grandfather said. "Just go. The sooner you leave, the sooner you'll be home."

Lily looked at Cecil, hoping for some kind of intervention from him, but he was peering at the horn and paying no attention to the conversation.

Mason was typically blunt. "If you don't wish for me to take you, all you have to do is say so."

Lily opened her mouth to do just that when one of her mother's guidelines sprang to mind: *A lady never argues in front of others*.

She shut her mouth and swallowed her words. However, she just couldn't make herself be so mannerly—as a good hostess would—as to flatter Donnelly with simpering cries of delight at the prospect of riding with him.

This was just one reason why she was afraid she could never shoehorn herself back into Boston society. The essential skills of flattery—and of charming dissimulation—had never taken hold.

Everyone was waiting for her reply. "Thank you," she finally said.

And that was that.

Her grandfather and Dickon bent over the horn again, nearly knocking heads in the process, and Cecil began pointing out the various shapes that suggested this was indeed a dinosaur remnant. Lily hovered, soaking in every word, until her grandfather saw her and said, "Off!"

Mason bowed her through the door. For a lout, he had a nice bow. She wondered where he'd picked that up in his travels.

But she swore she could feel his eyes on her backside again as she exited. As soon as he drew abreast of her, she very casually brushed her hand across her rear end again, but she couldn't feel anything that might have attracted his notice. Lord, it was probably an ink stain, then. She'd already ruined two skirts and one shirt this summer with her carelessness with ink.

He chuckled and said, "Now that we're alone—"

Lily stiffened. Would he begin with his snide remarks immediately?

"—you can tell me to go to the devil, if you like. I'm sure we can rustle up someone else to take you."

Oh. The twinkle in his eyes encouraged her to share his amusement, and she let some of the starch seep out of her spine. "If you don't mind taking me—and if you refrain from taunting me—I'm sure we'll scrape along just fine."

"I'll refrain from taunting you," Mason said after a moment, "if you'll refrain from attacking the pieces I've written."

She had forgotten about that. Her cheeks prickled with heat. "Sounds fair."

They managed to saddle their horses without too much rancor, though even to herself Lily had sounded a bit snappish when she had refused Mason's offer to do both her horse and his. When Cecil escorted her home, she always let him saddle her horse without demur. Mason's critical gaze put her back up, made her want to show she was strong instead of act the frail maiden.

The silence that stretched between them was jagged, uncomfortable, but Lily feared words would be even more harmful. Finally she cleared her throat. "How long do you plan to stay?" An innocuous question, she thought.

He grinned. "Already anticipating my departure?"

She gritted her teeth. He was like a cheeky schoolboy. As a teacher in Denver, she'd dealt with plenty of those.

"Mr. Donnelly." She waited until he looked at her, and then waited a beat more for his attention to truly focus. "I was making a pleasant inquiry. It would be polite if you made a pleasant response."

He grimaced, just as her schoolboys did. But this schoolboy continued to talk back. "If you want windy conversation about things of no matter, you'd be better off talking to someone else."

"Ah. Forgive me for boring you." First this man wrote snide things about her grandfather; then he made her regress ten years. She'd been doing an excellent job at being well-mannered until he'd shown up. His being here couldn't lead to any good.

Or maybe it could. A terrible, brilliant idea was taking shape in the back of her mind.

Mason tugged down the brim of his hat to shield his eyes from the swiftly dropping sun. "How long have you been out on the dig?"

"Three months."

"Really? You seem to know a lot for someone who's been here for only three months."

Pleasure unfurled in her chest. "Dickon is a very good teacher."

"And I think he likes teaching you," Mason said. The corner of his mouth quirked up, causing a tickle of suspicion, but before she could do more than frown, he said, "And do you like it?"

"Oh, enormously. The whole mystery behind the science is fascinating. We find shells and such out here, in the mountains, so far from any ocean. Why? It makes your head spin to realize how much we still don't know." She realized she'd been gesturing as she spoke, and she forced herself to be still. Ladies never waved their arms around in excitement.

"And what do you like best about it?"

"Sketching the fossils." And sketching the creatures she imagined they came from. And sketching Dickon as he squinted at a rock, his mouth pursed, and her grandfather as he sat by the morning fire, joking with the diggers.

"Is that your job here? St. John seemed to think he did most of the drawings."

She shrugged, a compromise between admitting that drawing the fossils wasn't her job and pointing out that her sketches were far better than Cecil's.

"And what exactly does Cecil St. John do here?"

"He's our expert. Did you meet Richter last time?"

Mason nodded.

"Then you know Richter is in charge of the dig as a whole, but he concentrates more on logistics than the science. St. John studies the bones. He's quite important, actually, in the geology field. As well-known in his field as you are in yours." A little bit of a compliment to soften him up. Now for her real concern. "Why are you here?"

"I enjoyed being here last time, so I decided to return."

"That's it?"

An expression she couldn't read tightened the skin around his eyes, but then he laughed. "That's it. I'm like a tumbleweed, going where the wind—or impulse—takes me. Can't remember the last time I stayed in one place for more than a week. Would anyone mind if I visited the dig site tomorrow?"

Lily blinked at the subject change. "No, I wouldn't think so. Please come."

The scheme that had begun to form hazily in her mind now sharpened. She doubted that Cecil would appreciate Mason accompanying them—even when they tried to hide their dislike for each other, men tended to be very obvious about that sort of thing—but Mason's ignorance about fossils would provide an excellent opportunity for her to display her knowledge. After Cecil realized how much she knew, surely he would be less dismissive of her work.

And . . . She eyed Mason speculatively. He was facing straight ahead, his eyes distant as he wandered through his own thoughts, giving her time to study him.

He was good-looking—when he wasn't laughing at her. In her grandfather's tent, when she'd really noticed him for the first time, her heart had hiccuped in her chest. Smoothly trimmed dark hair, eyes the blue of the sky when dusk turned to night, a rugged nose and chin, and lips that had snared her attention—

She gave herself a shake. Really, it didn't matter what his lips looked like. She couldn't say she cared for what came out when he flapped them at her.

However, Cecil wasn't blind. Mason Donnelly was a handsome man.

And therefore competition.

She'd seen it a thousand times in her schoolboys: males didn't back down from a rivalry. A little flirtation with Donnelly—while Cecil was nearby, of course—would make Cecil take notice and, hopefully, spur him into truly wooing her.

She'd been waiting for three months for him to move beyond occasional kisses to a more tender declaration. Now she would be leaving for Boston in only two weeks. Lily set her shoulders. If Cecil wanted her, he was going to have to win her.

"Mr. Donnelly." Her stomach did a little flip when he settled his gorgeous blue eyes on her. But she soldiered on. "May I flirt with you?"

Chapter Three

He should have said no.

Mason nudged his heels into his horse's ribs, provoking an overly dramatic wheeze from the beast, and followed Cecil St. John and Lily through a bottlenecked canyon. The girl was babbling away like she'd been snowed in all winter and had just met the first person who'd come through after the thaw. To his credit, St. John managed to keep an interested expression on his face. Mason felt a rush of pride at knowing that he'd been responsible for the turnabout in the Bostonian's attitude—and a wagonload of ill humor.

St. John twisted in his saddle to look back at him. "Still with us?"

Annoyance flashed. Mason was only thirty feet behind, hardly in the next county, and he had dropped back that far to give Lily a chance to work her wiles. Since St. John was sending him a contemptuous look that was at odds with his overly genial question, Mason guessed the man was trying to show Lily just how pathetic her other suitor was. Or maybe St. John simply disliked Mason as much as Mason disliked him.

"Just fine, old man," Mason replied, echoing St. John's false heartiness. "Just fine."

This was why he should have declined the princess's suggestion that he play Prince Charming. He'd come to the bone hunters' camp to get a grip on his writing, not to exchange sniping remarks with an overbred Bostonian. This recipe for entrapment that Lily had cooked up would throw him and St. John together more often than Mason liked.

He wasn't exactly sure why he'd said yes in the first place. Perhaps it was the way the princess had laid out her proposal. She'd tried to stare him in the eye as she spoke, but her entire face had turned the color of a tomato, and she was so desperate to get her proposition over with that she ran her final sentence together into one long, strange word: "Sowillyouhelpme?"

Perhaps it was because she'd been determined not to let her embarrassment stop her, or because he'd never had a wealthy eastern socialite ask him a favor. In any case, with no story to write, nowhere to go, and no other form of entertainment at hand, he'd finally said, "All right."

Today she wore over her hair a yellow scarf bright as a corncob. She looked like a very feminine pirate bent on pillaging the heart of the man riding beside her.

Upon waking this morning, Mason had had his doubts about whether her plan would work. He didn't any longer. When the three had met at the corral, he'd tipped his hat and given her a slow, appreciative survey that had made St. John scowl. Astonishment had crossed Lily's face, making her wide eyes widen even more, and then she recovered, apparently remembering her scheme. "Mr. Donnelly," she practically squealed, "I'm so happy you're joining us today."

And she *had* looked so happy, so utterly delighted, that Mason had felt his blood surge despite knowing this was all a sham.

Mason's horse stumbled, bringing his gaze up to his surroundings. A canyon had opened up before the three riders, and they approached the dig, where all the heavy work was being done.

The terrain was so rough here that it was almost impossible to tell the untouched cliff walls from the walls that had been scraped for fossils. Ten shirtless men wielding tools ranging from pickaxes to crowbars to small shovels were boring into the rock. Another group of men were wrapping large bones, some of them ten feet long, in burlap to cushion their trip back to camp. Still others sorted through the debris, piling the more promising-looking stones into small wagons. It was this debris that Dickon and Lily pored over later, Mason had been told.

And over all these activities ruled Richter, a balding man with a long torso that made his legs look shorter than they were. He used his legs to good effect, though, bounding toward them over rocks like a billy goat as soon as one of the sorters drew his attention to the mounted party. The rest of the men broke off from their work long enough to pull their discarded shirts over their heads. A digger glanced up at the sun, wiped his forehead, and sent a grimace Lily's way.

She appeared to be concentrating her full attention on Cecil St. John's blathering, but her smile slid south, and she whisked her eyes over at the disgruntled digger a few moments later. Hmm. She was more aware of what was going on outside her giddy little bubble than Mason had supposed.

"Miss Highfill!" Richter exclaimed, leaping to her side and holding her horse's head as she dismounted. "You honor us."

Mason wasn't sure which was worse: Richter's obsequiousness or St. John's (now restrained) condescension. Why didn't Lily threaten to punch either of *those* fellows in the nose? At least he'd treated her like she had a brain in her head. Well, mostly.

The overseer continued, "I heard from your grandfather that you made a wonderful discovery last night. Marvelous! A dinosaur, he said."

"It's too early to be sure," Cecil interjected, ruthlessly dampening the shorter man's enthusiasm. "In any case, we can't afford for one interesting find to throw us off pace, can we?"

"Of course not," Richter agreed, turning to wave to the men to keep working before stepping around Lily's horse. "Mason Donnelly, is that you? You're back, you rascal. I didn't think you'd ever show your face here after that article you wrote." But he chuckled as he said it, and Mason took that as an invitation to dismount without fear of being run off by a dozen men hefting pickaxes.

Lily turned back from surveying the men. "Oh, I'm sure Mr. Donnelly's handsome face is welcome wherever he takes it."

Undoubtedly she meant it to be a compliment, but it sounded so gushing—and so unlike something that she would say—that Mason couldn't resist quirking an eyebrow at her. Her cheeks pinkened, and she looked away.

"Did you read the article, miss?" Richter asked, oblivious to the byplay or her heavy-handed flattery.

St. John wasn't oblivious. Mason half expected steam to shoot from the man's nostrils.

Lily stroked her horse's neck, refusing to look at Mason. "I did when it came out. I meant to reread it last night."

Which meant that she had not reread it. Interesting. But perhaps she'd been too busy concocting devious plans to ensnare St. John.

Richter asked Mason, "Are you here to write another story?"

He would if he could, but his inspiration—and his words—seemed to have dried up like a stream in August. "No, I don't think so. Unless something interesting grabs me." No need to tell them that nothing interesting had grabbed him in more than six months.

"We're in a prime spot," Richter said, "so it's entirely possible that Miss Highfill's keen eyes will help us discover something even better than the horn. Perhaps that will whet your interest." Richter gallantly grasped her elbow to balance her as she picked her way through the tumbled rocks.

St. John had not yet followed his companions' examples by dismounting, so when one of the workers let out a shout and Richter scrambled to investigate the excitement, leaving Lily stranded in the boulder field, Mason had the perfect opportunity to play the eager swain. He leaped forward and tucked her hand in the crook of his arm.

The grateful smile she splashed over him would have made any man's bones melt.

"Your acting skills are admirable, Miss Highfill," Mason said in an undertone. "I never would have suspected."

Her hand on his elbow tightened. Mason guessed she didn't know if he was mocking her. He wasn't sure, either.

"I'm surprising myself," she replied, her voice low. "Do you think I'm being too obvious?"

Given that St. John had had to be smashed over the head with her big-eyed giggling and flirting before he'd realized that his grip on Lily was not as assured as he'd apparently assumed, Mason thought that anything subtle would have been ignored. "No, I think this is about right."

Experimentally, he tried out a leer. The expression felt ridiculous on his face. "You can be even more obvious if you like. I wouldn't mind."

This time her throaty giggle didn't sound faked. "You're an amusing fellow, Mr. Donnelly." And she raised her voice as she said it.

Mason imagined he could feel St. John's scowl punching through his shoulder blades.

The barely audible thump of boots hitting the ground behind them indicated that St. John had decided to follow. In fact, he joined them, taking control of Lily's free arm in a display of possessiveness that forced Mason to rub his hand across the end of his nose to obscure his uncontainable smile.

Lily juggled her two suitors with aplomb, balancing her attention—and her flirtation—between the two of them as they picked their way through the rocks. Her upper-crust upbringing had probably taught her how to entertain a roomful of bright-eyed men without breaking a sweat or speaking a single wrong word, Mason thought. But a flush began to creep up her neck, betraying her excitement at nearly landing her chosen fish.

However, the deft angler forgot her quarry upon drawing closer to the digging. As soon as they had emerged from the boulder field, she dashed forward to inspect the excavation more closely, her yellow scarf flapping like a single golden wing.

Had Mason liked the man, he would have exchanged with St. John a rueful and commiserating look. He kept his eyes on the princess instead. She was now standing about ten feet from one of the men attacking the slippery shale of the cliff wall—and too close to the little explosions of rock and dust for Mason's liking.

"Lily—" he started to say. But she had already taken two prudent steps back by the time her name left his lips, and when she turned to him, her expression questioning, he shook his head. "Never mind."

The digger, a young man in his early twenties, stopped and swung around. "Miss Highfill. Good to see you out here again."

She stepped forward again. "Good morning. Are you just bashing at the rock, or are you looking for something in particular?"

He laughed, as she'd clearly meant him to. "We've had a lot of good luck here—" He pointed to a whiter shade of rock that stretched from his feet to his shoulder. "Just trying to look around inside."

Beside Mason, St. John shifted his feet. "Lily, I need to speak to Richter about the categorization that's being done here. You and Dickon are finding so many worthwhile fossils in the debris brought back to the camp that I wonder what else these fellows are overlooking here. Our standards need to be higher." He paused, but Lily didn't reply or look away from the rock. "Will you join me?" he finally snapped out.

"In a moment," she said in a distracted tone, bending forward to look at something in the cliff wall.

Huffing a bit, St. John wheeled away.

Mason tried not to smile. St. John must be truly worried about the rock sorting if he was leaving his girl with a man who'd not so subtly expressed an interest in her.

The same thought must have struck the Bostonian, for his stride hitched and he glanced back at Mason, looking troubled, before resolutely continuing.

Mason drifted over to stand by Lily. The digger was still leaning on his pickax, waiting for her to stop poking at the cliff face.

Mason followed Lily's actions, bending close to the rock and squinting at it, but he had no idea what he was looking at, besides rock, or what he was looking for. "Do you see anything?"

She began chewing on the end of her gloved thumb, staring at the rock band the whole time. Finally she sighed. "No, I'm afraid not. Ah, well."

The digger said, "Try farther down the line. Some of the fellows have been pulling up some interesting stuff. Me, I'm finding a clamshell if I'm lucky."

"Thank you, Peter." Then she stepped back, allowing him to pick up his ax and give it a lusty swing.

Peter? That sounded awfully friendly. "Peter certainly seems to know quite a bit," Mason said as he and Lily moved away, more or less heading in Richter and St. John's direction.

"Oh, he's quite bright. He'll graduate from Yale next year." She pushed a wayward strand of hair back underneath her scarf. "Most of the Yale students have gone with Marsh, of course, on his dig—"

Othniel Charles Marsh, Mason knew, was one of the leading fossil scientists in the United States and had nearly singlehandedly created Yale's impressive reputation for paleontology.

"—but Grandfather managed to lure some Yalies here with promises to get them started in one of his businesses back east."

"Some of the less wealthy Yalies, eh?" The ones from well-to-do families would already have assured places in their family businesses, whatever they might be.

"I never asked," she said in such a haughty tone

that Mason killed his half-formed decision to offer her his arm.

He needn't have bothered. She reached out and took his arm anyway without waiting for an invitation. "Isn't it exciting out here? Dickon and I stay in camp and see only the least interesting of the most interesting rocks—the stuff that has been picked through twice already but gives the sorter out here at the dig site the strange feeling that he's overlooked something—so I have no idea what they are finding up here except when I take the time to visit."

Mason couldn't hold on to his disgruntlement in the face of such solemn-eyed eagerness. "How often do you visit?"

"Maybe once or twice every two weeks. Grandfather sometimes offers to take me."

Which meant that she usually invited herself.

A movement above made Mason lift his head. On the top of the rock face, forty feet up, a man stood watching them, a rifle hanging loose in his hand. One by one, the diggers stopped and looked up.

Lily shook her head. "Grandfather is going to be upset about this."

"About what? About him?" Whoever the fellow was, he wasn't a digger. Too old. Too frayed around the edges.

"There are a half dozen mines in this area, all played out."

Mason swallowed his smile. It sounded funny to hear mining jargon coming from those purebred lips.

"Most of the miners have moved on, but a handful

have stayed behind, hoping a mine would open again. They don't like outsiders who aren't miners, so they don't like us. A miner shows up about once a week to give us the evil eye, then fades away."

Sure enough, the man had vanished. Muttering among themselves, the diggers resumed swinging their pickaxes and wielding their shovels.

Lily added in a low voice, "No one is especially pleased by them always showing up armed."

No kidding. It had made him wish his rifle was in reach instead of in his saddle boot sixty feet away. "You don't mount guards at the dig site or around the camp at night?"

"Grandfather thinks it would just inflame the locals—make them think that we're challenging them or that we're hiding something." She hesitated. "I said that they show up once a week, but this is now the third day in a row we've been visited. They're becoming bolder."

"Why?"

She shook her head. "I don't know. We're leaving in a few weeks anyway, which everyone in town knows. Maybe they feel more confident that there will be no reprisals for bad behavior, or they want to hurry us up."

Or maybe too much time on their hands was leading to more mischief. Mason looked up at the cliff top again, but it remained bare. Still, he felt a tightness between his shoulder blades as he and Lily continued to walk toward St. John and Richter, who were chatting beneath the awning that created the only shade around.

Lily suddenly dug in her heels, tugging on Mason's arm to draw him to a halt. "Everything seems to be going quite well, doesn't it?" she whispered.

He didn't have to ask what she was talking about. "Yes, fairly well." Knowing that St. John had spotted them, Mason reached over and tucked a strand of hair behind Lily's ear.

She gaped at him.

Mason rolled his eyes in St. John's direction. "He's watching us."

"Oh!" Lily let out a high trill of false laughter. Then, perhaps seeing him wince, she quit her theatrics. But she remained where she was, forcing Mason to do the same.

"Thank you for helping me," she said.

"You're welcome. It's been fun."

"You think you'll be here for a week?"

"At the most." The last time he'd stayed anywhere for more than a week, he'd been laid out with influenza.

Her big eyes sparkled. "I'm not sure Cecil will be able to handle a full week."

Well, he wasn't sure about that. He glanced in St. John's way again. The man was still watching them, but he looked mildly annoyed rather than wild with jealousy.

"Lily," St. John called, "stop dawdling, would you? I want you to look at something here."

Was the fellow a complete idiot, addressing her as if she were a provoking child? If he was trying to win her affections, he was going about it the wrong way.

But maybe not. Lily practically skipped toward St. John, delight radiating from every line of her body. Apparently she didn't care what tone St. John used; she would dash to his side as soon as he snapped his fingers. And if St. John understood that, then he understood that he had the upper hand.

Well, they'd just have to see about that.

Lily seemed like a good sort, despite the drawback of her upbringing. She deserved better than to go into a marriage on such unequal footing.

They had a lot of work to do in less than a week.

"You're too easy."

"What?" Lily almost shoved her finger into her ear to scrub out the dirt that must have garbled Mason's words. "I'm *what*?"

"I said—" Mason stopped, then squinted as he recalled his words. "I meant to say, you're *making yourself easy*." He shifted his weight in the saddle. "This isn't going to work."

"Of course it will work. It's working already." She could see in her mind's eye the possessive stance Cecil had assumed in the corral that morning when Mason had begun his flirtation.

"Then why are the two of us merrily riding home alone together?"

"Oh." No good answer occurred to her. So she gave him a poor one. "Cecil is awfully busy."

She blew out a breath. Cecil might have begun the day by feeling threatened, but annoyingly that fear seemed to have worn off by noontime. She had spent the next two hours trying to gain his attention, but all that had led to was her now riding back to camp alone with Mason so that Cecil could stay behind to talk with Richter and "get some serious work done."

Shaking his head, Mason said, "You are sabotaging all your own efforts. And making me look like an idiot, too."

Lily tightened her grasp on her reins. The other option was to reach over and throttle the man. "You think you look like an idiot? How do you think *I* feel? I'm gaily bouncing between you two like a puppy looking for a treat. I look flighty. I've never been flighty!"

His eyebrows rose as if he were on the verge of disagreeing.

Lily stabbed a finger at him. "You don't know me well enough to contradict me, so take my word for it."

He laughed. "All right, you're not flighty. But you're still sabotaging yourself. To continue with your simile, it's obvious which man you'd prefer the treat from. And it's not me."

Of course it wasn't him. She wanted Cecil. How much easier her homecoming would be if she were engaged to Cecil. . . .

Lily voiced her fear. "You believe he won't marry me."

"Oh, no, he'll marry you, all right. But he'll do it for all the wrong reasons."

She knew what was coming. A noise of distress climbed up her throat, and she raised her hand to ward off his next words.

Mason continued doggedly, "He'll marry you for your money."

Lily tried to keep her spine stiff, though her insides were slumping with self-pity. "Any rational man would take my family's wealth into account. And Cecil is rational." Her money. It always came down to her money. Even after so many years in Denver, working at a school, living in a modest house, and acting like everyone else, she still sometimes saw her introduction to a newcomer followed by an explanation shielded with a cupped hand: "Of the Boston Highfills. And her stepfather is William Silas Grant."

Some newcomers would be impressed. Hah. If only they knew the real situation: that she'd been exiled from her home and family for eight years and was only now getting a reprieve.

She wasn't going to fit in. She just knew it. All the money in the world couldn't make her fit in.

The touch of Mason's hand on her elbow made her thoughts freeze. He said, "Are you all right? You look pale."

Lily shook her head. The landscape swam. For a hair-thin moment she thought she might be dizzy from the heat, but to her horror she realized that tears were blurring the jutting hills.

The last thing she wanted was pity from this man. She lifted her hand to her forehead, pretending to shield her eyes against the glare of the sun. "Just the heat and the dust," she said, and gave her cheeks a discreet wipe as she brought her hand back down again.

He wasn't buying it. His eyes narrowed beneath his hat's brim. "Did I offend you?"

Misery gave way to indignation. "Of course you offended me! How would you like to be told you're attractive only for your money? It's your ability to insult people every time you open your mouth that probably prompts you to leave any town after only a week's stay. I bet you have to leave in the middle of the night when you go."

"That's my girl," he said, smiling. "Up and swinging again."

She didn't smile back, but the knot in her chest loosened a little. What would Mason act like if he were really wooing her? Not like the silky-smooth talker he'd been this afternoon, she was sure. He'd act more like this—provoking.

Cecil's wooing—if she were generous enough to call it that—was wan in comparison.

Maybe she was making a mistake by encouraging him to propose to her. If he couldn't muster up enthusiasm for her before their wedding, what could she look forward to afterward? Not much.

Panic clutched at her chest. Cecil was the only man who had even come close to proposing to her. None of the Denver men had expressed an interest in her other than as a good dance partner.

"What if he's my last chance?" Lord, had she actually said that out loud?

Mason suddenly bent over and began to shake.

Good God. Was he having a fit? She grabbed his shoulder. "Are you all right?"

Lifting his head, he laughed in her face.

She yanked her hand back. "It's not funny!"

"You're . . . killing me," he gasped out between deep guffaws. "Believe me, you have nothing to worry about."

"No men in Denver liked me. My aunt said that it was because they were too intimidated by our family connections to even consider proposing, but—"

"Your aunt should have told you that they were idiots."

"—but if any of them had deep feelings for me, he would have proposed anyway, wouldn't he? So I have to conclude that no one had deep feelings for me."

He squinted as he considered that. "Perhaps. Did you have, ah, deep feelings for any of them?"

"Well, no."

"Then what's the problem?"

The problem was that she was stuck in the middle, between Denver men and Boston men. And so far neither had found her very appealing.

"I think I have to be more interesting," Lily said, and immediately felt like a fool. Mason would make mincemeat of her babbling.

To her surprise, though, instead of making a sarcastic remark, Mason said, "If you were more interesting, I'd bottle you as a cure for boredom."

What was that supposed to mean? Lily drummed her fingers on her knee and studied his expression. It gave nothing away. Perhaps he *was* being sarcastic.

Mason turned his blue eyes on her, but she still couldn't gauge his thoughts. "Look. If you still want to nab Cecil with the method we've begun, you have to pay much less attention to him. Stop giving him cow eyes and don't hang on his every word. Try not to talk to him at all tonight at supper. While at supper, we'll make a special date to go riding together tomorrow, and then I'll take you back to your rooms in town. Even if Cecil steps forward to do the honors, you'll agree to go only with me. All right?"

Just whose plan was this, anyway?

"You have to make him think that *he's* getting the prize, not the other way around," Mason continued. "He's too complacent right now. He needs to think that he could actually lose you."

"So you want me to give *you* cow eyes and acquiesce to whatever you want?"

He snorted. "If I had any belief that you could do so, I'd say yes. But I'll settle for just the cow eyes."

Lily opened her mouth to object, then slowly shut it. She wanted to disagree, but his idea did have merit. If she were honest with herself, she would have to admit that most of his ideas had been clever.

Something about him made her overreact. Breathing in deeply, Lily considered his request. "All right."

"If you'd push your pride aside . . . All right?" His brow furrowed. "Say that again."

"All right. Cow eyes it is." But she couldn't give in completely. "Unfortunately, I've never seen someone with cow eyes." She gave him her best helpless look. "Could you demonstrate?"

He stared at her, his features tight, his summer-storm eyes intense.

Then he blinked, and his face relaxed into its usual half-sardonic expression.

She demanded, "That was it? You looked like a murderer, not a lover."

"Probably a side effect of my current mood."

But then he grinned at her, and she grinned back.

The tops of the tents came into view. Lily sneaked a quick look beneath her lashes at Mason before kicking her horse into a canter.

Someone should have bottled Mason a long time ago.

After rubbing down her horse and setting it on a picket, Lily went to Dickon's tent. The fossilized horn was there, and she wanted to make a few good sketches before supper. But as she turned the last corner, her steps slowed. Oddly, the sorting and packing tent had all its sides rolled down. The poor man must be stifling in there.

She stepped inside and blinked against the heavy gloom. The chalky smell of wet plaster hit her nostrils. Ha. By going to the dig this morning, she'd managed to avoid her least favorite job: packing fossils in plaster.

"Lily." Dickon was seated at the desk far in the back. "Come here for a moment, would you?"

She'd heard Dickon shout with frustration, grumble about carelessness, and mutter curses under his breath. But never had she heard the troubled note that shaded his voice now. Anxiety tasted metallic on her tongue.

"Did I do something wrong?" Dickon didn't hesitate to point out her mistakes, even if she was the boss's granddaughter.

"No, no."

Good. She walked past the broad examination table littered with rock and fossil fragments, then past a smaller table where they sealed the smaller fossils in plaster and newspaper to protect them from rough treatment during shipping back east. Lily had put in her fair share of plastering this summer. Frankly, it was an unpleasant job. Sweaty hands and newsprint made a poor combination and left all her clothing smeared with black streaks. And the plaster remained crusted beneath her short fingernails for days. At least she didn't have to do the large plastering jobs. The diggers did those out in the field.

Lily looked down at Dickon's hand. A rough stone the size of a dime was nestled in his upturned palm. "What's that?"

Dickon nodded to her to take a better look.

She bent closer and squinted. She hated to say it, but she couldn't see anything special about the grayish-blue stone. "Um, quartz?"

"No, it's corundum."

It sounded like the name of a spice. When Dickon continued to look at her keenly, she shrugged. "I've never heard of it."

He snorted. "You're a Highfill—you've heard of it, all right. Probably seen one before, too. You'd know it as a sapphire."

"A sapphire?" This ugly rock? "It doesn't look like a good one."

"Most gems are rough like this. You have to cut them to make them into jewelry."

"Oh." She had forgotten that. "Where did you find this?"

"In yesterday's pile." Dickon bounced the sapphire in his palm. "Do you remember seeing it?"

Lily shook her head. "No. But I wouldn't have noticed anything special about it."

"Well, you might not know what to look for, but those boys out there should have recognized it, even if they are concentrating on fossils."

She sat on a stool and held out her hand. "Can I see it again?"

Dickon dropped the cool stone into her hand, and she bent over it to study it. The sapphire was the color of a cloudy sky.

Flipping through a journal on his desk, Dickon told her, "There've been reports of corundum finds in Montana. And two in the high points of the Colorado Rockies. But not around here."

Silently, she handed the sapphire back. Staring in the direction of the dig, Dickon bounced the gem in his palm, then finally closed his fingers over it and sighed. His mouth a flat line, he turned his attention back to her.

"You don't want me to tell anyone about this," Lily said immediately.

"Yes. Because I don't know what it'll do to the dig. I'll tell your grandfather and let him make the decision." Dickon rolled the rock between his thumb and forefinger, then held it up before her eyes. "Do you think you would recognize this if you saw it again?"

So Dickon believed there were more out there.

Lily tried to mask the excitement licking through her veins. "I think so."

"Good. Good girl." Dickon even reached out and patted her on the shoulder. "Remember, your lips are sealed. I'll speak with your grandfather and then let you know what he's decided."

As always, she was going to be shut out of the discussion. But at least Dickon had promised to fill her in.

He slid the sapphire into his pocket, then stood and began rolling up the sides of the tent.

The sunlight streaming in was almost as shocking as the darkness had been. Dickon suddenly chuckled. "Have you been playing in dirt, Lily?"

"No, I was just at the dig." She wiped her fingertips across her cheek. They came back dusted with gray grit. Lovely. She probably looked like a fossil herself. That would make a fine impression on Cecil and Mason. Of course, she had just ridden back with Mason, and he hadn't said a peep. Either he was being a gentleman or, more probably, he didn't care one way or the other.

"I'm going to wash my face," she told Dickon, backing out of the tent. She glanced down at herself and scowled. She looked like she'd been through a dust storm. She'd need to change her clothes as well.

"Fine. I'll see you back here."

Her pulse humming, Lily began winding her way through the maze of tents, heading for the little one in which she kept a few dresses and occasionally spent the night if no one could be bothered to escort her back to town.

A sapphire! Ninety-nine out of one hundred people

would have been delighted by the unexpected windfall, but the men here weren't gem seekers; they searched for old bones and imprints in clay. The news of sapphires would attract fortune hunters to these hills by the wagonload.

The news of sapphires . . . She groaned. What bad luck that Mason Donnelly had to be here, with his intelligent eyes that missed little and his easygoing demeanor that concealed a bulldog will.

Pushing aside the flap to her small tent, Lily shook her head. How was a girl supposed to flirt convincingly with a newspaper reporter while knowing that she held the knowledge of one of the biggest stories of the year?

Chapter Four

The cautious sideways looks Lily cast his way during supper—when she wasn't giggling, touching his arm as she spoke, and giving him soft-eyed glances—made Mason wonder what thoughts had been spinning through her head during the hours since he'd last seen her.

Her acting skills had improved. Of that there was no doubt. Hell, a few times he had found himself in danger of succumbing to the little fantasy she was weaving. He had had to turn to speak with the digger on his right just so he could reorder his thoughts and remind himself that her billing and cooing was for Cecil St. John's appreciation, not his.

The laughter and the flirtatious looks he could take in stride. But the way she touched his wrist to get his attention or to mark her admiration with something he had said simply wiped his mind clean of any thoughts. Too often he'd regained his senses only to find himself staring at her bare fingers on his arm like a cannibal with a particular hunger for women's hands.

She must have finally noticed that, for her little touches were becoming less and less frequent—only once every five minutes now. Unfortunately, the more time passed between her touch, the stronger the lightning flash of sensation of her warm skin on his.

Thank God the real target of Lily's flirtation was St. John. Mason figured that his own mind would turn to mush if Lily genuinely focused her charm on him. A few real smiles, real bursts of laughter, and real touches, and he would be a goner.

The Bostonian, however, seemed immune to the ravages of jealousy. He gave Lily fond smiles when he spoke to her, and he praised the increasing quality of her sketches. (Lily's own smile had slipped at that; Mason guessed she thought her sketches had been fine all along.) But Cecil did not try to gain the princess's attention, nor did he show any resentment of Mason.

Perhaps Cecil had seen the other, less loverlike looks that Lily had been shooting Mason's way. Wary looks. Looks that made Mason bristle inside. Just what was going on in her head?

The other possibility for the man's apathy was that Cecil truly did not care, either because he didn't want Lily as his wife or because he expected Highfill to eventually step in and put a stop to what would clearly be a mismatch.

The footloose newspaper reporter and the Boston heiress. What a pairing that would be.

As he watched Cecil and Highfill exchange easy words—words between equals—Mason bet on the latter reason for Cecil's uninterest: He knew he'd get Lily in the end.

Lily grazed the back of his hand with her fingertips, and heat skittered across his skin. He couldn't help himself—he flinched. And from the way Lily snatched her hand away, he knew that she had seen his reaction.

She leaned toward him, her lips fixed in a smile but her eyes sparking with a less amiable emotion. "Your obvious revulsion is not helping matters," she hissed.

Revulsion? She might be observant when sketching fossils, but not when deducing living people's reactions. "I was simply surprised," he lied.

"Well, next time try to appear pleasantly surprised."

He could think of a half dozen ways she could pleasantly surprise him, and at the top of the list would be forgetting about pompous Cecil. Right below that would be her attempting to ensnare *him*.

Idiot. He had come to the bone hunters' camp for a rest that would restore his mental agility, not for a doomed romance that would muddle his brain even more.

Mason tucked both his hands under the table. If she wanted to continue to play her touching game, she would have to venture into more dangerous territory. And he didn't think she'd be willing to go that far.

Cecil didn't seem to have noticed their little byplay. But Highfill had. A frown creased the older gentleman's forehead. When he saw Mason looking at him, though, the frown smoothed out. "How are you enjoying your stay with us, Donnelly?"

"Quite well, sir. I'm feeling a little extraneous, however. If there is anything you would like me to do, please put me to work."

"Let me consult with Dickon and Cecil and I'll let you know tomorrow morning. Don't be surprised if someone opens your tent door and thrusts a shovel into your hand."

"I won't." If Cecil had anything but ice water in his veins, the man should want to thump a shovel over Mason's head.

But Cecil gave him a good-natured nod. "Additional diggers are always welcome."

Beside him, Lily daintily dabbed her lips with her napkin before rising to her feet. "Gentlemen, I bid you all a good night."

Mason also rose. "Would you accept my escort to town?" He tried not to stare at Cecil. *Object, you fool!*

Lily replied after a slight hesitation, "Thank you."

Cecil broke off his conversation with Richter. "Lily—"

"Yes?" she said breathlessly.

Good. Cecil was finally rising to his duties. Even if the man believed Highfill would approve his suit over Mason's, he needed to show a little more enthusiasm. She deserved it.

Cecil pushed his chair back from the table. "Could you take some letters to town for me? They're sitting on my desk."

"Oh," Lily said, her tone faint.

When she didn't say anything more, Cecil said, "I can go get them for you. . . ."

Mason was so close, he heard her pull in a deep breath. "Oh, no, don't get up, Cecil." Her words were steadier now. She even managed a gracious smile. "I'll pick them up on our way to the corral."

"Thank you. You're a treasure—did you know that?" Without waiting to see if Lily did, in fact, know that, Cecil turned back to Richter and resumed his conversation.

Mason took a step back to allow Lily to pass before him. But she remained stuck in place, the smile on her face beginning to droop around the edges as she stared at the oblivious Bostonian.

A hard jab to the puffer's nose should grab his attention and reassign it to its proper place. Not that it was Mason's place to deliver such a punishment. From the way her eyes suddenly narrowed, he guessed that Lily was contemplating administering the penalty herself.

Well, as much as Mason would like to see that, it wouldn't quite suit her purposes. Cupping her shoulder with his hand, Mason steered her away from the long trestle table by the fire and toward the corral. "It's almost nightfall," he said, trying for a volume that was low enough to sound intimate yet loud enough to be heard by Cecil, "but if we dawdle on the way, we can look at the stars."

Lily pulled her lightning-bolt glare from Cecil. Luckily she reduced it to firecracker potency before focusing it on him, but Mason still blinked at the crackle that arced between them. "That's a lovely idea. How thoughtful of you."

"I'm just trying to imagine what would please you." They had walked far enough away from the table that those still lingering around it probably couldn't hear his words, but he kept playacting anyway. "A lady such as yourself has jewels aplenty, I'm sure, but the diamonds set in the night sky are unrivaled in beauty. Except, perhaps, by your ruby lips." His trite words could be beaten only by truly awful poetry. He tried for a bit of humor. "And your eyes would be like sapphires, except they're brown, so that doesn't work. Is there a brown jewel?"

Her eyes rounded to saucer size. Staring at him, her mouth open, Lily tripped over a tent stake and would have fallen to her knees if Mason hadn't grabbed her elbow.

Once she was upright and steady again, he slipped her arm through his. "Either you don't get compliments very often or you're ill. Are you ill?" He tried to press the palm of his free hand to her forehead, but she batted his hand away.

"I'm fine!" The last word barely squeaked out. She swallowed. "I mean . . . I'm fine. Just fine."

She looked stunned, though. It couldn't be from the compliment. She was pretty—more than pretty, when she laughed—and women were still thin enough on the ground out here that a pretty one would be showered with compliments. Plus, she knew he was only pretending to be enamored of her. So, why the flabbergasted reaction?

A feeling stirred in his chest, and it had been so many months since he'd felt it that it took him a few seconds to identify it. His reporter's instincts were rousing out of long dormancy. Lily was hiding something.

"We shouldn't forget Cecil's letters," Lily said, tugging him to the left and deeper into the tent town.

Mason snorted. "Yes, we should. Tell him tomorrow that you were having such a good time with me that you forgot to take his darn letters."

"But I promised I'd take them. And it wouldn't be nice to lie to him. Or to deliberately inconvenience him."

All true enough. But— "You're the prize here, not him."

"This has nothing to do with who the 'prize' is. I'm not going to be malicious just because Cecil isn't falling in with my plan the way I want him to."

She wasn't thinking of tactics, he saw, but right and wrong. Admirable, of course. It wasn't going to get her far in this love campaign of hers, though. Cecil undoubtedly was thinking tactics, which she had to be made to understand. "I'll tell you what I saw at supper tonight," he said. "First, I saw that Cecil is grooming you to be his servant. Second, I saw that Cecil is so convinced that he has your grandfather's approval that he isn't going to bother to lower himself to fend me off from his future bride. Meaning you."

She flinched, then pressed her lips together, looking as if she'd just tasted something nasty.

He recognized that expression. She was holding back a comment. "What?" he demanded. "No secrets here."

"No secrets about this."

Ha! He'd been right. She *was* hiding something.

A deep breath lifted her chest, and Mason found his attention momentarily diverted. Her next words snapped his eyes back up to her face. "I'm not sure I want to do this anymore." She waved her hand between the two of them. "It doesn't seem to be getting us anywhere, and it's dishonest. It doesn't feel right."

"Does it feel right to have Cecil treat you like someone he believes will come running when he snaps his fingers?"

She lifted her chin. "No. Nor do I particularly like your constantly flinging his disregard in my face. If you think it's such a bad match, why did you agree to help me?"

"Boredom."

He knew it was the wrong answer as soon as it left his mouth, leaving a sour taste behind. How stupid. And needlessly cruel.

"Ah." She disengaged her arm from his. "Well, I have better things to do than entertain you, Mr. Donnelly. Perhaps your time would be better spent in search of a circus than staying here with us. Good night." She gave him a chilly nod, then marched off into the dusk.

Idiot, he berated himself. *Ass.* He didn't want her mad at him; he wanted her mad at Cecil for taking her for granted.

Still, it would be best to let her go. He was finding it too easy to slip into the fantasy that she actually liked him for himself instead of as someone to make Cecil jealous. A few more days of her touches and smiles, and Mason would be pleading with her grandfather for her hand in marriage.

Great. That would give her two terrible choices for a husband: a snobbish, self-centered blueblood as one option, and a wandering frontier journalist as the other.

And . . . marriage? What was he doing, thinking about marriage? See, she was already muddling his mind. The last time he'd thought of marriage, he was seventeen and in the throes of a crush on an older, very sexy woman.

He was getting too far ahead of himself. Even letting his imagination run wild. The only real issue at hand was that he'd just insulted Lily.

He started after her, but she'd vanished among the tents while he'd been arguing with himself. Well, he'd just have to pick up his pace and hope to catch her at the corral. Some sort of apology would come to mind when he found her. She'd been insulted enough this evening.

However, at least she'd been in such a rush to get away from him that she'd left Cecil's letters behind. With a bounce in his step, he headed after her.

Chapter Five

Above the corral, the sky was the deep blue of a jay's wing. Darkness had gathered the nearest line of hills in its arms. It would be full night by the time she reached town.

Lily closed the gate behind her and took a deep breath. Thoughts leaped across her mind like stones skipped off the surface of a pond. The sapphire in the rubbish pile. Dickon's swearing her to secrecy. Cecil's obliviousness to—or lack of interest in—her flirtation with Mason. And Mason's admission that he was hanging around only because he found her love life entertaining.

At least *someone* was finding all this entertaining. Humiliating was the way she was starting to feel about it. Did she have to whack Cecil over the head with a chunk of rock just to get him to pay attention to her?

And even if that worked, was that really what she wanted?

No.

No, it wasn't.

She tilted her head back and sighed. All right. She'd finally admitted it. She didn't want Cecil anymore. Her mother would be disappointed, but it hardly made sense to wrestle a man into matrimony just to please her mother.

Lord, she felt like she'd just been released from a too-tight corset. Free.

Humming a little, she slipped a bridle onto her horse's head and gave the beast a pat on the neck. This would be the first time she would ride to town alone. Alone! She'd endured the constant presence of an escort to satisfy her grandfather and to demonstrate to Cecil that she was a lady—but, beginning tonight, she would do that no longer. She had been a circuit teacher in Colorado one year, riding from one town to the next, staying with families she didn't know. And all on her own.

No more playacting. She was going to do whatever she liked without worrying about what Cecil thought of her behavior.

A scuff of boot heels against dirt made her turn her head. Mason.

She returned her attention to her horse. There wasn't really much more for her to do—her mount was saddled and bridled—but she dawdled a little, checking the girth. If he didn't say anything intelligent in the next five seconds, though, she'd get up on her horse and head out.

The footsteps came closer, halting perhaps six feet behind her. "I'm sorry."

Well, that counted as something intelligent. "Sorry

for what?" she asked, still not facing him. She brushed a portion of her horse's mane over to the other side of its neck.

"Ah, now you're putting me in a difficult position, Lily. What if I'm sorry for the thing that you aren't even upset about? Then you'll be even angrier at me than you are now."

Did he think she was such a pudding brain that she'd fall for that? "Oh? So you're saying there's more than one thing you should apologize for? Well, why don't you just reel them all off, and we'll clear the air once and for all."

He laughed. She looked over her shoulder, and her pulse thrummed at how close he was. Despite the growing darkness, she could see the little crinkles around his eyes from his smile.

"I'm sorry for making you upset or angry," he said. "How's that?"

Not precisely what she was looking for—which had been more along the lines of *I'm sorry for making you feel unappealing by pointing out how Cecil ignores you, and Cecil is a complete idiot for ignoring a wonderful, beautiful woman like you*—but she'd take it. "All right." She twisted to face him, resting her elbow on the saddle.

"I think the problem has nothing to do with you—" *Finally.*

"—but because Cecil doesn't regard me as true competition. Your grandfather would never accept my suit, even if it was real."

She opened her mouth to tell him that it didn't

matter anymore—she wasn't going to ask him to continue their charade—but then the deeper meaning of
his statement sunk in.

Was it true that Grandfather wouldn't consider
Mason a proper suitor? Grandfather didn't talk much
about class, but that didn't necessarily mean that he'd
want any of his granddaughters marrying someone
outside the society they'd been born into. Discomfort
twisted inside her. "I don't know what Grandfather
would say," she hedged.

"Would any of the other fellows here be more likely
competition than me?"

She stared at the hollow of his throat while she
struggled to find something appropriate to say.
Pointing out that Cecil should feel threatened by a
blue-eyed man who had the singular ability to make
the breath catch in her chest when he grinned at her
was not appropriate. Nor was saying that daring girls
all over the world disregarded their families' opinions
about whom they should marry.

She should simply tell Mason that she had no interest in Cecil anymore. That there was no need for fake
flirtation between her and Mason, or between her
and anyone else. And if Mason had been serious when
he told her he was only staying to help her ensnare
Cecil, then Mason would leave. And if Mason left, she
wouldn't have to worry about hiding the news of the
sapphire find from him. Or about why she was spending more time thinking about him than about Cecil.

But when she opened her mouth, out came: "I'd say
you're the best competition in camp." And her words

had a distinct lilt to them. Heavens, was she *flirting* with him? Truly flirting with him, instead of pretending to?

He went still. Then he tilted his head to the side, as if he were trying to figure out what she was thinking.

What she was thinking was scaring even her. She swallowed, then breathed, "Should we find out for certain?"

"How—" he started to say. But she bobbed up onto her toes, braced her hand on his shoulder, and pressed her mouth to his, shutting off any more words.

Sensation jolted through her. Lord, it felt like every inch of her skin had suddenly become a thousand times more sensitive.

It was too much. She leaped back out of reach even as his arms started to come around her.

"Besides," she babbled on, taking another step away, "it was difficult enough to wring up the courage to ask for your help with Cecil. I can't imagine doing it again with someone else."

Not waiting for Mason to reply, she swung up onto her horse. "Can you get the gate for me?" she asked, turning her horse toward it.

"You did that well," he said.

Pleasure sparkled through her. Cecil had never complimented her kissing. She'd never complimented his, either, now that she thought of it. "Did what well?" she asked, feigning a casual tone.

"Mounted."

Mounted? She stared at him. She was obsessed with their kiss, and he was marveling that she'd managed to get on a horse? "I've ridden a horse before this summer, you know." And how did he think the saddle had gotten on the animal? That she'd snapped her fingers and it had flown over and strapped itself on? Sometimes he was as much an idiot as Cecil. Maybe all men wanted to shove her into a prelabeled box: helpless and silly.

"If you wait a few minutes, I'll take you in to town."

"No, I'll go by myself. I *want* to," she added when Mason began to object. As if she'd spend another moment in his insulting company. She nudged her horse to a walk, forcing Mason to back away a step. "The gate, please."

He went to the gate but didn't open it immediately. "What if I follow you in ten minutes or so? I want to see that article that I wrote about your grandfather. Refresh my memory."

"You do not. You just think that I'm going to panic or something if I have to ride to town on my own."

"So prove that I'm wrong by not panicking and arriving safe and sound. Instead of following you ten minutes later, I'll follow, say, fifteen minutes later."

He smiled then. It was a smile meant to persuade, and for a long, hypnotic moment it almost worked.

Lily straightened in the saddle. "No."

"No?" He tilted his head a bit. Oh, he could be a charmer when he tried. But he should have tried that a minute ago, instead of giving her compliments on how she mounted her horse.

"No," she said again.

His persuasive smile slipped just a hair. "Twenty

minutes. Twenty minutes is more than enough time for you to get into trouble and get yourself out again."

"No!"

"What about the miners?"

"The miners?" For a moment she had no idea what he was talking about, then remembered the armed man watching over the dig today. "They've never been any trouble. And when I'm in town, I speak to them in the general store and such. They have no reason to harm me."

"You're the expedition leader's granddaughter—"

"Mr. Donnelly." She paused, then shook her head. "It's been a long day. Let's not extend it."

This time his smile vanished entirely. He gave a little bow—an ironic one, she was sure—and pulled the corral gate open for her. "Miss Highfill, I'll see you tomorrow, then."

"Good night."

As he shut the gate behind her, she twisted in the saddle to face him. She didn't want to end the evening on sour note—a sour note that she was partly responsible for. "Thank you for all your help," she said to him. "I do appreciate it."

Before he could object again to her riding alone, she clucked at her mount, encouraging him first to a fast walk, then to a trot. When she reached the base of the steep trail that led up out of the valley, she glanced behind her. Night had stolen away all view of the small tent town. Only campfires, shining like rubies against a black velvet background, indicated the position of the bone hunters' camp.

A light night wind ruffled along her cheek, tossing a strand of hair across her eyes. She reached up with one hand to tuck the hair back into her scarf.

As her horse began its climb out of the valley, Lily leaned forward slightly to maintain her balance. Aside from the dull clicking of hooves over stone and the occasional shout of laughter from the invisible camp, not a sound broke the silence.

Lily sighed and stared up at the boundless black sky above her. Instead of focusing Cecil's attention on her, Mason's help in the fake flirtation—and that startling kiss—had focused her own attention on the lack of true compatibility and feeling between her and Cecil. Yes, she should be happy that she had figured it out sooner rather than later, but right now that was small comfort.

She thought back on the last several weeks and winced. She'd willingly endured tiny humiliation after tiny humiliation from Cecil in her attempts to get him to propose to her. Her own self-respect had dropped a few notches; the others in camp probably thought her quite foolish. At least Dickon didn't. He'd entrusted her with the information about the sapphire find. She wasn't sure even her grandfather would have done that.

A wash of stones rattled noisily down a nearby hill steeped in darkness. Lily pulled back on the reins. Her horse stopped, and silence cloaked them completely.

Long, tight moments passed. No other sound quivered through the black night.

Blowing out her held breath, Lily nudged her heels

into her horse, and they continued along, hooves clomping against the hard trail.

Then another rattle of stones, this time behind her.

All right. Something was out there. A coyote or rabbit, perhaps.

Or a local, trying to give her a scare.

Lily tried to steady her breathing. If it was one of the miners, he was certainly succeeding.

Suddenly her hardheadedness seemed foolish. She should have let Mason come with her, or at least follow her.

She didn't signal her horse, but it picked up its pace anyway, shifting into a fast walk. Straining with every cell of her being to hear any foreign noises, Lily slumped with relief when the lights of Milton twinkled at her as she crossed the last low ridge.

Within ten minutes she was ensconced in her snug room at the boardinghouse and lighting all the lamps. It was an extravagance, but after those endless moments out in the thick blackness, she needed to see everything around her.

She paced until her hands stopped shaking. Dumb. Tomorrow she'd take the escort of whoever offered— even Cecil. At least Mason wasn't here to tell her that he had told her so.

Sighing, she sat down at the rickety desk. Her aunt Evaline had read every one of Mason's stories, and had even chuckled over bits of the account he'd written about Highfill, Evaline's father—bits that had made Lily incensed at the time. Evaline would be thrilled to hear that Lily had actually met Mason.

She glanced at the hat box in which she kept letters from her aunt. Mason's story on Highfill was in there as well. She should look at it again, see if Mason had been as fair as he claimed. With a grimace, she pulled out a piece of clean stationery and a pen instead and began to write her aunt a letter. Mason had been right about enough things tonight. She could wait until tomorrow to find out if he was right about the story he'd written as well.

She had just finished scratching *Love, Lily* on the snowy white paper when the barely audible sound of hooves on the main street—which was really just a track—below her window made her lift her head.

She reached out and turned down the wick on her lamp until it was on the verge of fluttering out, then stood and went to the window, careful to stand to the side. Hopefully the lamplight was low enough that anyone outside wouldn't see her peering from the window.

The hoofbeats stopped, sounding like they had halted directly below her. Holding her breath, Lily slowly lifted a corner of the curtain away from the window.

The horseman stood like a war memorial statue in the middle of the street. Not enough light seeped from other windows on the street to illuminate more than his shape, but Lily knew him instantly. She exhaled with a hiss. Mason.

Darn it, he'd probably been the one who'd spooked her on the trail tonight. She pushed the curtain out of her way and shoved the window open. "What are you doing here?"

He looked up. A stray beam of lamplight from the boardinghouse's downstairs parlor cut across his features, highlighting his cheeks and nose but leaving his eyes in shadow. "Are you sure you want to be screeching out the window in the middle of the night? The hardworking people here must appreciate their sleep."

Ha. By now she was veteran of enough verbal duels with Mason to recognize a feint meant to throw her off target. "I told you not to follow me." The man had scared a few years off her life.

He shrugged, a careless gesture that made her grind her teeth. "It was a fine night for riding, so I figured I'd combine pleasure with duty and make sure you hadn't tumbled into a ditch or . . ." He paused and glanced around. The main street was clearly not the place to speculate aloud on the motivations of the local miners. ". . . or been snatched off as dinner by coyotes."

"How gallant of you, Mr. Donnelly."

"My gentlemanly qualities occasionally have the chance to shine through. But I can see you're perfectly fine, so I'll bid you good night." He started to pull his horse's head around to head back for the camp.

"Wait," she said, then wrinkled her nose. Why was she doing this? Maybe because he had, after all, taken the time to check on her. "Would you, ah, like to come into the parlor?"

When he gave her a single nod, she shut the window and pulled the curtains closed.

She'd not yet undressed for bed, so she simply pushed her unbound hair off her shoulders before leaving her room and descending the stairs.

Halfway down the staircase, Lily stopped. Her heartbeat pounded in her ears like a muffled war drum, and a gentle twisting sensation in her stomach made her press one of her hands to her belly.

Nervousness. Excitement. Anticipation.

She shouldn't have kissed him. Now she would feel this way around him every time she saw him. Well, she would just have to pretend that she didn't.

Taking a deep breath, she continued down to the ground floor.

Mason was already in the parlor, his hat in his hands, his uncovered head making him seem suddenly domestic—a dangerous thought, for if there was anything Lily was certain of, it was that he was not the stay-at-home type.

Lily put on her best hostess smile. It felt a little rusty. "Welcome."

"Thank you."

His eyes swept over her. Goose bumps, quite a delicious kind, sprung up in their wake. Lily brought one hand to her mouth, took a single nibble from her thumbnail, then forced her hand back down.

He frowned. "You didn't bring my article."

"Your article?"

"About your grandfather."

"Oh." Of course. *That* article. The article they'd been arguing about for almost two days. "Would you like anything to drink? Some cider? Then I'll get the article."

"Cider would be fine."

Lily almost ran for the kitchen to get the jug of

cider the landlady provided for her guests. When she picked up the jug and two glasses, she was relieved to see that at least her hands weren't shaking anymore. The twirling in her stomach had settled as well.

In the parlor, she sat on the worn settee, and Mason chose a chair opposite her. When she poured the cider and pressed a glass into his hand, he said, "I didn't expect you to invite me in."

Lily sipped at the cider. It tasted stronger than she remembered. "I didn't expect you to follow me home, either." Especially since she'd specifically asked him not to. But after the scare she'd had riding home, she wasn't going to throw down that gauntlet. "So it's a night full of the unexpected."

There: the perfect opening for him to say something about the kiss they'd shared earlier. She held her breath.

"Don't misunderstand me—I'm in favor of the unexpected. It's how I've found my best stories."

She wanted to throw her head back and heave a sigh. So he was going to ignore it. Fine. She could do that, too.

He hesitated, then held up his glass to her. "Here's to the unexpected."

His blue eyes grew intense, and for a moment it seemed like he was leaning his whole body toward her. But he only stretched his arm out and clinked his glass against hers.

"The unexpected," she repeated, and took a larger swallow of her drink than was polite.

Then an awkward silence fell. Lily glanced at her

cider, at the modest bookshelf beneath the parlor window, at her boots—even at Mason's boots—but she couldn't dredge up from her brain anything to say to him. It was humiliating enough when one man had little interest in kissing her. When two men weren't interested . . .

"So, where will you go next?" she finally asked. "When you're through with us here."

"I haven't decided."

"Is that how you usually manage things? Without thinking them through?" Not the most diplomatic question, she realized as soon as the words left her mouth, but she was feeling a little cranky.

He didn't take offense. "I write stories about people, and there are endless numbers of stories available. We all make up new ones every day. Sometimes I discover the story, and sometimes the story discovers me. It's not a science, like your digging is. Or an art, like your sketching. More . . . well, more like luck, I suppose. Out of my hands entirely."

"I occasionally read your stories when I was in Denver. Out here, we don't always get the papers on time, so I haven't seen what you've written lately."

"Your grandfather told me that Dickon uses the newspapers to wrap the fossils."

Lily smiled. Only last week she had caught Dickon sneaking out of her grandfather's tent with a large handful of newspaper—papers most likely not yet read. "Grandfather is lucky to have Dickon with him, and he knows it. Ultimately, wrapping the fossils properly is more important than keeping current with the news. But ever since you wrote about my grandfather, your stories—"

"Is this your first summer on one of your grandfather's expeditions?" Mason cut in.

"Yes. And my last, I suppose."

"You don't think Cecil will take you along after you get married?"

She didn't want to talk about Cecil. Her realization that they would not suit felt too new to delve into. "Even at the beginning of the summer I'd planned to move to Boston when the dig was over. My mother and my two younger sisters live there. My mother thinks it's time I return to the fold."

"You're going back to Boston? I hadn't realized." Mason tilted his head as he examined her. "Were you such a bad sheep that exile was necessary?"

Lily made a face. "I was a brat. A loud brat. I stomped a lot."

"Hmm. I guess some things never change."

She surprised herself by laughing. "Enough about my shameful childhood," she said. "Tell me about yours."

This felt too much like a regular social visit—as if he were really courting her.

Stretching his long legs out in front of him, Mason took a draft of his cider. "Hell towns."

"I beg your pardon?"

"I grew up in hell towns, and as a result became a bit of a—" He broke off his words, obviously remembering that he was in a parlor with a young lady, not in the woods with lumberjacks.

"Hellion," Lily supplied, smiling.

He raised his glass to her. "Precisely."

When he didn't continue, Lily frowned at him. "That's it? That's all you're going to tell me?"

"You gave me even less. All I know is that you were a brat and shipped off to Denver. And that you have two sisters and a mother. No brothers? What about your father?"

"My father died when I was nine, and it was due to my mother marrying William Silas Grant that I became a brat." That sounded like she was blaming her mother for her own bad behavior. "I mean, I was spoiled and said nasty things to her and to Mr. Grant when I learned they were to marry, and after a bit of discussion with the rest of my family—"

"Including your grandfather?"

Lily nodded. "—including my grandfather, most thought that I'd be better off for a year or two out in Denver with my father's sister. A year or two turned into eight." Lily settled back against the lumpy settee and crossed her arms over her chest. "Now you." This was less like a parlor visit and more like a parlor game.

"My mother died having my younger brother, so I don't remember her at all, and my brother died soon after. My father raised me while he helped lay the railroad across the country. You get to see a lot of the country that way, but he was so busy laying track and I was so busy running around with water for the crews that neither of us had any time to look around. I remember my first look at the Rockies, though." He shook his head, his eyes distant. "Absolutely magnificent."

"I remember my first time, too. I had had no idea that mountains were made that high."

The smile he sent her was so warm, Lily's toes curled.

Mason placed his empty glass on the rickety old table at the elbow of his chair and then stood. "Could I see that article? Even borrow it for the evening?"

She had begun to hope that he had forgotten about the article. She hadn't read it again after making her accusation the night before that it was an unfair portrait of her grandfather, and now she was afraid to. After she had spent the day with Mason, a niggling suspicion had swelled in her mind that she had been too defensive—and perhaps too strident in that defensiveness. "Are you so determined to prove me wrong?" she asked, attempting a light tone as she rose to her feet.

"No, I merely want to read it. I'll give it back to you when I'm done, and then we can go at it hammer and tongs if you like."

Lily shook her head. "That's not necessary. Why fight about it?"

One dark eyebrow lifted. "Now I'm worried. Only twenty-four hours ago it seemed to be your life's mission to fight about it."

"Well . . ." Lily spread her hands in a gesture that was a plea for peace. "I'm willing to call a truce."

He suddenly grinned. "You've read it, haven't you?" Bracketing his hands on his hips, he allowed his smile to stretch even wider. "And you were wrong."

Lily shook her head. "You certainly know how to woo a lady, don't you, Mason?"

"Sorry, I'm—" He broke off his apology. "But I'm not wooing you."

"Nobody is." How marvelously self-pitying. She rushed out her next words. "I'll get the article now."

She tiptoed up the stairs to avoid waking her fellow boarders. Had she been wrong about his article? She was wrong often enough, Lord knew. She should be used to the feeling by now.

The article lay facedown on her desk, and she picked it up. It was cowardice, she knew, but she didn't read it before she handed it to Mason, who was waiting at the base of the stairway. "I want it back," she told him.

"Tomorrow."

A stealthy rush of pleasure tugged at her like an undertow. Her face heated. Good Lord, was she blushing? Just because he said he'd see her tomorrow? Of course she'd see him tomorrow. The camp was small. There was no way they could avoid each other, even if they tried.

Mason settled his hat on his head. "Maybe tomorrow St. John will have come to his senses."

Come to his senses. She liked that. But she still didn't tell him that, sensible or no, Cecil was no longer the man she wished to spend her life with. "Perhaps. But he's been singularly stubborn so far."

Mason adjusted his hat—unnecessarily, as far as she could tell—and then rubbed his thumb over his chin. Finally he said, "Something to think about, maybe. Marriage is hard enough without one of the partners being stubborn and lacking sense." A final tug on his hat. "Thank you for the cider."

She was glad he'd come, so she added ungrudgingly, "And thank you for looking after me."

"Well, you clearly didn't need it."

She smiled. "I was just about to say that."

He nodded, slipped through the door, and vanished into the night. Moments later she heard his horse's hooves thudding against the hard-packed road, moving in the direction of the camp.

Giving in to impulse, she shoved the door wider and poked her head out. Her eyes took several seconds to adapt to the inky blackness, but by the time they did, Mason was gone.

She'd see him tomorrow, she reminded herself, then went into the kitchen to return the cider bottle to its place and wash their glasses.

As she placed the dried glasses on the shelf, she suddenly stilled. Mason had arrived in Milton at least twenty minutes after she had. Unless he'd ridden several circles around town before entering it—and she couldn't think of a reason why he would have—he wasn't the one she'd heard following her on the trail.

Chapter Six

Mason stroked the ragged edges of the article he'd written, his gaze fixed on the gilt lip of the sun trembling over the choppy hills to the east. Voices bubbled to life in the tents around him, waking to the new day.

He had written this?

He hadn't concerned himself much with the article's subject—though he'd realized on the first reading that his description of Highfill had not been an overwhelmingly positive one. In truth, his descriptions seldom were. Con men, cheats, snake oil salesmen, and the like made more vigorous stories.

No, what had seized his amazement were the words. The rhythm, the cadence, the easy humor that gave each sentence a bounce, effortlessly launching the reader into the next.

Where had that gone?

He pulled out a sheet of paper he'd stuck in his pocket. It was the last piece he'd had published, and it couldn't be more different. Each word was a misshapen lump, a stone that only made the reader stumble. Even he could see the utter lack of interest that pervaded every syllable.

Mason crumpled his last article into a ball and tossed it into a dark, musty corner of his tent. He was lucky his paper hadn't fired him months ago but had agreed to give him a few months off to get himself together.

Writing used to be exhilarating. A challenge. His desire to entertain and to educate forged into articles that people would want to read.

But his soul had a hollow ring to it now. No passion burned beneath his writing.

Could he force himself to relight the fire by sheer willpower alone? Or should he continue to just wander across the country until he found something interesting?

He could write about Lily.

Mason stretched his legs out in front of him. Interesting? *Interesting* was an adjective that didn't begin to cover her. *Muleheaded, naïve, aggravating, beguiling* . . .

Terrifying.

Terrifying?

That kiss last night had been terrifying, singing through him from his scalp down to his toes. And when he'd been in her parlor, civilly sharing conversation, he'd had to smother a dozen impulses to yank her against him and continue the kiss she'd unexpectedly begun.

But she had just been experimenting, or acting out her anger against Cecil. As much as he didn't want to believe it, Mason was smart enough to know that ladies like her didn't normally kiss men like him. So it was a kiss better forgotten.

Lily: the Boston heiress exiled to the rougher society of Denver, now working on a dig in the last summer of her maidenhood before her triumphant return to the East. He'd leave out any mention of her giggly but steel-nerved stratagems to capture Cecil's attention. If he published that, she would track Mason down and give him a tongue-lashing he'd richly deserve by betraying her trust. He'd also leave out her ability to rock a man with a simple kiss that had lasted as long as a single heartbeat. He might be a fool for getting snagged in her unwitting web, but he didn't need everyone else to know it, too.

Could he really write a story about Lily? He certainly thought of her often enough. Sentences about her should be spinning out of his busy brain.

Unfortunately, each sentence that did form was sentimental and softly rounded—not his clean, sharp-edged style at all. Just another indication that his career as a writer might be finished.

Damn it. All this thinking was getting him nowhere. He had to *do* something.

Mason climbed to his feet and tucked the article on Highfill into his belt. He'd go to Dickon's tent, see if Lily was there. An interesting subject was the heart of a good story. The writing . . . well, he could fix the sentimental hogwash into crisp, biting images during his second draft. Anyway, it was only a practice story. Something to get the juices flowing again.

As he rode to Milton the night before, following Lily to her boardinghouse, he'd started thinking about heading out soon. Now, though, it made sense to delay his departure. Stay a few more days. And if she wanted to experiment with kissing him again, he'd certainly hold still and let her do it.

Anticipation tingling under his skin, he strode toward the center of the camp.

"She's not here," Dickon greeted Mason when he stepped into the tent's shade. All the canvas walls had been rolled back so that the large sorting table and the equally large packing table stood open to the light breeze. "She rode away with St. John right around sunup."

Annoyance rose—at Dickon's assumption that he was mooning after Lily, of course, not because she'd gone off with that supercilious bastard.

"I came to see you," Mason retorted. But Dickon rolled his eyes, and Mason realized he'd answered a beat too late. Perfect. Now he'd reinforced Dickon's belief that he was trailing after Lily like some softheaded swain.

Well, what of it? That was the role he was supposed to play. He just didn't like playing it when neither Lily nor Cecil St. John was around to appreciate it.

So when was Lily coming back?

Mason gestured at the tables. "With Lily gone, do you need any assistance?"

A strange expression darkened Dickon's face. Suspicion?

Dickon turned back to a pile of rubble at the end

of the sorting table. "What do you want to help me with?" he threw over his shoulder.

"Packing, if you need it. I'm no good at looking at rocks." He knew what coal looked like—he'd spent one miserable summer shoveling coal into a train engine's boiler—but that was the limit of his geology knowledge.

"Fine." Still acting a little distant, Dickon gave Mason a thorough lesson on how to wrap and label the specimens being sent back east. Within a half hour Mason was covered in plaster up to his elbows. He could feel a few heavy chunks dangling in his hair, left behind from when he'd unthinkingly scratched his head.

Talk about the ongoing range war between cattlemen and sheep farmers filled the morning. The greedy noon sun had swallowed up all shadows by the time Mason casually asked, "When is Lily returning to take over her job?" He should get a prize for patience, which wasn't one of his usual traits.

A frown cut a line between Dickon's brows. "She didn't say."

Mason shrugged as if he didn't care much, and wrote the address of Highfill's small museum on a bone he'd just finished plastering. He hadn't waited long enough for the plaster to dry, and the pen's nib clogged with white paste.

After several moments Dickon relented enough to add, "I didn't talk to her this morning, but Highfill said that she was going out with Cecil to one of the dig sites for the day."

Nice. He wished she'd told him her plans last night, when they'd been sitting so cozily in her parlor. But maybe she didn't want him around today.

Right now she was probably hanging on every one of Cecil's upper-class syllables as if he were a preacher promising eternal salvation. Eternal misery, more like, if she believed Cecil's interest extended beyond her wealth to who she truly was. Mason had dropped plenty of hints to her about the fellow's real goal. If she didn't trust Mason enough to believe him, that was her loss.

The plaster on the next package was dry, but Mason bore down too hard when he wrote, clogging the pen nib again. Swearing, he wiped the nib clean with a piece of newspaper. Then he paused.

It was his newspaper, or rather, the paper he used to write for. He hadn't picked up a copy since he and his editor had agreed to a temporary parting.

What was this? In the place where his stories usually ran, another fellow's byline had been set.

Mason shook his head at himself. Of course they had filled his space with something else. They could hardly leave the space blank, could they?

His eyes skimmed over the column, his focus sharpening as he began to follow the story. This new fellow, Gregory Cutler, was good.

No, better than good. Far better than good.

A chill tightened Mason's stomach. Maybe his future as a writer had been taken out of his hands.

"Anything interesting?" Dickon asked.

Mutely, Mason held up the paper.

"You looking at Cutler? Good stuff. He makes me laugh." Dickon cocked his head. "Come to think of it, I haven't seen any of your stories lately. Have you moved to a different paper, maybe one we don't get?"

Mason tried to laugh. "Not yet."

"Hmm. Do you even still work for the *Tribune*, Donnelly?"

Great. That was the last question he wanted to answer while still reeling from learning that his paper had apparently found a replacement for him. Maybe that was why he replied with blunt honesty: "I have no idea."

Dickon pressed his lips together. "Looks odd," he finally said. "A jobless man trailing after an heiress."

Mason's breath turned solid in his chest. He hadn't considered Dickon to be a staunch friend, but that comment hurt.

Dickon held up his hand, blocking Mason's response before he even had time to clear his thoughts to form one. "I shouldn't have said that, because I don't believe that's what's happening here. Look, lad, I'm proud to know you. Delighted to spend the morning talking to you, a knowledgeable, personable fellow who's seen more of this country in one year than I will in my entire life. But an older man's wisdom is not something to discard just because you don't like it. And I'm telling you that you and Lily just wouldn't suit."

Mason's backbone stiffened until it was as straight as a lodgepole pine.

Dickon softened his tone. "I know what I'm talking

about, believe it or not I was in a similar situation, oh, twenty years ago. And it led only to disappointment."

That was a little too vague to be the basis of an entire theory on the incompatibility of social classes. "What happened?"

"Our lives were too far apart. I knew I'd be awkward in her social circles, and I didn't feel comfortable bringing her into mine. And one day she didn't show up at our usual meeting place. I never saw her again." Dickon grimaced. "Maybe things are different these days. But I doubt it."

"You never saw her again at all?"

"Nope. Met my future wife a year later, and I never looked back."

Based on the ferocity of Dickon's advice, Mason guessed Dickon had probably looked back quite a bit. Too bad there had been no one there to return his gaze.

"I know the flush of young love must be scrambling your brains so that neither of you can think straight—"

Young love? That *did* scramble his brain for a moment. "Whoa," Mason said before Dickon could go into more detail. "You're putting the wagon before the horses. I like the girl, make no mistake. But we're only having a bit of fun."

The older man's hands fisted at his sides. Whoops. *Only having a bit of fun* wasn't a phrase that was comforting Dickon.

Mason hurried on. "She knows as well as I do that it's just a flirtation. She's told me so, in fact."

"Just a flirtation, eh?" Dickon's hands relaxed and he began picking again through the diminishing pile of rubble on the table. "And she said so, too? That's reassuring."

"Plus, she's going back to Boston in two weeks, isn't she?" Mason found himself mesmerized by Dickon's hands darting through the scrap rocks like fish. "That should reassure you even more."

Dickon's hands paused, then one closed over a stone so quickly that Mason didn't have time to see any details.

He stepped toward the table. "Found something?"

"No! I mean, no, nothing of importance. Just a pretty rock that my daughter would appreciate." Dickon slid his hand into his pocket, and when he withdrew it again, it was empty. He even displayed his open palm to Mason, like a magician showing his audience that he had no scarves dangling out of his sleeves. "If I have time tonight, I'll mail it off to her."

Dickon's ridiculous lie made Mason's senses flare like those of a wolf that had unexpectedly come across the path of a wounded rabbit. He had enough experience to know that he'd stumbled on something big.

Forget writing the practice story about Lily. There was a real story here.

He could smell it.

"If you give the stone to me, I'll pack it up," Mason offered, turning half away as if he didn't care one way or the other.

"No! I, uh, may want to write a letter, too."

Forget all this dancing around. He was too impatient to play the game. "Can I see it?"

Dickon blinked, then played dumb. "The letter?"

"No, the stone." And he waited.

"Well . . ." But Dickon had apparently run out of excuses, for after a moment he pulled the rock out of his pocket.

Mason held out his hand, and Dickon dropped the stone in his palm, where it gave a soft bounce.

Holding his breath, Mason raised the stone to his eye.

Damn it. He hadn't been joking the other night when he'd told Highfill that he couldn't see why one rock was more interesting than another. This one had a pretty light-blue cast and looked a little like quartz, but that was about it. He tossed the rock back to Dickon, who stuffed it into his pocket.

There must be something important about that rock. He was just too ignorant about geology to recognize the significance of it.

But Lily might know.

And he'd worn out his patience, waiting for her to return from the morning excursion with her Bostonian.

"Where's the other dig site?" he asked Dickon.

Dickon seemed as eager for Mason to leave as Mason was himself. "Two or three hills southeast from the one you went to yesterday. Head toward the first site, but take the right-hand path when it splits about a mile outside of camp. Maybe two miles later, the path splits again, and this time take the left track, which is pretty steep for about fifteen minutes. At the bottom, go right. The site is about a mile farther. Because of that steep path, we've had a lot of trouble transporting any finds out of the site. Luckily—if you want to call it that—we haven't found anything spectacular there."

Mason had stopped paying close attention after the directions. "Any messages for Lily?" he asked as he headed for the sunshine outside the tent.

Dickon sent him a sharp look. "No, no messages for Lily. But I have one for you: Better to leave while your heart's still in one piece." Then he turned back to the table and resumed his sorting.

Mason snorted as he left the tent. Both Lily and Dickon seemed to have romance on the brain. It would have made him laugh, except both had cast him in the role of the ineligible, lucklesss swain. Not something that boosted a fellow's self-confidence. Even though he wasn't really angling after Lily—at least, not when his brain was in control—it still smarted.

At the corral, it took him a few minutes to find his saddle, as it wasn't where he'd left it. Someone must have moved it this morning. Both Lily's saddle and Cecil's were missing, but Highfill's sat on top of a box, the leather gleaming.

He paused, staring at Highfill's saddle. If most of the digging took place at the main site, and Lily and Cecil were at the second site, that might mean that they'd been alone for the entire morning.

He had to make an effort to unclench his jaw.

Maybe several hours of unadulterated Cecil would put Lily off the man completely.

Maybe.

Or maybe Cecil had woken up to the possibility that

he might lose her and had spent the morning being his charming best. Which, considering his upbringing and bluest of blue bloodlines, was probably disgustingly charming. Would Lily be fooled by that?

Either way, they'd had plenty of time together. He wasn't going to feel bad about bursting into the middle of their little party.

Following Dickon's directions, forty minutes later he found himself at the top of a rocky path that dipped sharply, hugging the edge of a vertical-sided hill.

Mason tapped his boot heels against his horse, and they started to descend.

Swiftly the path went from steep to approaching treacherous. No wonder Dickon had mentioned the difficulty in moving fossils up this path. As his horse took an awkward step, Mason leaned back in his saddle to help the animal keep its balance. Flicking its ears, his mount took the next two steps quickly and then stumbled again.

"Whoa," Mason murmured, leaning back farther and giving the reins a tug at the same time. The horse had to slow down on such rough terrain.

Ears flattening like fans against its head, the horse half leaped forward, then threw a twisting buck.

Shit. He grabbed for the horse's mane as he flew over, but the beast was just a brown blur, and his fingers seized only air. A whisker of a second later, the wall of rock thumped the air out of his lungs and knocked him to the ground.

He blinked his eyes open in time to see his horse spin around on its rear legs like a Wild West show trick horse and thunder up the path, disappearing within moments.

Better and better.

Wheezing like a fish that had been thrown upon a rocky beach, Mason closed his eyes and concentrated on getting air into his lungs. Painful aeons later, his breathing settled into a regular pattern and his vision stopped graying out at the edges. He shoved himself up into a sitting position. After two more minutes, he climbed to his feet.

He felt like crap. Crap that had been run over by a locomotive, picked up off the track by a vulture, and then dropped onto very hard rocks from hundreds of feet up.

So. Walk down the path to the second dig site, or walk back up the path toward the camp? Assuming his legs would carry him more than ten feet, which he wasn't entirely confident about.

Well, at least his legs were still attached. Had his horse twisted the other way when it bucked, he would have taken a long fall off the hill onto the nasty-looking boulders gathered hungrily below.

He would have to walk back to camp. Though the second site was closer, only a mile or so away, Lily and Cecil might have moved on to the first dig site. And Mason certainly didn't want to climb down this stupid trail, discover Lily wasn't at the second site, and then have to climb back up the trail.

Sucking in a deep breath, he pushed off from the wall and started slowly up the path.

The path itself wasn't too bad, although sheets of

loose rocks occasionally slipped beneath his boots, causing a minor heart attack every time he lost his balance. He huffed out a relieved sigh when he reached the top of the trail and stopped for a quick break.

The rest of the walk back, though, was a brutal march through the wastelands of hell.

The steep path had been shaded in many places by the hill. Out here, where the earth ran flat, the sun crashed down like a hammer on an anvil. He'd had a full waterskin on his saddle, but of course that didn't do him any good now. And no matter how much wishing or cursing he did, his horse didn't helpfully return to pick him up.

A line of sweat tickled his temple. Damn, it was hot. And his body wasn't holding up as well as he thought it would.

For the first time he considered the possibility that he might not make it.

Lily shaded her eyes and tried to look interested in what Cecil was saying. "Uh-huh," she said when he paused and looked at her.

The sun was a distraction, a hot, heavy hand smothering her. She took her hat off to let cool air comb across her scalp, then flapped the hat in front of her face, stirring up a local breeze.

When she was in Dickon's tent, sorting or packing or sketching or labeling, she wished she were out here with the diggers. Now, out here, she wished she were back with Dickon in the cool shade. She was fickle, she supposed.

And not just about her surroundings but about the company she kept.

"Quite, quite intriguing, don't you think?" Cecil said.

"Quite," she murmured.

"Even revolutionary, one might say."

Lily nodded vaguely. He was talking about something involving agriculture on his family's country estate fifty miles outside of Boston—a subject she would have been thrilled to learn more about yesterday, but one that held little interest today.

"I say, you're looking rather done in." Cecil peered at her. "Shall we go sit in the shade for a few moments while you recover?" Not waiting for her agreement, he pulled her hand through the crook of his arm and guided her to an awning set up to provide some shade, as careful with her as he'd be with a delicate blown-glass vase. When he pointed out and steered her around a small, ankle-high pile of rubble that was no more dangerous than a newborn kitten, she had to remind herself that snapping the head off one's escort wasn't the decent way to repay his effort.

She did gently pull away, though. "I can manage now. Thank you."

Once under the awning, he fussed around until he had a blanket positioned on a stool just right—her womanly nether parts needed more cushioning than a man's did, apparently—and then coaxed her to sit and drink a cup of water. "Slowly," he cautioned, as if she were the newcomer to Colorado summers, not he.

They had spent the entire morning at the small dig

site farthest from the camp, taking a few of the Yale diggers, including Peter, with them. But they hadn't done any real digging—Cecil had just wanted to check out the lay of the land again—and had returned to the major dig area just after lunchtime.

And Cecil had paid attention to her the whole time, conversing with her, asking her opinion, praising her for the sketches she had made of the odd fossilized horn she'd found.

Too little, too late.

Lily shifted on the stool and wondered when they would return to camp. Mason had claimed to be like a tumbleweed, moving on when the impulse grabbed him. But he wouldn't leave without telling her first, would he?

"My sister Anne—oh, you'll like her when you meet her." Cecil gave her hand a few pats. Lily scrounged up a smile. "She is quite the hostess, known for a hundred miles around for the table she sets. Why, she wrote in her most recent letter to me that she'd met—"

All day he had peppered his conversation with names of famous or infamous people he or his family knew. Another attempt to impress her, she supposed. Only her mother's strictures on politeness had kept her tongue behind her teeth.

"What is it that you do when you aren't fossil hunting?" she interrupted. "Do you help your brother with his business?"

"It's the family business, not my brother's," Cecil snapped. He took a deep breath, then forced a smile. "My brother and I have our differences on how to run the company. I doubt I'll be able to put my ideas into effect until after he dies."

Lily blinked. What a strange thing to say. "Is he much older than you? Or ill?"

"No, no." His eyes left hers for a moment. "He's an avid sportsman, though, and inclined to take risks." Looking back at her, he added, "My mother has been predicting a bad end for him since he was five and nearly drowned in a pond at our country house."

Cecil abruptly leaned forward, his face taut with an emotion she couldn't identify. Aggression? Anger? Hate? Lily couldn't suppress her instinctive start backward.

He dropped his voice. "Dickon said you were there when he found the sapphire."

Dickon had told her that he'd inform her grandfather of the find, and her grandfather must have told his top two men, Richter and St. John.

She looked around to locate Richter. St. John shook his head, apparently reading her thought. "Richter doesn't know," he said. "No one knows, except you, me, your grandfather, and Dickon. And it must stay that way."

Dickon had given her the same warning. Did they expect she would scribble letters about the sapphire to all her friends? "I understand that public knowledge of the find would hinder our dig," she said stiffly. "We'd have gem hunters underfoot, getting in our way and possibly destroying invaluable fossils."

Cecil smiled. "Good girl. You do understand." He hesitated. "I would never attempt to dictate your actions, but it would be wise if you kept your distance from Donnelly until he leaves, which hopefully will be any day now."

Well, it had taken Cecil long enough to display any signs of jealousy. Unless . . . "Why?"

"He's a reporter. A good reporter, your grandfather says, which means he ferrets out people's secrets. We don't need him here." Cecil looked away for a moment, then solemnly returned his gaze to hers. "You may think it crass of me to mention it, but the fellow appears beguiled by you. If you don't encourage him in his infatuation, he will leave all the sooner—and leave us in peace."

She should have known that Cecil's worries about Mason centered on his being a reporter. "I'll have to speak with my grandfather about this. Mason is his guest, and it would be rude for me to ignore him just on your say-so."

"'Mason,' eh?" Cecil seemed about to say more, then shook his head. "I think that if you speak with your grandfather, you'll find we are in complete agreement. The reporter must leave. And you, my lovely girl, are the one who will make him go."

Slapping his hat against his knee, Cecil stood. "I have a few things to see to in camp. Are you ready to go?"

She had been, five seconds ago. But she just couldn't take another moment in Cecil's company. And she wanted some time to think. "No, I'd prefer to stay here for a while longer. But you should go ahead."

As he left, she could've sworn she heard him mutter something like "Stubborn."

Alone and able to be herself, Lily closed her eyes

and groaned. What a disaster. Cecil was right—if Mason knew about the sapphire find, he would grab the story and write it. And with his wide readership, the camp would be immediately overrun by gem hunters. It might not impact this season, as they were already winding down, but the gem seekers could do enormous damage to the dig sites and the fossils yet to be uncovered if they bashed their way into the rocks, searching for more sapphires.

Lily opened her eyes and looked around her at the busy dig site. Her grandfather planned to dig here for another two seasons at least. If the gem seekers came here, all their painstaking work would be ruined.

Of course, the trouble with Cecil's instruction that she stop flirting with Mason so that he'd be discouraged and leave was that Mason knew her flirtation was fake. Whether he stayed or went was out of her control. All she could do was make sure that he didn't learn about the sapphire from her.

Sighing, she climbed to her feet. This fake flirtation business had seemed so straightforward when she had first thought of it. Now it had more twists than a coiled rattler.

She left the shade cast by the awning, taking her sketchbook with her. Picking a nice, flat rock near where Peter and a few other Yalies were working, she sat down and began to sketch them.

Just a rough sketch—nothing more than a few lines to denote a bent back, an upflung pickax, and the cliff face into which the men bored. As she lifted her eyes again to the scene, she let out a little gasp.

A man was standing on top of the cliff, the sun behind him shading his features.

Peter lifted his head at the sound of her gasp, followed her gaze, and grimaced. "Another damn miner. I'm getting tired of them popping up, trying to look menacing. Don't they know that we're leaving in only two weeks? Why bother with the intimidation?"

Last night she'd found their intimidation tactics to be quite effective. She shivered but kept her mouth shut. The last thing she wanted was to be forced to leave the dig early over concerns about her safety. She'd just make sure to have an escort for the ride back to Milton tonight.

As they watched, the miner turned and disappeared behind the ridge.

"Are you looking forward to going home?" Lily asked Peter.

He leaned against his pickax—not stopping precisely, just pausing. "Sure am. I've never gone so long without seeing my family. Letters from them are nice but aren't the same as seeing their faces across the supper table. What about you? Oh, but I forgot. You're from here."

"I'm from Boston, too, and I'll be going there after the dig closes up." And then she'd finally see her family's faces across the supper table instead of subsisting on their letters, as she'd done for years.

Her sisters, Annabelle and Emily, wrote her every two weeks. And her mother wrote once a week, sometimes enclosing a short note from Lily's stepfather. But it wasn't nearly the same as speaking with them and laughing with them.

Not that she'd laughed very much during her last disastrous visit home.

This time would be different, though. She wouldn't be a brat—she had outgrown that. And she'd remember enough of her manners to get by without embarrassing her family too much.

Shaking out her skirts, she stood. "I need to speak with my grandfather about some things," she said to Peter. Things such as whether Cecil's command to discourage Mason had originally come from her grandfather. "I'll see you at supper tonight."

He tipped his wide-brimmed hat. "A pleasure, Miss Lily."

She felt a smile tilt up the corners of her mouth as she swung up into her saddle. Though she hadn't considered it before, Peter was just the sort of young man—minus the big hat and sweat-stained shirt and pickax, of course—who her mother would expect her to charm while in Boston. Although charming Peter was beyond her reach, she always held her own with him without getting flustered. Very reassuring.

Maybe returning home wouldn't be so difficult after all.

Two hours after he'd been tossed off his horse, Mason reached the fork in the trail that led to the first dig site. The tent town was now a ripple on the horizon, luring him on.

Hoofbeats echoed to his left. Mason turned, his perspiration-soaked shirt pulling at his shoulders. A single rider approached from the first dig. Lily.

Mason stopped, sat down on the nearest boulder, and waited. He was just too damn tired to feel anything other than a niggle of embarrassment at his predicament.

Her face twisted in concern, Lily pulled her mount to a halt before him. Mason coughed at the little dust cloud kicked up by its hooves. "Lord above," she said, swinging down to the ground. "What happened to you?"

As she dismounted, her skirts frothed around her knees in quite an interesting fashion. Hmm, very nice, he thought. Getting tossed off his horse was almost worth this.

"My horse threw me," Mason answered, climbing to his feet. God, he felt awful. "Did you happen to see it running around?"

"Are you hurt?" Lily asked, reaching out a hand as if to touch him, then dropping it quickly.

"Nah. Just a bump on the head." A bump that was the size of one of the Rocky Mountains.

She scrutinized Mason as if she didn't believe him, then finally nodded her acceptance. Fumbling with her waterskin, she unfastened it from her saddle and handed it to him.

Warm and dusty-smelling, the water was the best he'd ever had. "I love you," he said, finally returning the waterskin to her.

She rolled her eyes. "Now I know the secret to gaining eternal devotion. Find a man who's parched."

"Your being pretty helps a lot, too."

Another eye roll. "Thanks."

"And smart."

This time she cocked her head and didn't respond.

He had to watch his mouth better. Without Cecil here as an excuse, he was going to get himself into trouble. Avoiding her eyes, he made a production of taking his hat off, wiping his brow, and then putting it on again.

"I think you should ride my horse," she said.

"And let you walk?" He shook his head and started down the road on foot. He went only twenty paces before the edges of his vision began rolling in. Damn. This just might kill him.

"Stop that!" She caught up to him, pulling her horse along behind her. "Why are you being so stubborn? Just get on the horse."

"Sorry." One foot, then the other. The camp looked closer already.

"Or we can ride together," she said, grabbing his elbow and yanking him to a stop.

Any other day he would have put up more of a fight. But black spots were beginning to flicker across his vision, and when he stood still, as he was doing now, he could feel an embarrassing wobbliness in his knees. The possibility of making it to the tent camp on his own steam was almost zero.

And if he did end up crashing to the ground like a shot buffalo, that would leave Lily to deal with the mess of hauling him back to camp.

"All right. Let me mount first, then you climb up behind me."

He felt like an old man, all creaking joints and

flabby muscles, as he stuck his foot in the stirrup and swung up on the horse. Lily adjusted the stirrup length so that his knees wouldn't knock against his teeth. Wrapping her fingers around his wrist while he held hers, she placed her foot on his boot—again displaying a fair amount of petticoat—levered herself up, and awkwardly mounted behind him. Without hesitation, she circled his waist with her arms.

Maybe this wasn't such a bad way to travel after all. He considered telling her that, then reconsidered and finally pressed his heels into her horse in silence.

"This is truly uncomfortable," she said after only ten seconds. "It sounds so much easier in dime novels. I mean, in *Moriarty's Last Stand*, he even had one girl in front of him and one behind him, and they chatted merrily the whole way."

"I guess that's why it's called fiction."

"Well, now I know. So, where did you lose your horse?"

An aggravating way to put it. "On my way to the second dig site, on the trail down."

Her arms tightened. He'd thought having her hug him had felt good before. This felt even better.

"The trail down?" Her voice rose. "The *steep* trail?"

"Yep, it was pretty steep. My horse took fright at something, bucked me off, and hightailed it out of there."

"Lord above," she whispered, her breath tickling his ear. For a moment there was a new pressure against his shoulder blade. Was she pressing her cheek against him? "You're lucky you're not dead."

As well as lucky to be where he was now, with Lily's arms wrapped around him like he was a box and she was the bow.

Or he was her beau.

He cleared his throat. Any speculation along those lines would be sheer fantasy, and he'd best keep that in mind. "Any progress with Cecil today?"

"Hmm, I think some progress was made, yes."

His innards slid down into his boots. Not a pleasant sensation when combined with the dizziness he still felt from being thrown to the ground and after his sun-scoured two-hour walk.

"Yes . . . progress," she repeated. "There is now doubt in my mind that if I married Cecil, I would kill him within a year. Maybe rig something to make his horse buck him off in a nasty place, like yours did today. I consider that realization to be great progress, actually."

He found himself grinning like an idiot. And somehow he suddenly felt much healthier. "I do, too."

She poked him in the shoulder. "That's because you dislike him. I don't dislike him. I just find him tedious."

Well, that seemed like a fast switch. Two days ago she'd asked for Mason's help in ensnaring Cecil. Yesterday she'd trailed after Cecil like a puppy. Today she was declaring that her interest was over.

Suddenly the air tasted sweeter, the sky looked deeper, the clouds appeared puffier.

Today she was free to be pursued.

But he had to be practical. "Have you told him this?" he asked.

"No, of course not. Should I say out of the blue, 'Cecil, you haven't paid attention to me in weeks, so I no longer will marry you, even though you've never asked me'?"

That didn't reassure him. "He's dropped hints that he would propose, hasn't he?"

"Yes. But not recently."

"But if he resumed dropping hints tomorrow—"

"You think I'd change my mind?" In his peripheral vision, he saw her shake her head. "No. I gave him lots of opportunities. I even roped you into trying to make him jealous. He missed his chance." She sighed, then shrugged. "Ah, well. Live and learn."

The camp was now so close that Mason could pick out details such as a man's boots lying in front of one canvas doorway. To the right, Highfill's tent rose like a palace.

"Were you coming out to the second dig site to see me?" Lily asked.

He'd almost forgotten. "Dickon found something today. A blue stone."

Her arms tightened around him. It felt delicious. "He showed it to you?"

"I saw him find it and I asked to see it. *Then* he showed it to me. I think he would've been happier if I hadn't seen it at all."

She hesitated before speaking again, and her next words sounded more cautious than curious. "Did he say what it was?"

Mason wished he could see her face as he answered. "All he said was that it was a gift for his daughter."

Until she sagged against him, he hadn't realized

that she'd been holding herself so stiffly. "That makes sense."

"Does it? Why be so secretive about a stone?"

"Who knows? But it's Dickon's business, not ours."

If a story was there, it was Mason's business, too, whether he still had a job with the paper or not.

How much did Lily know about this strange stone? Well, she was the granddaughter of the expedition's financier, Dickon's assistant, and formerly the fossil expert's near fiancée. If there was something special about that stone, there was no way she could be unaware of whatever was going on.

In a bright, let's-change-the-subject voice, Lily said, "Oh, look." They were nearly at the corral. "There's your horse."

Someone had taken care of the animal, for his saddle had been removed and he had been rubbed down. Lily jumped to the ground, landing with an "Oof," then gave her abused rear end a quick rub, making Mason's mouth go dry so fast that he reached for Lily's waterskin again. The princess wasn't even trying, and she made him crazy.

His eyes were glued so tightly to her butt that it took him a few moments to notice that Cecil had exited from Highfill's nearby tent and was approaching them. Mason slid off Lily's horse and took a little step closer to her.

"I was about to send someone to go looking for you, Donnelly," Cecil said, concern oozing from his upperclass accent. "Never a good sign when a man's horse precedes him home. Get tossed?"

Unless his horse had taken the scenic route, the animal had been back here for at least two hours. Plenty of time for Cecil to have sent someone out to look for him.

Of course, if Mason was after a girl and the girl appeared to be falling for someone else, maybe Mason wouldn't be quick on the trigger to search out the missing rival, either. If Cecil's horse had come back riderless . . .

No. Mason would have sent out a few searchers immediately. These lands could kill you fast.

Lily, frowning to herself, gave her rear end a final swipe. Cecil's eyes followed her movement, then tightened their focus. Bastard.

"Thanks for taking care of my horse," Mason said loudly.

Cecil blinked and pulled his gaze back to Mason. "Of course. Lily, your grandfather wants to see you."

Cecil started for Highfill's tent. When Lily didn't follow him immediately, he halted and glared back at her. "Now, Lily."

"Are you certain you're all right?" Lily asked Mason, her wide eyes fixed on his face.

Her attention alone was a balm to the soreness settling in his muscles. "I'm fine. But thanks for bullying me onto your horse."

"The cook also serves as a doctor of sorts. Maybe you should visit him."

"Lily!" Cecil said again.

"I'm not a dog who comes when you call, Cecil," she snapped. "I will join you in a few moments."

Heaving an irritated sigh, Cecil crossed his arms over his chest and waited.

"You'll see the cook?" she said, not really asking a question.

"All right." And his reward was the glowing smile she gave him.

"See you at supper." With one last smile, she turned away and entered her grandfather's tent, a grim-mouthed Cecil on her tail.

Now that she was out of sight, Mason gave him-self a little inspection. His torn-up elbow and scraped hand should be washed out, which the cook could help with. Not much to do for his twisted knee. And he couldn't see his own face, of course, but it felt like he had a few nice deep scratches there—probably caused by the bush he'd half landed in when his horse had de-cided to displace him.

Entering the corral, Mason ran his hands over his horse. Cecil had rubbed it down, amazingly. Mason had assumed that Cecil's dislike for him would have extended to his horse as well.

His fingers caught on a rough patch. What was this? Pushing the hair aside, he saw new scabs spot-ting his horse's skin right about where the back edge of his saddle lay.

Damn it, there'd probably been a burr or a stick caught in his saddle blanket, and when he'd leaned his weight back as they'd descended the steep trail, the object had jabbed into his horse, causing it to buck. It was his own fault for not checking his saddle blanket.

But when he went to remove whatever had stuck to the saddle blanket, he couldn't find anything there.

>>>·<<<

Not only was her grandfather waiting for her in his tent, but Dickon was there as well. Cecil followed her inside and twitched the tent flap shut, enclosing them in humid, airless gloom.

Lily stifled a sigh. Why didn't they just hang a sign outside saying SECRET MEETING IN PROGRESS?

Dickon patted the stool next to him, and Lily settled onto it.

"What the devil were you doing with Donnelly?" Cecil demanded before anyone else could speak. "You were plastered all over him, Lily. You're supposed to encourage him to leave, not encourage him to stay."

Her grandfather cocked his head. "What's this?"

Huffing with indignation, Cecil said, "When I heard Lily riding up, I discovered her riding double with Donnelly, her arms around his waist."

Lily gripped the edge of the stool. "That's the way one rides double, Cecil. Would you have preferred *him* holding *me* around the waist?"

"Why were you riding double in the first place?" her grandfather asked.

"His horse ran off after throwing him." She paused for dramatic effect. "On the steep trail down to the second dig site."

"Good God. He's lucky to be alive."

"I simply encountered him as he was walking back." And then browbeat him into getting on the horse. And then gave in to impulse and laid her cheek against his shoulder. But she didn't think her grandfather would appreciate those details.

Time to move the conversation along. "Another sapphire was found, I understand."

"And Donnelly saw it," Cecil confirmed. He looked at Dickon. "Was Donnelly with you when you found the sapphire?"

"He was helping me pack up specimens."

"Does he usually do this?"

"No, it was the first time."

Cecil grimaced. "I think he already knew that something is going on. Why else would he be in the right place at the right time?" He swiveled his head to stare at Lily.

He was lucky that her mother had taught her never to assault people, no matter how provoking they might be. "I haven't told him a thing," she said steadily.

"But every time I look at you, you two have your heads together, chatting."

Dickon chuckled. "St. John, there are plenty of things for a smart fellow and a pretty young lady to discuss other than fossils or gemstones."

A flush began creeping up Cecil's neck like a rash. "I'm aware of that, thank you. I just wanted to remind Lily where her loyalties should lie."

They certainly did not lie with *him*. "I'd never do anything to hurt my grandfather or this expedition. And that includes telling Mason about the sapphires. But does he suspect something is going on? Yes."

Her grandfather leaned forward. "What does he suspect?"

"I don't know. He thought that Dickon being so secretive about the sapphire he found today was strange.

I told him that if it wasn't a fossil, then it was Dickon's business and not ours."

"Good girl," her grandfather said, settling back again into his chair.

"I'll keep Donnelly out of my tent," Dickon told them. "With luck he'll have moved on in a day or two, and he'll be out of our hair."

Her lungs seemed to tighten, and she had trouble drawing a full breath. But of course Mason would move on in a day or two. He'd been warning her of that since she'd met him. It shouldn't feel so much like betrayal.

Cecil nodded at her. "Lily could help encourage him to leave."

Was Cecil determined to make her drive Mason away because he thought it the most effective method to get Mason to leave? Or had his pride been wounded by her apparent preference for Mason? Cecil's heart certainly hadn't been damaged.

"That hardly seems fair—" Dickon began, but her grandfather rode over him.

"A good idea. Lily dear: Try to convince him to hasten his departure. Cutting down on those chats you have together would be a good place to start."

Mason's words popped into her head: *Your grandfather would never accept my suit, even if it was real.* Was this the true problem, not the sapphires?

"But—" she started to say, then snapped her mouth shut at the flint-sharp look in her grandfather's eyes.

Whatever the reasons behind his suggestion, this *was* a test of her loyalty.

She exhaled slowly. "Yes, sir."

Chapter Seven

Something had changed.

Nodding in agreement to whatever the digger beside him had just said, Mason mentally flipped through reasons for the sudden cold shoulder he was getting from Lily.

Up near the head of the supper table, seated between Cecil and Peter-from-Yale, Lily smiled and laughed and generally behaved like she was having a wonderful time. All good.

But although Mason was on the other side of Peter-from-Yale, Lily had spared him barely a word or a glance since she'd sat down at the trestle table ten minutes ago.

Something had changed. And Mason didn't like it.

The digger to his left was a local fellow. "Two places you need to see here," he told Mason. "The hot springs that lie a few miles north of Milton, and the mines that run through this ridge."

Mason pushed his lumpy potatoes around on his plate. "I've been in mines before." He'd written a number of stories on the terrible working conditions involved in mining, and how the lure of gold pulled men into the earth—and sometimes into their graves. "What's special about these?"

The local man chuckled. "You'll see. I don't want to spoil it for you. Make sure you bring a half dozen candles with you."

A half dozen? "Just how far into this mine do you expect me to go?"

"You'll see," the digger repeated. "And you won't have to go very far at all."

Lily spoke up from several seats down. "It is impressive, Mason. You should see it before you leave. Maybe tomorrow."

Before you leave. Not a subtle hint.

Anger bubbled in his veins, and he looked away quickly before she could see it in his eyes. No need to advertise that she affected him.

He had to push emotion aside and tackle this the same way he had tackled every other situation he suspected concealed a fantastic story: by being relentless. If that meant pushing Lily to tell him what she knew, then that's what he would do.

He forced his attention back to the discussion. "What about the miners?" Mason asked the local digger. "Won't they object to my poking around in their mines?"

"Oh, those fellows don't even mine anymore—they just talk about when they did. No one will even know you're there."

Mason glanced over at Lily. She had her gaze on

Peter-from-Yale, but from the way she kept her head slightly cocked, Mason knew she was following this conversation. "I saw a fellow yesterday who was watching you men digging," Mason said. "He didn't look pleased to see you there."

The local man pulled at his mustache. "One or two— all right, a good dozen—don't like outsiders messing around near the mines. The mines ran out long ago, and everyone who worked on 'em sold their shares in the mine and the land around it, but some still think of the place as theirs. They keep an eye on things."

Mason looked away from the digger and found himself locking stares with St. John. He had also been listening. "Have you been there, St. John?"

"When I first arrived. He's right: You should see the mine before you go." St. John turned his head, dismissing him.

Apparently everyone would be happy to see his back as he rode over the horizon.

Night fell in ever-darkening layers over the camp, plates got shoved aside, and elbows rested on the table as the bone hunters finished their dinner and settled into socializing. Mason launched into a Can-you-top-this? competition with some of the diggers about blizzards they'd lived through. At the top of the table, Highfill, St. John, Dickon, and Lily sat with their heads together, speaking in low tones.

Secrets. They lurked all over this place. And whatever the big one was—the one that Mason had been blindly pursuing when he'd gone down that trail and been thrown by his horse—Lily knew it.

He shifted his shoulders, then winced. He was going to be hurting for days. It wasn't any worse than when he'd gotten beaten up on the wharves in San Francisco by a bunch of sailors when he was sniffing out a story that the U.S. Navy was transporting contraband and lining their own pockets, or when a madam in a Reno brothel sicced half a dozen bottle-wielding girls at him, but the pain he was feeling now was no fun at all. All his instincts were screaming at him that there was a story here, and so far his instincts had never let him down. They'd gotten him into trouble, but they'd never let him down.

He stared down the trestle table at Lily. She was trouble personified, wrapped up in the most delicious possible package.

Clearing his throat, he said loudly, "Miss Highfill must have some good blizzard stories to tell."

Her head jerked up. "What?"

"You've lived through your share of blizzards. Tell us about one."

She delivered a distant smile. "I'm not a good storyteller."

Perhaps not, but she'd been a hell of an actress these past three days, pretending friendliness with him so that she could play her games with Cecil. She had clearly won the Bostonian over. His eyes fixed on her face, he had been hanging on her every word all evening.

As she twisted away to return to her conversation, Cecil laid his hand over her wrist. She immediately reached for her glass of cider, flicking his hand off in the process.

All right. So maybe he was wrong and Lily had been serious that afternoon when she'd said that she had no more interest in St. John.

Mason scowled. He didn't understand why she was now giving him the cold shoulder, though. That little kiss she'd landed on him at the corral last night hadn't been for the benefit of the crowd or for St. John. Was she simply flighty?

No—he'd made that assumption in the beginning and had had to quickly take it back. Something else was going on. Mason just didn't have all the pieces to figure out the puzzle.

A few of the diggers began to shove back from the table and disappear into the night. Soon it turned into a full-fledged exodus, leaving Mason, Lily, St. John, Highfill, and Dickon as the final stragglers. The cook's assistant started tossing the tin supper plates into a bucket of water, sending up splashy clangs.

Mason couldn't wait any longer. "Miss Highfill, do you need an escort home tonight?"

"I—"

St. John interposed smoothly. "Lily already asked me to take her home tonight, Donnelly." He smiled, showing a lot of white teeth. "Better luck next time."

"You go too far!" Lily snapped as soon as she and Cecil were out of earshot of the supper table. "There was no need to lie like that."

"The other option was for you to turn him down. But I thought you might turn soft at the end and allow him to ride back with you."

She might not have let Mason escort her to Milton. Oh, who was she fooling? She'd started to tell him yes before Cecil spoke over her. For the past hour, she had sat within six feet of Mason. Not being able to talk to him had eaten away at her, taking away her appetite and adding a sharp edge to every word she spoke. Toward the end of supper, even Dickon had begun avoiding engaging her in conversation.

"You don't seem to understand the potential for disaster," Cecil continued. "If word gets out that sapphires have been found here, the expedition is ruined. As both an outsider and a reporter, Donnelly is the one who's most likely to take this information public. We have to make sure he doesn't learn about the sapphires at all."

They had reached the corral, and Cecil began saddling both horses. Within a few minutes they were on the trail to Milton, the stars overhead looking like beads of silver against inky satin.

"As you know," Cecil continued, "your grandfather wants to return here next season." He paused. "I hope that you and I will return here next season as well."

If she'd been walking, she would have stumbled. But the horse beneath her continued to plod steadily along, clearly oblivious to the almost-proposal that had just left Cecil's lips.

She turned her head to stare at him. The starlight revealed that he was looking straight ahead, a smug smile pursing his mouth.

Thank God, thank God, thank God she'd come to

her senses last night. For if she had to wake up to that smug smile every morning, she'd be driven to murder by their second anniversary.

"I'm glad Grandfather invited me to join him here this summer. But next year seems so far away. I don't know if I'll be in Denver with my aunt or in Boston with my family." A parry to his assumption that they'd be together.

His smile widened. "Oh, don't be coy, Lily. You'll be in Boston, and you'll be the toast of the town."

"I'm not being coy. The last time I visited Boston, I lasted only a few months there. Any impact I made on the social scene was decidedly a negative one."

"You were young. Besides, this time you'll have me at your side."

Lord, the arrogance! She wasn't sure which was more offensive: his assumption that she'd so easily forget that he had ignored her for the past few weeks, or his belief that his consequence was more than enough to offset any social blunders she might make.

"Cecil . . ." She paused. As much as she itched to point out all the reasons he annoyed her—plus a few occasions when he'd outright insulted her—a gently worded rejection would better maintain the ties of friendship between their families.

"Cecil, I've enjoyed your company this summer, but I do not believe we suit each other."

His smug smile vanished. "Your family would never let you marry a roaming reporter."

"I never said anything about—"

"You'd be cut off."

"Cut off?" She could hear herself growing shrill, but she couldn't stop it. "I've been living in Denver without my mother and sisters for eight years, Cecil. How could I become more cut off?"

He snorted. "Your mother talks to my mother all the time. I know that you're taken care of in Denver."

"I wasn't talking about money. I was talking about having my family around me."

Somehow they'd reached Milton without her realizing it. Good—this conversation wouldn't last much longer.

As she turned toward the livery stable, Cecil continued to speak. "If you want your family back, the first thing you should do is get rid of Donnelly. He's going to ruin your grandfather's dreams."

"I'm trying!"

They both dismounted at the stable, and Lily handed her horse to the livery boy. Cecil, surprising her, did the same. "I'll be back in an hour or so," he told the boy.

"My room is only a minute away," she reminded Cecil as they began walking.

"I thought I might spend a little time with you. Because the second thing you can do to get your family back is to marry me."

He stroked his palm down her back, curling his hand around her hip.

She sidestepped fast, and his hand dropped away. An hour. She had to endure an hour of this sort of love play, she suspected. She was torn between wanting to laugh and smacking him.

She lifted her chin and stared him in the eyes. "For my grandfather's sake, I'm willing to encourage Mason to leave. But I will not marry you, Cecil. That's my final decision."

His lips narrowed. "Try bringing him home, Lily. I'd love to see the reception he gets."

"My aunt, for one, would love him!" she snapped, then immediately regretted it. She took a deep breath. "This has nothing to do with Mason." It had *everything* to do with Mason, as he'd helped open her eyes to how poorly Cecil was treating her and realize that she deserved better than that. Still, the fact that she caught herself staring at Mason's mouth every few minutes during supper wasn't relevant to this argument. Because Cecil was right about one thing: Mason was a roving reporter who had no intention of settling down.

"Your aunt is in Denver for a reason," Cecil sneered. "A reason that has everything to do with her loving the wrong man."

Lily blinked. What was he talking about? She shook the question away. Whatever it was, she wasn't going to get sidetracked. "I don't believe you and I would be happy together. And I would appreciate it if you wouldn't bring up the subject again."

There. The onus of behaving properly was now on him.

They were at the boardinghouse door—finally. "Good night," she said, and entered the building. As she turned to close the door, he slapped his hand on it, stopping her.

"I'm a nice fellow," he said. "I'll give you one chance to change your mind." His smile didn't look nice, though. Lily took a step back.

He finally released the door. "Sweet dreams." And he melted into the night.

Chapter Eight

Talking to Richter was like talking to a friendly dog: He was very happy to see you but couldn't answer your questions. Mason tried again. "You've got a good crew down there." He gestured at the shirtless young men digging away at the cliff face under the sun while he and Richter sat in the luxury of shade under an open-sided canvas tent on a hill, catching the occasional breeze.

Richter gave an agreeable nod. "A good crew."

Mason continued, "Maybe even better than last year's. Has that made a difference?"

"A little, I think. They're good boys."

"They must be excited by the possibility of a new find."

"Every day is filled with possibilities for these boys!"

Enough with dancing around what he wanted to know. "And have they found anything?" Mason asked baldly.

The dig foreman blinked at him. "You arrived the

night we found the fossilized horn, didn't you? Quite a find. *Quite* a find."

Mason squinted at him. "Anything besides that? Some interesting stones, maybe?"

"Stones? Not that I know of. But Mr. Highfill and Mr. St. John have a better idea about what's important and what's not. Well, Mr. Highfill has some idea. Mr. St. John is the real expert." Richter gave a self-deprecating shrug of his wide shoulders. "I'm just here to oversee the diggers."

Richter either was a master of deception or he truly had no concern about what was or wasn't found during the dig.

"Do you get a percentage of the proceeds?"

Richter pulled his eyes from his diggers and grimaced, his first sign of disgruntlement since Mason had shown up in midmorning to delicately probe him about the goings-on of the dig. "The proceeds? There are no 'proceeds': Everything goes into Highfill's private collection. He'll sell some of the lesser pieces to other museums, but that doesn't bring in much money. I get a fee for the season. A good fee, for Highfill isn't stingy about the things that are important to him."

"And St. John is getting a fee, too, you think?"

"Well, if Highfill's sold him on taking a percentage, the fellow is going to a have a shock at the end of the season." Richter's eyes crinkled at that, as if he wouldn't mind Cecil being disappointed.

Mason smiled back, but questions were boiling inside him.

Was he chasing a figment of his imagination? If he

could no longer write and no longer properly interview someone, did he even still have a story instinct—"the nose," as his mentor had described it?

Well, if he gave up now, he'd never find out. Or, worse, he'd find out he was right by reading someone else's story on it.

Richter scratched his bearded jaw. "It's been a funny summer, I have to admit. My boys down there are excited, of course, about the finds we've made. But Highfill and St. John don't seem to be in the spirit of things."

"Why?"

"Highfill's an important man; he probably has other things on his mind. I don't know St. John well enough to speculate."

Hmm. Maybe Mason could find someone who was willing to speculate. He turned the conversation away from the dig. "How are your children? You have two, don't you?"

Richter's eyes lit. In the next twenty minutes he made up for his earlier taciturnity—with interest.

"That daughter of yours sounds like a real fire-cracker," Mason broke in. "Oh, look, there's Peter . . ." He couldn't remember the Yale kid's last name or if he'd even been told what it was. "I need to ask him a quick question. Good luck today."

"You're leaving soon, right?" Richter said. His eyes sharpened. "That's what you said last night at supper."

He'd made no promises at supper. Interesting that Richter believed that, though. "I'll leave at some point, sure. Why?"

"No reason. It's just that things get busy at the end of the season. Wouldn't want you to think you're in the way."

If he hadn't thought that before—and he hadn't—Richter was doing his best to plant the idea in his head. "Hmm, that hadn't occurred to me." Mason frowned. "Maybe I could help out more, give you a hand—"

"No! I mean, no, but thanks all the same. I'd spend more time telling you what to do than if I did it myself."

Mason nodded, but his thoughts churned behind his agreeable smile. Just why did everyone want him out of here? There was something going on. He just needed to find it. . . .

"Good day, Mr. Donnelly." Richter turned back to what he'd been doing before Mason had interrupted him. Writing a letter to his children, Mason now saw.

Mason stepped out into the sun and started strolling toward the diggers. He should be thinking of questions to ask Peter—questions that might get him closer to finding out what everyone was trying to conceal—but all he could think about was that he couldn't remember the last time he'd written a letter to someone other than his editor or his friend Old Joe.

His father had been his last surviving family member. Everyone else had been wiped out during the potato famine or had moved from Ireland to America and then vanished into its vast interior without a trace. *Donnelly* wasn't an uncommon name. A few times after his father had died, Mason had tracked down a few Donnellys to see if they were relations of a sort. He'd soon figured out that looking for cousins and such would be like searching for a specific blade of grass in the prairie.

His father had been too tired after a full day's work on the railroad to summon the energy to discuss family history. And Mason, caught up in the colorful lives of the other railroad workers, hadn't pushed any questions on him. Too late, he'd realized that he'd probably cut himself off from any family through his ignorance.

Old Joe was the closest thing he had to family now. A curmudgeon who lived in Mason's house in San Francisco as its "caretaker," because he refused to accept any charity, Old Joe had taught him the ropes of journalism. The least Mason could do was give him a place to live and send him a letter once a month. Mason returned to his house so seldom that he probably saw Old Joe only two or three times a year. Well, the way things were going with his writing, the two of them might be living together full-time soon.

Lily wrote to her family in Boston; she'd mentioned her mother's and sisters' letters several times.

Where was Lily? He had expected her to be here by now, riding at St. John's elbow. Despite her claim yesterday afternoon that she'd decided that she and Cecil wouldn't suit, she'd clearly changed her mind again by the time supper rolled around. She'd even ridden off with Cecil to her place in town. Mason had happened to be near the corral when Cecil returned, so at least he knew that Lily hadn't asked him in for cider the way she'd asked Mason in the night before.

He gave himself a shake. He shouldn't be thinking

about Lily's butterfly resolve. He should be trying to figure out just what was going on with Highfill's expedition and whether it was a story good enough to get him his column back. Assuming he could write the story.

He wandered down the line of diggers, all of whom were already covered with a fine veil of yellow dust, until he found the young man from Yale. "Morning, Peter."

The fellow turned and grinned. "Hullo, Mr. Donnelly. Hot work here today." But he said it cheerfully even as he dragged his tanned forearm across his sweat-shiny forehead. "Want to give us a hand?"

Mason laughed at the cheerful jibe. "I already put in my time, working on the Central Pacific railroad as a boy. So I'll pass on your offer—thanks."

"One of my uncles worked on the Union Pacific for a few seasons. Brutal work, he said."

Mason grinned at him. "Where's St. John today?"

Peter looked at him sideways. "Why?"

"I'd expected to see him here by now." And Lily as well, though he didn't need to let Peter know that.

"He went to Denver for a few days, maybe a week."

"Oh." Mason tried to keep his satisfaction from his expression.

"A little strange that he'd hie off so close to the end of the season," Peter said, "but I'm sure you don't mind. Lily is working in Dickon's tent today."

"What does Lily have to do with anything?" He'd suspected the kid was sweet on her, and his bringing her name up for no reason now proved it. He narrowed his eyes.

Shrugging, Peter said, "I'm just telling you where she is."

He started to ask why, then stopped. He'd forgotten—he had been playing the flirt with her. Of course Peter believed Mason would want to know where she was.

Damn. He did want to know—that was the aggravating part. And not just so he could pin her down so he could ask her questions. Though the idea of gently pinning her against a tree or on top of a bed and sealing her mouth with his sparked his imagination.

Over the past few days, the line between playacting and reality had blurred. Too many times, standing next to Lily and breathing in the scent of her sun-warmed hair, he'd wanted to lift her chin and kiss the sense out of her. Well, he was the one who'd lost his sense, thinking that way. She was a virgin heiress from Boston, for God's sake.

And with Richter being oddly uncommunicative, she was also Mason's best shot at finding out what the importance of that stone was.

"Thanks, Peter." Mason turned away.

"Going to see Lily?" Peter asked.

"Yes."

"Good!" Peter slapped him on the back. "My money's on you."

Mason swung around. "What?"

"Some of us have bets going on whom Lily is going to chose."

"And you put your money on me?" Flattering, if stupid. He shook his head. "Bad choice, I'm afraid."

"Cecil St. John isn't right for her."

He wouldn't argue with that. "I think I look good only in comparison."

"Maybe, sir. I bet just a nickel."

Great. He was sure Lily would be appalled to learn that the diggers were placing nickel bets on the identity of her future husband. Still, he couldn't resist asking, "So, who's ahead?"

"You have thirty cents on you."

Thirty cents. So that was probably six diggers who—

"And Cecil St. John has a dollar twenty on him." Peter shrugged. "Some fellows bet more than a nickel. Richter, for instance, has got a quarter riding on St. John. A business decision, he said—nothing personal."

That quarter probably explained Richter's interest in encouraging Mason to depart quickly: Richter wanted an open field for St. John so Richter could win the bet. So that lead had hit a dead end. Now Mason was left where he had started out today, with only a few strong suspicions that something strange was going on at the bone hunters' camp but no real proof.

Oh, and he'd also learned that Cecil St. John had left—which was good—and that St. John had four times as much support among the diggers for marrying Lily—which was bad.

Mason growled under his breath. Who cared who was ahead in the betting? It wasn't like he was going to ask Lily to marry him. God, even the diggers thought that a long shot.

"What happens if she doesn't marry either one

of us?" he asked Peter. A little hint that putting additional money into the betting would be a waste of cash.

"Well, maybe a third candidate will appear and surprise everyone."

Mason dug into his pocket, found a dime, and handed it to Peter. "Here. My money is on you. But what if none of us wins the fair lady?"

"We'll all spend the pot at the saloon in Milton."

Mason chuckled, clapped his hand on Peter's shoulder, and headed for his horse.

Mounting up, he realized he wouldn't be around to learn the outcome. Maybe, after he'd left, he'd check the society columns every so often to see if Lily's engagement had been announced. Perhaps Peter *would* be the lucky fellow. Stranger things had happened.

No. Checking the society columns would be like poking at a sore tooth with his tongue just to feel the pain. Better to leave it alone and hope never to stumble across Lily's engagement notice to Cecil, to Peter, or to whoever finally captured her heart.

"If you're not going to pay attention," Dickon said, "you might as well join your grandfather in his tent. Even Mason was doing a better wrapping job yesterday."

Lily sliced her knuckle on the edge of a sheet of newspaper and hissed a curse.

Dickon frowned. "I heard that. If you were my daughter, I'd give you a real talking-to about how ladies don't swear."

The paper cut wasn't the only thing she wanted to swear about; it had simply been the handiest. Irritation and a sense of unfairness chewed at her thoughts, causing her to make dumb mistakes as she labeled some of the smaller fossils.

She hadn't looked forward to facing Cecil's anger—and his arrogance—and this morning she'd lain in bed for a half hour after waking, imagining all sorts of hideous, embarrassing situations upon their first encounter today. Relief had filled her when Dickon told her that Cecil would be away for a few days on business for her grandfather.

That relief had been short-lived. Her grandfather had stopped by Dickon's tent a half hour after Lily had arrived. "Remember," he said after the "Good mornings" had been exchanged, "it's your job to try to convince Donnelly to leave."

She'd nodded silently. But she hadn't pursued her job with any enthusiasm. In fact, when Mason had stopped by Dickon's tent on his way out to the dig site, she'd scuttled out the back before he saw her.

Well, she couldn't avoid him forever. Perhaps this afternoon she'd try to talk him into leaving.

Her chest buckled in on itself at just the thought.

Or maybe she'd talk to him this evening.

Lily swept the trailing end of her bright blue scarf off her cheek, where the gauzy material was clinging like a kiss. "If Cecil is away, who will be overseeing the dig?"

"Richter, of course."

"I mean, who will be looking for, ah, unusual finds?"

"You and I will. The first two got past Cecil, so his being gone doesn't change much. But we shouldn't talk about this," Dickon said, glancing at the rolled-up front of the tent. "Your pet journalist could come in here at any minute."

He was hardly a pet. She had seen a fierceness in his eyes once or twice that reminded her of the hardest men who'd walked down Denver's streets. And he certainly wasn't hers.

Still, when he wasn't aggravating her, he was making her laugh. And if her stomach gave a little shiver when he fixed his gorgeous blue eyes on her, well, that just added to the pleasure of his conversation.

Lily picked up her quill, then put it down again and sighed. Persuading him to leave shouldn't be too hard—he'd said more than once that he wasn't the type to stick around in one place for long. But she didn't want to be the one to make him go. They'd been allies in her campaign to win Cecil. Now she felt like they were enemies. Mason just didn't know that the battle had changed.

She wandered over to the sorting table, where Dickon was peering at a lumpy rock the size of his fist. "You're right—I'm just making a mess of the labeling. Do you want help with cleaning anything?"

"No. Not much came in yesterday." His eyelids flickered as he seemed to remember the second sapphire, and then he frowned. "Nothing *I'm* interested in, at any rate." He bent back over the rock.

Lily sat at the little rickety desk Dickon kept in the back corner of the tent. A breeze tiptoed under the canvas tent sides and brushed the scents of sage and dust under her nose. She'd miss the smell of Colorado when she returned to Boston.

Leaning over, she swiped a newspaper from the packing table. Only a week old—not bad. In fact, it was recent enough that Dickon had probably stolen it away before her grandfather had had a chance to read it.

She began to read. When she reached the letters to the editor page, she jolted upright and spread the newspaper out on the desk so that there was no chance she was misreading it.

"Mason Donnelly Missing?" was the headline, and the two letters following asked the paper where their favorite writer was. The editor's reply stated, "Mr. Donnelly is no longer writing for the *Herald* and is taking a much-deserved vacation. Although we do not know what his future plans are, rest assured that we're grateful for the many years he's spent with us, uncovering corruption and the poor working conditions many people suffer in their occupations, as well as giving us insights on the lives of scores of Americans, from the lowliest bootblack to the wealthiest railroad owner."

Mason wasn't working for the *Herald* any longer? Was he working for any paper at all? Her brain was buzzing so loudly, she could hardly hear her own thoughts.

"Dickon, look at this." She stood and passed him the paper, pointing to the headline.

"Hmm." Dickon read for a few seconds, then looked up. "Poor fellow was fired, huh?"

Lily snatched the paper back. "It doesn't say that."

"I can read between the lines as well as any man." He flicked a corner of the paper. "And between the lines, it says that they asked him to leave. He's not working anywhere else, is he? They either would have mentioned that or not printed the letters at all."

Lily read the editor's response again. "I still don't see it."

"You don't want to see it."

Lily gritted her teeth. "My point in showing you this is not that he was fired or not fired but that he's not working as a reporter anymore. So—"

She shut up before she could say more. *So we don't have to worry about him writing a story about the sapphires* was what she'd been going to say, but even in her mind that sounded incredibly optimistic. Maybe he was already working for another paper, but the *Herald* didn't know it yet. Maybe he was taking a break from writing but would jump back in as soon as he found a story that interested him. He was possibly still dangerous to the expedition's future.

Well, the only way to find out if he was still a reporter was to ask him. If he wasn't . . . then maybe he wouldn't have to leave.

"If you don't need me for anything . . ."

Dickon waved her off. "Go."

"Are you sure?"

"Out!" he roared. "But don't bring that Donnelly fellow back with you when you return."

She must be as transparent as glass. Her face heating, she left.

Though she doubted he'd be there, she checked his tent first, calling his name and then scratching on the canvas. No one answered, so she went to the corral, saddled up her horse, and headed out to the dig site.

She met Mason halfway along the rugged track between the dig and the camp. He smiled when she pulled her horse to a halt next to him. The sun suddenly felt extraordinarily warm, and Lily flapped her hand in front of her face to stir up a cooling breeze and to dissipate the ridiculous flush that had sprung up again.

Mason tugged at a dangling corner of her scarf. "Blue today?"

"Only colorwise." Though that could change if she really did have to convince him to leave.

"Good." He looked away, staring out at the rock ridges that rippled off to the horizon. "I heard that your beau has gone to Denver for a few days."

"*Cecil* has gone to Denver for a few days," she corrected. "I told you yesterday that it was over."

Still not looking at her, he gave a single brief nod. A nod that silently said he didn't believe her.

Well, she *had* let Cecil escort her back to Milton last night, so she shouldn't be upset by Mason's mistrust. Still she said loudly, "He practically asked me to marry him last night. And I said no."

Finally. He was no longer staring at the horizon but looking at her, his blue eyes making the backs of her knees suddenly sweat.

"Really?" he asked. The corners of his mouth twitched a few times, then rose in a grin.

She wrinkled her nose at him. "Of course, really. Do I look like a liar?"

"Well, good for you. You can do better than him. For instance, there's Peter—"

Lily rolled her eyes. Was he deliberately trying to aggravate her? "Peter is a child."

"I thought him close to your age."

"Perhaps," she allowed. "He's a child in worldly experience, I mean."

Raising his eyebrows, Mason asked, "And just how worldly is your experience?"

That darn blush attacked her cheeks again. She was probably starting to look like a sunstroke victim. "I was speaking of traveling, of seeing places outside one's hometown." But she found herself focusing on Mason's lips as she spoke. She jerked her eyes away.

"Then that may make me the most worldly man in the camp."

Now she should ask him if he was no longer a reporter. Instead she asked, "How are you feeling? From your fall yesterday."

"Better than I had expected, to be honest. Your grandfather doused my insides with some fine whiskey after you and Cecil left together, and it must have had magical properties."

"I bet it just gave you a good night's sleep."

"Whatever works suits me. My horse has been a bit skittish since yesterday, though. I had a tough time saddling him this morning. So, are you on your way to the dig?" he asked.

"Yes. Well, no. I was looking for you."

"And you found me." He glanced around. "Where is the famous mine I've heard about?"

Lily pointed to the east. "A mile that way—not far at all."

"Want to go with me?"

She should have said no, Mason thought, watching her out of the corner of his eye. She rode beside him, her face tilted toward the sun, her expression pensive. Didn't she realize that, now that he had her alone, he was going to do his best to pry the camp's secrets out of her?

Beside him, Lily sighed.

"What?" he asked.

"Oh . . . I, um, was just thinking about what to write my mother. About Cecil."

Not what she was thinking about at all, but her response was a somewhat decent recovery. When she'd asked him if he thought she was a liar, he'd almost said, *Not a good one.* She had trouble throwing herself into a role. She was too much herself.

But he responded to her lead. "Tell your mother he was no good for you. A complete waste of your time. I can't imagine why she steered him your way in the first place."

She frowned at him. "You're very negative about Cecil all of a sudden."

"Oh, I disliked him from the first. But you seemed set on him, so . . ." He shrugged. "No one wants to hear bad things about the person they're in love with."

She looked even more cross. "I wasn't in love with

him. And in the future you should tell me things like that. What if I'd married him? I'd be miserable for the next thirty years."

"I put my faith in your good sense."

"Oh." Her frown vanished, and she beamed at him.

His lungs lost all their air and his brain seized. Damn it, the woman, with her blinding, reason-erasing smiles, was a menace.

She seemed oblivious to his reaction. "What would you write to your mother if she expected you to marry a particular person and you had decided not to?"

"I don't have a mother."

"Everyone has a mother."

"I mean, my mother's dead. She died when I was very little."

"Well, who would you write to, then, if you needed advice on marriage?"

"Joseph Richardson." When Mason had met him in San Francisco almost twelve years ago, he'd generously passed on all his knowledge and advice about sniffing out a story and then writing it. A good story wrote itself, Old Joe had said. But go at the story from another angle and it would become a great story.

"Old Joe helped me break into journalism. Helped me talk to the right people, get some work."

"Does he know that you're no longer working for the *Herald*?"

Mason's thoughts cartwheeled and shattered. "What?" The word came out as a croak.

Her eyes widening, she asked, "Didn't you know?"

"I thought it was just temporary." Mason rubbed

his forehead. "I asked for some time off." Well, his editor had suggested time off, but taking time off was different from leaving the paper altogether. Had he been fired without being told? "How do you know this?"

"There was a letter from the editor in the *Herald* explaining your absence from the paper." She bit her lip. "The letter said that you were on vacation, but also that you weren't working there anymore. Is that true?"

"I . . . I'm not sure." In fact, he didn't think he'd ever felt more unsure, off balance, in his life. "What did the letter say, precisely?"

"'Mr. Donnelly is no longer writing for the *Herald*.'"

An invisible boot seemed to swing into his guts. "Seems clear enough, then," he said, trying not to show anything on his face. He'd been fired. *Fired.*

He'd been the *Herald*'s top writer for five years. Had that new fellow, Cutler, insisted that Mason be fired so he could hog the spotlight? Then Mason blew a breath out. Blaming Cutler felt good, but Mason hadn't delivered a single decent story in six months, so he shouldn't be surprised that the *Herald* had run out of patience.

But he was onto something here at Highfill's expedition—something big. And in the last several days the words that had been locked deep inside had started to break free. During the rides between the tent town and the dig sites, he found himself composing sentences in his head, and they were good. Some of them were even great, and he'd scribbled a few down in the notebook he carried in his coat pocket. He felt like a man who'd lost his appetite during a long illness and was now sampling the most delightful mouthfuls of food again.

Only to have the plate yanked out from in front of him.

Well, the *Herald* wasn't the only paper out there. Even some national magazines had approached him in the past. As long as he could write a great story, he could find a place for it.

If he was sure of anything in this whirlwind, it was that.

A large black hole in the side of a tall ridge wall now loomed up before them. He'd forgotten for a few moments where they'd been heading. "Is this the mine?" Mason asked, pointing toward the hole with his chin.

Lily nodded, her troubled eyes fastened on him.

He'd deal with the paper later. He needed a distraction now. "Then let's go in."

They dismounted. Several metal rings had been driven into the rock face, but most had rusted through. Mason looped his horse's reins through the ring nearest the mine entrance, but Lily had to turn the corner into a small, dead-end passage before she found another ring that would hold.

Reappearing from inside the passage, she walked to his side and took his hand. Her hand fluttered against his for a moment before she squeezed his fingers with her own, pressing their palms together. "I'm sorry I upset you."

Her hand felt strangely right in his. "You didn't upset me; the news did."

When she loosened her hold, he wouldn't let her

go. Instead, he began walking into the mine, pulling her along behind him until she took a few quick steps and caught up.

They halted before stepping into the blackness of the mine, and he glanced down at her. She wasn't smiling, but she wasn't frowning, either. And she hadn't tried to reclaim her hand.

She looked up and caught his eye.

"Ready?" And this time she took the lead, tugging him by the hand into the maw of the mountain.

Chapter Nine

L ily shivered. She'd forgotten how cool the mine was inside. The light from the entrance guided their steps for a dozen more feet, but within those dozen feet the temperature dropped thirty degrees.

She moved closer to Mason. He seemed unconcerned by the chill and radiated heat like a furnace. Warmth traveled from their clasped hands and up her arm, settling deep inside her.

A dozen more feet, a turn to the right, and blackness closed around them like a fist. After a brief pause, she continued forward. She'd visited here perhaps a half dozen times, and the path deeper into the mountain was as straight as a needle.

"Do you know where you're going?" Mason asked. He didn't stop following her blind walk through the dark, though.

"I've been here many times. It's quite safe."

"All that talk at supper last night made me wonder if a disgruntled miner may have booby-trapped the mine against casual visitors like you and me."

"Oh." She stopped, and he stopped, too. "That hadn't occurred to me."

"Not in your worldly nature to distrust folks, huh?" But she could hear the smile in his voice. "Did you bring a candle like we were supposed to?"

"No—I didn't know we'd be coming here. But the only people who need a candle are those who haven't been here before." She proceeded more cautiously now, her eyes open wide, but she couldn't see a single thing. She held her hand straight out in front of her, then slowly drew it back toward her face. Even when her hand touched her nose, she couldn't see it.

Being utterly blind was a strange feeling, exhilarating and terrifying at once. But with Mason's hand anchoring hers, exhilaration quickly shoved aside the terror, and she found herself smiling.

Twenty paces past the turn, she stopped again and fumbled in her pocket for the box of matches she always kept with her. Her fingers touched a little folding knife, a needle wrapped with thread and stuck in a cork, and a handkerchief before finding the matchbox. "I need both hands for this," she whispered.

Loosening his hold, Mason curled his fingers around her wrist, then glided his hand up the full length of her arm until his palm settled on her shoulder. Goose bumps sprang to life where he had touched her. "I wouldn't want to lose you," he teased.

She fumbled the first two strikes, producing only sparks that sizzled briefly against her skin. At the third strike, the match flared brightly, as astonishing in the tar-black mine as a lightning flash would have been, and illuminated the rock encircling them.

Beside her, Mason sucked in his breath, and his hand clamped down on her shoulder.

All around them glowed thick seams of mica woven into the stone, making them feel as if they were enclosed by a gleaming tunnel of silver filigree.

She'd been expecting the sight, but her heart thumped hard in her chest and her eyes grew tight with unshed tears. The continual pull of air toward the mine entrance made the match flame dance, and the whole corridor seemed to undulate.

Lily glanced up at Mason. He looked thunderstruck, and she would have bet he didn't feel that very often.

"Like it?" she asked, knowing the answer already.

As if he couldn't bear to pull his eyes away, it took him a few moments to look down at her. And when he did, his only response was an ear-to-ear grin that caused her heart to give another wild thump.

The fingers holding the match got suddenly warm. With a yelp, Lily gave her hand a snap to extinguish the flame. Darkness slammed down around them again.

"Just a minute . . ." she said, sliding the matchbox open to retrieve another match.

"Leave it." Mason sounded as if his mouth was right next to her ear, and a warm puff of breath tickled her cheek. Lily stopped fiddling with the matchbox and froze.

Then she blindly turned her face toward his and leaned forward.

He was even closer than she'd expected, for she didn't have time even to pucker up before her mouth grazed a slightly stubbled cheek.

She pulled back immediately and murmured, "Sorry," but she wasn't sure if she was apologizing for slapping a limp-as-oatmeal kiss on his face, or for missing his mouth, or for kissing him at all. Well, he could take it whichever way he wished.

He must have assumed she was apologizing for missing his mouth, for his hand slipped from her shoulder to cup her chin, and his lips captured hers.

Fireflies began to dance in her stomach, and she sighed his name as she kissed him back. She threaded her free hand through his hair and held him in place in case he got any terrible ideas, like moving away.

He did finally move away, though. She could hear him breathing hard in the darkness. "You kiss like the devil."

"Really?" she asked, pleased. Cecil had never said anything like that to her. But neither had she fisted her hand in his hair and moaned his name into his mouth, so perhaps she kissed like the devil only with Mason.

"Really. Are there any candles in here?"

Darn. The kissing portion of the mine exploration must be over. Sighing, Lily struck another match and held it aloft.

Mason blinked in the flaring light and raised his hand against the dazzle. Backing her up a few steps until her shoulder blades nearly touched the wall of the tunnel, he reached over her shoulder and took from a ledge carved in the stone a candle stub that a previous visitor had helpfully left behind. The damp wick sizzled for several moments in the match flame before catching, and Mason replaced the candle on the ledge he'd taken it from.

Shaking the flame from the match, Lily dropped it to the ground. Again the silver in the rock streaked all around them, but she couldn't pull her eyes from Mason's face.

"Now," he said, "I can see you when I kiss you."

Did all Boston heiresses kiss like this? Mason wondered as Lily again sank wholeheartedly into his kiss. If so, he'd been overlooking a small but remarkable segment of the female population. Not that he'd spend any amount of time in Boston just to kiss the blue-bloods there. He'd been to Boston once and disliked it heartily.

But Lily probably considered herself a Denver girl.

Still, he'd never kissed a girl from Denver like this, either.

He felt as if their actions were taking place in slow motion, allowing him to savor every nuance—every graze of his lips against hers, every slow, thorough lick that had Lily curving her body into his. Even his pulse seemed to beat slowly in his ears.

He could kiss her like this forever. In fact, if things really were moving in slow motion, perhaps he could kiss her forever while only five minutes passed in the real world outside the mine.

He had her backed up against the stone wall and

was nuzzling her neck to get better access to the delicate skin behind her left earlobe when a bead of hot wax splashed against his nape.

He yelped and knocked heads with Lily. Lily's skull cracked against the rock, and she let out her own "Ow!"

From kisses to concussions, all in a single second. Giving the candle a glare, he grabbed her hand and pulled her away from the wall.

"We should go," Lily said, rubbing the back of her head. "People will wonder where we are."

It was a reasonable excuse to leave, but she had avoided his eyes when she'd given it. Mason swallowed his sigh. Maybe this was why he hadn't kissed any Boston heiresses before. Regrets too soon crowded out the giddy satisfaction.

"I'll leave the candle here," he said, then added, testing her, "We may need it again."

"Mm-hmm."

With more force than necessary, he blew out the candle. Darkness smothered them, and he was suddenly grateful. Now he didn't have to look at her carefully blank expression any longer.

She did take him by the hand, though, as she led him back to the entrance. He wondered if she'd drop his hand like a hot coal as soon as they reached the light.

Keeping his grip loose so she could pull away at any time, Mason stepped into the half circle of sunlight that fell inside the mine entrance. A sting bit his cheek, then a crack split the air.

He wheeled around and hauled Lily back inside

the mine before he brought his other hand up to his cheek. His hand came back wet and warm with blood.

"Someone took a shot at us," Lily hissed.

He wiped his hand on his pants. "I know." The side of his face had turned numb, and the vision in his right eye had gone fuzzy. He didn't think he'd been shot in the head, but he'd heard plenty of tales of men who'd walked around with bullets in their skulls for hours before realizing what had happened. Turning to her, he said in as normal a voice as he could manage, "Is my eye all right?"

She stared back at him, then pulled a handkerchief out of her pocket and wiped his face. He could see the handkerchief fluttering as she cleared away the blood but could barely feel the material pressed against his skin.

Lily said steadily, "Your eye is still there and I can't see anything wrong with it, but I won't be able to tell for sure until we're out in the sunlight. I think the bullet hit the wall nearby and sent some rock chips into your cheek and forehead. Do you want to hold the handkerchief against the cuts, or do you want me to do it?"

She really was a Denver girl, Mason thought, then passed out.

He came to in what felt like only a blink of an eye later, but he was sprawled on the ground with his head in Lily's lap.

He flailed a bit and, with Lily's help, sat up so they were shoulder to shoulder against the wall.

"Are you all right?" she asked.

"Fine," he said shortly. Heck, he might pass out again from sheer embarrassment. He'd better have at least two bullet holes in his head to justify fainting on her like that.

"I've seen that happen before." She shifted beside him, settling in more comfortably. "One of my children got his finger smashed between a yoke and an ox's neck. He was fine for a minute or so, then turned white and keeled over. But nothing was wrong with his finger except a bruise."

His brain must still be fuzzy. "What do you mean, one of your children?"

"I taught school in Denver. Was even a circuit teacher for a year." She paused. "I don't think he's out there any longer. I heard a horse galloping away soon after you, um, fell down."

She was being gentle with his self-esteem. "Are there other exits from the mine that you know of?"

"One, but it's an exit that everyone knows. Maybe whoever shot at us went around to that exit, expecting us to try to escape that way. He could be waiting for us there."

"Or he could have ridden off noisily to make us think he's left, and then crawled back quietly to this exit," Mason pointed out.

"That's true."

They lapsed into silence.

What was the best way to get out of this? Maybe he'd learn that if he could figure out who had shot at them.

The digger last night had said that the miners had

been angry by the camp's presence and seemed to blame the bone hunters for the mine being shut down, although the mine had closed years before the diggers had arrived. Maybe it had been an old miner firing off a warning shot—a shot of frustration. Not a killing shot.

He shared his theory with Lily.

"Well, that shot across our bow came awfully close to your bowsprit," she said, lightly drawing her fingertip down his nose. Then she put her hands back in her lap and laced them together, cutting off his half-formed idea of holding her hand. "I don't know," she said. "But we can't stay here forever."

"At what point will someone come looking for you?"

"No one might realize until suppertime that we're not at either the dig site or camp."

At least two more hours, then, of crouching like rabbits with a fox lurking outside their burrow.

Trying to act as if he weren't looking at her, he studied her out of the corner of his eye. It would be the highest flight of fancy for him to imagine that he might convince her to pass the time with him doing what bunnies did best.

She moved his hand aside and gently pulled the handkerchief away from his cheek and forehead. "The bleeding's stopped. How's your eye?"

"Seems to work well enough, thank God. It'd be difficult to be a blind reporter."

"If you are no longer working for the *Herald*, will you go work for another paper?"

"Yes." He hoped so.

"Oh. So, then, when do you plan to leave?" She gave a shrug. "If you were staying to help me with Cecil, you're now free to go."

"I was always free to go." In fact, he'd been more free to go before, when they were only playing at courtship, than he was now, after he'd kissed Lily like a madman. And there were the secrets here, of course. The secrets he'd planned to discover by bringing Lily here alone. Instead, he'd kissed her, then gotten shot. Hardly the hallmark of a fine reporter.

"I think I'll stick around for a while longer," he said. "It's a bit of a novelty to stay in one place for so long. Plus"—he gave her a glance, then looked out the mine entrance at where a would-be assassin might still be lying in wait—"things are just starting to get interesting."

Things were just starting to get interesting? Lily didn't know whether she should panic or be flattered. What, exactly, did he think was interesting? Her kisses or getting shot? And he still didn't know the most interesting thing of all, which was that the land they were digging in seemed to be rife with sapphires.

Honestly. She had been given just one job by her grandfather—to get rid of Mason—and what did she do but throw herself in his arms?

She chewed on her lip. For the first time all day, she wished that Cecil were still around and she hadn't rejected his marriage proposal. Then maybe she would be able to convince Mason that kissing him had been another move in her battle to incite Cecil's jealousy.

But probably not. After all, they'd been kissing in a pitch-black mine with no one else around. It would be difficult to argue that she'd been trying to make Cecil jealous.

She sighed. And found herself staring at Mason's mouth again.

Perhaps he'd hypnotized her. She could come up with no other reason why she was so fascinated by his lips. Aside from the fact that he kissed like the very devil, too, and had sparked a number of heated thoughts, unleashing a molten hum low in her stomach.

She needed to stop thinking about his delicious mouth and start concentrating on the danger they were in.

"If the shooter was trying to kill us, wouldn't he come in after us to finish us off?" she asked.

"Maybe he doesn't know if I'm armed."

"*Are* you armed?" She didn't think so. Surely she would have felt a revolver either while they had been pressed together in the darkness or when she had frantically searched Mason for bullet holes after he had gone down like a felled tree.

"No. But there's a rifle on my saddle."

"That doesn't do us much good in here. Why don't I go get it? I don't think he'd shoot me."

"Why? Because you're rich?"

She clenched her fists in the near dark. Was that the first thing that came to mind when Mason thought of her? That she was rich? "No," she bit out. "Because I'm a woman. And because all those miners know me.

I go to their church on Sunday, I use the same general store, and I speak with them when I meet them at the post office. You're a stranger. It's much easier to shoot at a stranger than someone you know."

Mason began shaking his head before she'd even finished talking. "It's still a bad idea."

Another bad idea was staying in this mine with him, where she'd be tempted into more kisses. She stood and stepped away, placing herself out of reach. "You've been shot in the head—"

"I wasn't shot!"

"—so I'm the one who's going to do the thinking."

"You're not thinking at all."

"I'll be back." And she headed for the mine exit.

He made a grab for her but missed. "Lily!"

I won't get shot, she told herself, forcing her legs to keep moving. *I won't get shot.*

Plus, she felt pretty sure that the gunman had left. At least she really, really hoped he had left.

The sunlight streaming through the entrance made her blink and slow her pace. But a scuffling behind her, the sound of Mason getting to his feet, propelled her out into the open.

She didn't run—after all, if she was moving too quickly for the gunman to realize who she was, she might get shot accidentally. But her heart beat madly as she strode briskly to Mason's horse, yanked the rifle out of the boot it rested in, swung around, and headed back for the mine.

Mason staggered out into the sunlight to meet her. No shot cracked the peace of the afternoon.

When she came close, he grabbed her by the upper arms and wheeled her about so that he stood between her and where he guessed the shooter was, his broad back an easy target.

Still no shot.

Lily knocked his hands away. "Stop manhandling me."

Mason's eyes blazed in his blood-speckled white face as he grabbed the rifle from her. "Well, when you don't listen to reason, sometimes there's no other choice."

Bristling, Lily demanded, "Reason? Who was right here? No one shot at me."

"He must be gone."

"That doesn't mean that I was wrong."

"It doesn't mean you were right, either."

She threw her hands up. "Fine. Let's agree that he's gone, and that we're now safe."

Still careful to keep her shielded by his body, Mason escorted her back to her horse. "Let's agree that we should get back to camp."

"You were *what*?" Highfill roared, his white beard quivering as if equally outraged.

Mason found himself moving a step closer to the chair where Lily sat, her grandfather and Dickon looming over her like the Rocky Mountains outside Highfill's tent.

"Shot at," Lily whispered, looking at her feet.

"What were you doing out there, getting shot at?"

Mason slid another step closer and rested his

hand on the back of Lily's chair. Concealed from the other men by the flow of her blue scarf, his fingertips brushed her spine.

It was one thing for him to yell at Lily for taking chances with her life. It rubbed him the wrong way to listen to her grandfather do it. Though, as the head of her family, Highfill had more right to yell at her than Mason did.

Highfill had so far heard about only the last part of their adventure at the mine. Mason didn't doubt that Lily would judiciously edit the kiss from her story.

He brushed his fingers against her again, hoping to remind her that she wasn't alone. She could depend on him. Lily momentarily leaned back, pressing against his hand in return.

"What were we doing out there?" she repeated. "We spoke of the mine last night at supper. Mason wanted to see it before he left. Which he plans to do quite soon."

Mason jerked his hand away. What? He'd told her that he was staying.

Highfill turned his stare on Mason. "Leave? We'll be sad to see you go, but you must have plenty to do elsewhere, my boy. Heading out tonight or tomorrow?"

Mason cleared his throat. "Actually, I hadn't intended to leave immediately. Unless you'd rather I do. . . ."

"No, of course not," Highfill said. But he looked at Dickon as he said it, and the other man gave a slight shrug.

Interesting. Did Lily, Highfill, and Dickon all wish

him to leave because something was going on here that they didn't want him to know?

Or did Highfill and Dickon want him to leave because they didn't want him romancing Lily?

Both possibilities could be true at the same time, of course.

Why Lily suddenly wanted him to leave, though, was harder to fathom. Unless she'd decided that kissing him—twice—had been a bad, bad mistake.

If he'd knocked his head or passed out before their kissing episode, he might have concluded that he'd imagined it. The edge of embarrassment to her words and a slightly red patch low on one of her cheeks that signaled whisker burn were also evidence that those wild moments hadn't happened only in his head. He scowled at the back of Lily's head.

Highfill crossed his arms over his chest. "I'm going into town to talk to a few of those folks and put the fear of God in them. If anything else like this happens . . ." He didn't finish the sentence, but he was a powerful, wealthy man: Mason had no doubt that the punishment he could inflict was brutal.

After being out of the line of fire for so long, Lily must have felt it safe to speak. "Grandfather, you could ride with me to Milton tonight—"

Highfill made a chopping motion with his hand. "No. Until I find out who shot at you, you're staying here in camp. And you don't ride anywhere, even around here, without an escort. Two, if possible."

"Grandfather, I don't think the man was aiming at *me*."

"Yes, you've mentioned that before," Mason murmured. If he'd been furious with Lily for waltzing out of the mine under such a harebrained impression, he could imagine how her grandfather would react.

Lily threw a panicked look over her shoulder. Mason grinned at her a little maliciously. Payback for her unflattering attempts to encourage him to go.

"I think we should let Mr. Donnelly get the cuts on his face cleaned out," she said, returning her attention to her grandfather.

Mr. Donnelly. It sounded so formal after she'd breathed "Mason" in between kisses.

Highfill nodded and waved toward the pinned-back tent flap. "The cook will fix you up. See you later, Donnelly. Thanks for taking care of Lily."

He'd collapsed at her feet and then hadn't been fast enough to prevent her from walking out into what he believed had been deadly danger. If that could be called "taking care of Lily," then he'd done a smashing job. Mason grimaced.

But Lily also turned to him, her eyes clear and sincere. "Yes, thank you."

He almost assumed she was thanking him for not revealing that she had dashed out of the mine. But then the faintest blush softened her cheeks.

Hmm . . .

Mason left the tent smiling.

As soon as Mason's footsteps were swallowed by the background noise of the camp, Lily swung to face her grandfather and Dickon. "Did you find anything today?"

"Don't go trying to change the subject, my girl," Highfill said. "I thought you were supposed to get rid of that . . . that . . . *journalist*—not go on sightseeing trips with him!"

"Grandfather, I wasn't sure he was a journalist any longer. That's what I went to ask him about."

"Come again?"

Dickon broke in. "Seems he was fired from his paper. Just wandering around without a job now."

"Huh. I wish he'd wander around somewhere else." Highfill pointed at her, his long finger reminding her uncomfortably of a rifle barrel. "Go break his heart or something so that he'll leave us alone. Whether he has a job or not, I don't want him here."

She swallowed. "I don't think he's actually given me his heart to break," she began.

Highfill snorted. "That's not what Cecil said before he left this morning. And Cecil believed that it had been a fair exchange—that you'd been equally generous in giving your heart to Donnelly." Shaking his head, her grandfather said, "I can't believe you'd have so little sense."

"Grandfather, I haven't. I was trying to—"

"Cecil left because of you," her grandfather interrupted. "You know that, don't you?"

Lily dropped her head. She could hear the disappointment through his gruffness, and it ground into her side like a sharp stick. "Yes. But I thought he was coming back. Isn't he?"

"Of course he'll be back. He has a great deal of unfinished business here." He bent his gaze on her. "Perhaps even with you."

"I don't think so, Grandfather."

"All it would take, I think, is a pretty apology from you—"

From her? Indignation spiked inside her. What about an apology from Cecil? An apology for ignoring her for the past month, for his disrespect toward her sketches, for spreading rumors about her falling for Mason when she rejected Cecil's advances. Yes, she had kissed Mason. And had loved every minute of it—until they'd cracked heads. But that had come *after* she'd turned down Cecil.

She looked up to find her grandfather staring at her and realized that she'd missed whatever else he had said.

"I'm not going to apologize to Cecil," she stated, "as I do not wish to patch things up with Cecil."

"Good for you," Dickon said, earning himself a glare from Highfill. The edge softened on the glare when Dickon added, "But stay away from Donnelly, too. You may believe that he isn't enamored with you, but he watches you all the time. So either he's honestly enamored or his interest is not so honorable."

"You think he's interested in my inheritance," Lily said hollowly. Was that all that people saw when they looked at her? Her money?

Dickon chuckled. "No, sweetheart, not in your inheritance."

"He might try to bed you, but he wouldn't wed you," her grandfather said more bluntly.

Oh. Lily could feel every inch of her skin turn scarlet. She did *not* want to have this conversation with Dickon and her grandfather.

She hurried on. "While I believe that Cecil is interested in my inheritance and little else."

His frown reappearing again, Highfill said, "Your mother likes him a great deal, and so do I. Do you think that we would approve of someone whom we believed would make you unhappy?"

"No, Grandfather. Not at all. But there is a large difference between being someone who won't make me unhappy and being someone who will make me happy."

He huffed but didn't disagree. "Well, when Cecil returns, at least be pleasant to him. Let him speak to you in private if he likes. Maybe he'll have reconsidered his priorities and come back a changed man. A man you'll like better."

She nodded. To give in to this request would merely inconvenience and irritate her, causing no real damage.

She stood. "I would like to wash up before supper."

Surprising her, her grandfather embraced her and pressed a kiss to her forehead. "I'm glad you're all right."

She kissed his white-bearded cheek, nodded to Dickon, and strode out into the fading daylight.

It had been a few weeks since she'd stayed overnight in her small tent in camp. She'd have to tidy it up, make space for all her belongings now in Milton. And she did want to scrub off the grime that she could feel coating her face and arms. Mason had pushed them and their horses at a brutal pace back to camp. She'd probably eaten half the dust in this part of Colorado during the ride.

The shortest way to her tent took her past the tent Mason was using, and as luck would have it, he was exiting it just as she walked by.

The cook had cleaned off the blood and done a neat job of patching up the worst cuts to his cheek and above his eye. His shirt had several top buttons undone, and the collar of his shirt was wet, sticking to his skin. She immediately wanted to kiss him again, and she took a step toward him before she could check herself. They were in the middle of her grandfather's camp, for goodness' sake. And she was supposed to be sending him away. "You look better," she said.

"Healthy enough to leave?"

Of course he'd bring that up. "When *are* you leaving?"

"Maybe when everyone stops telling me to."

"Ah. Then I'll be sure to never mention it again."

The banter felt good, easy. And a buoyancy filled her when the corners of his mouth twitched into a grin.

"Are you going to your tent?" he asked.

"Yes."

"Will you need help later moving your possessions to another tent?"

"Another tent? Why?"

"You're permanently moving here, right? Isn't your current tent too small?"

So he knew which tent was hers. She smiled at him and asked, "Too small for what?"

He looked at her as if she were a muttonhead. "Too small for a millionaire's granddaughter."

Humiliation rushed up like a flash flood. Dickon had been wrong. When Mason looked at her, he did think of her money. She turned away without a word.

"Lily."

She sensed him reaching out and she dodged.

"Princess—"

"I'm not a princess!" Whirling about, she planted her hands on each side of his face, got up on her toes, and fused her mouth to his.

His arms closed around her and hauled her up tight against him. He angled his head, deepening the kiss. She shivered.

He took two steps backward, dragging her along with him, and his tent flap dropped behind them, sealing them in the dusky interior, where no one could see them.

She let her eyelids droop and concentrated on the taste of him. After only those few minutes in the mine, his taste was as familiar to her as if they'd exchanged kisses a dozen times. Sighing, she tunneled her hands deeper into his hair.

He pulled back a little but not entirely. "Why," he murmured between gentle sips at her mouth, "are you so eager to see me leave one minute, then kissing me the next?"

Oh, God. She thrust away from him. "That was an accident."

He rubbed his knuckles against his forehead and sighed. "Let me get this straight. You're deliberately telling me to leave, but then accidentally kissing me?" He stepped closer and feathered his fingertip over her eyebrow and then down her cheek, finishing with a little tap on her lips. "I think I'd prefer it the other way around."

She thought that she would, too. No, she *knew* that she would. She wrapped her arms around herself. "Yes. You really should leave."

"Why?" Even in the dim light, she could see that his eyes were intense. "Lily, I'll be honest with you. More honest, I think, than you're being with me." He paused. "I couldn't write anymore. I don't know what happened, but the words . . . they wouldn't spring into my thoughts the way they used to. Every sentence was a struggle, and readers can tell. My editor could tell. That's why I don't have a job now."

He turned away and settled cross-legged on a mass of blankets that served as his bed. When he pointed at an overturned wooden box by the bed, Lily sat on it. "Is there more?" she asked when he didn't immediately speak again.

"This is the more difficult part. I don't want to hurt you," he said after another pause, "but I want to be clear what my priority is."

Lily's heart sank. Whatever his priority was, it clearly wasn't going to be her.

Cecil's priority hadn't been her, either. When was she going to find someone whose first priority was *her*?

Giving herself a shake, she reminded herself that her priority was to get him to leave, not to make him happy. Why should she expect his priorities to be different?

Well, those kisses, for one.

But she'd initiated the kisses every time. Perhaps she didn't understand her priorities as well as she should.

"I think that my writing is coming back. Finding a big story helps make the words come again. You see, being excited about a story triggers a need to tell people about it, and that excitement is where the words come from."

He leaned forward. "I sense that there's a story here."

She froze.

"Am I right? Is there a story here, Lily?"

Chapter Ten

N o," she said.

Mason flopped back on his bed and covered his eyes with his hand. She was lying. He could tell. She had hesitated. She had spoken no louder than she'd needed to. And she'd glanced away immediately afterward. She really was a terrible liar.

And he couldn't bear to look at her when she lied to him.

"No," she said again, even louder than before.

Mason pushed himself up on his elbows so he could see her again. "I don't believe you."

Her head snapped back at his cool tone. She opened her mouth as if to speak, then shut it.

The supper bell set up a racket on the other side of camp. Before the last notes died away, she stood. "I still have to clean up." Without another word, she slipped outside, the tent flap falling shut behind her.

He dropped flat on his back again, jarring his skull. A headache blossomed behind his eyes. Crap. He'd been thrown nearly off a cliff yesterday and shot at today. Neither explained why he felt like a railroad spike had been driven through his chest, though.

Between damage done by his horse, crazy miners, and Lily, he'd be lucky if he lived out the week.

Why the hell hadn't she just told him what was going on? Or at the very least said that she couldn't tell him?

And now he'd blown his hand, telling her that he knew something was going on here and he planned to write about it.

She was probably going to Dickon and Highfill right now, passing along the information. Highfill didn't really need an excuse to kick Mason out of the camp. But if Highfill did need one, Lily could always tell him about their kisses in the mine.

Kisses that Lily had begun, if Mason remembered correctly. He hadn't been so charmed by a girl in a long time, and he'd allowed himself to get sidetracked from the story. That had never happened before—never. Had she done it on purpose? Or was it an accident, as she'd claimed? Really, could he trust anything she was telling him? If she cared for him at all, she wouldn't have lied about there not being a story here.

By the time supper rolled around, his headache was squeezing his skull like a starving anaconda, and he burned with cold indignation. Lily shouldn't have lied to him, and that was that.

Supper was much the same as the night before, but with their roles reversed. Mason ignored Lily as much as he could without being dramatically rude, but he could see from a few sideways glances that Peter was giving him that the youth was rethinking his decision to put any money on Mason winning the girl.

He didn't want to win her anyway, he told himself. He left the supper table before the cook brought out the apple crumble dessert, and returned to his tent, where he collapsed onto his cot, lies and strawberry-sweet kisses buzzing through his mind until he fell asleep.

Lily pushed her hand through her hair, lifting a hank off the back of her neck to allow the faint breeze a chance to cool her. But the air was still as death inside Dickon's work tent. She dropped her hair with a sigh.

"Are you working or daydreaming?" Dickon asked from directly behind her, causing her to jump.

"Daydreaming." Or day-nightmaring. As much as she tried, she couldn't force the image of Mason's disappointed expression out of her mind. She'd thought that her grandfather's disappointment had been painful. Mason's disappointment settled inside her like food poisoning, twisting her stomach and radiating through her in a full-body ache.

"Well, daydream on your own time. Richter must be working those boys like slaves, based on the amount of debris and samples they brought us yesterday."

Piles of rock chunks lounged in the dark corners of the tent, waiting to be sorted. Ninety percent of it would be junk, but they had to make sure they found the worthwhile ten percent, meaning that they had to look through all of it. Another pile sat on the sorting table, and Dickon, after giving her a sharp stare, bent over it again, his fingers pulling the scrap away from the treasures.

"Did Mason say anything to you this morning about leaving?" she asked as casually as she could.

Dickon didn't look up. "No."

"No?"

"No. I'm guessing that he didn't say anything to you, either."

"No. I think he's, ah, not speaking to me."

Dickon grunted. "I noticed that last night at supper. Should make your grandfather happy."

"Yes," she agreed, but it didn't make *her* happy.

Last night she'd been so distracted by Mason's ignoring her that she'd had trouble paying attention to her grandfather's decree that no one leave camp alone. Lily had considered pointing out that she and Mason being together hadn't stopped the shooter's attack. Then she'd thought better of it and kept her mouth shut. After all, perhaps the miner had thought Mason was alone. His horse was the only one left out in front of the mine; hers had been deeper in a side canyon, probably out of the shooter's sight. And she had to admit that even a raving-mad miner would know better than to shoot at Charles Highfill's granddaughter.

"As much as I appreciate your company," Dickon said, "your help with sorting these rocks would be even more appreciated."

She stepped up to the edge of the table and began dividing the pile into possibles and junk. She'd go through the possibles more carefully later.

For a moment yesterday—well, several moments,

most of which involved her mouth plastered to his—she'd imagined that Mason might fall into the category of "possible." But his focus was on the secret he was, correctly, thinking she knew about and was hiding from him. Had he been kissing her to find out more?

Or rather, had he been kissing her *back* to find out more? Had she been the kisser, and he the kissee? And if he'd been trying to find out more by kissing her, why had he told her flat out what his "priority" was? Oh, blast it. If he thought about the situation at all, he had to realize that she couldn't tell him anything that might hurt her grandfather or the expedition. To even ask her was unfair.

The whole blasted situation was unfair.

She sighed again. When she looked up, she discovered Dickon staring at her.

"What?" she asked.

"Lily girl, you just placed another one of those damn sapphires in the junk pile."

Dickon snarled under his breath during the entire ride out to the dig site. Lily didn't know whether to blame the sapphire or the horse for his bad mood. Dickon disliked riding. His legs stuck out straight like a scarecrow's, and he painfully bounced in counterpoint to the horse's gait. From the way the horse's ears were twitching, Lily guessed the horse was equally displeased with the rider he was saddled with.

Dickon shook his head in disgust. "Seven years of fossil hunting, and now this!" Grumble grumble. "And what sort of training are those boys getting that they let sapphires fall into the scrap pile?" Grumble grumble. "And once word gets out, this place will be mobbed with speculators. The digging season will be over whether we like it or not."

Dickon suddenly focused on Lily. "You're not to say a word to Mason Donnelly about this, you hear?"

Did he think she had to be reminded every hour? She wanted to point out to Dickon that she hadn't broken down and told Mason about the sapphires after kissing him several times yesterday, so it was unlikely that she'd break down and tell him today. But she thought she wouldn't get an apologetic response. Apoplectic might be more accurate.

Upon reaching the dig site, she and Dickon dismounted. Both Dickon and his horse let out a gusty sigh at the same moment, then glared at each other.

Lily allowed herself one quick scan of the diggers. No sign of Mason.

Her hands went clammy, and her belly writhed like a ball of baby snakes.

Had he simply left?

Had he decided that she had been telling the truth after all and then, with no story to hold him here, departed?

A movement at the end of the line of diggers caught her eye, and she jerked her head around to look. Mason, with Peter on his heels, rounded an outcropping of rock.

Relief made her heart cramp. She began to lift her hand to wave before remembering that they were here about a sapphire and the last thing she should want was to gain his attention. She let her hand drop back down to her side, but she couldn't pull her eyes away from him for the life of her. He had his shirt off like most of the men, but his pale skin shone like a lamp among the suntans the other diggers had developed during the hot summer. But while he lacked color, he didn't lack muscles. When he raised his arm to run his fingers through his sweat-darkened hair, Lily's mouth went dry.

Mason half turned back to laugh at something Peter had said, then abruptly paused.

He had seen her.

"Lily," her grandfather hollered from the shade of Richter's crude pavilion. Dickon had already reached the shade and turned around to see what was keeping her.

Wonderful. She had been standing out here all alone, drooling over Mason like he was a treat in a confectionary shop, and everyone had probably noticed.

"If you could join us when you get the chance . . ." Her grandfather's words were polite, but his tone impatient.

Her ears must be burning as bright as a pair of torches. Lifting her chin, Lily turned away from Mason and picked her way over the uneven ground.

The sooner Mason left, she thought, the sooner her peace of mind could be restored. And her dignity.

Her mother had often said that clothing was what made people civilized. And Lily had descended into an altogether uncivilized state of mind for a moment upon seeing Mason's naked strong chest and shoulders.

Lily narrowed her eyes against the sun and risked a glance behind her. Mason now had his shirt on—and his back to her. And she was maintaining a firm grasp on her wits.

As usual, her mother was right.

Her eyes traveled back to him again. Even with his pale skin covered so that the contrast between him and the other diggers was indiscernible, he still stood out.

"Lily!" No longer a request from her grandfather but a command that she join him *right now*.

Lily pulled her gaze away from Mason and entered the pavilion's shade.

Her grandfather waved her over to a chair under the canvas awning. With an equally terse flip of his hand, he indicated that Richter should leave. His expression surprised, then sullen, Richter turned and left the tent, an excuse about checking on the diggers floating behind him.

Tapping his fist on his thigh, her grandfather strode back and forth in the confines of the tent. "This is outrageous," he said. "If we're accidentally finding sapphires every day, how many are out there just waiting to be found by gem hunters who are looking for them?" Highfill ran his hand through his hair, leaving it standing up like whitecaps on the sea.

Silence smothered the pavilion. Highfill continued to pace. Dickon's face twisted as if he'd tasted too-strong cider. Lily found her gaze drifting back to the line of men digging into the cliff.

Ah, there he was. At the end farthest from the tent.

From her. He had bent over to take a closer look at something.

He straightened up abruptly and shoved a nickel-sized rock under the nose of the digger to his left. Lily's stomach plunged. Had Mason, of all people, found another sapphire?

The other digger peered closer at the rock Mason held, then threw back his head and laughed. He took the piece of stone from Mason and showed it to the digger on the other side, who also chuckled.

Not the sapphire, then. From the way the rock was being passed down the row of diggers, accompanied by a wave of merriment, Lily could only assume that the stone was of some sort of sexual nature. She'd spent too many years around giggling schoolboys not to recognize the signs.

He still hadn't turned around to look at her. Lily chewed on her lower lip.

"Are there even supposed to be sapphires around here?" her grandfather was asking behind her.

"I checked a few journals, and there have been minor finds in the area," Dickon replied. "Our bad luck to discover them here."

"It does complicate things," Highfill answered. "But it might not, after all, be such bad luck. Lily?"

"Hmm?" She turned back. Mason was angry with her. That was the only explanation for why he hadn't glanced even once toward the tent.

Her grandfather was giving her his pay-attention-to-me-young-lady stare. Lily obediently focused on him, but a spot between her shoulder blades began to tingle.

"Lily, I noticed that Donnelly is still here. And not only is he here, but he's working with the diggers. How did that happen?"

Suddenly she'd had enough of being the one who was responsible for forcing Mason out of the camp. "If you wanted him gone, you could've asked him to leave last night. Or this morning, when you arrived at the dig. It's your expedition. Your camp. And I'm not the one in charge of the diggers."

She thought her grandfather was going to blast her with his fury, but his voice was reasonable when he said, "If I asked him to leave, then he'd know we wanted him gone. And then he'd be determined to stay. We need to be subtle, manipulate him into leaving."

"But this little secret—"

"'Little secret'?" Dickon's face turned an intriguing shade of red. "Young lady, we've made some of our greatest finds this season, and this 'little secret' could destroy our fossil field. Gem miners couldn't care less about being careful about unearthing fossils when their greedy blood is screaming at them to find gems and gems and more gems. This 'little secret' could destroy everything we've worked toward for years!" He stopped to take a deep breath, and his color drifted back toward normal. "Pardon me for yelling, but I feel strongly about this." He turned to Highfill. "I don't advocate deception usually, but I agree that we have to get Donnelly out of here before he suspects anything."

"Suspects?" Lily repeated. "He doesn't suspect. He practically—"

"Lily," her grandfather said. "No more, please. Your

insistence that Donnelly is as harmless as a babe is quite naïve, as you'd know if you thought about it for a few moments."

She took a step back. She'd been going to say, *He practically knows,* not try to convince them that Mason should stay.

She took another step backward, pulling herself out of the conversational sphere. Highfill and Dickon kept talking about the sapphire finds while she ran her mind back over the past week.

This wasn't the first time her grandfather had cut her off or ignored something she'd said. She didn't expect him to agree with her all the time, but she did expect a certain amount of, well, respect. Her grandfather acted a little too much like Cecil sometimes. He didn't pat her on the head and say, "Go off and play," but that was the essential message.

An awful thought came to her. Perhaps the disregard Cecil showed her sprang from her grandfather's disregard, not the other way around. Perhaps Cecil thought that manner acceptable because that was how her grandfather treated her sometimes.

She scrubbed her palms up and down her arms. Suddenly it felt chilly beneath the awning.

Dickon's voice intruded into her thoughts. "How long can we wait before notifying the owner of the land? I assume we have a deal with him about the fossils but not about other finds."

Highfill rubbed his chin. "The owner already knows."

"How?"

"The owner is me."

That solved everything, then. "If this is your land," she said, "then no one can mine here and ruin the fossils."

"I wish you had told me that before," Dickon said. He let out a relieved laugh. "I've been tossing and turning all night ever since the first sapphire was found. But if you own the property—"

"During the past ten years, I've tried to buy most of the property we've dug on." But Highfill didn't return Dickon's smile, appearing contemplative instead. He nodded shortly, as if answering his own thought. "Well, we can wait until the end of the season before making any sort of decision."

"You're the owner!" Dickon repeated happily.

But a shiver corkscrewed through Lily's chest. Her grandfather hadn't said that he wouldn't open up the land to gem hunters, only that he would decide what to do later.

Dickon clearly thought Highfill would continue his fossil dig on the site, but Lily had been listening to stories about her grandfather's business sense all her life. And an excellent businessman didn't let such a prime opportunity slip through his fingers.

"Dickon—" she began.

"We'll see, we'll see," Highfill said over her. "I want to talk to Cecil about this before I make any decisions."

The joy faded from Dickon's face. For a moment Lily thought that he'd back off from the subject. Then Dickon's chin went up.

Lily silently sighed.

"What decision is there to make?" Dickon demanded. He gestured at the string of men working the cliff face. "These fellows have been breaking their backs for you all summer, and you're considering cutting the dig short for a few bucks?"

Dickon's voice had approached the volume of a moose's bellow toward the end. The diggers closest to the tent stopped digging and leaned on their spades. In a chain reaction, the rest of the diggers followed suit. The ones toward the end, including Mason, no doubt couldn't hear a word. But Dickon's arm waving and head shaking would make it clear that a drama was being staged under the awning.

At least Mason was finally looking in this direction, even if he wasn't looking at her. Well, she'd just pretend that he was.

Ugh. She was growing more pathetic by the minute. If she wanted to talk to him, maybe even apologize to him, though she wasn't sure exactly what she'd be apologizing for, she should go over and speak to him. Not stare at him desperately.

"That's not what I said. I said that I'd make a decision at the end of the season. Nothing is being cut short," Highfill told Dickon, his tone reasonable. And soft. *Highfills don't air their dirty laundry in public,* her mother often reminded her in letters, usually after Lily had related a scene to her in which she had had a verbal altercation with a shopkeeper or a child's parent. *But,* her mother always added, *Highfills never back down. Good for you.*

Her grandfather had no intention of backing down

this time, either. "And while I appreciate your thoughts on this matter, Dickon, it's not your decision to make."

Dickon jerked back as if he'd been backhanded. His face flushed a deeper scarlet, then went nearly white. "I have work to do," he said, sounding strangled. "You know where to find me."

Turning on his heel, he exited the tent.

All the diggers watched him stumble across the rugged ground to his horse. Then twenty pairs of eyes swung back to the tent.

Lily shifted her weight on the balls of her toes. She wanted to go with Dickon back to the sorting tent. But she had to stay and show support for her grandfather's decision. In any case, Dickon wouldn't want to see her until after he'd calmed down. She'd follow in fifteen minutes.

"Do you think he'll sabotage the dig?" her grandfather said, staring at Dickon as he mounted his horse.

Of all the stupid questions . . . "Dickon? He's been by your side longer than I've been alive."

"Yes, true."

"But you could have been nicer to him," she stated. *Highfills never back down,* she reminded herself. Just because her grandfather ignored her opinions didn't mean she wasn't going to stop giving them.

"I suppose."

Hmm. So she wasn't being ignored all the time. That was good.

Her grandfather sat down in one of the folding camp chairs. "I just didn't like his suggestion that I didn't give two shakes about those fellows out there."

Lily obligingly looked at the diggers. They were back at work again, so all she could see was Mason's back.

It was an awfully nice back. She'd run her hands all over his back yesterday.

"Lily?" Her grandfather made a big show of waving his hand in front of her eyes. Her face heating, she swatted his hand away. Thank God Mason wasn't looking at her now. How humiliating that would be.

"You know, Cecil is mighty worked up about this affection you seem to have for Mason Donnelly."

"Affection?" she squeaked. "There is no affection." How could there be affection when the man wouldn't even look at her?

Highfill shrugged. "Or whatever you young folk call it these days. Cecil wants to marry you, you know." He jerked a thumb at Mason. "What does *he* want?"

To write a big story. To break through his writer's block. To kiss her a few more times—she hoped. But she doubted he'd do that again, given the opposite positions they were now in.

Her grandfather took her hand. "Lily, my sweet, Cecil loves you."

She let out a bark of laughter. "I'm not convinced he even likes me, much less loves me. Grandfather, I told Cecil that I wouldn't marry him."

"I asked you to reconsider."

"And I did!" For all of half a second late last night when she'd been flipping from side to side, trying to sleep. But she knew from experience that many bad ideas were conceived in the short hours of the morning, and she'd dismissed the thought almost before it could fully form.

Another bad idea had been to sneak over to Mason's tent. He was angry. Disappointed. She understood why, but she hoped that he could see past that—could talk to her again. Maybe hold her hand. And kiss her until all thoughts of conflicting loyalties and sapphires slid away.

Luckily, she'd tossed out the idea of visiting Mason almost as quickly as she'd tossed out giving Cecil a second try. Her grandfather and Dickon were suspicious enough of her "affection" for Mason. Finding her crawling into his tent in the middle of the night would cinch it.

Not that she really would. Kissing Mason was one thing. Additional, ah, adventures were outside her expectations of correct behavior, especially when the other person had already been clear that he was going to ride away as soon as he got his story.

"Have you truly thought this through?" her grandfather asked. "Cecil is the brother and heir to a very wealthy shipping line owner."

Lily stared at her grandfather. "And I am a Highfill." She would have to marry into European royalty to rise any further in the eyes of the Boston social and financial scene.

Her grandfather stood and planted a kiss on her forehead. "So you are. All right, I won't say anything more about it. Except this: Your mother will be disappointed."

Her mother. She still had to write her mother and break the news. "When is Cecil returning?"

Highfill's eyes brightened. "Tomorrow, I believe."

Tomorrow. She would have her letter to her mother at the post office before Cecil arrived at camp. By writing her mother of the end of her not-quite-engagement, she'd make her decision final—and not allow either her mother or her grandfather to nag her into receiving Cecil's suit.

"I should go help Dickon with the sorting," she said.

"Get one of the boys to take you back. I don't want you wandering around alone."

One of the boys? Her focus shifted to Mason, as it had so many times since she'd arrived at camp.

"And have you retrieved all your things from town yet?" her grandfather asked.

"No."

"Well, I'll ask Cecil to help you with that after he returns. Remember, no one rides anywhere alone."

She'd ask even that trigger-happy miner to help her move her belongings before she'd willingly spend so much time in Cecil's company.

At the end of the line of diggers, Mason stopped shoveling and straightened. He rolled his neck and shoulders to loosen them.

Imagine if he were doing that without his shirt on . . .

"I'll see you at supper," Highfill said, turning to some sketches she'd penned by lamplight after supper last night. Not her best work: She'd been distracted by Mason's anger. "Send Richter back in here if you see him, won't you? And have someone take you back to camp."

Well, her choice of an escort was easy. Whether he'd want to fill that position was another question entirely.

Painting a smile on her face, she tiptoed through the rough ground until she reached the end of the line of men. Peter glanced up, saw her, and swept her a gracious bow.

"Hello, Peter . . . Mason." She was trying to look at Mason and not look at him at the same time, and it was giving her a headache. Finally she just gave in and really looked at him.

And he was looking at her back. "Morning," he said. But his raised eyebrows made his astonishment at her presence clear. Hadn't he even noticed that she was here at the dig?

She kept her smile still affixed, but it was beginning to stiffen like a dead lizard baked in the sun. "I need an escort back to camp. And help moving my belongings from town into my tent."

She waited. He had to offer, damn it. She couldn't ask him without making her grandfather and Dickon furious.

But all he said was "Ah." And leaned on his shovel.

Fine. "Peter, could you possibly help me? My grandfather said it was all right," she added, in case he though she was shanghaiing him on her own initiative.

"Sure can." He rested his shovel against the rock wall. "That beats digging up chunks of stone any day. Wait here while I go to tell Richter, all right?"

He hurried off before she could protest or yell, "For

God's sake don't leave me with this man whose shirt I want to tear off his body. And then maybe strangle him with it."

She watched Peter dodge past his fellow diggers, but finally she had to turn and face Mason. "I didn't see you at breakfast. I thought you might have left."

His eyebrows crawled even higher on his forehead. "Disappointed that I didn't?" he said challengingly.

Given her cool behavior the night before, he had every right to make that assumption. "No. Disappointed, perhaps, that you'd think that, though." She held his stare until he looked away.

Peter ran up, sleekly handsome and glowing with perspiration from his sprint. Too bad she couldn't imagine ripping *his* shirt off. That would make her life ten thousand times easier. "I'm ready," he puffed.

Lily had reached her horse before she realized she had not said good-bye to Mason. Another strike against him: He unraveled her composure so thoroughly that she couldn't even remember the basic social niceties.

She mounted her horse and, under cover of pretending to lean over and check her stirrup, glanced back at Mason.

He was already working again, his dark head bent and his shoulders curved with power as he thrust the shovel into the ground.

Lily shivered, then rode with Peter back to camp.

Chapter Eleven

Mason was in a foul mood. Maybe it was due to the sunburn tight across his shoulders. Maybe it was the half dozen blisters studding his palms like rubies, stinging every time he forked a bite of steak or potatoes into his mouth. But it was definitely not because Lily had her head close to Peter's as she spoke to him.

Mason chewed his mouthful of steak and swallowed. He tried to look away, to strike up conversation with the fellow to his left, but he couldn't pull his eyes from Lily on the other side of the table and six seats away. At least she glanced in his direction every so often. He'd caught her eye once or twice, but after one little nod, she'd ignored him.

The evening had started out so promising, too. He'd cleaned his blisters, had the cook wrap them up—it was growing to be a bit embarrassing how often he visited the cook to be patched up—and then gone back to his tent to write down a few character sketches of the men he'd worked shoulder to shoulder with all day.

The words had poured out of his pen like they were rushing toward freedom. He'd filled four pages with notes before the supper bell snapped him out of his trance—the trance he remembered well from when he was in the grip of a story that wouldn't let him go. A trance he hadn't experienced in six months.

But even a man in a trance had to eat—especially a man who'd spent the day out in the hot sun, plunging a shovel into gravelly earth, and so he'd followed the bell's summons and gone to supper.

And now this.

For all Lily's talk of how Peter was too young, she certainly didn't seem to mind spending time with him. Of course, Mason could take full responsibility for that. He'd practically shoved Peter at Lily earlier today when she'd come to ask for help moving her things.

So, what the hell was his problem?

Down the table, Lily cocked her head at something Peter said. She began to twirl a corner of her scarf— the red one Mason remembered from the first day he'd met her—around her forefinger as she listened.

The problem was that he wasn't angry anymore. And he wanted to forget about the damn story bubbling underneath this expedition, return to his tent with Lily, and resume kissing her as if he'd never been so stupid as to ask her to reveal secrets that almost certainly weren't hers to reveal.

At the end of the table, Highfill stood, signaling the end of supper. Most of the men had finished long ago, and many had left behind a fair amount of the watery potatoes. The cook wouldn't be happy tonight.

Dickon was another fellow who was clearly unhappy. As he rose after Highfill and followed the older man from the table, the fossil cataloger's outthrust jaw signaled he was angling for an argument.

Mason had seen Lily shove her jaw out in much the same way. Had Dickon picked up the mannerism from her, or had she copied him?

As Mason stood, Peter appeared beside him and gave him a friendly slap on the shoulder. Mason let out a grunt.

Peter frowned. "What's wrong?"

"Sunburn."

Peter's expression lightened. "I thought maybe you had greater effects from being shot than you'd admitted to anyone."

"Being shot *at*," Mason corrected. Not quite the same thing. "So. Have a nice day with Miss Highfill?"

Peter's ears reddened and he looked away. "As I've said before, she's a nice young lady, and . . ."

And? And she could make a man's thoughts do sommersaults? And she could kiss in a way that could cut your knees out from under you?

Mason waited, but Peter didn't elaborate.

Well, maybe she and Peter hadn't found themselves in the cozy situation of a cold cave. Or a dim tent. Though if Peter had moved her belongings from town to here, they must have been alone together in her room at the boardinghouse.

Mason's blistered palms began to burn. He relaxed his clenched fists. Just a stab of jealousy. Nothing life threatening.

Across the table, Lily finished her conversation with Richter, stood with a grace that made Mason's throat tighten, and began threading through the group still milling around the table. Mason pushed himself up on the balls of his feet to follow her with his eyes, but he lost her in the crowd.

"A few of us are going into Milton to the saloon," Peter said. "Want to join us?"

Brilliant. A bunch of pressed-pants easterners versus a town full of angry miners. That would give the cook more patchwork to do in the morning. "No, thanks. I've been beaten up enough in the past few days. Just try to make sure no one gets killed. Don't bring any guns."

"*They* might have guns."

"Yeah, but they probably won't shoot you all if you're unarmed. If you're armed, all bets are off."

"Huh." Peter considered that for a moment. "I'll talk to the other fellows about it."

"Good." Mason gave him a nod, then started his hunt for Lily.

He found her in the sorting tent, sitting at the desk in the back with a lit lamp tossing a veil of light over her, her pen scratching against a page. The tent's sides were still rolled up, opening the interior to the darkening night. And to the eyes of any curious passersby. Not a good place for kissing, unfortunately. But perhaps an excellent place to try to worm his way back into her good graces.

She looked up at the sound of his footsteps on the dirt floor. "Oh. Hello."

She wasn't smiling. Well, he deserved that. "Hi."

He drew closer, then dropped to his haunches next to the chair she sat in. She shifted away a little to keep space between them. Not a good sign.

Well, he was notorious for being relentless. He'd be relentless now in trying to convince her to let him be close to her again. He didn't know what he wanted exactly, but it wasn't the chilly wall that existed now between them.

No, he was deluding himself. He wanted far more than to melt that wall.

"How was the move this afternoon?" he asked.

"Easy enough. I didn't have much with me." She shot her chin out the same way Dickon had done only a few minutes earlier. Spoiling for a fight. "I'd like the article on my grandfather back, please."

"Of course. I should have given it back to you days ago." He paused. "And I should have offered to help you this afternoon."

The chin dropped a fraction. "Peter did a good job." A shadow of a smile. "Didn't break anything."

Taking a deep breath, he reached out and drew his fingertip along the fine bones of her hand resting on the chair arm nearest him. She flinched, but didn't jerk away. "I'm afraid I may have broken something yesterday. The friendship between us."

Her cute chin settled back into its usual position, but her big eyes remained wary. "In what fashion exactly? Are you referring to our kiss—"

"Kiss*es*."

"—or your belief that there's a big story here?"

He was glad that she'd phrased it that way instead of saying that he believed she had lied to him. Because he knew darn well that she had lied to him, and he didn't want to touch the subject again.

"I'm referring to my asking you to tell me something that you probably can't tell me."

"Oh." Thankfully, she didn't press it further. Or declare that she knew nothing.

Silence passed, but an easier silence than before. "What are you working on?" he asked. "Another sketch?" But it looked like a letter to him.

She handed him the sheet of paper. "Read this and tell me what you think."

Mason pulled over a canvas camp chair and settled beside her. "I'm not a good letter writer," he told her. "I write maybe one a month, to someone other than my editor." Former editor.

"Really?" She blinked at him. "I write about one letter a day. Sometimes two, as I'm now also writing to my aunt, while before I was living with her and of course didn't need to write to her."

Mason glanced at the letter in hand. It was addressed to Mrs. Grant in Boston. "Then who is this?" He gave the single page a shake.

"My mother. She lives in Boston with my stepfather."

"Do you plan to return to Denver?" He came through Denver fairly often. He liked Denver. He could take her out to supper the next time he was in town, and then maybe to the Friday-night dance at William Green's Emporium. They could sneak out the back door and linger in the shadows of the building, returning to the dance later with their clothes mussed.

"I don't know. It depends on how well I do in Boston this time." She made a face. "It was a disaster the last time I visited. I returned to Denver after only a month."

"How old were you?"

"Seventeen. And as awkward as a newborn goat."

"Well, you should have no worries about that now. I've never seen a lady snatch a rifle off a saddle with as much grace as you did yesterday."

She blushed, then laughed. "Read the letter. And tell me how I should fix it."

He obediently dropped his eyes to the page in his hand.

Dear Mother,

> *I write you this letter knowing that you will be disappointed but I am unable to find a solution that will make both of us happy. Though I know that you think quite highly of Cecil St. John, after spending much of the summer in his company I have realized that we would not suit. We disagree on several issues of importance.*

Mason tapped the page. "What are the 'issues of importance' that you and Cecil disagree on?"

"Do you think I should specify them?"

Telling her he was only curious might not get him the answer. "Maybe."

She began ticking points off on her fingers. "One, he thinks that when he says 'Jump,' I should eagerly jump."

"As if you don't have common sense of your own."

"Exactly. Two, he doesn't trust me."

"About what?"

She wouldn't meet his eyes. "That's not important."

Now his curiosity sank its claws in deep.

"What's important is that although I swore something up and down, he refused to believe me. What sort of marriage is it when you start off not trusting each other?" She didn't wait for his answer. "Three, I don't think he believes I'm intelligent. Perhaps this is vanity speaking, but *I* think I'm intelligent. I may not be as intelligent as he is—"

"No, don't think that. You have a brain, and you use it. I could see that the first time I met you." He grinned at her. "And your tongue was just as sharp as your mind, if I recall."

"Because Cecil had maligned my sketches."

Mason added softly, "And no one defended you."

"No, they didn't." She half closed her eyes, apparently thinking back. "You tried to save my sketches."

"They were good sketches."

Her smile started in her eyes and transformed her face. "They were, weren't they."

He could kiss her now. He could see it in the invitation in her slightly tilted chin, in the relaxed line of her shoulders. And he was beginning to lean toward her.

He exhaled, reversed course, and settled back onto his chair. His own intelligence had to be in question if he had so easily forgotten that they were in full view of the camp.

Lily said, "So you think I should tell my mother what the important issues are that Cecil and I disagree on?"

"What do you think? You've seen your mother in two different marriages. Does she believe in a husband respecting his wife's common sense, trustworthiness, and intelligence?"

She thought about it. "Yes."

"Then put it in there." He read on.

I'll give you more details when I see you, but please believe me when I say that I will not change my decision on this. Both Cecil and I will be happier with other people.

Looking forward to seeing you after so long. Although I will not be coming to Boston with the husband that you liked, I hope you'll be proud of me when you see me again.

Love, your daughter,
Lily

Lily's being afraid that she didn't live up to her mother's expectations seemed odd. She had a lot of pluck and smarts. But perhaps pluck and smarts weren't as prized by Boston mamas as they were by him.

"So?" she asked.

"I think you need to write the whole thing over."

"Being more specific about why I won't marry Cecil?"

"In a way. Take that pen and write what I tell you to."

She gave him a suspicious look—another example that she was intelligent—but did as he said.

"'Dear Mother, I have wonderful news,'" Mason dictated. "'I discovered before making the misstep of marrying Cecil St. John that he is a toad and unworthy of a princess like me. I quite bravely kissed him a few times, and he neglected to turn into the prince I deserve.'"

He'd half hoped that she would say she'd never kissed St. John. "You know I hate it when you call me a princess," she said instead. But she was scratching the pen across the paper, and when he leaned forward, he saw that she was writing what he had said.

"It worked with the fairy tale theme, though," he said. "No one could remain a princess after living so long in Denver."

"And I take it from your tone that you think that's good?"

"I find it easier to talk to non-princesses than princesses."

"If you've just discovered that I'm not a princess, then I tremble to imagine the outpouring of conversation I'm going to receive from you."

He hadn't exactly been stilted in his speech since meeting her, so she had a point. "Well, you were the most likable princess I've ever met."

"Hmm."

"Your mother recommended that Cecil marry you?" he asked. When she nodded, he said, "Then write instead: 'the prince I deserved and the prince that you promised me.' After all, she should have known better."

"He can be charming," she said, not writing the words.

"Funny. He's never that way with me."

Her mouth quirking, she bent her head and scribbled another line.

Mason cleared his throat. "'I've found another fellow who stirs up all sorts of feelings in me.'"

Her pen continued to move across the page.

"'His name is . . . Peter.'"

She rolled her eyes. "Don't be silly. Peter is a puppy."

"He'd be hurt to hear you say that."

"That's why I'm saying it to you, not to him."

"All right. 'His name is Mason.'"

She started writing again. "If you're referring to feelings of indignation and exasperation, I agree."

"'Mother, this wonderful man saved my life yesterday, throwing himself in front of me to take a bullet.'"

She penned the words. "An exaggeration, but nonetheless, you were wounded."

"'But even before that I knew he was special, for only moments earlier, we were embracing with a passion unlike any I'd felt before.'"

"I think I'm going to write *kissing* instead of *embracing*. *Embracing* sounds like it's only a hug, and that wasn't the situation."

Mason leaned forward. Her pen etched the words into the page. "You're really writing this down?"

"Well, that, at least, is truthful. Unlike your throwing yourself in front of a bullet meant for me."

She didn't look up at him. A good idea. If she'd looked at him, he would have given her an ambushing she'd never forget.

"'And,'" he added, his voice scratchy, "'he trusts in me, my common sense, and my intelligence.'"

Lily scrawled the last words, then put her pen down. She gave the letter a little push with her fingertip. "This confuses me." And she finally looked up at him.

There was a question in her eyes, but he couldn't tell what she was asking.

He answered the question that he wanted her to ask. "I like you a great deal. And I want to take you to bed." His heart's self-preservation instincts then kicked in. "As does almost every man here."

She shook her head. "I don't think I'm quite as in demand as you do. But let's imagine that we did go to bed together. And then what would happen?"

He swallowed. "I can't marry you, if that's what you mean. We're too different."

Her gaze held steady. "I'm not sure I agree with that, either. But if you believe that, then there's not much point, is there?"

"We'd both enjoy it immensely."

"I've heard that it's not always so enjoyable for a virgin. Is that true?"

A blush dusted her cheeks, but she still didn't look away.

"That's true."

"So then you'd get immense enjoyment out of it, while I might not. And if I'm not enjoying it—

immensely—then I think that you might not enjoy it so much, either."

It was said so bluntly, he could see that she didn't have much reason to sleep with him. Who was he fooling? Even if she wanted to sleep with him, any "good" reasons for doing so would be thin on the ground.

"I think I'm being dosed with your vaunted common sense," he said, trying to tease her.

She grinned. "I'm dosing myself as well, you know."

"I know." And that made everything—almost—all right.

Lily picked up the lantern and returned it to its hook by the sorting tent's front door. She turned down the flame until it went out.

"Will you walk me back to my tent?" she asked in the darkness.

Mason hesitated by the desk for a moment, then moved slowly through the crowded tent, banging his hip only once on the corner of some table. Reaching the tent entrance, he took her hand. "I'd be happy to."

She threaded her fingers with his and squeezed.

Voices hushed by canvas sidings drifted around them as they wound among the tents. The moon popped out from behind the thickening cloud cover every once in a while, but at times the darkness was nearly absolute, wrapping them together in anonymity.

She led him onto a path he didn't travel often and stopped. "This is my new tent," she whispered. "You were right, though I hate to admit it. The old one was a little too small after I had to bring all my things here."

The moon made another bow. Mason could see that the other tents nearby didn't have laundry floating off their guylines. Lily had been set within a circle of tents empty except for rocks and fossils.

As if hearing his thoughts, she said, "Peter had to clean this one out for me before I could use it. It's still a little dusty inside."

The words broke out before he knew he was going to say them. "You could share my tent."

She slapped him gently on the shoulder. "Stop trying to lure me into your bed, please."

He took the hand she had slapped him with and the hand he was already holding and settled them on the back of his neck. Then he released her hands and slid his palms down her arms, her sides, to her waist, where he tightened his hold.

If she pushed him away after a minute, he could live with that. She'd already told him she wouldn't go to bed with him, so a no was the only conclusion he was going to receive at some point anyway.

But she wasn't saying no right away. She leaned forward into him, her breasts pressing against his chest. Mason let his hands drift down until they cupped her perfect rear end, and he pulled her hips tightly against him.

Her breath sighed out, and then he ducked his head to capture her lips with his.

He didn't know how she did it, for she certainly wasn't doing anything special. But the whole world faded away until his only gravity was her mouth.

Finally—maybe minutes, maybe hours later—her

hand slid down from where it had been toying with the hair at his nape and settled against his chest. She pressed a kiss to his throat and whispered against his hot skin, "Thank you."

Then she disappeared inside her tent, leaving him alone with the night.

If her aunt could have seen her, she would have dubbed her "chipper as a grasshopper." Lily couldn't bear to staidly walk anywhere—she had to bounce. At one point, when no one else was on the path she was taking to the sorting tent, she even did a little pirouette.

"Another daydreaming day, huh?" Dickon grumbled when she practically danced through the door.

Oh, without a doubt. Lily went to the end of the table, where Dickon had assembled a group of pieces to be shipped back.

"As my assistant," he said, "you should check in with me before you take the afternoon off."

Lily put the rock she had picked up back down on the table. "I thought that yesterday afternoon I was Highfill's granddaughter, not your assistant. You certainly didn't encourage me to come back here with you."

"Maybe so. But next time, let me know."

"Yes, sir." She bit her lip. Dickon had championed her work several times to both her grandfather and Cecil. To dash away whenever she felt like it didn't show him very much respect. "I'm sorry."

Dickon waved off her apology. "No harm done. I'm not sure how much more time we have left here anyway." He dodged a look at her.

"I don't know, either. I left the dig yesterday soon after you did."

"All right. But what do you think will happen?"

Dickon wasn't going to like this, but he'd like a wishy-washy statement from her even less. "I think my grandfather is a businessman first, a fossil hunter second."

Dickon sagged. "My thoughts, too."

"But that doesn't mean the dig will be shortened this season." She gestured at the contents of the tent. "We have weeks' more work here to do."

Her original plan had been to leave when her grandfather did, and he always left when the digging part was over. But Dickon had always stayed behind for an extra week or two, shipping back the last of the finds and the camp equipment. Perhaps she could convince her grandfather that she should stay. And perhaps Mason would want to stay as well. . . .

She'd thought about this quite a lot last night as she'd stared up at the canvas ceiling of her tent. She'd been of marriageable age for several years and not one of the gentlemen—or even ruffians—she'd met in that time had sparked any strong interest from her. Flickers of awareness, yes. Sparks, no.

The sensation she felt when she was with Mason wasn't sparks: It was a lightning strike. Perhaps during his endless travels he, too, had simply never found the right person.

Not that his desire to bed her indicated anything more powerful and lasting than simple lust. She was worldly enough to know that. At the same time, it didn't rule out the possibility that there could be something more than lust. On her side, anyway, there was more. Vastly more.

Well, even if Mason didn't remain after the end of the digging season, she wanted to. At the very least, it would put off her return to Boston and facing her mother's disappointment, now guaranteed. And it would give her a handful more days in Colorado.

She started wrapping a fragile jawbone in newspaper. Mason's old newspaper. He'd signaled last night that he wouldn't press her for more information about the story he sensed here, but she didn't doubt he'd continue his search.

"I was mad yesterday about your grandfather thinking about shutting down the dig," Dickon said, resuming the conversation, "but that's not what's bothering me today." He shoved out his jaw in a way that Lily had seen so often. She'd mentally dubbed it his bulldog face. "It's all this sneaking around. All the uncertainty. Let's just decide what we're going to do, and do it."

"I agree," she said wholeheartedly.

"And I don't know why you're the one who's supposed to be driving Donnelly away. You're the worst liar I know, and he's clearly besotted by you. Your grandfather is well-known for choosing the best people for the job, but in this case he's chosen the worst."

"I agree," she said again, though more dryly. Plain speaking could sometimes have a sandpaper edge that abraded one's ego. Not that she was convinced that Mason was "besotted."

"How's your aunt doing?" Dickon asked abruptly.

"Fine. I received a letter from her a few days ago."

"Does she—" He coughed. "Does she know I'm here?"

Lily blinked. "I'm not sure I ever mentioned you to her by name."

"Oh."

"Why?"

He shook his head as if he weren't going to answer her, but said, "I knew her before she moved out here."

Dickon had been with Grandfather's company for as long as she could remember. He must have met her aunt in Boston before she moved to Denver.

"Maybe I'll write to her," he mused, "and maybe I'll drop by to say hello before I catch the train back east in Denver."

"She'd probably like that. When I first moved out to live with her, she told me that the one thing she missed about Boston were the friends she'd had to leave behind."

"I'll do that, then. Post a letter tomorrow."

"I'm going into town to post a letter today. If you write it now, I can send it out."

"Oh, I took your letter to town this morning. The general store had hardly even opened—"

Panic knocked hard in her chest. She looked over at the desk. The surface was empty except for pen and ink. "Which letter did you take?"

"There was only one there. You'd signed it, so I folded it up, put it in the envelope, and mailed it off."

She'd left two letters on the desk last night. Her first letter that she'd asked Mason's opinion on, and the second silly letter that had gotten out of hand toward the end.

Good God. Which letter had Dickon mailed? And where had the other one gone?

"Did you happen to read the letter?"

Dickon gave her an offended look. "Of course not."

"I thought I had left two letters there last night, and I just want to make sure the wrong letter didn't get sent to my mother." Somehow her voice came out normal instead of in the shrill tones echoing in her skull.

"There was only one. It did say 'Dear Mother'—I saw that." He smiled. "So don't worry. Your letter went to the right person."

The right person, but perhaps the wrong letter. She could just imagine her mother reading her description of kissing Mason "with a passion unlike anything" she'd felt before.

Dickon rubbed his chin. "I didn't see a second letter, though. Could a gust of wind have stolen it?"

Which would be worse? Having her mother receive such an outrageous letter, or having one of the diggers discover it floating around the camp?

She tottered over to the desk chair and plunked down. Oh, Lord. Please let the letter Dickon sent be the right one.

Dickon hovered over her. "Are you all right?"

Another voice came from the front of the tent. "Is something wrong with Lily?"

Typical. Cecil thought she was so helpless that she couldn't even answer a question about her own health.

Anger's edge snapped through the noose of panic. "I'm fine. Or did you want Dickon to answer you?"

"No, your answer is fine." But he strode into the tent, exuding an easy and somehow offensive elegance, and asked Dickon again, "What's wrong?"

Dickon leaned against the desk and placed his big hand on Lily's shoulder. Comfort, and an alliance. "We had a little excitement while you were gone. Someone took a few shots at Lily and Mason Donnelly out at the mine. And we made another, uh, find."

Cecil's face bleached of color. "Say that again."

"I was shot at," Lily said, "and we found another you-know-what."

"Dear God." Cecil stared at her.

If she'd liked him, she would have felt quite gratified by his shock. Only a week ago she would have been overjoyed by his reaction at her brush with death. But now irritation was her main response.

"Dear God," he said again, then shook his head like a dog shaking off water. "But you were unharmed?"

"Yes. Mason was slightly injured, but—"

"Is he gone now?" Cecil interrupted.

"No, he's out with the diggers again today." She'd sat with him at breakfast, not saying much but smiling a great deal. He'd walked off to the dig site with the other men, turning and giving her a wave before disappearing around the first bend. She'd been half-embarrassed to be caught waiting and watching, and half-delighted that he'd looked back for her.

Cecil was saying something to her, but she'd lost track of it. "Pardon me?"

"I said," Cecil growled through clenched teeth, "just what were you doing there with Mason Donnelly, anyway?"

Lily heaved a sigh. "Oh, Cecil, probably what you imagine we were doing there."

Dickon lifted his hand to cover a cough, but not before Lily saw him grin.

Cecil exhaled a long breath. "Lily, I know that you're unhappy with me, but you don't have to throw him in my face." Then he shook his head again, this time playfully. "I see I have a great deal of ground to recover and penance to make." He raised his hand in farewell before striding away in the direction of her grandfather's tent.

Dickon started to chuckle. "Poor fool doesn't understand the meaning of rejection, does he?"

Chapter Twelve

When Dickon found the fourth sapphire, Lily thought she'd never seen anyone so disheartened. His shoulders slumped as he rolled the stone on his open palm, looking at it as if he wished he could cast it into a well. But if they'd found four sapphires in five days, odds were that another one would show up tomorrow, making his attempts at denial fruitless.

Dickon closed his hand around the gem. "Let's go."

Both her grandfather and Cecil were in her grandfather's tent, speaking in low tones. Dickon swept in without calling out a greeting. "Found another one." He tossed it to Highfill, then rubbed his palm against his leg as though he were trying to scrub off a smell.

Highfill looked at Cecil. "We can't put off this decision much longer."

"Give me a few more days," Cecil said. "A few more days won't matter one way or the other."

Highfill nodded, but he looked grim.

"This still remains a secret." Cecil seemed to be

speaking to everyone, but Lily thought that his eyes had settled on her a little bit longer than on the others. She stiffened. Did he still believe that she couldn't control her mouth?

Vivid memories of last night welled to the surface. Well, maybe she couldn't always control her mouth. But she at least knew not to blab about secrets that weren't her own.

Dickon propped his hands on his hips. He said to Highfill, "What exactly does that mean that he has a few more days? Does that mean that I, too, have a few more days? Should I be readying the camp for packing up?"

"We're two weeks away from the date when we said we'd leave," Highfill said, his tone mild. "I assumed that you are already beginning your preparations for closing up the camp."

"There's a difference between two weeks and two days."

"We can't close up the whole camp in two days, Dickon."

Lily knew an evasion when she heard it, and so, apparently, did Dickon. He sucked in a deep breath and almost visibly counted to ten.

"Will you give me a few days' notice as to when we're closing up?" Dickon asked. "Or is this it?"

Her grandfather hesitated and glanced at Cecil.

Lily frowned. How odd that Cecil seemed to have such a strong say in this decision, while Dickon, who'd been with Grandfather for twenty years, was in the position of pleading for information.

"No, this isn't it. And I'll give you enough notice for you to do your job properly."

Dickon jerked his head at her and she followed him out of the tent. Much better than yesterday, when he'd strode off in a huff and relegated her to the side of the enemy.

Without looking at her, Dickon said, "Let's start packing up."

Lily stopped dead. "But my grandfather—"

"I believe your grandfather when he says that he'll give me a few days' notice, but he's also right in that I'll need more than that. If we begin packing up today, we'll be in good shape when he announces the closure of the dig." Dickon turned and faced her, his spine straight. "I can't work on one thing while thinking another is going to happen. We're packing up, Lily girl."

That meant her chances of staying later to help Dickon ship the dig equipment back east were fading fast. How else could she delay her trip to Boston? Mason wasn't going to be around forever—he'd been frank about that—but a few more days with him . . .

"I could introduce you to my aunt," Lily said.

Dickon blinked at her.

"I mean, I could take you to Denver with me for a few days, and you could be our guest during that time. And then you and I could go back to Boston together."

"Hmm." Dickon rubbed his chin and started walking again toward the sorting tent. Lily had to dash a few steps to catch up with him.

"I don't know, Lily girl. I appreciate the offer—more than you know—but I may take some time to explore the area a bit more. You know, I've spent the last five summers out west, and I've seen only the inside of a tent or a dozen dig sites. I'd like to see more."

Lily was dazed. "You aren't coming back to Boston?"

"Not immediately, I don't think. But I haven't really thought this through yet." He shook his head. "Too many secrets right now. I can't think straight."

Lily nodded in understanding. Her grandfather was concealing from his diggers and the public possibly the biggest gemstone find of the century, and Lily was concealing from just about everybody that she was falling hard for a frontier reporter who believed that uncovering the first secret was his path back to his career.

The high-society drawing rooms of Boston were starting to look less complicated than this.

Shadows streamed out behind the tents around them as the sun stubbed its toe against the western horizon. The mashed potatoes had been runny again, Lily thought, and drew a little frown with a tine on her fork in the potatoes that were left on her plate.

Highfill cleared his throat, drawing Lily's attention from her doodling. "Thank you, gentlemen," her grandfather said, and stood, signaling the end of supper.

Lily looked down the long table again, but nothing had changed. Mason still wasn't there.

Her stomach dropped under the sudden pressure of the disappointment she'd managed to shove aside during supper, telling herself that Mason would arrive only five minutes late. Or ten minutes late. Or an hour. But he wasn't late. He hadn't shown up at all.

Where in blazes was he? Didn't he realize that her entire afternoon of wrapping and plastering had been brightened only by her expectation that she'd see him at supper? And she'd entertained the idea that perhaps he'd looked forward to seeing her after a backbreaking day of shoveling out rocks.

Maybe his tent had fallen on him and he was trapped there, unable to come to supper. She didn't like to wish ill luck on anyone, but she hoped that that was what had happened.

Dickon, though not a big talker by nature, had been unusually quiet, and a pall of silence had fallen over the table during much of supper.

Her grandfather's big hand descended onto her shoulder. "Lily, how would you like to share some tea with me?"

A cup of tea was part of her grandfather's nightly ritual. He'd invited her to it a few times at the beginning of the summer, but more often he shared his teatime with Cecil.

As she stood, Lily glanced at Cecil to see if he was going to be invited as well, and she caught a meaningful look being exchanged between the two men.

She barely managed not to groan out loud. First Mason had failed to show up, and now she had to deal as well with the irritation of having to fend off the attentions—apparently to be conveyed by her grandfather—of a man she disliked?

Cecil, perhaps demonstrating the intelligence that

Highfill had supposedly hired him for, hadn't made any attempts at charming her during supper, which had lulled her into imagining that he'd given up.

Lily stood. "Yes, I'd love some tea." Perhaps if she drank it very quickly, she could escape before the subject of Cecil came up.

Inside her grandfather's huge tent, he gestured for her to take a seat. "Cecil is head over heels for you, you know."

Lily sank down in a chair and briefly closed her eyes. Her grandfather hadn't even put the tea in the pot yet and he'd launched into his campaign to support Cecil.

"So, what do you think of that?" he asked when she didn't answer.

"First, I don't think that's true at all. Second, if it is true, it would've been more convenient if he had been head over heels for me at the same time I was head over heels for him. But he wasn't. And now I'm not."

"But just because you keep, ah, missing each other doesn't mean you should dismiss the idea outright, as you seem to be doing. Perhaps the timing will be right soon."

Yes, perhaps, but most likely in the opposite way her grandfather assumed. Lily suspected the time would come when neither one would be head over heels for the other.

"But if you persist in not giving him a chance," Highfill continued, "in five years you'll think back and say, 'I should have found out if Cecil and I could've had a wonderful marriage.'"

"I would hope that in five years I'd still be so happy with the marriage I do have that the thought wouldn't cross my mind."

Her grandfather smiled. "Sweetheart, the thought will cross your mind whether or not you're happily married. I'll bet a hundred dollars on that."

"Fine. Imagine that I did marry Cecil. According to you, five years in, I'll think, *What if I gave Bill in Denver a chance?* I'll always wonder about a man I didn't marry. So I'm not sure I follow your—" She almost said *logic* but bit it back. That sounded too belligerent. "—your argument."

"You're trying to be difficult," Highfill said mildly. "So of course you won't follow my argument. You don't want to."

Lily squirmed. She suddenly felt all of twelve years old.

Her grandfather poured the tea and they sat sipping in silence.

The faint sound of singing drifted in through the canvas walls. The diggers were belting out their favorite songs while they shared mugs of hard cider. A brief but brutal scuffle last night at the Milton saloon had convinced them to confine their drinking to the camp. She thought she could hear Peter's voice among the singers'. Really, he was such a nice boy.

"Are you still angry with your mother for sending you to Denver when you were younger?" her grandfather asked.

"No." Even to her ears, her answer sounded too quick, defensive. "Well, I was in the beginning. For the first year, at least. But once I found my place in Denver, everything grew much easier." She took a swallow of tea to give her time to organize her thoughts. "Aunt Evaline is so different from both the Boston ladies and the Denver ladies. She is a daily example of independence and independent thinking. Her example helped me make my place in Denver instead of finding my place."

"She always did have a streak of independence as wide as the sky," her grandfather muttered.

"And I think Aunt Evaline was very happy to have me with her, so of course I can't regret that part of moving to Denver. Besides, I know that I acted atrociously when Mr. Grant started courting Mother. I'm sure I deserved to be sent out to Aunt Evaline." It was being sent back to Denver the second time that had truly wounded her, even though she'd practically demanded it by moping around her mother's house for weeks.

Eight years of exile. Her aunt had suffered worse, though. More than twenty years had passed since she'd left Boston, and she hadn't returned once. Nor, as far as Lily knew, had anyone come out specifically to visit her. Grandfather—Aunt Evaline's father—had stopped in on his way somewhere else, but that was it. If Dickon did visit Evaline, he'd be her first real visitor from home.

Highfill scratched his beard. "So your first answer was correct. You aren't mad at your mother."

"Yes. Well, mostly. I do wish she'd visited me and Aunt Evaline at least once."

"Hmm."

"What?"

"Oh, I was just thinking that maybe you were dismissing Cecil because your mother liked him so much, and you were tallying the balance from when she sent you to Denver."

Lily was speechless.

"I wouldn't think less of you if that were the case. Completely understandable. But you'd be cutting off your nose to spite—"

"I almost wish I did like Cecil more," Lily interrupted, "for that would make everything far easier." She wouldn't worry about disappointing her mother and would return to Boston with the fiancé her mother approved of. She would not be so undone by Mason's missing supper. And she wouldn't feel so adrift as she did now.

"Then why not give Cecil another chance?"

Lily sighed into her tea. Persistence, she was coming to realize, must be one reason for her grandfather's success. He never accepted no as the final answer.

"Cecil's mother is your mother's closest friend," her grandfather told her, as if she didn't know that. "Given the friendship between your family and his, it'd be courteous of you to give him one more chance. A real chance, Lily."

How could she say no?

He must have read her acquiescence in her expression, for he exclaimed, "Wonderful, wonderful. How about an evening picnic tomorrow?"

A pinch in his stomach reminded Mason that he was mortal. He lifted his eyes from the sheets of paper in front of him. Outside the open flap of his tent, the sky had turned the color of a violet's petals.

He'd missed supper.

And he'd missed Lily.

But he'd caught the magic again.

There was no other way to describe it. Today the words didn't flow as they had yesterday. Instead, they tripped out of his head in a drunken stagger. But the ideas behind the words stretched back deeper into his brain. The character sketches he had written yesterday were coming together into a larger work. Not a newspaper story—whatever he had buzzing in his head was bigger than that. But if he wanted to, he could throw together a compelling newspaper story about young eastern men who came out to the West in their first test of their manhood. He could work all night, revise the story in the morning, and then have it in the mail to his old editor by midafternoon. There was no guarantee that he'd get his regular spot back, but he was convinced he could at least sell this story.

The thing was, he didn't want to.

He raised his arms above his head, pressing his palms to the sky. His backbone popped and he settled back into his chair, stretching his legs out in front of him.

He stared at his boots—boots dusty with the rock litter he had stood in all day before racing back to his tent at the end of the afternoon like a schoolboy who knew he had a cookie waiting for him at home.

And inside those boots were feet that usually began to grow restless after only a few days of planting themselves in one spot.

Mason counted back. Six days. It had been six days since he had ridden into the bone hunters' camp.

He gave his feet a shake.

Nope, nothing. No tingling. No twitching. No jittery tapping. His feet were happy to stay where they were.

So. Maybe it was time for a change. Time to stop dashing out newspaper stories. Time to stop rushing from place to place.

Of course, he couldn't stay here. But he did have a place in San Francisco.

Unfortunately, San Francisco was a long, long way from Boston.

He dragged himself to his feet. He would just make himself crazy thinking along those lines. All right—so he could write again. He hadn't been completely sure yesterday, but today he was convinced that whatever he'd lost was back. He could get a job at another paper without much difficulty. And he certainly didn't need to uncover the secrets sliding beneath this expedition in order to write a story or get a job.

But there was a big difference between being a journalist again and being . . . well, being Lily's beau. He'd been one of the top three frontier journalists for more than five years now. That distinction wasn't going to get him very far, though, as he sat in the Highfills' Boston parlor, his hair slicked back and wearing an uncomfortable new suit. There was success . . . and there was success. His sort of success barely registered in Lily's family's world.

He was getting too far ahead of himself. What if he woke up tomorrow with the overpowering urge to trot over the horizon and see what was worth writing about? All this thinking about settling down was hasty.

He should get moving now and see if he could grab any leftovers from the cook, then seek out Lily.

Ten minutes later, while munching on a cold drumstick, he halted in front of Dickon's sorting tent. The lantern hanging from a hook threw strange shadows over the piles of ancient rocks and Dickon's hunch-shouldered shape.

"Don't you usually close up shop by now?" Mason asked from the doorway. He'd given Dickon and his grimaces and snarls a wide berth for the past two days, but anything unusual—like Dickon working past dusk—drew Mason like a moth to a candle flame.

Dickon looked up and scowled. "Oh, it's you." Then he shrugged and waved him inside the tent. "Saw that you've been digging with the boys."

"Getting in their way, more like."

"I thought you grew up on the railroad."

"I did. Hardly touched a shovel, though. I took care of the horse teams and carried water out to those digging or laying track."

"How would you like to work here with me tomorrow? I could use an extra set of hands."

He'd get to spend the day with Lily. "Sure, I'd like that."

"Thought you might."

Mason couldn't tell from his tone whether Dickon was being sarcastic or friendly.

"You missed supper tonight."

Mason nodded and took a bite of chicken.

"And," Dickon continued, "Lily missed you."

Mason almost choked. After finally swallowing the chicken, he stared at Dickon. "I thought you didn't, ah, approve. What, do you have money bet on me, too?"

"Put twenty cents on you tonight. You're better than the alternative."

Should he be flattered or insulted? Almost anyone would be a better alternative to Cecil.

Not that it mattered. He wasn't wooing Lily. Kissing her, yes. And looking forward to finding her tonight so that they could spend a little time and conversation together.

But not wooing. Wooing meant that he believed they could have some kind of future together. Lily had a whole different future with her highbrow family—and undoubtedly a slew of highbrow suitors—in Boston.

"Besides," Dickon added, "you seem to find trouble when you leave camp. First getting thrown by your horse on the steepest bit of trail hereabouts, and then getting shot at. Not a good track record. Better stick close."

Behind him, Lily said, "Oh. Here you are. You passed up some more bad potatoes tonight."

Dickon had said that she'd missed him. That gave Mason a shot of courage. He took a step close to her. "I missed you more than I missed the bad potatoes," he said, low enough that Dickon couldn't hear him.

Her eyes glowed with mischief. "I'm honored. However, I see that you found food before you found me."

"I thought I should restore my strength before tangling with you."

She raised her brows at him, but her mouth relaxed into another grin.

"So this is where everyone is." Cecil stepped into the circle of light. He nodded to Dickon and Mason, but his gaze swung back to Lily.

Mason tried to control his frown. It was clear that "everyone" wasn't Cecil's interest; Lily was.

Why the fellow wanted her now didn't take more than a smidgen of knowledge of human nature to figure out. As soon as Lily had stopped running after him, she became interesting.

"Can I walk you back to your tent?" Cecil asked Lily. "When you're finished here, of course."

Mason silently swore. He should have asked her the same thing as soon as she'd appeared, but he'd been caught up in their banter and hadn't expected Cecil's visit. Maybe tomorrow he could ask Lily if she'd let him walk her to her tent every night until the digging ended.

No. That would seem like he was wooing her. And he didn't know if he'd get the need to start traveling again. He couldn't ask her to save her evenings for him when he didn't know if he'd be around to enjoy them.

Lily said to Cecil, "I only came to say good night to Dickon, so I'm ready to go."

She didn't have to sound so cheerful about it. He'd

just told her that he'd missed her, and now she was waltzing off with someone else? No, not just someone else, but Cecil.

Cecil bent his arm for Lily to take, but she shook her head. "However, Mason already asked me."

Mason didn't bother to hide his grin.

Lily waved at Dickon and then ducked out of the tent, not waiting for Mason to genteelly escort her as Cecil had attempted to.

Because she didn't think Mason knew how to, or because it didn't even cross her mind that he might want to?

He was being ridiculous. And all this worrying about what Lily was thinking or not thinking didn't matter in the end.

"Dickon asked me to work with the two of you tomorrow," he said, taking two quick strides to catch up with her. At the same time she slowed down, and they knocked elbows.

Smoothly Mason tucked her hand in the crook of his arm and then smiled to himself in the darkness.

"Dickon invited you back into the sorting tent?" Lily shook her head. "That doesn't make sense."

He hadn't expected her to shout with joy, but he hadn't expected this perplexity, either. "Dickon isn't a supporter of Cecil's," he said, trying to be delicate. "And he knows that I annoy Cecil because of, well, you."

She gave her head another shake. "That still doesn't make a great deal of sense."

Frustration snipped at the edges of his thoughts.

Did he have to spell it out for her? "Dickon thinks that you like me. Dickon does not like—"

Her fingers against his lips trapped his words. "I understand *that*. And if things were normal, I'd believe that was Dickon's only reason. But things aren't, well, normal."

Ah. The secret.

Well, forget about the secret. He could write again. He didn't need any secrets to stoke his pen. "Let's not talk about it anymore."

They had reached her tent. With no living residents in the tents around hers, quiet enfolded them.

She stopped and stared up at him, her big eyes dark pools in the dusk. "You are quite a gentleman, aren't you, Mason Donnelly?"

She didn't have to sound so surprised. "Sometimes," he said. He settled his hands on her hips and drew her body flush up against his. "And sometimes not." Then he lowered his mouth to hers.

Chapter Thirteen

Five years ago, Mason had stood on the Kansas prairie and watched a monster summer storm bear down on him, lightning flashing like teeth and the thunder an endless growl. One thunderclap had detonated what felt like a dozen feet over his head, pulsing down through his body and nearly knocking him out of his boots.

That thunderclap slammed Mason again as Lily opened her mouth under his and tangled her fingers in his hair. He staggered and gripped her hips for balance. Then he deepened the kiss, and she responded with an enthusiasm that intoxicated him.

Maybe fifty feet away, a bucket clanged and a man cursed. Mason pulled back a half inch. "Anyone could see us." Her lips were so lovely and so close, he couldn't resist kissing them again. A few moments later, when he came back to reality, he added, "I should probably go."

Her eyes went a little unfocused, as if she were thinking hard about something. Then she brought her gaze back to his. "Or you could come inside my tent." She smiled. "I've seen your tent. You've never seen mine."

If he went into her tent, he'd have to leave at some point unsatisfied. But he was a strong-willed fellow. He could handle it.

And there was always the possibility that she'd change her mind. . . .

He nodded, and she led the way inside.

Of course, it was black as onyx in the tent. He stopped just inside the entrance, letting the canvas door flop shut behind him.

"We shouldn't light a lamp," he said softly.

"I know." Her hand, small and warm, brushed against his arm, then slid down to his wrist, tugging him farther into the tent. She led him around obstacles unseen in the dark. A chair or stool whispered against Mason's pant leg once, but her sense of direction was unerring.

Negotiating this course blindly reminded him of their venture into the mine. He grimaced. Hopefully tonight wouldn't end with him nearly shot in the face.

She stopped. He took the opportunity to step up against her back and nuzzle her nape. A breathy giggle flew out of her. "That tickles a little."

"Oh? What about this?" He tiptoed his fingers up her ribs, prompting a few more giggles, then slowly feathered his hands low over her belly before pulling her snugly against him. "Turn your head so I can kiss you."

Moving languidly, she did as he asked, and he took her mouth with all the urgency that was coiling tight inside him.

God. This desire was like an undertow threatening to pull his feet—and his good sense—out from under him. Five more minutes. In five minutes, he'd kiss her good night and then leave.

She pulled away a half inch, licked his lower lip, then swirled her hips against him, wedging his manhood firmly against her back.

All right. Ten minutes. Maybe twenty.

"Do you know what you're doing?" he whispered against her mouth.

She stopped her delicious movements. "Why? Am I doing it wrong?"

"If you want to make me leave anytime soon, then you're doing it wrong. If you want to make me crazy for you, you're doing it right." He kissed her again. "This would be better if we lie down on your cot," he said, hands low on her belly and pressing her backward against his penis.

"It's awfully small," Lily said, sounding uncertain for the first time.

He hoped she meant the cot. "We could put a blanket on the floor instead."

She shrugged, her shoulders moving against his chest. He had to kiss her neck a second time. "There isn't enough space. My things are all over the place."

Mason withdrew his lips from their feast and stepped around her, locating the cot by barking his knee against it. He sat down on it, then stretched out on his back. She was right: It *was* small. He filled the entire bed. "All right, I'm ready."

Lily's hands fluttered across his chest and shoulders as she tried to figure out how she was going to brace herself while she climbed on top of him. The cot was too wide and her skirts too cumbersome for her to swing her leg over the entire bed and straddle it so that she could slowly lower herself onto it. Onto him.

She swallowed. The lovely sheen of kissing and rubbing was wearing off, and the prickle of awareness and embarrassment was taking its place. The impulse to think clearly was also trying to reassert itself. They really, really, really shouldn't be doing this. Never mind her grandfather's demand that she act coldly toward Mason to encourage him to leave: It was a little too late for that. More important was the fact that Mason was a wanderer, someone who never stayed in one place. And she was going to Boston.

"Lily?" he said.

Maybe if she could put one knee on the cot, she could brace herself enough to control her descent instead of flopping on him like a huge landed fish. She reached down and felt around where she thought his hip might be, to see if she could find a place on the cot to plant her knee, and encountered his hand there instead, curled around—

She jerked her fingers back. "Sorry!" But why in the world was he holding himself?

"I don't want you to accidentally knee me in the dark," he said.

Considering that that was where she'd almost put her knee, he had good cause for concern. "I'm not sure this is going to work."

"It has to work. Maybe if I rolled onto my side—"

"No, I don't think so. Move your, um, hand."

"Why?"

"I'm going to sit there." If she sat sideways on his lap and held his shoulders, she could lower herself onto his chest.

She gave him a few seconds to follow her request and then gingerly sat on him. Good Lord, his erection had never felt so, well, prominent.

She wiggled to change her position. Mason made a choking noise, and then his hands came out of the darkness to seize her shoulders and pull her down flat on his chest. "Straighten out your legs," he commanded.

Moving carefully, she did as he asked, one of her legs coming to rest between his and, more disconcertingly, one of his legs resting between hers. But then his lips grazed the corner of her mouth, pushing away all jittery thoughts.

It didn't take more than one kiss for her to admit that he'd been right: Kissing while lying down was much better. No longer having to worry about keeping her balance, she could concentrate on sensation. And the length of their bodies molded together seamlessly, with the exception of Mason's erection jabbing into her hip.

He traced the curve of her cheek with his lips, spurring a shiver, and murmured against her ear, "Move your left knee so that it's outside mine."

Her left knee? He was thinking clearer than she was if he could tell his left from his right—and, even more impressive, what *her* left was. But she figured out what he meant and pulled her knee over his thigh so that both his legs rested between hers and his erection now pressed against her belly button.

Although she was accustomed to riding horses, this felt much different. No saddle, just a few layers of material between her and Mason.

Mason wrapped his hands around her waist and tugged her several inches higher on his body. Lily wiggled to settle herself, then froze. His erection had settled between her legs, and the pressure had changed. It no longer felt slightly painful. The discomfort had changed into a different beast altogether.

Lily licked her lips. "Is this proper?"

What a stupid question. Her mother could name without thinking a dozen improper aspects about this situation. Lily could, too.

Mason swiveled his hips, and the unusual pressure set off a shudder. Lily's eyes crossed. "Depends," he said, sounding breathless. "It's proper for many things, and improper for other things. It's very proper for kissing on a bed."

"A cot," she said. As if that made a difference.

He thrust against her, and her thoughts fractured.

"We could go to my tent instead. There's more room on the floor."

At that, her thoughts reknit—fast. "Mason, I can't run across the length of the camp to go to your tent. It's bad enough that you're in here."

"Bad?" he echoed. He stopped the interesting movements he was doing with his hips, and his hold on her loosened. "What do you mean by *bad*?"

She pushed herself up so that she was no longer sprawled across his chest. "I mean improper."

"Of course it's improper. Do you always have to be proper? Follow the rules?"

"Not always. But—"

"One more minute. Give me only one more minute and I'll leave."

She didn't want him to leave. She just needed him to understand that they couldn't go dodging from tent to tent. "The reason why people follow proper behavior—"

His fingers began working at the buttons on her shirt, popping them open.

"Um . . . proper behavior is that it often coincides with common sense. In this case, both proper behavior and common sense—"

He tugged her unfastened blouse down so that it hung at her elbows.

"—dictate that moving to another location might lead to discovery—"

He pushed the straps of her chemise off her shoulders, then peeled the material down.

"—ah, to discovery or to unexpected complications like—"

His warm hands settled on her bare waist and then stroked upward, knocking the final word *marriage* out of her mouth in an unintelligible squeak.

Oh, sweet heaven. Now she knew why she had

breasts. It was so that she could place them in Mason's magical hands.

His thumbs skidded over her nipples. She let out another squeak.

"Quiet," he whispered.

He was rubbing his hands all over her hot skin, and he expected her to be quiet? Well. She let her weight settle deeper on his erection and gave her hips a little pulse. It felt so lovely that she leaned into Mason's palms and did it again.

Mason groaned.

"Quiet," she teased, and laughed.

"Lily . . . either we stop now, or we don't stop at all."

But he was still touching her, his fingertips whispering over her breasts and stomach, sending quivers racing up her spine. This was so unfair. Why couldn't she just throw away common sense, her upbringing, and the rest of her clothing and make love to him?

Make love to him. But was this love or infatuation? She had known him only a week. It couldn't be love. Lust, yes. Love . . . well, she'd never know. With her grandfather probably shutting down the camp early, she would likely be leaving within the week.

"We should stop," she finally said.

His hands fell away, and chilly air wrapped around her. But instead of lifting her off him, he pulled her down on top of him and folded his arms around her. She nestled her face into the crook of his neck and sighed. How was she supposed to give him up when he finally left?

"That wasn't a minute, you know," she said. "That was only maybe twenty seconds. We have forty more seconds."

He smoothed her hair with one hand. "I think you're the most dangerous girl I've ever met."

She liked the sound of that. "You're such a flatterer."

"No, it's true."

"Well, I feel dangerous only with you."

"Now you're flattering *me*." His choppy breathing slowly evened out, and he continued to stroke her hair.

She shifted against him, seeking a more comfortable position, and something in his chest pocket crackled. She started to lift herself away. "I think I broke something in your pocket."

Tugging her back down on top of him, he said, "Nah, it's just your letter."

"What letter?"

"You know. The one you wrote your mother last night."

"The *kissing* letter?"

"Right."

She smacked him on the shoulder. "I've been worrying myself into an early grave about that letter all day, thinking that Dickon had mailed it to her. Why did you take it?"

"I don't know." He paused. "I liked it."

This man was going to make her crazy. Crazier than she was already for being here like this with him.

He started stroking her hair again, and she relaxed in his arms.

She must have fallen asleep, for when she opened her eyes to darkness again, he was sliding off the cot and settling her in his place.

An endless kiss branded her lips. Then the tent flap rustled, the scent of the mountains coasted in on a gust of fresh air, and he was gone.

His wildcat from last night blushed scarlet when Mason sat down next to her at breakfast. "Morning," he said, then popped a piece of buttery biscuit in his mouth. He nodded to Cecil, Highfill, and Dickon, but kept his attention on Lily.

"Hello." The word came out breathlessly, and her blush fired up across her cheeks again.

Cecil shot Mason a suspicious stare. Mason ignored him but groaned inside. If she wasn't careful, the entire camp was going to know they'd been snuggling in her cot last night.

She had already finished her breakfast and sat with her hands tucked under the table in her lap. Very lady-like, and very convenient. As soon as Cecil turned his focus elsewhere, Mason covertly reached under the table and threaded his fingers through hers.

Instead of blushing again, she flashed a smile at him and her shoulders relaxed. "Dickon has been bragging for the last five minutes about how he's going to make you work harder with us than you did with the diggers."

"Plastering?"

She nodded. "All day."

Mason heaved a dramatic sigh. "If I have to."

Cecil was not amused. "Donnelly, you can dig with us today instead. We also need all the help we can get."

"Thanks, St. John, but I told Dickon I'd be his slave today."

"Tomorrow, then."

Persistent bugger. Mason shrugged. "Perhaps. If I'm still here."

Lily's hand quivered in his, then went limp.

Damn. That line had been meant to draw Cecil out, not wound Lily. Guilt bit him hard. But she knew he'd be leaving at some point. Plus, he wasn't sure he could survive letting her go if he stayed around much longer.

Cecil looked at him, then at Lily, who was staring off in the distance as if she were thinking of other things. "Interesting," he said. "Where will you go?"

He had no idea, so he said the first thing that popped into his head. "The Dakotas."

Lily flinched.

"I've heard the landscape up there is quite fascinating," Cecil said. "But winter comes fast."

An unsubtle hint that he should leave immediately.

Lily began to tug her hand away. He couldn't hold on to her without making a scene, so he let her fingers slide from his. Free of his grasp and in defiance of the good manners she seemed to live by, Lily set her elbows on the table, keeping her hands well out of his reach.

"Boston is also nice," Dickon said. Both Cecil and Lily glared at him, but he seemed not to notice. "Beautiful around Christmastime."

"Eastern cities seem to suck the soul out of me,"

Mason said honestly. "I don't think I could last more than a few days in Boston."

"You said yourself you don't stay long anywhere, so what's the difference?" Lily asked, a snap in her voice.

"The difference is that no matter how long or short my stay, I prefer to enjoy the place. And I don't enjoy Boston."

"Been there, then?" Dickon said.

"Once, about seven years ago." It hadn't been Christmastime; it had been the hot, smelly, humid summer. All the buildings piled one on the other trapped the heat in the streets, making a man willing to give the last nickel in his pocket for a whisper of cool air.

"Ah, well," Dickon said, "it hasn't changed all that much since then. I myself am thinking of spending a week or more in Denver after this dig is over."

Highfill, who had been eating voraciously throughout this exchange, looked up from his food and finally joined the conversation. "Really? Whatever for?"

"I've never seen the place. I've been out to the West six times and never done more than get on and off the train in Denver."

"He may visit Aunt Evaline, too," Lily put in. "They used to know each other in Boston."

Highfill frowned. "How did you know Evaline? You began working for me after she moved west."

"She and my mother worked for the same immigrant aid society, helping single ladies find employment," Dickon said. "I believe my mother invited Evaline over for tea one afternoon." With a strange note in his voice, he added, "Your daughter was very beautiful. Unforgettable, in fact."

Cecil took one of Lily's hands and kissed it. "Clearly those qualities run strong in the family."

Mason gave the man three seconds to relinquish Lily's hand. Otherwise Mason was going to reach across the table and punch him in the nose. One, two—

Lily pulled her hand away and held it in her lap. Then she gave Mason a sideways look and folded her arms across her chest, tucking her hands out of reach of both men.

"So you knew Evaline when, exactly?" Highfill asked.

"Twenty-some years ago." Dickon shifted in his seat. "Why?"

"There was someone—" Highfill said, then stopped and shook his head. "Her mother and I didn't know all the new friends she met through the aid society, and we sometimes worried. But it was a long time ago."

Dickon grimaced. "I know what you mean. I tried to keep an eagle eye on my two daughters, and I still ended up with a son-in-law who's so dumb, he couldn't pound a nail into a snowbank. Ah, well. Time for us to get to work." Dickon shoved half a biscuit into his mouth and stood.

Lily jumped to her feet, nodded to everyone at the table, and headed for the sorting tent without waiting for Dickon or Mason. Her gorgeous backside disappeared among the other tents within a few moments.

Dickon excused himself, rose, and began to leave,

and Mason followed suit, falling in step with the older man. As soon as they were out of earshot of those still at the table, Dickon remarked, "I'd say that you were so dumb you couldn't pound nails into a snowbank, too, if I didn't know better."

Mason didn't bother to pretend to misunderstand. "So you think I should lie to her? Spin some fairy tale? Tell her I'll be by her side forever, when it'll be a few more days at most?" As much as Mason wanted to tell himself that this newfound feeling of settling in would last, he had years of experience saying that it would not.

"If that's the case, then of course not. But why are you rushing away, Donnelly? You have no job, if I'm not mistaken. Why not come to Boston at the end of the summer?"

"And if I'm not mistaken, you're the same fellow who told me only four days ago that the social difference between Lily and me is too great."

Dickon exhaled. "I've been rethinking that. Rethinking a lot of things."

"Obviously." Mason stalked along for a few more steps, then said, "If she were your daughter, would you want her with me? Honestly?"

"Want her *with* you? No. Want her *married* to you? Well, she could do worse."

Mason let out a short laugh. "Hardly an enthusiastic endorsement."

"Well, my endorsement shouldn't matter anyway."

"And I doubt Highfill would be overjoyed by the idea."

"He shouldn't matter, either. You and Lily are the only ones who count."

No, Lily was the only one who counted. And he didn't want her to be stuck with anything but the best. A transient frontier reporter was not, for her, the best.

"I'll give her about a half hour to cool down," Dickon said, "and then I'm going to go get a fresh cup of coffee. You can fix things then."

"It isn't a question of fixing things, Dickon." Mason took a deep breath. "I'm still leaving."

Dickon sighed. "All right. But you can tell her that—and tell her why. If you simply leave without letting her know why, questions are just going to buzz around in her head for months, maybe years." Dickon rubbed his jaw. "It's not fair to her to make her keep thinking about you long after you've moved on."

The selfish thought rose that he wanted her to keep thinking about him. For years, if possible. He certainly wouldn't be able to get her out of his mind immediately.

They reached the tent and helped Lily finish rolling up the canvas flaps so that a breeze could blow through the tent. Dickon set Mason to wrapping and plastering and Lily to sorting. Lily's voice held a chill whenever she had to speak to Mason, but by the time thirty minutes had rolled by, she had lost her frosty edge.

Dickon stretched and groaned. "I'm off to get coffee. Anyone want another cup?"

"I'll help you get it," Lily said quickly.

"Do you want a cup?" Dickon asked her.

"No."

"Mason, you?"

Mason shook his head. "No, sir."

"No need for your help, then, Lily girl. You stay here in the shade." He strode out before she could mount another argument.

Mason's heart picked up its pace. "Lily?" he said, putting down a half-wrapped rock. Now that the time had come to talk to her, all he could think about saying was *Maybe Boston isn't so bad after all*. But he wouldn't say that. She was an heiress, for God's sake. He had no place in her world. No—he had no wish to live in her world.

Lily looked up and sighed. "I'm not angry, Mason. I was, but I'm not anymore. You've said over and over that you're going to leave. I simply forgot." She shrugged. "It's my own fault for being upset."

Now he felt even worse. "I'd like to take some of the blame, too, if you don't mind."

"All right." She smiled at him. "I'm a generous woman. You can take half."

"Thank you."

Her smile slowly slipped away. "When are you leaving? Today? Tomorrow?"

Though he'd told Cecil maybe tomorrow, tomorrow would be far too soon. "Not today. But I don't know when."

She took a deep breath. "It'd be easier if I knew exactly when you're leaving."

Tomorrow would kill him. A week from now would kill him, but in a different way. Maybe somewhere in the middle . . . "How about four days from now?"

She looked downward, and for a brief, terrible moment he thought she was going to suggest that he leave sooner. But she raised her gaze again and smiled past the shadows that lurked in her eyes. "Four days it is. And Dickon is right: Boston is beautiful during Christmas. If you're anywhere nearby, you should be sure to visit."

Visit the city, or visit her? But he'd never be near Boston; he'd probably even take pains to avoid it. But he said, "If I am nearby, I'll do that."

Resting her forearm on Mason's shoulder, Lily leaned over to see what he was working on. "A mollusk?" she guessed as he bundled it in paper.

"Don't ask me. You're the expert here." He turned his head and kissed her fingers before reaching for another fossil. Lily glanced over at Dickon, but he was peering at a rock and paying no attention to them.

"Ah, you've been practicing your flattery," she told Mason.

He flashed a grin at her. "Remind me again why I'm doing this. Fame? Fortune?" He dropped his voice and waggled his eyebrows. "Promise of future rewards?"

Lily laughed. "If so, those are rewards we'd share."

This flirtation came so naturally. She had had a difficult time this morning holding on to her hurt that he hadn't changed his mind about pursuing his footloose existence. But she hadn't asked him to, had she? Nor would she. He was Mason Donnelly, fearless frontier reporter. To ask him to give that up would be like him asking her to give up her love for her family.

Still. Four days. Given his reputation for always being on the move, four additional days was far more than she had expected, and that caused its own singular ache.

Four days. She bit her lip. How was she supposed to hold out against his intense eyes and her own body's clamoring for four days? Did she really want to hold out?

Mason reached over to grab a sheet of paper, and his arm grazed her breast. Her breath stopped and her senses spun.

"That's unfair, you know," she murmured when she could think again.

His smile was smug. "What is?"

"I can't counterattack, can I?" She lowered her eyes to the front of his pants. "It'd hardly be proper."

"I never thought I liked proper girls, but you've managed to prove me wrong. Though I admit that I sometimes like you better when you're less proper."

Like last night. Well, she sometimes liked herself better then, too. No, not liked herself better. Enjoyed herself more. Enjoyed the boldness that flowed through her. "You still owe me forty more seconds," she told him.

He jerked his chin toward her chest. "That didn't count as one second?"

"All right, now you owe me thirty-nine seconds." She moved a step back, out of reach. "But you can't do that thirty-nine more times."

"Hmm. I'll see what I can come up with." He slid her a smile. "Later."

A noise at the front of the tent made her look away from the promise in Mason's eyes.

She stifled a sigh when she saw who was there. Cecil. The one good thing about the end of this dig was that she would no longer have to see Cecil several times a day. How had she ever imagined that she wanted to spend the rest of her life with him? She glanced at the shadows creeping across the hot ground. And what was he doing back so early from the dig site?

Her heart plummeted. Oh, no. The picnic. She'd forgotten it. And forgotten to tell Mason about it.

Not caring what Cecil thought, she grabbed Mason's elbow. "I promised my grandfather I'd have supper tonight with Cecil," she hissed.

"You mean sit with him at the table?"

"No, I mean go on a picnic somewhere with him."

Mason's eyebrows darted down into a scowl. "Alone?"

Cecil had finished saying hello to Dickon and was walking toward them.

"Yes, alone," Lily whispered swiftly. "But it doesn't mean anything."

Mason stared at her but she couldn't decipher his expression. "I'll wait up," he finally said.

And then Cecil was there, standing at Lily's shoulder. "Are you ready?" he asked her, nodding to Mason but not offering even the slightest pleasantry.

"Yes."

Cecil ran his eyes over her. "You have ink on your hands and bits of plaster on your skirt. I can wait, if you want to change."

"Oh, but this is just an informal picnic, isn't it?" Lily shook out her skirt, dislodging some of the plaster but not all. She'd spent several weeks worrying about what to wear to catch Cecil's admiration. She wasn't going to spend another moment on such idiocy. "I think this is informal enough."

"Fine." His mouth pressed in a tight line, he offered her his arm. When she took it, he led her out of the tent.

Lily glanced over her shoulder as she stepped outside in the sun, but Mason was bent over his work.

After saddling their horses, Cecil took her to a pleasant little canyon about a mile away and spread out the picnic bounty on a large, soft blanket. Then he stretched out on the blanket and gazed up at her with warm eyes. "Beautiful Lily."

She hoped she wouldn't have to listen to this drivel for the next several hours. She tried to change the subject. "When the dig is over, what will be your plans?"

"That depends on you. I hope to escort you to Boston. Once there . . ." He donned a bashful smile. "Lily, you must know that I adore you."

Oh, heavens, she *was* going to have to listen to this drivel.

He waved in the direction of camp. "The dig and especially these strange recent finds have taken up so much of my time that I fear I neglected you too much and perhaps even drove you away."

Neglected her "too much." As if he believed there was an acceptable amount of neglect but he had accidentally crossed the line.

"But if we travel to Boston together," he continued, "maybe you will reconsider your . . . your . . ."

For a moment she wondered if he'd say *stupidity* or something similar, but he continued smoothly, ". . . your decision that we do not suit."

She'd try politeness first. "Thank you for your kind offer, but my travel plans are not yet settled, and I do not want to delay yours."

"It would be no trouble to wait for you. It would be a pleasure."

Lily shook her head. "No, I insist."

When Cecil smiled, he showed a great number of teeth, and his smile did not touch his eyes. "No, *I* insist."

Without replying, Lily reached for her napkin. The sooner they finished this meal, the better. And if he believed that she would meekly fall in with his plans, then he was in for a surprise. She'd behave with abominable rudeness and sneak out to the train station in the middle of the night if it meant she could escape Cecil's presence during the long trip to Boston.

She glanced at the tops of the canyon walls. Where was a crazy miner when you needed one? A harmless volley would send her and Cecil back to camp lickety-split.

The cook had provided cold ham and rolls. Cecil's mouth turned down as Lily divided the food between two plates. "I'd expected, well, more," he said, prodding at the ham with his knife.

"You can have some of my portion."

"No, no, I mean I expected it to be more roman—" He stopped and gave her a wary look. "Elaborate."

Cold ham was as romantic as she wished to get. "This is fine for me. Are picnics in Boston such elaborate affairs?"

She succeeded in distracting him from any more discussion of romance or traveling to Boston, and additional questions about his life in Boston, delivered with a wide-eyed interest she did not feel, kept him occupied with talking about himself during the rest of the meal.

But he could not talk and eat at the same time, and it was several hours past full dark when he finally popped the last bit of ham in his mouth. Before he'd even swallowed it, Lily suggested that they pack up and return. "It's rather late," she added.

"Nonsense."

Lily bristled. She hated when he said "Nonsense" in that self-assured tone, as if any opinion other than his was worthless.

"Your grandfather wouldn't mind if we stayed out later," he continued. "And look at the stars! Almost as beautiful as you." The candle he'd brought along cast a soft glow on his charming smile.

"Thank you, but it's been a wearying day." Lily began to return the dishes to their wicker basket. Grandfather might not mind if they stayed out later, but she suspected that Mason might. And *she* certainly did.

They rode back to the camp in silence. Cecil offered to unsaddle her horse and turn it into the corral for her, and she accepted. If she had to spend one more minute in his tedious company, she was afraid she would snap his head off.

"Lily, wait," he said as she turned away to walk to her tent. When she swiveled back to face him, he circled his arm around her waist and tried to pull her close.

Lily jammed her forearm against his chest, keeping their bodies separated as much as she could. "What are you doing?"

He gave an indulgent laugh. "Giving you a good night kiss, of course."

"Thank you, but no." She tried to twist away, but he wouldn't release his grip.

She took a deep breath. All right. She could threaten to bite him if he put his mouth anywhere near hers, which would undoubtedly lead to a big scene, or she could stand still for three seconds, let him kiss her, and then be free.

She stood still. He kissed her with ten times as much passion as he had a week ago, but the part of her that had responded to him was now cold. With a frustrated huff, he ended the kiss.

She pressed back against the cage of his arms, and this time he let her go. "Good night," she said, and left the corral. As soon as she was sure that the darkness concealed her movements, she scrubbed her hand across her mouth.

Ugh. What an evening. It ranked among the worst five in her life. Her steps picked up speed. Mason had said he would wait for her. Was he in her tent?

But when she pulled back the flap, he wasn't there. Lily tapped her forefinger against her lower lip as she thought. No, he wouldn't wait in her tent—that was too risky. Perhaps he had meant he'd wait at Dickon's sorting tent. That was where she had discovered him yesterday evening.

As she approached the sorting tent, her heart began a slow, downward slide. No lamp glowed within the tent. She would go inside to be sure, but she knew even before she entered that he wasn't there, either.

She sat in a chair at the desk and tried to think. Where was he? He said he'd wait up, hadn't he? Yes, he had. She knew he had. His promise was the only thing that had gotten her through this awful evening, and she'd replayed it in her mind every time Cecil said something that made her want to stuff a corner of the picnic blanket in his mouth to shut him up.

Though if she had stuffed his mouth with the blanket, maybe he wouldn't have insisted on kissing her before they parted.

She began to give her lips another scrubbing with her sleeve, then froze.

What if Mason had been waiting at the corral?

And seen Cecil kissing her?

Oh, Lord. Now she wished she had kicked up a fuss, refusing to let Cecil put his mouth anywhere near hers, instead of giving in.

A wave of heat scorched through her body. It took her a moment to realize it was fury—fury at herself. She *always* gave in. She'd given in to her mother's expectation that she'd want to marry Cecil, though she had to admit that she was equally to blame for that disaster. She'd given in to her grandfather's insistence that she have a picnic with Cecil. And she'd given in to Cecil's silly kiss.

When was she going to stop giving in?

She stood.

Now. She was going to stop now. And she was going to track down Mason.

She strode through the darkened camp, her skirt making *whup-whup* noises as it whipped around her legs. A few of the diggers dodged out of her path as she marched to Mason's tent. When she reached it, she stood tall in a splash of moonlight and scratched on the canvas, made golden by a lit lamp within.

The sound of movement inside. The tent flap jerked open.

Without waiting for an invitation, Lily entered.

Chapter Fourteen

The light of the lamp dazzled her. Then Mason stepped in front of it, and she was able to see his face. He wore the same impenetrable expression he had adopted when she'd told him that she'd promised to picnic with Cecil.

Had Mason seen Cecil kissing her? She couldn't tell.

"Thank you for waiting up." When he didn't immediately invite her to sit, she shrugged to herself and dropped into the only chair in the tent. He was going to have her company whether he liked it or not. "I haven't had to endure such a tedious evening in a long time." She made a face, but underneath her grimace, her heart began rat-a-tatting like a snare drum. "He even kissed me at the end of it."

Mason lost his poker face—fast. "He kissed you?" His scowl would have made even Medusa wary. "And you let him?"

Whoops. Maybe Mason hadn't seen the kiss. He certainly was reacting with surprise. She sighed. "I didn't want him to."

Mason began to pace. "But you let him. I thought . . . I thought . . ."

"You thought what?"

He spun around and nailed her with his blue eyes. "I thought you were done with that stupidity."

Stupidity? Maybe so, but she didn't appreciate hearing it from his mouth. She could feel her temper begin to warm. "I *am* done with Cecil. Look. Where am I?"

"What do you mean?"

She made a sweeping gesture that encompassed him, her, the tent. "I'm here. I'm with you. I'm in your tent at nighttime, for goodness' sake. I'm *not* with Cecil."

He pressed his lips together as if determined not to argue with her further, but then burst out, "Yes, but what about tomorrow? I thought yesterday that you were done with him, and then I find out today that you had planned a special little supper together." He planted his hands on his hips, and his eyes flashed. "So, what's happening tomorrow?"

If he weren't being so belligerent, she might find his uncertainty endearing. "Nothing is happening to-morrow."

Mason sat down on his cot, rubbed his hand through his hair, and exhaled. "I'm here for only four more days. What will you do after I leave?"

Her first impulse was to snap that if he wanted her all to himself, then he should reconsider leaving her. But she swallowed her retort and said instead, attempting to keep her tone light, "For a man constantly on the move, you can be quite possessive." She let him think about that for a moment, then added, "I'm sorry I didn't tell you about the picnic. Last night my grandfather asked me to go on one final supper with Cecil in order to hear him out, and I agreed. I should have told you when you were escorting me back to my tent that night, but I, um, got distracted."

Mason's lips twitched. "Is that what you call it?"

"And then I forgot completely. It wasn't until Cecil showed up this afternoon that I remembered."

After a moment he nodded grudgingly. "All right." He added, "It makes me annoyed to watch him suddenly pay attention to you after ignoring you all that time."

Clearly. Though she guessed that he was more jealous than annoyed. "If you're annoyed, imagine how *I* feel. Annoyed *and* insulted."

"You sent that letter to your mother?"

"Yes."

"Then that's that, right? It's over. Cecil will have to leave you alone."

Lily raised her eyebrows at him. He sounded as if he were trying awfully hard to convince himself that Cecil would go away. Jealousy and insecurity. These were two very good signs. "Actually, Cecil expressed his intention of escorting me to Boston after the dig closes down."

Ah, the Medusa-worthy scowl again. "He has a lot of nerve," Mason growled.

She could sit there all night and watch him steam. Really, he looked quite lovely doing it, and it created an exquisite buzz in her chest. But it wouldn't be fair to play games with him. Mason had been painfully blunt with her about his intentions, or lack thereof. She admitted, "I'm considering writing my aunt and asking her to come to Boston with me so at least I won't have to be alone with him."

Surprising her, Mason reached out and took her hand. He began running his knuckles over her palm, sending a shiver darting through her. "If your aunt doesn't show up, let me know, and I'll come back in the dead of the night and kidnap you."

Lily's throat tightened. A delicate moment. She wanted to press it and force him to think about the possibility of her in his life beyond his departure four days from now. But if she pushed too hard, she was certain he would back off. And tonight she didn't want him to back off.

However, she could nudge. Gazing at him from beneath her lashes, she said, "So let's imagine that you've kidnapped me. Now what would you do?" When he didn't respond immediately, she said, "Turn the lamp down a bit, I would think."

His eyes widened. Then he reached for the lamp and turned it down until darkness pooled around them.

Standing, he pulled her to her feet as well, then settled his hands low on her hips. Lily quivered. "I would have to keep you from calling for help," he said, his tone smoky.

He lowered his head. Instead of seizing her mouth, he barely grazed her lips, dropping a kiss at the corner of her smile, on the high ridge of her cheekbone, on her temple, on both her closed eyes, and then drifting down to her lips again, which he finally caressed with his own.

Lily sighed against his mouth. She'd waited all night for this. She nudged his arms up so that they encircled her. And this.

"You're a mighty passive kidnapping victim," he said.

"Really?" She nibbled on his stubble-roughened chin. "I thought I was being quite active."

He reached up and slid his thumb over one of her eyebrows, then the other. She felt as if she were being marked, or anointed. "You make me laugh," he said.

Lily looked down, afraid that he'd be able to see her feelings for him in her eyes. "Oh? I thought I made you mad."

"If you mean crazy, then yes, you do that, too." He gently pressed her head against his shoulder and she rested there, listening to his heartbeat and his breath shuddering through his chest. After a long moment he ran his hand down her spine and then held her slightly away from him. "Do you want me to take you back to your tent now?" he asked. His face reflected smooth sincerity, but his eyes burned.

"No." It came out more as a gasp than a confident statement, so she sucked in a hasty breath and thundered out, "No!"

She was tired of saying yes when she meant no. She wanted this. She wanted him—wanted to be close to him in a way she'd never be close to anyone else except her future husband, whoever he would be. Mason was sure it wouldn't be him, but she had four days to prove him wrong.

"Oh." He stared at her, suddenly nonplussed.

Lily choked back a giggle. They both had what they wanted: She was here and in no hurry to leave. But now neither of them knew what next to do.

She broke eye contact to look around. "You're right: You do have more space here than I do. Weren't you going to put blankets on the floor?" She was trying to sound casual, but she was afraid that the blush scalding her cheeks was giving away her nervousness.

"Blankets?"

Darn it, she'd hoped he would pick things up from there. She hadn't imagined that coaxing him into lovemaking was going to be so difficult. So, well, embarrassing. She didn't know how he had gotten up the courage in the first place to ask her to go to bed with him.

Well, she had plenty of courage, too. And she was going to seduce him.

She plucked at his top shirt button, and it popped free. "You owe me forty-five seconds," she reminded him.

"Forty-five? I thought it was thirty-nine."

She undid another button. "I." Then the third button went. "Charge." The fourth button. "Interest." And the fifth and final button slipped away, and his shirt gaped open, revealing a hard chest. Holding her breath, Lily reached out and splayed her hand against his heated skin.

Mason pressed his hand on top of hers, trapping

her there. Not that she had any interest in removing her hand. "And I," he said, his dark eyes intense, "try to give two hundred percent, so we're about to have a memorable minute and a half."

His tent was bigger, but not much bigger. Without removing her hand, he managed to pull a blanket from the cot and layer it on the floor. For a half second he looked doubtful, and Lily wondered if he was going to do the gentlemanly thing and insist upon escorting her back to her tent mostly untouched. Well, if he tried to make her leave, she would sit on the floor, wrap herself around his ankles, and refuse to let go.

But he said, "If I knew you were coming, I would have gotten hold of more blankets. This might be even less comfortable than your cot."

He wasn't being very encouraging. It was one thing to seduce Mason when he wanted to sleep with her, and another to cajole him into bed against his will. "Do you—" She swallowed and lifted her chin. "Do you *want* me to go?"

Somehow in the next three seconds she ended up down on the blankets with Mason half sprawled on top of her and her mouth sealed to his. When he finally broke off, gasping, he let out a little laugh. "God, no, I don't want that. But . . . who is going to be the sensible one tonight?"

He was right: The ground was hard. But it was still better than the alternative, which was no ground at all. She wriggled an arm free and began tugging his shirttails out of his pants. "Neither of us. I was sensible two nights ago. You were sensible last night. I figure we both get the chance to be insensible tonight. Or unsensible. Whichever happens first."

Mason laughed. "Well, I'm not sure exactly what you had in mind, but I think unsensible would be a better initial goal to strive for."

"I'm already there," she told him, and pushed his shirt off his shoulders.

He sat up, straddling her, and removed his shirt completely. His skin was still paler than the diggers' bronzed torsos, but it was somehow even more attractive. He was as much an outsider here as she sometimes felt herself to be.

She trailed the backs of her fingers up his rib cage and his chest, pausing at his nipples. She liked it so much when he touched her nipples; she wondered if he'd feel the same.

She made light little circles with her fingertips. Mason's eyes half closed, and a smile curved his mouth. Good.

"Are you counting yet?" he asked.

"Counting what?"

"The seconds. We have a minute and a half."

"Oh. One . . ."

He furiously began unbuttoning her shirt. With her help, he soon had it and her chemise off. Partially resting his weight on his elbows, he lowered himself over her. Lily gasped as his mouth dropped a hot kiss on her shoulder, then the swell of her breast, and then on her nipple. Each astonishing stroke of his tongue made her eyes cross.

"Two," she forced out.

She stopped counting at fourteen, when they both had all their clothes off and were lying on their sides, madly kissing each other. It was difficult to count aloud while kissing, and near impossible to concentrate on counting when Mason's hand was cupping her hip and his thumb was stroking back and forth along the outer edge of her triangle of dark hair. She kept holding her breath, willing his thumb to slide off course and delve into places that ached for his touch, but the only thing she was accomplishing by holding her breath was making kissing him difficult.

Well, perhaps she would have to be bold again.

Giving him plenty of time to move away—though she wasn't sure why he would—she reached down between them and, after mustering the courage, wrapped her hand around his stiff penis, which had been nudging against her belly.

Mason made a strange noise, half sigh, half grunt. His kisses became downright ravenous, and his hand finally slid off her hip and dipped lower.

Even though she'd been expecting his touch—craving it, even—she flinched at the first slide of his finger between her legs. This felt very strange. Was it supposed to feel strange?

Another half dozen strokes. Strange suddenly became wonderful, and his finger glided more easily against her. She lifted her hips in counterpoint to his strokes. That must have been the signal he'd been waiting for. He gently guided her onto her back and covered her body with his, his hips pressing against hers and his penis settling where his finger had been.

Hmm. This was nice—she especially loved the feeling of all that skin touching skin—but she missed what he'd been doing with his finger. She bit her lip, trying to decide if she should mention it. Then he flexed his lower body, and his penis rubbed deliciously hard against her.

She let out a yelp and grabbed his hips. Good Lord.

Mason froze. "Do you want me to slow down?" He swallowed. "Or stop?"

"It's—it's—" Heavens, her thoughts were so jumbled that she couldn't even be coherent. "It's too much. Like an ache that just keeps tightening up."

His expression relaxed, and he even grinned at her. "It's supposed to feel that way." And he moved against her again, wiping away forever any chance for her to put together a complete sentence.

But conversation wasn't necessary, for their bodies were communicating just fine. His penis nudged her core, and she wrapped her legs around his waist, opening herself to him. He began to push into her.

Was it supposed to feel like this? And the whole idea of him inside her suddenly seemed ridiculous.

"Mason," she started to say, but at the same time he gave a powerful push, and the breath hissed out of her. The strange, exciting ache had been replaced by a painful one.

Well, she knew what *that* was. She had just lost her virginity.

"Are you all right?" Mason whispered. He reared back so that he could see her more clearly, and the concern in his eyes began to chase away the pain.

"I think so." The ache wasn't too bad anymore.

"Let's give it a few more seconds," he said. Keeping himself unmoving within her, he resumed kissing her, his tongue soon making interesting forays into her mouth.

Trailing her fingers through his hair, she kissed him back. This was familiar territory. If she concentrated hard enough on his delicious mouth, she could almost forget that he was still lodged intimately inside her.

And then a restless heat started to build, and she didn't want to forget. Why wasn't he doing anything? She nudged him with her hips. And he slid deeper.

Oh, my.

She nudged her hips against him again. This time he met her motion, and the strange ache roared back to life, stronger than before.

"This must be the nice part," she gasped in his ear.

He laughed, throwing their rhythm off. He started to say something, but his eyes went unfocused and he increased his speed.

She couldn't keep up, so she held herself still while he rocked in and out, feeding the ache. Her sight beginning to blur around the edges, she tried to keep her eyes on Mason's face above her. One more hard thrust, and the ache inside her pulled taut, then snapped, shimmering fiercely through her.

He arched above her, his eyes shut and his expression tight, and then sagged, catching himself on his elbows before he flattened her. His chest knocked against hers as he pulled air into his lungs.

Lily raised one limp hand to his hair and began to feather her fingers through it again. "That was the strangest experience of my life." Had she really said that? She probably should have come up with something more complimentary, like *Darling, that was wonderful*.

But he laughed as he rolled to the side, sliding out of her but keeping her body snug against his. "That was definitely among my top five life experiences, too."

She propped herself up on her elbow. She was suddenly feeling quite chatty. "What were some of the other ones?" Maybe other women, she realized a second too late. Which wasn't exactly what she wanted to hear about at the moment, with her body still singing.

"Let's see. . . . The first time I saw the Pacific Ocean. Huge waves smashed onto the beach, and all I could see were more and more waves stretching out to the horizon. And one winter a few years ago, I came face-to-face with a grizzly. I was so scared, my heart damn near stopped in my chest. He must've been just as surprised as I was, because he didn't follow when I turned and ran." He smiled, caught her hand playing with his hair, and kissed her wrist. "So it looks like you and I are actually among the top three."

A good answer—and if numbers four and five were Betty in Topeka and Virginia in Santa Fe, he should stop talking right now.

His expression turned thoughtful. "I guess I'd round it out with the first earthquake I felt while in San Francisco, and the first time I was paid for an article I wrote."

So Betty and Virginia were probably six and seven.

Still, she liked the idea that she was sharing his top five with an earthquake. Because that's the way she felt—as if the entire world had shifted beneath her, leaving her body, her mind, her heart, in a different place from where they had been only an hour before.

She rested her cheek in the hollow of his shoulder, turned her head an inch or two and kissed his skin, then settled back into place. She could grow accustomed to this very easily.

But she had only four more days. No, three days: It must be after midnight. If he left after three days, her heart would be torn to pieces.

But other people had survived heartbreak. Her mother had survived her father's death and found love a second time with Mr. Grant. Whatever happened in three days, Lily would survive it. And she was determined to have no regrets. She had made her decision, for better or for worse.

"Cold?" he asked, and she realized she must have trembled.

She pushed a bright note into her voice. "Hardly. Are you?"

"You could boil water on me, I think. How many seconds did we use?"

"Um, I lost count."

He stroked her hip. "Then I guess we did it right," he said, a smile in his voice.

"But I'd say no more than twenty seconds."

He stopped stroking. "Twenty *seconds*?"

"So that leaves us with at least twenty-five seconds left."

His stroking resumed. "Plus, you charge a mean rate of interest."

Lily tilted her head to kiss his jaw. "Yes, I do."

"Are you available for more repayment tomorrow, then?"

Good, she hadn't had to spell it out for him. "I haven't taken you to the hot springs yet."

Mason plucked her hand from his chest and began placing a light kiss on each finger. When he reached her pinkie, he retraced his travels, but she sensed the kisses had become automatic as his thoughts shifted. Two more trips back and forth across her knuckles, and then he intertwined her fingers with his and rested their hands on his stomach.

"You promised your grandfather that you'd have supper with Cecil last night," he said. "Do you think you could make me another sort of promise? That you won't have supper—or lunch, or breakfast, or afternoon tea—alone with him during my last four days here?"

"Three days," she corrected.

Mason went still.

Oh, her big mouth. The low lamplight made deciphering his expression difficult. "Of course I promise." Had she hurt him? She got the sinking feeling that she had.

But perhaps that was good. If the thought of leaving bothered him so much, he could rethink it. He could stay.

She dusted kisses on his cheeks, chin, and nose until she felt him smile again. "Let's not talk about

Cecil or when you're going to leave. Both subjects are too depressing. Tell me instead about working on the railroad. What was the best part about it?"

"The best part? The camaraderie, I guess," he said slowly. "We all lived in a boxcar that would creep down the track just as fast as we laid it. . . ."

Lily closed her eyes, listening to his words rumbling inside his chest, and smiled.

Mason hunched over his cup of excellent coffee—there was a lot to be said for having a millionaire bankroll a fossil dig—and tried to figure out what his problem was.

He should be ecstatic, beaming with great goodwill at his fellow man, unable to remove the smile from his lips. But that wasn't the case, and it was pissing him off.

Last night, after Lily had suggested he throw blankets down on the floor, he hadn't been able to think of a single good reason why he shouldn't stretch her out and kiss her all over, and a thousand reasons why he should. Now those thousand reasons had dwindled down to one very selfish reason—he simply had wanted to kiss her, undress her, get inside her—and the reasons why he should have stopped had grown in number and weight.

One: They had no future together.

Mason pushed his hand into his hair and gave it a frustrated tug. That had never stopped him before, though. He'd been honest with her about his intention to leave, just as he'd been honest with other girls he'd met and taken to bed. So, why was it bothering him now? Because she had refused to sleep with him earlier for that reason? She had apparently gotten over her reservations.

Two: Their lives were so different.

But what did that have to do with anything? See reason number one, above: They had no future, so any issues about different lives were inconsequential.

Three: He was severely imposing on his host's hospitality by sleeping with the host's granddaughter, especially since Highfill wanted her to marry another fellow. Mason's father hadn't bothered teaching his son a great deal about social niceties, but if he had, not sleeping with his host's virginal female relatives probably would have been one of the lessons.

Four: Lily had been a virgin.

Several of Mason's lady friends—some of them women he'd slept with, and some of them friends' wives whose tongues had wagged after too much wine—had mentioned that many women didn't come to their husbands as virgins, though most pretended to be. Mason supposed that ladies in the higher social classes would succumb just as easily to the pleasures of sex before marriage. But still, it was important, and he wanted to show his appreciation to her for choosing him. Leaving in three days wasn't a good way to demonstrate that appreciation.

"Morning." Lily sat down beside him on the bench, cupping her coffee in her hands. She gave him a conspiratorial sideways look, then smiled up into his face.

That smile. It knocked out of his head all of his

good reasons for not sleeping with her, and the reasons why he had came flooding back: her quick, open grin; the mischief that made her give him fake wide-eyed looks when she thought he was saying something ridiculous; her laughter, which made him answer her with his own laughter. And her remarkably luscious rear end, which had been just as marvelous last night as he'd dreamed.

Oh, hell. He might as well admit it: He was completely besotted. By a girl who moved in the refined social circles of Boston. Never what he had expected would happen—but he had never expected anyone like Lily, either.

"A fine morning," he replied. And somehow it had suddenly become so. He glanced around. Aside from the cook grumbling over the fire, the camp was quiet; most people were not yet up to greet the dawn. This felt like a fairy tale in which an enchanted sleep had been laid on those around them so that he and Lily could snatch a few more minutes together.

He wanted to set aside his coffee cup, pull her into his arms, and rest his chin on the top of her head as he stroked the graceful curve of her spine. But the cook was with them, so Mason settled for giving the scarf she wore today—a green one—a little tug. "I'd even say it's a gorgeous morning, actually."

"Then why the frown you were wearing only a few minutes ago?"

He might be head over heels, but that didn't mean he'd lost all his brains. Telling her that he was having second thoughts was not a smart move. So he picked the least of his worries to confide in her. "It struck me this morning that it's the worst sort of behavior for me to, ah, spend so many good moments with you while I'm your grandfather's guest."

"Oh." Her eyebrows scrunched together. "That hadn't even occurred to me." She thought for a moment. "Do you want to just stop?"

As if this attraction, this crazy good feeling he got when he was with her, could be switched on or off so easily. Just stop? But maybe she didn't feel the same way. "Do *you* want to stop?"

She rolled her eyes as if he'd asked a stupid question. That reassured him more than her answer did. "No."

"Then I guess I'll have to ignore my conscience for the next few days."

Lily started to reply, but Dickon approached and sat down at the table with them. "Lovely morning," he said around a yawn. "Are you helping us out again today?" he asked Mason.

"Yes, sir." Who would work at breaking up rock in the blistering sun when the alternative was to work in the shade of a tent, doing nothing more strenuous than packing crates?

But the real reason for staying here in camp was Lily. They didn't have nearly enough time left together. He wasn't going to squander what they did have.

Dickon got to his feet. "Then let's get moving. No rest for the wicked."

When Dickon turned his back, Mason gave Lily an exaggerated leer. She leered in return—and not very well—and then giggled. "Dickon," she called as she stood, "we're going to go to the springs early this afternoon. Is that all right with you?"

Dickon snorted. "Based on how you asked me that question, you clearly are going whether I like it or not. So I guess it'll have to be all right." But he didn't sound nearly as caustic as he had during the past week, and he even slid Lily a wink. Someone must have dumped a solid dose of happiness into Dickon's coffee this morning.

Lily's fingers skittered against the inside of Mason's wrist. When he glanced at her walking beside him, she gave him an innocent look, then reached over and tickled his wrist again.

Mason felt the rock of anxiety that had been in his stomach since he woke begin to soften and melt. He didn't know how it was going to happen or even what the outcome would be, but he was going to enjoy every minute of the next few days and try not to think about what came next.

"Didn't you say you were going to go to the springs?" Dickon suddenly said. "I can finish this up myself if you want to go."

Mason looked up. He'd been packing and labeling for only an hour, and even he could see that there were still several full days' worth of work to be done just plastering and packing. How did Dickon expect he'd "finish this up" on his own?

Dickon turned away, and as he did so, he slipped his hand into his pocket.

Mason slowly straightened. Dickon had found

something he didn't want anyone to know about—again. And he wanted Mason and Lily out of the way.

But then Dickon and Lily exchanged meaningful looks.

No, Dickon didn't want Mason and Lily out of the way. He wanted Mason out of the way. Lily, though she was doing an excellent job at keeping her expression blank, knew what Dickon had found.

This damn tent town was knee-deep in secrets.

"Let's go," Mason said abruptly to Lily. One secret—his and Lily's—was all he cared about right now. If Dickon wanted to hide things in his pocket, that was his business.

Lily stood. "All right." She preceded Mason out of the tent, but she threw one last glance over her shoulder at Dickon before she stepped outside.

The sunlight struck Mason like an anvil, and he squinted against it. "Maybe our nice, cool mine would be a good place to visit instead," he said as they walked to the corral.

Lily shuddered. "And risk running into that madman again?"

"Did your grandfather ever find out who it was?"

"No, and he talked to the townspeople until his tongue almost fell out. Bought a lot of whiskey at the saloon, hoping to loosen tongues, but all it did was loosen wits."

In the past, Mason had made a number of inquiries at saloons himself. Rundown, nearly broken men would trade any tale for a few glasses of liquor. "That was smart," he said.

Lily grinned at him. "Thanks. It was my suggestion. Denver," she reminded him when he stared at her. "Plenty of saloons there."

Mason shook his head. "I keep forgetting how much time you spent out here," he admitted.

"Must be due to my natural glamour."

Mason opened the corral gate and motioned her through. As she passed, Mason mentally took a step away and studied her. No, he couldn't say that she shone with the sharp sophistication that most city girls had. Her smile spread too wide and her laughter spilled out too often. And although she shivered now at the thought of the miner who had shot at them, she'd been cool at the time, even when he'd passed out at her feet. It was only when she had to deal with Cecil that she had faltered, displaying her inexperience.

Mason narrowed his eyes. If he hadn't known that she was Highfill's granddaughter, would he have guessed that upon meeting her? Probably not. No, definitely not.

She wasn't going to last more than a year in Boston, he suddenly knew. And she'd be uncomfortable after the first two weeks.

She'd move back to Denver. And he could visit her in Denver. Mason swallowed. He might even be able to live in Denver.

He blew out his breath. One night in bed with her, and he was the one reacting like a virgin, spinning rosy fantasies of happily ever after.

Lily settled her hands on her hips. "Are you coming, or are you going to stand there thinking?"

Mason started moving again and picked up his saddle. "Since my thoughts are worthless, I might as well come with you."

"Don't overwhelm me with your eagerness." But she threw him a smile, and he knew she was teasing him.

His arms full of saddle and gear, he walked up to her and gave her what he hoped was an intense look. "I was saving my eagerness for later."

Her lips trembled and her eyes shone so bright, Mason bent down to kiss her, but common sense intervened and he caught himself. Kissing her in broad daylight in the corral could lead to complications if anyone saw them. Better to escape to the solitude of the spring, where he could kiss her at his leisure.

He saddled both their mounts in record time, helped Lily onto her horse, then swung into his saddle. "Let's go."

Chapter Fifteen

Mason nuzzled Lily's neck, then drifted upward to capture her soft mouth in his own. She was slow to respond, which made him smile even as he continued to kiss her. "Tired?" he asked.

"Exhausted."

He dolloped a few more kisses on her, then rolled off. Their sweat-slick skin slid like silk against silk. "How many seconds do we have left now?"

"Hmm. Funny, but it's now sixty seconds."

"Sixty?" Mason propped himself up on his elbow to gaze down at Lily—naked, boneless, and trying to look solemn instead of mischievous. The way she widened her big eyes at him was a dead giveaway that she was pulling his leg. "I thought you were a schoolteacher. Don't you have to learn your sums before you're allowed to teach children theirs?"

"Of course. But I'm fining you for more seconds."

"Fining me? For what?"

"You snore."

"I do not."

"I heard it last night. You snored for hours, actually. A really tough lady would fine you for every minute you snored instead of giving you a small fine like I did."

"No one has ever told me that I snore."

Lily shrugged her pale shoulders. "Then either you just started snoring or no one thought to mention it. Almost all the men in camp seem to snore. But it's only the men whose snoring is as loud as stampeding buffalo who get ribbed about it."

"And I don't snore like a buffalo stampede, I take it."

"No. More like a . . ." She scrunched up her nose and appeared to be thinking of a good comparison.

"Stop," Mason said. "I don't want to know."

"Then make me."

"What?"

She laughed up at him. "Make me stop. Let's try again. 'When you snore, you sound like—'"

Mason grabbed her shoulders and yanked her to him for kiss that swooped from hot to playful, to hot again, and then eased away into gentle sips.

"Thanks for giving me a second chance after I missed my cue," he said.

"I'm not sure I've seen you miss anything." Lily rolled onto her side and tucked the edge of the blanket over herself.

"You don't have to do that on my account."

"I'm trying not to get sunburned."

Mason looked up, and the sun speared him. Wincing, he glanced away. "I've made plenty of mistakes," he said. "See, I just made another one: Who but a fool stares straight at the sun at noontime?" And who but a fool lets his heart get stolen away without putting up a fight to keep it—or to keep her?

"So, why are you all fired up to go to Boston?" he asked, keeping his tone casual.

"My family's there." She gave him a small frown. "You know this."

"I do. I was just reminding myself."

Confusion etching her face, she squinted at him.

"Tell me about your aunt in Denver," he said quickly. "How did she come to live there instead of Boston?"

"She knew she wanted to move west, but she didn't know where. So she set off for San Francisco but fell in love with Denver as soon as she saw it. She stopped there and never made it to San Francisco." Lily laughed. "She's been in Denver for more than twenty years now, and she's always complaining about how crowded it now is. I'd like to be able to convince her to come to Boston for a visit. Then she'd be reminded of just how crowded a city can get, and she'll appreciate Denver more."

Maybe Lily would react the same way to Boston and find a new appreciation for Denver. "What are you looking forward to the most in Boston?" he asked. "The smell, the buildings squashed together, the hordes of people—"

She wrinkled her nose at him. "Seeing my mother and my sisters. It's been five years since I last saw them. I love my aunt—she's like a sister and a mother rolled up into one—but I don't think she ever expected that I'd live with her for eight years. And I never expected that I'd grow up without my real mother and sisters in the house with me."

"But you like Denver, right?"

"Oh, yes."

"I like Denver, too. I, ah, stop by there whenever I'm in the area."

She nodded but looked puzzled by his sudden enthusiasm.

He'd have to be more straightforward. "If you ever return to Denver for more than a day or two, let me know. I'd like to come meet you."

She looked away and didn't say anything for a long moment—a moment that seemed to stretch into years, decades, centuries.

Then she let out a long exhale.

Damn. Whatever she was going to say, he didn't want to hear it. How much of a coward would he look like if he clapped his hands over his ears?

"Ignoring for the moment that we wouldn't have nearly as much privacy in Denver as we have here, how would I contact you?" she asked.

Oh. That hadn't been so bad, except for her assumption that he wanted to see her only to take her to bed. He answered the direct question before diving into muddier waters. "Write to my paper." Then he winced. "No, that won't work any longer. Write to me in San Francisco."

"Why San Francisco?"

"I visit there more often than anyplace else."

"So I'll come from Boston and you'll come from San Francisco, and we'll meet in the middle at Denver?"

"Assuming that I get your letter in time."

"Or we could pick a date right now. Early January?"

"I don't know what I'll be doing in January."

A smile curved her mouth, but her eyes stayed serious. "So, no promises."

"I guess . . . no." He couldn't promise. Who knew what the next few months would bring? She might marry a Boston blueblood. He might decide to write a book about the Yukon. The only thing that was certain was that he was leaving in three days.

She cleared her throat. "I hope you know that I'd like you to call on me if you're ever in Boston, though I know it's unlikely that you will be. You've said before that you dislike the city."

Mason arched an eyebrow. "Your mother would want you to entertain a wandering journalist?"

"I have no idea. In any case, you'd be my guest, not my mother's."

"In your mother's house."

Lily lifted one bare shoulder. "As long as she doesn't find us kissing in the drawing room, I don't see what she could object to."

Looking at her lounging nearly naked on a blanket with a mass of gray-green scrub forming a backdrop behind her, Mason had difficulty imagining her perfectly coiffed, stylishly dressed, and politely cool as she stood in the middle of a fancy drawing room. And he had even more trouble imagining himself taking such a fashionably packaged creature in his arms.

Especially if she had an equally perfect husband standing beside her.

"What if you're married?" he asked.

She frowned. "You'd discover whether I was upon inquiring for me at my mother's house. It would be up to you if you wanted to see me. But I—" She stopped.

"What?"

Heaving a sigh, she said, "I don't know how to put this. But you made me see how wrong Cecil was for me. It'd be unbearable if, after I was married, you also made me realize that the man I married was wrong for me as well."

He turned that over in his mind, looked at it this way and that. "I can understand your not wanting to entertain an old lover while you have a new husband," he said slowly. "But I don't understand why you think you'd marry someone not right for you."

"I almost married Cecil," she pointed out.

"You would have realized your mistake soon enough. The man was acting like an ass."

Lily fiddled with the edge of the blanket. "But if he weren't such an ass . . . maybe just half an ass . . . then I'm not sure I would've realized my mistake before it was too late. Everyone was encouraging me to marry him. No one was suggesting that I not."

"Dickon dropped a few heavy hints."

"But my family . . ."

Mason stroked her shoulder, but he could feel his anger building. No, her family had not looked out for her very well. He didn't know her mother and what she considered to be important, but he had expected better from Highfill. Cecil might be a good paleontologist, but it didn't take much to see that he wasn't a good man.

"Your family might not have the wisdom you should depend on when it comes to marriage." He paused. "You're a sensible girl. Why not rely on yourself?"

Lily rubbed her forehead as if trying to ease away a headache, then gave a short laugh.

"What?" he asked, when she didn't say anything.

She stopped rubbing her forehead but let her hand remain there, covering her eyes. "I like *you*. But that's not sensible, because you're leaving in three days."

The words popped out before he thought about them: "I could come back."

Her hand slid away from her face, and she looked at him gravely. "But for how long?"

He didn't have an answer. He wanted to say, *Forever*, but he could see the obstacles standing between them. Her family would want better for her, and Lily cared deeply about what her family wanted. As for him, he had never been in love before. How long would this need to be with Lily as much as possible last? Maybe tomorrow he'd wake with a buzz along his soles and an unquenchable desire to see what lay over the next hill—and then the hill after that and the hill after that.

Or maybe, his mind whispered, his rambling days were over. Maybe he had finally found where he was supposed to be.

"I don't know," he finally answered. "I honestly don't."

She put her hand to her face again—to conceal tears, he realized. In a rough voice, she said, "I didn't expect anything else, really. It's part of who you are. But I had to ask."

He had never felt so helpless. And unworthy.

"Your family would never accept me," he said a little desperately.

She dropped her hand and laughed past her tears. "That's a terrible argument. I thought you just told me that I shouldn't listen to them."

"Well—"

She gave him a smile that he realized was meant to be reassuring. "We're traveling in different directions. I'm just glad we intersected here in Colorado."

He pushed her hair off her face, thumbed away the tears drying on her cheeks, and whispered, "So am I."

Chapter Sixteen

Lily wished her aunt were there to advise her.

If she were having a social problem, like how to smooth over an accidental insult or how to gently let her hostess know that her drapes were about to catch on fire, Lily would have consulted her mother. But this problem involved men—well, a man. Mason.

How did you know if a man was in love with you?

Aunt Evaline was an expert on men falling in love. She had every unwed man in Denver wrapped around her finger. Lily had long ago stopped being surprised when her aunt announced during supper, "Oh, nice Mr. Jones asked me to marry him today." Or Mr. Douglas. Or Mr. Snider. Or Mr. Winterbourne. She'd never accepted the proposal. When Lily had asked why, after a particularly loving, handsome, and successful suitor had been turned down, her aunt had replied, "I'll know the right man for me when I see him. And that wasn't him."

Lily watched Mason riding in front of her on the trail back to camp, his shoulders set, his back straight, the ends of his short, dark hair brushing the edge of his wrinkled collar. She suspected her clothes were just as disheveled.

She hadn't known that Mason was the right man for her when she had first seen him. She'd argued with him, then cajoled him into playing a lovesick swain in order to spur Cecil's competitive instincts. Now she wished Mason would return to acting lovesick. At least then she'd have a better idea of where she stood in his affections.

Well, she did know, actually: She was front and center—for the next three days. Beyond that, no promises.

He'd offered to meet her in Denver. That was something, wasn't it? A hint of a hope for a chance beyond a weeklong romance?

He hadn't been willing to commit to meeting her in January, but that didn't mean she couldn't be there—just in case.

Just in case he hoped for something beyond a weeklong romance, too.

Just in case he loved her.

She took a deep breath and tried to slow her runaway heartbeat. Someone had to be the first to say *I love you.* There was no reason why he had to be the one who said it—except that it'd be easier on her that way.

She swallowed back her nervousness. All right. She'd tell him tonight. What did she have to lose?

Ahead of her, Mason reined his horse in and waited for her. Lily brought her horse to a halt when she reached his side. Below them, the tent town spread out like lichen on the Colorado landscape. Mason pointed. "Isn't that your grandfather?"

She didn't see him at first; she was looking for him at his large tent. Then she dropped her gaze. His bare head shining like burnished silver in the afternoon light, her grandfather sat on a sturdy pony on the trail halfway between where they were and the point where the trail fed into the camp.

"Yes, that's him." How strange. She'd never seen her grandfather anywhere except at camp, in town, or at the dig site. He hadn't shown her around the land when she had first arrived—Dickon or Cecil or Peter had done that—because he claimed to not like to ride. "I wonder why he's there."

Her grandfather waved at them. Then he beckoned imperiously, turned his pony, and rode back into camp.

Oh. He'd been waiting for them.

Her stomach gave a twist and her hands went clammy. She looked at Mason. "Do you think he knows?"

"About what?"

She huffed out an exasperated breath. "About us." If that wasn't the immediate thing that came to his mind, maybe she was being idiotic in planning to return to Denver for January.

"I don't know." His tone still calm, he added, "I hope not."

Half of her hoped not, too—the stubborn half that didn't want her grandfather making the decision about who she married and how. She hadn't spent much time daydreaming about her wedding day, but whenever she had contemplated it, a shotgun had never played a leading role.

But the practical half recognized that if her grandfather insisted that Mason marry her, it might be her only chance to wed him with her family's blessing—angry and reluctant as it might be.

Mason watched her grandfather disappear among the tents, but he didn't move to follow. "Don't give in to guilt and confess before he even asks us anything."

"I don't feel guilty," she told him. "Do you?"

"If he does know, I'm going to feel guilty for putting you in a difficult position." He pulled free a twig that had gotten tangled in her scarf, then gave her a smile that sent her heart thudding madly. "Otherwise, no."

But still he didn't heel his horse forward. "Lily, I don't know if . . ." He frowned and started again. "I expect that if Highfill does know about us, he'll give me two options. One is to accept a generous offer."

"An offer? You mean he'll pay you to marry me?"

His eyes flashed. "I'm not Cecil, Lily. A girl's wealth doesn't affect whether I want to marry her."

"At all?" In her more delusional moments, she realized, she'd hoped her family's affluence might swing his thoughts on marriage in her favor.

"At all," he said firmly. "In any case, your grandfather's offer would be in exchange for my leaving at once, staying away from you, and keeping my mouth shut."

She winced. "Then what *does* affect whether you'll marry a girl?"

"A gun at my back."

Wonderful. Lily closed her eyes. Why was she even worrying about how to tell him she loved him? It was hopeless. "If you're so dead set against marriage, then you might as well take the offer."

When he spoke again, he sounded angry. "You don't think much of me, do you?"

She snapped her eyes open and stared at him in disbelief. "I think the world of you. But you're leaving anyway. So, why not take whatever deal he offers?"

"Because whenever you thought back on my leaving, you'd associate it with your grandfather paying me off, that's why. And eventually, so would I. That's not the way I want to leave."

"How do you want to leave, then?" she demanded.

"I'm not sure I want to leave at all." He ran his hand through his hair, leaving dark clumps poking up. "You're the one who made me pick a day to go."

She had done it in order to protect her heart, but that battle had been lost a long time ago. "So don't leave," she said softly.

"That's the other option, of course." His midnight blue eyes searched hers. "Ever thought about being a frontier journalist's wife?"

Only in her most optimistic moments—of which she'd had about a thousand during the last several days. Keeping her eyes locked with his, she nodded.

He exhaled sharply. But with delight? Or with disbelief?

"Then, if your grandfather gives me that option, I should say yes?"

She nodded again, then cleared her throat. "Yes."

"All right."

Not the most enthusiastic response. When he didn't add anything, she sagged a little inside.

Then he reached over, took her free hand, and brought it to his mouth. "You're a lovely girl, Lily."

Her knees quivered in disappointment. It wasn't *I love you*, but apparently it was the closest she was going to get in this situation.

Mason released her hand and heeled his horse into a walk. "Come on. Let's see what the future has in store for us."

Chapter Seventeen

Her grandfather was at the corral, waiting for them. He opened the gate to let them through, then helped Lily down from her horse.

Her nerves began to buzz, and she avoided his eyes. She wouldn't regret being with Mason. She couldn't. Still, she dreaded the coming conversation.

"Had a good ride, sweetheart?" her grandfather asked.

"Yes, to the springs." Lily covertly studied her grandfather as he unsaddled her horse. He wasn't acting like someone who'd discovered his granddaughter dallying with a man he would certainly consider unsuitable.

"A beautiful spot," her grandfather said. "I should get out there before we close up camp. I haven't been there yet this year."

No, he was definitely not irate. She looked at Mason. He gave a small shrug.

Well, so much for worrying about being found out. And so much for marrying Mason.

She rubbed her forehead and sighed. She should be glad that Mason wasn't going to be forced into marrying her. That wasn't the way she wanted to win him. But she couldn't summon the emotion.

"Have you had a good time while you've been here, Donnelly?" her grandfather asked.

"Yes, sir. Learned more than I did the last time I was here." Mason nodded at Lily. "And of course I had the unexpected pleasure of meeting your granddaughter."

Her grandfather held the corral gate open, motioning them through. "When you rode into camp, Donnelly, I didn't expect you'd stay here more than a few days, but I think you'll be pleased that you extended your stay past your usual time. I have a bit of a surprise for you."

Lily looked at her grandfather sharply. Was this friendliness just an act? Perhaps the surprise was Dickon holding a shotgun and the local preacher sweating over his Bible.

Mason tossed his saddle blanket over the top rail of the fence, then followed Lily and her grandfather out of the corral. "I'm in your hands, sir."

Lily blinked when she stepped inside her grandfather's tent, and she slammed to a halt. Dickon *was* there.

But no shotgun, and no preacher. She sighed and then saw that Cecil was there. Oh, joy.

"Cecil," she murmured, nodding to him.

He nodded back but didn't speak. Though the flaps on two sides of the tent were rolled up, allowing in sunlight and a taste of a breeze, his expression was in shadow. When he sat after she did, she finally saw that his face was tight with tension.

Goose bumps cascaded over her arms. Whatever this surprise was, Cecil was unhappy with it. And an unhappy Cecil was not a pleasant companion.

In contrast, Dickon looked the happiest she'd seen him since the first sapphire had been found.

There were several empty chairs and stools. Mason dropped onto the stool nearest her chair. Cecil's frown dug blacker grooves along his mouth, while Dickon appeared much more relaxed. "Have a good time at the springs?" Dickon asked.

"You went to the springs?" Cecil demanded before Lily could respond.

She didn't bother to hide her irritation. "Yes. And yes, we had a wonderful time."

Cecil turned to her grandfather, who had settled into his large canvas chair. "Did you know they were at the springs?"

"Of course. That's how I knew where to find them."

Cecil's mouth twisted. He opened it, but Mason cut him off. "So, what's the reason for this powwow?"

Her grandfather nodded at Dickon.

"Catch," Dickon said to Mason, then flipped him a rock he'd been concealing in his hand.

Mason grabbed it out of the air. Lily's breath caught in her throat. The stone was another sapphire.

Mason held it between his thumb and forefinger, rotating it in the light. There wasn't much to see, but his eyes narrowed. "This is why you pushed us out of the tent this morning?" he asked Dickon.

Lord, he was quick-witted.

Dickon grinned. "This morning, plus one or two other times."

"Uh-huh." He eyed the stone again. "So, is someone going to tell me why the hell this rock is so important?"

His tone reeking of condescension, Cecil said, "It's a sapphire."

Mason silently stared at the blue stone. Then he glanced at Lily.

Her stomach clenched. She wasn't looking forward to this.

"You knew about this?" He shook his head. "Of course you did." He turned his eyes back to the stone before she could see what was there. Reproach? Understanding?

Mason bounced the sapphire on his palm, then closed his hand over it. "So," he said to Highfill. "Why tell me?" Suspicion gave his words an edge.

Lily's grandfather laced his fingers together, rested them on his stomach, and leaned back in his chair. Lily recognized this posture, although she'd seen it only a half dozen times. He was readying himself for serious bargaining. "We found too many of them. It was going to come out sooner or later. And with your nose for stories . . ."

Mason nodded. "But you do know that I'm not working for a paper any longer, don't you?"

"Of course. That doesn't mean the instincts turn off, though. Dickon said you were suspicious. And you've stayed around far longer than anyone thought you would. I figured you were pursuing the story, paper or not."

A thread of doubt wove through Lily's mind. She shook it off. No, Mason hadn't stayed longer for the story. He'd stayed here because of her.

Hadn't he?

Mason reached over and dropped the sapphire in Lily's lap, causing her to jerk in surprise. She gingerly picked it up and gave it to Dickon, who began to toss it from hand to hand, still grinning.

She understood the reason for Dickon's grin. No more lying or sneaking around. No more waiting for her grandfather to make his decision about what to do with the sapphires and the expedition. And for her, no more conflict between encouraging Mason to stay and, at her grandfather's order, making Mason leave. Finally everything was out in the open.

"This isn't the first one, you said." Mason leaned forward, his eyes on Highfill. "So tell me about finding the first one."

Lily raised her hand to cover a yawn. For a fairly small story about an isolated gem strike, her grandfather and Cecil had had a great deal to say about the find. Dickon didn't contribute much except the bare facts about when he had found the sapphires and in which piles of rubble, but he never stopped tossing the sapphire from one hand to the other. Lily finally had to turn her eyes away from him or risk tearing the stupid stone away from him.

And with every word spoken by her grandfather and Cecil, Lily could feel Mason growing more remote. The lover had faded away, to be replaced by the famously tough reporter.

Darkness had wrapped around the camp more than three hours earlier. Lily had left the tent only to get plates loaded with supper from the cook. Cecil had, of course, offered his assistance, but she'd refused him in an uncompromising tone. His back stiff, he had turned to Highfill for support, but her grandfather had been so busy relating his surprise at finding yet another sapphire that he'd either missed or ignored Cecil's appeal.

". . . and that's it in its entirety," her grandfather said. "Amazing, isn't it?"

"Interesting," Mason replied, his enthusiasm not nearly at the same level as Highfill's. "How will this affect the dig? When people hear about your finds, they're certain to flock to the area, aren't they?"

"That's another reason why we were keeping this information close to the vest," Highfill admitted. "There's no way we can run a dig with gem seekers crawling about. We'd have to post a guard at the site every night to keep out pesky folk, and even that might not be enough. And I don't want any of my boys dying for a bunch of rocks."

"Do you mean the fossils or the sapphires?"

Highfill stared. "The sapphires."

"What about the miner who shot at Lily and me?"

"Whoa, boy, one subject at a time. What about him?"

"Wasn't he a danger to the diggers, too?"

"Of course, but I can't shut down a dig because of a lone crazy man. A dozen crazy people is another story altogether." Highfill frowned. "Look here. This isn't going to be another one of your stories where I end up being the bad guy, is it?"

Lily shut her eyes. She was exhausted. The last thing she wanted to listen to was her grandfather nit-pick an article that had been printed last year.

A hand closed over hers, and Lily opened her eyes to find Mason close to her, his eyes on her face.

"What?" she asked, and was startled to hear her voice come out as a croak.

"You fell asleep. Why don't you go to bed?"

"We don't need you here," Highfill added.

No, and they never had needed her. He and Cecil hadn't wanted to include her in the sapphire discussions in the first place, and now, suddenly, she wished they had continued to keep her in the dark. Then she'd be able to look Mason in the eye and know that she hadn't been a part of deceiving him.

Lily rose. All the men got to their feet as well. Mason slid his hand up her arm to steady her, then let go.

Lily covered another yawn. "Well, then. Gentlemen, good night."

"Lily, I can—" Cecil started.

"I'll walk you back," Dickon said loudly. "Still have to be careful of that miner running around."

Saved by Dickon, as usual. "Thank you." Lily nodded to her grandfather and to Mason. She tried to send Mason a message with her eyes—*Come visit me later*—but his polite expression didn't change and she didn't know if he'd understood her or not.

Maybe he understood but wouldn't come.

She and Dickon ducked out of the tent and into the night, thick with humidity.

"Though I still want to spend a few more weeks in the area, traveling around, I am looking forward to going back to Boston," Dickon said as they walked along the paths between the tents. "It's muggy there, but at least there's a breeze off the ocean. Does your aunt ever miss the Boston breezes?"

"Not that she's mentioned to me. Dickon, what do you think will happen now?"

Dickon shook his head. "I don't know. Your fellow—he's a wild card. Your grandfather and Cecil believe that he'll meekly write a story about the find and file it with some paper." Lily had gathered that herself, and the assumption had surprised her. Mason was known for digging deeper than the surface, for looking beyond what people told him was the truth.

"And you don't think he'll write what they want?" she asked.

"Of course not. If you want that boy to do what you want, the best way is to tell him that you want the opposite. I've seen that stubborn streak in my own daughters." Dickon laughed. "Heck, I see it in you."

They had reached her tent. Lily ducked into the pitch-black interior, fumbled with the lamp and matches by the opening, and successfully lit the lamp. "Good night," Dickon called from outside, and then she heard his footsteps thumping away.

Lily turned the light down as low as possible so her silhouette would not be visible from outside the tent. She and Mason had bathed in the spring before returning to camp, but she splashed water on her face to rinse away the dust kicked up by her horse.

She hesitated, then opened a large valise that held several stylish dresses she'd packed for Boston and a lacy silk nightgown she had often worn during hot summer nights in her aunt's home. She hadn't worn it since Denver, though, as she was uncomfortable with the idea of wearing such a revealing garment while sleeping near strangers. Undoubtedly a fire would break out at the boardinghouse during the one night she wore it, and she'd have to dash downstairs nearly naked. But she pulled the silk and lace nightgown free from the valise, shrugged out of her skirt and shirt, and dropped the nightgown over her head. It whispered over her skin, and the hem licked at her ankles.

She sat on the cot, then swung her legs up on it and stretched out. She owed her aunt a letter, but she would rest for just a moment.

A hand stroking her hair woke her. She blinked sleep away to find Mason crouched by her cot. He continued to smooth her hair, but she could see in the lamplight that he didn't smile.

"I wasn't sure you'd come," she said. Her voice had a ragged edge to it—from sleeping, she told herself, then realized there was no point in deceiving herself. Or him. She rose up on one elbow. She heard the same desperation in her voice when she asked, "Are you mad at me?"

He stood, and his hand fell away from her hair. One stride brought him to the lamp, and he turned the knob. The flame, already flickering on the edge of life, died away without a struggle.

Lily sat up. Was he leaving without saying a word to her? But as she began to get to her feet to go after him, she heard the rustle of clothing, then the thump of a boot falling on the ground, then another. In the darkness, he sat down beside her again, causing the cot to sag. Curling an arm around her waist, he coaxed her down onto the cot, lying with his bare chest molded against her back. His heat enfolded her. He dabbed a kiss on her shoulder, and she stroked the arm he had wrapped around her.

"Are you mad at me?" she asked again. This time her voice was calm. If he were furious, he wouldn't be here with her. But she had to hear him say it.

She felt his breath on the nape of her neck. "For a few moments at the beginning, I was. I hate being ambushed like that."

Ambushed. She hadn't thought of the meeting that way, though she could now see how he would have felt that.

"I would've appreciated a warning," he added.

She relaxed. If the only thing that bothered him about the whole meeting was that he believed she knew about it, then her worries were over. "I had no idea they were going to tell you. Your being here at the dig made them nervous, to tell you the truth. They thought you'd find out everything on your own."

"I almost did. You distracted me."

The barest hint of a question flavored his last statement. Lily stopped stroking his arm. She had relaxed too soon.

"What do you think? That I did it deliberately?"

His sigh cascaded over her shoulder. "Not really. It's just that at one point after you left, Cecil said something before Dickon glared him into silence."

"Said what?"

"I can't remember the exact words—"

Her indignation redoubled. "You're a journalist. You quote people for a living. *What did he say?*"

"That you'd done your job well in keeping me occupied."

What a bastard. Cecil knew that she was supposed to make Mason leave—he'd reminded her of that often enough. "I didn't—I mean, I wouldn't have—"

"Don't worry. I don't think you slept with me in order to keep me so befuddled that I wouldn't see what was going on around me practically in plain sight."

She couldn't tell if his dry words ridiculed her or him. Maybe both. "I didn't even kiss you for that reason!" She struggled to turn around to face him, but his arm tightened, holding her in place.

"I know that, Lily. It just threw me for a minute."

"I was supposed to hustle you out of here—that's what my grandfather really wanted me to do," she confessed. "See how well that worked? You must know that I hardly tried."

His silence didn't reassure her. But the kiss he pressed to her shoulder did.

Lily took a deep breath. She thought about trying to shift around to face him again, but an undercurrent of cowardice kept her where she was. "I think . . . that is, I'm fairly sure . . ."

Her throat seized up. Mason bit her shoulder very lightly, then soothed the spot with a feathery kiss.

". . . thatI'minlovewithyou," she finished in a rush.

He froze, his mouth on her skin. A heartbeat passed. Then two. Three.

"Let's get some sleep," he said. "Today was a long day, and full of surprises."

She blew out a long breath and waited for him to get up and don his clothes. Instead, he kissed her shoulder again and settled deeper into the cot. His breathing slowed.

All right. She needed to look on the positive side.

He was going to stay. He didn't love her, and he wasn't going to make love to her, but he would stay.

A voice, thick with sleep, rumbled in her ear. "I have to leave."

Lily cracked her eyes open. Gray light crept in under the tent flap. Dawn was near. "I'll see you at breakfast," she mumbled, and shut her eyes again.

He shifted against her, and she realized he was shaking his head. "No, I won't be at breakfast. I'm going to Denver."

Chapter Eighteen

Under his hand, her heartbeat sped up. Lily scrambled into a sitting position, knocking his arms away in the process. "Denver? What's in Denver?"

With her hair mussed, her eyes wide, and a nightgown he'd never seen before clinging to every curve, she looked good enough to eat. Mason brushed his palm down her side, the silk turning buttery warm. "Did you have this marvelous thing on last night?"

She would not be sidetracked. "What's in Denver?" she repeated.

He paused. He didn't know what he'd find in Denver; he had only a few suspicions propelling him there. And to tell her why he was going would upset her, possibly needlessly.

"Something I need to look into. It shouldn't take long. Maybe three days." He curled a finger under the nightgown's lacy strap and edged it over her shoulder. "Would you wear this for me when I come back? I was too tired last night to properly pay attention to it—and to you."

"Three days?" she repeated.

"Or thereabouts." He ducked his head and kissed her on the mouth.

She responded, but he could feel her hesitation, a holding back.

He grabbed her by the shoulders and held her away from him so that he could see her expression. Doubt shaded her big eyes.

Wonderful. She thought he might be running away—spooked, probably, by her telling him she loved him. He brushed his thumb over her cheek. If he returned with good news from Denver, he'd be able to echo her words back to her. "Lily, I'll be back. I promise. And you know I don't make promises lightly."

She smiled slowly. "Good."

He kissed her one more time, then rose and got dressed. Raising his hand briefly in farewell, he slid through the tent opening and stepped into the newborn morning.

Lily nestled another fossil into the straw-filled wooden crate, then rested her elbows on the edge with a sigh.

Seven days had passed since Mason had left her at dawn in the blankets they had shared all night. It was now four days past the day he'd promised to return.

"That's the last one," she told Dickon. "If we have the men load this into the wagon this afternoon, we can get it to the depot by tomorrow morning."

To the depot and on its way to Boston. Her own trip to Boston would begin only a few days after that.

Lily looked out of the sorting tent one more time. Not a half hour had passed in the last four days in which she hadn't lifted her head at the sound of a horse's hooves or a man's voice.

But there was nothing out there—or at least nothing she cared about—just as there had been nothing out there the last fifty times she had checked.

"Good job," Dickon grunted. He was poring over notes he'd scribbled, transcribing some into a clearer hand. He dipped a pen into an inkpot and laboriously wrote out a few more lines. "I must have been drunk when I wrote this," he muttered.

Lily wiped her forehead with the edge of her scarf. The heat had become oppressive. Or maybe it was her thoughts.

She didn't know any longer whether Mason was coming back. A week ago she would have crossed her heart and sworn on a Bible that he'd return, but each day that passed after his promised three had eroded her confidence.

She had assumed during days four and five that weather or something else beyond Mason's control had delayed him. That wasn't uncommon. But yesterday the thought had crept into her mind that maybe he wasn't coming back at all. Perhaps he had truly believed he'd return when he had told her so that morning in the tent. But once free of her—and her grandfather's schemes—maybe he had reconsidered the situation and decided a clean break would be better.

Oh, he'd been sincere when he said he would come

back—she had no doubt of that. She had tasted his sincerity in his kiss. But a man could change his mind later.

Lily wrapped her arms around herself. Even if he did return, she had learned something about herself. She wouldn't be a good stay-behind wife. She had thought that she could be content making a home for them both while he ventured off for weeks or even months at a time in order to track down newspaper stories, but she knew now that so many uncertain homecomings would stress and eventually fracture her heart.

Not that he wanted to make her his bride. He didn't even love her. But if he did love her and did want to marry her . . .

"There's Mason," Dickon said.

Lily dashed to the tent entrance and lifted her hand to shield her eyes from the sun.

Yes, it was Mason, on his ragged horse.

And he had someone riding alongside him: a woman.

What was Mason doing with another woman? Riding away and deciding never to come back was one thing. But returning with a new woman was quite another—and, if she got past her anger for a moment, seemed vastly out of character.

Her palms starting to sweat, Lily waited as they drew nearer. Recognition jolted her. "Good Lord, Dickon, that's my aunt. Whyever is she with Mason?"

"Your aunt?" Dickon sucked in a breath and tried to cough at the same time, propelling himself into a brief choking fit. Lily absently pounded him on the back, her eyes on the riders, until Dickon twisted away. "I'm fine," he wheezed.

Their shadows streaming out in front of them, the two riders reached the edge of the camp. Instead of swinging toward the corral near Highfill's tent, they angled through the camp, heading straight for Lily and Dickon.

Mason looked older, weary, as if he'd spent the last several days straight on horseback instead of in the comfortable beds of Denver's hotels. His mouth was folded in a straight line that hadn't turned up in a smile in too many days.

Lily wanted to run out to greet them, but fear froze her in place. She didn't need Mason to speak to know that something was terribly wrong.

Then her feet moved, and she reached up to help her aunt dismount. "What happened?" Lily blurted out.

"Oh, sweetheart." Her aunt hugged her, but Lily couldn't lose the stiffness in her spine. "Don't look so terrified. Everything is fine."

"My family? My mother and sisters?"

"All well, last I heard."

Her knees suddenly shaky with relief, Lily turned to Mason, who still hadn't dismounted. "Then what's going on?"

Mason swung his leg over his horse and dropped to the ground. He grabbed the saddle for a moment, as if his legs had threatened not to hold him, then stepped toward Lily. "I ran into your aunt and convinced her to come out here with me. You had told me that you wished she'd go with you back to Boston, and I wanted to give you the chance to convince her in person."

He was lying. She knew it as surely as she'd known he was sincere when he pledged to come back.

She wanted to shake him until the truth came out. She wanted to kiss him until her mouth was bruised.

She held a trembling hand out to him. He pulled off one of his heavy riding gloves with his teeth and grabbed her hand in his. Then he tugged her to his side and, despite the presence of her aunt and Dickon, layered his arm across her shoulders. "Can we speak alone?" he asked softly.

No, she almost said. Whatever it was, she didn't want to hear it. She swallowed and gave him a short nod.

Mason didn't escort her away immediately. "Dickon," he said, "this is Miss Highfill. Would you please keep her company for a few moments?"

"Abner Dickon," her aunt said. "I never thought I'd see you again."

"Uh, hello, Evaline. Miss Highfill, I mean."

Lily allowed Mason to steer her away. Instead of moving them only out of hearing distance of Dickon and her aunt, Mason led her through the camp.

"Where are we going?" Lily asked, resisting his guiding arm.

"Your tent."

In broad daylight? That couldn't be good.

When they reached her tent, he flicked open the entrance flap and Lily ducked through. He rolled the flap up and tied it in place so that they would be clearly visible to anyone passing by. Protecting her reputation, she understood. Her uneasiness grew.

"Do you want to sit down?" he asked her.

"Should I?"

"Perhaps. In any case, if you do, then I can." He smiled, but his eyes were exhausted.

She perched on the cot, and he settled onto a stool, stretching his legs out in front of him with a sigh.

He pulled off his dusty hat, revealing damp corkscrews of dark hair, and dropped the hat in his lap. "I don't know how to say this. I rehearsed it for the past day or so, but I still don't know how to say it. Lily, your grandfather is a crook."

A crook? Ridiculous. She giggled out of sheer relief. "He's a businessman. I know some people—usually people who didn't get the better end of the deal—think that businessmen are dishonest, but—"

"The gem find is a swindle. Your grandfather, probably with Cecil St. John's help, planted those gems. Their scheme was to announce the find and then sell off shares in a gem mine. Worthless shares, at least to everyone but them."

"My grandfather has no interest in gems," she protested. "Neither does Cecil. I've been working with them all summer. They were shocked by the gem discovery: It meant we'd have to shut down the dig early. Plus, they didn't discover the first gem. Dickon did. Or do you think that Dickon is in on it, too?" The sheer absurdity of the idea of Dickon as a criminal made her laugh again.

"If he is, I couldn't find any proof of it."

The implication of Mason's words made the laughter die in her chest. The skin between her shoulder blades tightened. "Then what proof did you find?"

"Your grandfather and Cecil co-own this land."

Lily snorted. "That doesn't mean they're planting gems in the ground. If that's your so-called proof—"

"The night when I was told about the sapphires, I asked your grandfather whether he always bought the land on which he put his digs. He said usually, but not always. I checked that out, and he wasn't lying."

"I don't see—"

"However, all the land he did purchase, he purchased during the past year—not before he dug on them. And he's been doing these digs for six or seven years now. He's trying to establish a record of owning the land he digs on, when that's not truly the case. He probably thought that if he found gems on the first piece of land that he 'coincidentally' owned, investors would start asking questions. So he went back and bought the other land that he had dug on. But, Lily, he bought the other land before the sapphires were found. If it were an honest discovery, why would he do that?"

"That's not proof," she said weakly. "Just a bunch of suspicions."

"Also, when Cecil went away for those few days, he went to Denver to register a new business: St. John Gems."

"But that's Cecil. That doesn't mean my grandfather is involved."

"The application shows that he's Cecil's partner. The majority partner in the company."

Lily felt as if the air had been punched out of her lungs. It couldn't be true. Her grandfather couldn't be trying to swindle people. He had plenty of money from his other businesses.

It just wasn't possible. She didn't know why Mason had gone to so much trouble to dig up all these "facts" when the truth would vindicate her grandfather—

The story. The big story that Mason needed. An eastern financier finding gems during a fossil dig wasn't a big story. But an eastern financier planning to swindle hardworking people out of their money was. No matter that it was all lies.

"Lily—"

Her face felt stiff. "No."

"Lily, listen to me. You and I, we could leave here—"

"You're trying to ruin my grandfather's reputation and you expect me to want to leave with you?" She choked out a bitter laugh, then stood. "Out. Get out of here."

He rose to his feet. "All right. But I'm going to send your aunt—"

The reason why he'd brought her aunt from Denver crashed over her. He had thought Lily would be so devastated by his "proof" that she would need her aunt to cling to. Was that something a weaver of lies would consider?

Her certainty about her grandfather's innocence wavered like a candle flame hit by a gust of wind. Then it burned bright again. "I don't ever want to see you again. Go! Just go away."

Without another word, he slammed his hat on his head and left.

Chapter Nineteen

God, he'd handled that badly. Not that there had been a good way to handle it. But even in his head, while imagining what he would say, he had never blurted out, "Your grandfather is a crook."

Mason stomped along the camp path until his weary legs sent him the signal that his body wouldn't put up with much more. He'd spent thirty hours in the saddle over the last four days, tracking down the deeds or the former owners themselves of the land that Highfill had purchased in the past year. Telegrams had gotten answers to most of the questions, but he had ridden out to talk to as many people as possible in order to fill in the details.

Damn it. He'd told himself over and over that Lily would be angry at him for pulling together evidence that her grandfather was trying to con people into buying bogus mine shares. But he hadn't really believed she'd side with her grandfather against him. Not until she'd told him to get out, her eyes burning with disgust.

His feet suddenly wouldn't take him any farther.

He kicked over a bucket lying in front of one of the tents, sat down on it, and rested his head in his hands.

He must have been insane to think that she would consider running off with him after he told her what he had found. But that's what she had done: make him think crazy thoughts and do crazy things.

After the story ran, maybe she'd reconsider. . . . No. A man couldn't call a woman's grandfather a crook in front of the whole country and then hope to win her love back. Especially when her loving him—before he had decided to kick her family in the teeth—had been a miracle in the first place. A miracle he hadn't properly appreciated until he'd thrown it away.

Two pairs of legs appeared in front of him. Mason raised his head to peer at Dickon and Lily's aunt frowning down at him.

Mason moistened his mouth before he could speak. "I think that Lily might need you now," he told Miss Highfill.

"Well, that's why you dragged me out here, so I won't dawdle." She caught Dickon's eye. "Give him a hand, will you, Abner?"

Mason watched Miss Highfill stride away. Then he looked up at Dickon. "Abner?"

"My first name. I knew her back in Boston a long time ago, before I got married. What delayed you so long? I thought my Lily girl was going to climb the walls, waiting for you."

Well, that would be the last time she'd do that. "I was looking deeper into this gem business."

"And? Have there been other finds around here? I

hadn't heard of any before this summer, but I hadn't been looking, to be honest. The bones are my interest."

Mason hesitated. Although he was as sure as he could be that Dickon wasn't involved in the gem mine swindle, he didn't want to say anything before he had a chance to speak with Highfill and Cecil St. John. "I didn't turn up news of other recent finds, no."

"Well, recent finds isn't necessarily the issue, is it? These rocks have been here for millions of years. Are you going to see Highfill now?"

"If he's around."

"Oh, he's around. Not much digging going on these days. Some of the boys even left yesterday. I expect St. John will be with him, too." Dickon reached down and pulled Mason to his feet. "Let's go."

Mason followed Dickon, listening to him with only half an ear as he talked about how busy they'd been, packing the finds. Until Dickon had mentioned it, Mason hadn't noticed the stillness that pervaded the tent town. Flaps that hadn't been secured undulated in the finicky wind, giving Mason glimpses of the bare floors inside. Laundry still hung on a few tents' guy-lines, but the rare patches of color only emphasized how empty the rest of the camp was.

Two sides of Highfill's tent had been rolled up to allow breezes to blow in, and Mason could see both Highfill and Cecil St. John inside, lounging in chairs. Cecil said something too low for Mason to catch, and Highfill chuckled in response.

"Ahoy, Captain," Dickon called. "Permission to come aboard—or enter your tent?"

Half turning, Highfill raised his hand to beckon him in, then saw Mason and turned his gesture into a wide, welcoming wave. "My boy, where have you been? We were about to send out a search party for you."

Cecil, ever the sycophant, laughed, but his eyes hardened.

Mason nearly smiled. Cecil clearly thought his return was not cause for celebration. For once, Cecil was right.

Mason ducked inside. "I had to tie up some loose ends." Like bringing Lily's aunt here so Lily would have someone from her family to lean on when all hell broke loose. Like telling Lily the truth and making her hate him. Like eliminating any possibility that he and Lily could make a future together.

Highfill pointed to a chair next to Cecil, and Mason took it. Dickon continued to stand by the entrance.

"And there were a lot of details to chase down, so that took time." Mason crossed his legs and hooked his hat over his knee. "Company filings, property purchases, and so on. I went back quite a ways."

"Sounds tedious," the white-haired financier said mildly, but Mason had seen him stiffen. "But I guess that's why you do what you do and why I do what I do."

"Yes, these past few days did give my pride in being a good journalist quite a boost."

Highfill half smiled at the sally, then turned to Dickon. "Dickon, would you please close up the side of the tent before you leave?"

Ah. So he had been right. Dickon wasn't involved in the mine swindle.

His shoulders tight with resentment, Dickon undid the ties holding the rolled canvas with sharp jerks. The tent side swung down and hung loosely against the framework, and the interior of the tent became as dark as late dusk. Mason blinked rapidly to help his eyes adapt.

A match flared. Highfill lit a lamp and set it on the table next to him. If Mason wanted to look at Highfill, he had to squint.

Muttering under his breath, Dickon stomped out of the tent.

"Maybe you should give us the details of what you found," Highfill said, leaning back in his chair as if he did not have a care in the world. But he tapped one finger on his knee as he waited.

Mason expected to be filled with satisfaction. This was the moment when he was going to reveal that he'd toppled Highfill's plan to bilk hundreds of people out of their money. But satisfaction never came, only another pulse of regret.

He had always assumed his and Lily's affair would end, and he'd gotten some of the details right: Lily was angry with him, and guilt was slicing him raw. But he'd never imagined it would end with him threatening to publish a story about her grandfather's criminal schemes.

Mason took a deep breath and tried to pull his mind back to the present conversation. "You told me several days ago that you always bought the land you worked on, because you'd had problems in the beginning with farmers and such trying to renege on their promises to let you keep what you found. And you do own the lands you've worked on: I checked that out."

Highfill nodded, and Cecil began to relax into a smile.

"However"—Mason leaned forward—"you didn't buy most of that land until this year or last year. In some cases you waited more than five years after you'd done your digging on it to purchase the property."

Cecil lost his smile fast. "You must have gotten the dates wrong. Or people were lying to you."

"I saw several of the deeds for myself. You're right: The dates on them were fine. But the handwriting was not. The deeds had obviously been backdated by the current land-claim clerks. For instance, though one of those clerks had been working at his post for a year and a half, your deed with his handwriting on it had supposedly been filed six years ago. Another clerk had started work only this spring, but his handwriting was on a deed dated two years ago." Mason raised his eyebrows at Highfill. "You must have paid them both very well, for it took me quite a while to pull the story out of them." Turning to Cecil, he said, "And you featured prominently in both tales. Both clerks identified you well enough."

Mason waited for a reaction from Highfill, but the financier only murmured, "Fascinating," as if he were listening to a story about someone else.

"The gems were planted," Mason said bluntly. "You and St. John here planned to sell shares of a worthless mine, making thousands of dollars in the process."

Cecil, his face turning splotchy, opened his mouth,

but Highfill waved him into silence. "That's quite a leap in conclusions," Highfill said to Mason. "And, of course, unprovable."

Lily had said something similar, but of course she had assumed that her grandfather was innocent. Though Highfill hadn't admitted to the scam—he hadn't grown rich by being stupid—he wasn't wasting anyone's time by denying it, either.

"Unprovable, but damaging enough to scare off your mine investors."

"We should get rid of him," Cecil burst out. Jumping to his feet, he closed his hand around the butt of a pistol hanging by his side.

Mason froze. His rifle was still hanging off his saddle—not the most helpful place for it. Highfill had a shotgun resting near the entrance to the tent, but Mason would have to knock Cecil aside as he lunged for it—

"Settle down," Highfill snapped. "We are civilized men, Mr. St. John." He waited until Cecil dropped back into his chair, then turned his flinty stare on Mason. "Do I take it that you're threatening to run the story? Even though you have no proof?"

Mason let out his pent-up breath. Cecil was still heeding his master's commands—for now. "I wouldn't write the story unless I was convinced it was true. And the doctored deeds are proof."

"But you cannot say that you saw either me or St. John place a gem in a rubble pile and then sit back and wait for it to be discovered, can you?"

"I don't need to. The readers will draw their own conclusions—the right conclusions."

He should get up and walk away. The only reason why he had come back to the bone hunters' camp was to give Lily fair warning and try to persuade her to come away with him. It was time to cut this short and go.

But something in the way that Highfill tapped his fingers against his mouth as he thought—a gesture Mason had seen Lily make countless times—kept Mason in his chair.

"Every business hits a few bumps on its way," Highfill said slowly. "This is merely one of them, and not a very large one."

Only as large as the Rockies. But Mason kept his mouth shut. Now for the negotiations. Too bad Highfill and Cecil had nothing to negotiate with.

Highfill's bright blue eyes clamped on Mason. "Do you like Lily?"

Mason's brain stuttered. Luckily, Highfill didn't wait for him to respond. "I believe she has a strong liking for you. And I know that her mother would like to see her married before the year is out. . . ."

A deaf man wouldn't be able to mistake Highfill's meaning. A howl started clawing its way out of Mason's chest, but he didn't know if it would erupt as laughter or tears. He swallowed it down. "Sir, she would not have me—"

"She would come around. She's a biddable girl."

Biddable? This time Mason did laugh.

"Mr. Donnelly, I fail to see the humor. This is serious business."

"Serious business indeed," Cecil rasped. "You promised Lily to me, Highfill."

Highfill flicked a glance at Mason, but Mason didn't show surprise. He had guessed about this aspect of the two men's partnership as soon as he had put the pieces of the swindle puzzle together. It was another reason why he had brought Lily's aunt back to the camp with him. Shattering any possible future with Lily was one thing. Shattering that future and then allowing Cecil to get his paws on her was another. Her aunt would travel to Boston with Lily—she had told Mason so.

"Lily won't have you," Highfill told Cecil. "Though I've lobbied hard on your behalf, she's told me that she refuses to spend another meal alone with you, much less marry you. You messed that one up yourself by ignoring her for so long. Donnelly here did not ignore her." Highfill raised his eyebrows at Mason. "Well? Do you want her?"

Seven days ago, without knowledge of the swindle, he would have been pumping Highfill's hand and grinning from ear to ear like a man who'd just won the lottery. Now . . .

The tent flap was yanked up, and golden light flashed across the tent like the beam from a lighthouse lamp, blinding Mason for a heartbeat. He blinked, then recognized the silhouette in the entrance.

"You're still talking?" Lily asked, sounding amazed. "What is there to talk about?" She flipped her wrist. "Just throw him out."

Him clearly meaning Mason. "I was just leaving." He rose and faced Highfill. "Sir, thank you for your hospitality and your, ah, last offer, but the story has already gone." A lie—he hadn't written the story yet, though he'd start as soon as he reached Denver. Better say he had, though, as a form of security. Highfill's shotgun and his own rifle were still too far away, and Cecil was practically vibrating with fury.

Mason turned to Lily but couldn't look her in the eye. Couldn't stand to see the hatred there. "Miss Highfill, your servant, always."

Then he strode out the door and into the fierce Colorado sunshine. Its intensity was no match for the regrets blazing in his chest.

Lily crossed the tent and threw herself into the chair Mason had just vacated. She could still feel the warmth of his body in the canvas seat, and she squirmed.

As he'd passed her in the doorway, she'd involuntarily inhaled, breathing in his scent. And it had hit her like a fist, cramming memory upon memory until she thought she'd crumple under the weight of them. How could she have been so stupid? She'd known from the first article Mason had written that he didn't respect her grandfather, but Mason's show of courtesy toward her grandfather had dispelled her suspicions. She should have known better—should have known that he was just biding his time, looking for another way to stab her grandfather in print. Her grandfather, who had apparently been generous enough to try to negotiate with the scoundrel, based on Mason's words.

"What was the offer?" she asked her grandfather.

Highfill shook his head as if snapping himself out of his thoughts. "Sorry, my dear?"

"He thanked you for your last offer. What was it?"

With a snort, Cecil settled back in his chair. "You."

Lily straightened. "Me? What about me?"

"Your hand in marriage, you silly cow."

"I understand that you're angry," Highfill said sharply to Cecil, "but if you insult my granddaughter again, you will regret it."

Cecil snorted again but kept his mouth shut.

Wait a moment. "You offered me to Mason?" she asked her grandfather.

He shrugged. "It would have been dependent on your agreement, of course, but I wouldn't have suggested it if I hadn't believed you might be enthusiastic about the idea. In any case, he said no."

"But . . . why make the offer at all?"

Cecil cast a disgusted look at her. "To shut him up, of course."

"But he has no real proof. He knows he can't write the story, doesn't he?" She turned to her grandfather. "You must have persuaded him of that."

"You heard him. He's already written the story, my girl, and sent it off." Highfill pinched the bridge of his nose. "Damn. I should have just sent him on his way when he first arrived, but to have the announcement of our new mine made through him seemed like too good an opportunity to pass up. But he dug too deep."

Lily went still. *No. Oh, no.* "What did he find?" She almost didn't recognize the thin voice as her own.

"A few backdated deeds. Rather poor forgeries, it seems. A bit of business gone bad." Tapping his fingers against his lips, Highfill stared off into space again.

Gray seeped into the edges of her vision. Closing

her eyes, she breathed deeply until the faintness passed.

Mason had been telling the truth. And her grandfather had lied, using her and Dickon as dupes so he could set up a fake mining company. And when confronted, her grandfather had tried to buy Mason off with the offer of her hand in marriage.

She opened her eyes and stared at Cecil. Had her grandfather made Cecil the same offer as part of their business deal? Is that why her grandfather had kept pushing her at Cecil even when she'd said that she had no interest in him? Lily shuddered. She couldn't ask that. She could live with uneasy ignorance but not the ugly confirmation of her suspicions. The gem mine swindle was all she could handle at the moment.

"Well." Highfill stood and opened a trunk, from which he pulled three glasses and a bottle of Scotch. Uncorking the bottle, he poured two fingers' worth of whiskey into each glass, then passed one to Lily and one to Cecil. "I toast both successes and failures when it comes to business deals. Because a failure can sometimes be a better lesson than success." He clinked his glass against Cecil's. Lily tried to pull her glass out of reach, but her grandfather frowned at her. "Highfills never give up, girl. And Highfills always stick together." He grabbed her wrist and held her hand still so that he could tap their glasses together. Tipping his head backward, he tossed down the liquor.

Cecil also swallowed his Scotch, then grabbed the bottle and gave himself a generous refill.

Her drink untouched, Lily slapped her glass down

on the table, ignoring the whiskey that sloshed over the rim onto her fingers and the papers covering the table. She would not be a part of this.

"Here's a lesson learned." Cecil hoisted his drink. "Next time you have the bastard in your sights, don't miss."

Her grandfather frowned. "You hardly could have killed him in cold blood in the middle of my tent, St. John. That would have only given his story credence."

"Not just now. At the mine. Before he wrote the stupid story." He glared at Highfill. "The story that will toss us in prison."

"There's not enough proof, and if we don't issue the stocks—"

"You were the one who shot at us at the mine?" Lily interrupted. "That was you? Not a crazy miner?"

Cecil gulped his Scotch, then pulled a handkerchief from his pocket and wiped his mouth. "I knew he was going to be trouble, and I almost got rid of him—twice. I put some tacks in his saddle that would jab the horse once they started going downhill, but he managed to survive being thrown. And then I missed him at the mine. Fellow has all the luck."

Lily stared at him. He sounded almost rational as he talked about his attempts to kill Mason as coolly as if he were explaining a fossil's age. Her hands in her lap began to shake.

Highfill rose to his feet even as his voice dropped to a deadly hush. "Are you telling me that you shot at Lily? You shot at *my granddaughter*?"

"Not at her. I didn't even know she was there. At

him. Poking his nose around where it didn't belong. Even in Lily's direction, though she was mine! He wasn't good enough for her—"

Lily snatched up her glass and pitched it at Cecil. Cursing, he dodged, and the heavy tumbler thumped against the canvas wall behind him and dropped to the ground.

Evaline Highfill ducked through the half-open tent flap. She accidentally kicked the shotgun leaning there and grabbed it before it fell to the ground. "What on earth is going on in here? It smells like a saloon. Is this how you usually run your expeditions, Father?"

Cecil didn't seem to notice the intrusion. His eyes boring into Lily's, he levered himself out of his chair. "I've had enough of you." One hand dropped to his pistol.

"Don't touch that gun," Highfill barked.

All noise receded, and Lily could see only Cecil— and his hand drawing his pistol from its holster.

Half rising from her chair, Lily scrabbled on the table for anything else to throw but came up with only a handful of sketches she had made. Her heart jammed up in her throat, she tossed the papers at him. They exploded into a blizzard of white, and Lily threw herself down to the ground and began to crawl toward the tent sides swaying loosely in the light breeze.

A blast thundered through the tent. Papers spun crazily in the air like huge confetti. Cecil crumpled to the ground, blood freckling his face. The left side of his torso had disappeared into a gory mess.

The sketches settled, some sticking to Cecil as he lay unmoving.

Lily rose shakily to her feet, clamping her teeth against the urge to retch. The world flipped end over end once, as if she'd done a cartwheel, and she grabbed the center tent pole for support.

Her aunt lowered Highfill's shotgun from her shoulder. "No one," she told Cecil sternly, "tries to shoot my daughter."

Chapter Twenty

Lily rested her forehead against the window of her family's private Pullman car and watched the Massachusetts countryside flash past in a smear of green. As the patchwork of farmland gave way to clusters of houses and then to compact towns, the muscles along her spine tightened. It was with a great deal of effort that she kept her gloved hands—*a lady always wears gloves*—loose in her lap instead of curled into fists.

In her lap also lay the very first article Mason had written about her grandfather, its corners worn soft. The last lines she now knew by heart: *Even while his bright blue eyes sparkle with enthusiasm for his fossil finds, he cannot conceal the acquisitiveness that beats through his veins. Should the avarice of the businessman come in conflict with the generosity of the expedition financier, the businessman will always emerge the victor. For Charles Highfill is a natural moneyman, but not a natural philanthropist.*

When she had first met Mason, she accused him of

making her grandfather seem selfish. As it turned out, Mason had come the closest to identifying the weakness in her grandfather's character. But even Mason had underestimated his greed.

There was a knock at the door, and a conductor poked his head into the car. "Ten minutes to Boston."

"Are you anxious?" Dickon asked from the seat across from her.

Lily turned her head to reply, but Dickon was staring at her aunt Evaline—no, her mother—and waiting for her reply.

"A little," Evaline said. "It's been twenty-two years since I left." She touched a forefinger to his hand resting on the seat between them and traced his knuckles. "But I have other, happier thoughts preoccupying me."

Lily bent down to inspect the hem of her skirt so she could conceal her expression, afraid that her simmering anger would show on her face. During the past week, in Denver and on the train, Evaline and Dickon had been mooning over each other like first loves. When Dickon wasn't around, Evaline would talk to Lily about how wonderful Dickon was. When Evaline wasn't around, Dickon would sing her praises to Lily.

She didn't begrudge them their happiness. But the lies—always the lies—continued to sting like a raw wound.

She must have made a noise, for Evaline wrested her gaze away from Dickon and reached over and patted Lily's hand. "Everything will be better once we're in Boston. Your mother will keep you so busy that—"

"My mother?"

Evaline didn't look away. "I'm used to calling her that. You're used to calling her that. Why should we rearrange everything?"

"Because it's important!" Lily crossed her arms over her chest. She knew she looked like a mutinous twelve-year-old—and it was also the way she felt. "Don't you think it's important? Don't you care?" The last was a low blow. Her aunt had raised her for eight years and had last week killed a man with a shotgun for her. Of course Evaline cared.

Dickon started to rise. "Maybe I'll give you ladies a little space—"

"Oh, no you don't." Lily stabbed a finger at him. "If I'm not mistaken, you have an equal share in this conversation about my parentage." She waited a beat. "Or am I wrong?"

This was the final secret—the one that had remained hidden even after Evaline's impromptu declaration that she was Lily's mother: Dickon was Lily's father. The whole truth had been revealed in the way Dickon hadn't been able to take his eyes away from Evaline except to throw looks at Lily that were a mixture of tenderness and astonishment.

Dickon settled back in his seat. He glanced at Evaline, then back at Lily. "No, you're not wrong. Do you want to hear the story, or have you figured it all out yourself?"

The last bit of gruffness sounded like the old Dickon she knew. "I think I understand the major points. You two met, Evaline got pregnant and was sent out to Denver, and my mother"—even she was having trouble calling Mary anything but her mother—"raised me here in Boston. What I don't know is where you were during all this."

Dickon rubbed his chin. "Let me fill in some of the details. Maybe that'll explain more. Twenty-some years ago, Evaline was helping recently arrived immigrants at an international aid society, where she met my sister. Eventually I met Evaline through my sister and, uh—" He coughed.

"You had a whirlwind romance?" Lily had meant the words to sound sarcastic, but they came out wistful instead.

She'd had her own whirlwind romance—although a hurricane romance might be a better description of it, given the destruction that it had wrought in the end. No, that made it sound like no one had made any choices and that devastation had been inevitable. She had made those bad choices. She had mistrusted Mason and told him she never wanted to see him again. And he had taken her at her word.

Evaline curled her hand in Dickon's. "My father, needless to say, was not happy, especially when I refused to name the man I'd been with. Before I knew it, he had lined up half a dozen desperate men willing to take on a pregnant bride. The Highfill name outweighed their discomfort with my situation. But I wouldn't have any of them." A smile flickered across her eyes. "Those were some battles, believe me. But your mother came up with a solution. She had been having trouble conceiving, and she suggested that she raise you as her own. So I, your mother, and my brother—

your 'father'—went out to Denver for several months. They returned to Boston with you, claiming you as their own. I remained in Denver."

"But my mother—Mary—had her own children afterward," Lily said.

Evaline shrugged. "That happens sometimes."

"Meanwhile," Dickon interjected, "I was in Boston, trying to find Evaline. But no one knew where she was. I even joined Highfill's business to try to track her down. There were rumors that she'd gone west, but no one had any details, and Highfill wouldn't talk about it, even after I'd plied him with a full bottle of good Irish whiskey one night. But when I hadn't heard from her or seen her for a full year, I decided that she'd lost interest—found someone else, most likely. I didn't know about you, Lily, until just a few days ago."

Secrets! Always secrets in this family.

Evaline leaned forward, her eyes intense. "Lily, there's another reason why I referred to Mary as your mother. Because in the eyes of society, she still is." Evaline paused. "You may not want to hear this right now, but your chances of an advantageous marriage are far better if you're known as Mary's legitimate daughter than my illegitimate one. The Highfill name is only so strong."

Lily could feel her lip curl. "A marriage to a man like Cecil St. John? Thank you, but I'll pass."

"If your mother were here," Evaline said calmly, "she'd tell you that a lady does not sneer."

"A lady does not swear, either," Lily shot back, knowing that her voice was far less calm than Evaline's, "but if the subject of an advantageous marriage is raised around me again, that's likely to be my response."

Evaline pressed her lips together and fell silent, but Dickon leaned forward. "One bad apple does not taint the whole batch."

"That bad apple twice tried to kill Mason—and then tried to kill me! Forgive me if I'm not inclined to leap back into being courted by greedy bluebloods."

Besides, Mason was still out there—somewhere. All she had to do was find him and persuade him to give her a second chance.

She snorted. Yes, that was all. Too bad the country was so darn big and she had little idea of how to find him in it. Even if he did get another newspaper job, he'd be constantly on the move. He had told her so time and again.

And finding him was the easy half of the equation. Convincing him to forgive her and take her with him was a task even Hercules would have shied from. He had been a reluctant suitor even before she had tossed him out of her life.

"There are fellows out there without a greedy bone in their body," Dickon said. "Take Peter, for example. That boy is head over heels for you. He comes from a very fine family, and—"

"Dickon, did you tell your other daughters how important social prestige was to a happy marriage?"

He glowered at her. "I told them to mind their manners, and that honey would catch more flies than vinegar. Advice I'm entirely willing to pass on to you, Lily girl."

Flushing, she turned back to the window. She shouldn't be here, on this train to Boston. She should have stayed in Denver and tried harder to find Mason. She'd asked for him at the telegraph office, the livery stables, and the hotels, but she hadn't uncovered a trace. He'd vanished as abruptly from her life as he had entered it. But in the crazy days after Mason's accusation and Evaline's shooting of Cecil, and without any easy way to find Mason, Lily had mistakenly taken the easiest solution, following the path already laid out.

Unfortunately, a few minutes outside of the Boston train station was the wrong time to have the realization that she should have remained in Colorado.

Also, had she remained in Colorado, maybe she wouldn't have had to acknowledge that she was a daughter twice unwanted—unwanted by her adoptive mother, who had sent her to Denver eight years ago; now unwanted by her real mother, who refused to claim Lily as her own. The double rejection sank like a barbed fishhook into her heart, causing pain every time she mentally touched on it.

"Lily, it's not that I don't want you as my daughter," Evaline said, as if reading her mind. "You *are* my daughter. I know that, you know that, and Mary and Abner know that. But the world doesn't need to know that. Even your sisters, Emily and Annabelle, don't need to know." Evaline shuddered. "And your grandfather absolutely should not know who your real father is. I can't imagine what he might do to Abner. Even though Abner has quit, and your birth is twenty years past, your grandfather would find a way to get revenge on him."

Oh. Put that way . . .

"Don't worry about me," Dickon said. Gruffly, of course.

Evaline continued, gazing at Lily, "Also, your mother—Mary—raised you. I watched you reach adulthood, but it was Mary's letters full of advice and encouragement that you listened to, not me."

Evaline's voice twisted at the end of the final sentence, and Lily frowned. Had she really disregarded Evaline's advice? She hadn't thought so. In fact, she thought that she'd paid far more attention to Evaline's words than to her mother's letters.

But there had been a handful of times when her mother's advice and Evaline's had collided. And Lily had invariably followed her mother's suggestions instead of Evaline's.

And as much as Lily didn't want to admit it right now, each letter from her mother *had* contained praise of some sort, even if it was about something as minor as Lily improving her penmanship. Of course, every letter had concluded with *Remember your manners, darling.* But in her mother's mind, that phrase was the equivalent of *Be good and safe.* Not uncaring letters. Not at all.

Had her mother not wanted to send her to Denver eight years ago? Had Evaline requested that Lily be sent out to her?

Lily opened her mouth to ask that question, but the carriage lurched, and she grabbed Mason's article on her lap before it could slip off. The train slowed, grumbling. The people on the fringe of the crowd on the station platform slid past their window, and soon smiling faces and merrily waved handkerchiefs filled Lily's view. One more touch of the brake, a half dozen clacks of the rotating wheels, and the cars wheezed to a halt.

Pain shooting through her hands made Lily look down. Her hands were clenched into tight fists. Taking a deep breath, she flexed her fingers and stood.

Dickon pushed the door open and leaned out. "I see the carriage," he called over his shoulder. "I'll go get our baggage headed in the right direction. Be back in a few minutes." He leaped down into the swirling throng, swallowed from view almost immediately.

Lily smoothed her dress, then stepped to the open door. Her mother's blue and white carriage shone like a jewel among the drab black and brown carriages that surrounded it. Lily scanned the crowd, searching for her mother's tall driver, a skeleton-thin but tough-as-wire man named Mick.

There he was, shouldering his way through the mass of people on the platform. And her sisters, Emily and Annabelle, were just behind him. When they caught sight of her, they began waving their arms over their heads in an unrefined manner their mother would have scolded them for. Lily laughed and waved back.

Mick must have developed a limp or another infirmity since Lily had seen him last, for he kept stopping every few seconds and glancing down, perhaps to catch his breath. The threesome's progress through the crowd was agonizingly slow.

"Emily and Annabelle are here with Mick," she told

Evaline as she turned and went back inside the car to gather the little things she'd brought with her. She folded Mason's article carefully and slipped it into her reticule.

"Where is your mother?"

"She always refuses to come to the station. Too noisy, and too many people. She will undoubtedly have tea and sandwiches waiting for us when we arrive at home."

Evaline smiled. "She hated the train trip to Denver that we took before you were born. I wondered for a few months if we'd ever manage to get her on a train going back east. I think she wrote me letters for years about the horrors of train travel."

A footstep scraped on the little ladder at the door. "So this is what Highfill's private car looks like inside," a musical and very familiar voice said. "I've often wondered."

Lily spun around. Her mother—short, plump, marvelously garbed, and of course wearing gloves— beamed at her. "Welcome home, Lily darling." Eyes beginning to glisten with tears, she held out her arms.

"Amazing." Mason's former editor, Bill Thornton, placed the article down in the center of his desk with the reverence he might show a relic of a saint. Then he stabbed the page with his forefinger. "*This* is what I knew you could do. I'd hoped that seeing Gregory Cutler's name in your place would get your juices flowing again, but I had no idea you'd come back with anything like this."

Right. If his editor had truly hoped to nudge him

into writing better stories, he wouldn't have fired him.

"Glad you like it," Mason said dryly.

"Like it? It's the most astounding story you've written in three years."

And the most painful. With every word he wrote about Highfill's campaign of deception, he saw Lily in his mind, telling him to get out. He should have known that her loyalty to her family would overrule her love for him. Even after she read this story, she would probably still believe in her grandfather's innocence.

"Since I'm no longer on the *Herald* staff, I'm looking for a flat fee."

"Who said you weren't on the *Herald* staff?"

"The *Herald*, last month. Remember the editor's note about it?"

"Oh, that." Bill waved his hand dismissively. "A misunderstanding. I tried to fix it before the paper was printed, but it was too late. You know how that can happen. But it was probably a shock for you to see that. So let's give you back pay for, say, six weeks, as compensation."

"No, let's admit that you did fire me without having the courtesy to inform me directly. And then you can give me two hundred for the article."

"And you'll be back on staff after this."

Mason smiled. "No."

"No?" Bill laughed. "Then what's in it for me aside from one measly article?" His eyes narrowing, he demanded, "Who are you working for next? The *Sun*? The *Telegrapher*?"

"No one. I'm taking more time off." Mason stood. "But if you think I should take this article to the *Telegrapher* instead—"

"Oh, sit down. We know each other too well to do this. One fifty."

"One ninety, and I promise not to write for the *Telegrapher* or the *Sun* for three months."

"Fine, fine." Bill held out his hand and Mason shook it. "It's the most expensive article I've ever bought, you know. But the way it ends, with this Cecil St. John's being 'accidentally' killed, will have our readers gasping."

"Yes," Mason said neutrally. He'd heard about Cecil's death while he'd been in Denver, but no one could supply him any information beyond that the gun had gone off "accidentally" in Evaline's hands.

He had been nearly finished writing his article when he had learned of the shooting. He had almost tossed the story in the fire—had almost convinced himself that, with Cecil dead, Highfill would be less likely to succumb to the insatiable greed that had spurred him into the mine swindle. But Highfill had been the leader of the plan, not the follower. How many other crooked business deals had Highfill executed, ruining innocent investors? This way, with the article published, Highfill's power would be tamed, at least momentarily.

But for a crazy second, Mason had stretched the article toward the flames. With the article gone, he could return to the bone hunters' camp and take Highfill up on his offer of Lily's hand.

Brutal truth had pulled his hand away from the

fire. No matter how much he wanted her, Lily did not want him. Even if she did finally accept that her grandfather was a crook, she wasn't going to thank Mason for exposing that.

Also, he'd never killed a story just to make life easier for himself. He had enemies from the Mississippi to the Pacific who could testify to that. This story might reduce to impossibility any chance of him persuading Lily to forgive him, but there were others out there whom he needed to protect: the people who'd happily give their life's savings to Highfill when he concocted his next illegal scheme.

But now he knew what his mentor Old Joe had meant when he said that idealism wouldn't keeping him warm at night.

"So, if you're not writing for me, what are you going to do?" Bill asked as he stood. It was a casual question, a prelude to good-bye, but Mason answered anyway.

"I think I'm going to write a book. And spend a few months in San Francisco. See what it's like to live in one place."

Bill chuckled and opened the office door for him. "Good luck. And let me know when you want to come back to work for me. Oh, wait, there's just one thing."

"Yes?"

"The girl. Highfill's granddaughter. You mention her once or twice but don't say what happens to her or what she knew about the mine swindle."

Mason froze. "I don't know what happened to her. And she didn't know anything."

"You're sure about that?"

"Pretty sure." Absolutely sure.

"Then I'm going to cut her out of the story. She seems irrelevant, and the way you have it now, you'd leave people wondering about her."

"Ah." Irrelevant? He almost laughed. She had been the focus of his world. If anything, the mine swindle had been the irrelevant part of his time spent at the bone hunters' camp—except that, in the end, that swindle had wrestled Lily away from him. "Go ahead. Cut her out of the story." Too bad she couldn't be exorcised from his heart so easily.

Chapter Twenty-one

L ily glanced up from the newspaper at the first click of icy snowflakes against the sitting room windows.

Unlike those in Denver, where blizzards roared into town with little warning, Boston storms gave fair notice of their arrival. The temperature dropped, the air turned tight, and the windows rattled. Then, after all this fanfare, the snow came.

She dropped her eyes to the train timetable in the newspaper. Even though it was late December, with January right around the corner, she hadn't thought of snow. She needed to make a decision soon, or the weather would make the decision for her.

Her mother picked up her cup of tea and took a sip. "Seeing snow outside always makes me appreciate drinking tea inside," she said.

In the chair beside her, Evaline nodded. "Much as a hot summer day makes me appreciate a cold lemonade fortified with whiskey."

"Evaline!" her mother exclaimed, but then laughed.

From their spot on the settee near the fireplace, Emily and Annabelle giggled. Dickon, practically a fixture in the house, let out a deep chuckle.

Lily smiled. Her mother and Evaline's delight in each other's company was infectious, bringing extra sunlight into any room they entered. This little salon that hosted the afternoon ritual the ladies had fallen into—her mother embroidering, Lily reading the newspaper, her sisters exchanging gossip, and Evaline writing letters to friends back in Denver—was often filled with laughter. If Dickon was available, he'd stop by to join in the merriment. He was no longer working for her grandfather, but her mother Mary had made it very clear that Dickon would always be welcome in her house.

Her smile dimmed. If she left, she'd miss this.

Three months in Boston had reconciled her to her strange, secret parentage almost without her noticing it. Dickon and Evaline had not claimed Lily as their own, even within the family. And her mother, aware that Lily now knew the truth, had not changed their relationship in the slightest, doling out encouragement and social advice as enthusiastically as she had before—and just as she did with her two blood daughters, Lily could see now. Lily was as likely to get scolded for pouring tea improperly as Annabelle was for being too chatty with gentlemen.

Another blast of snow skittered against the window, and Lily glanced outside again. This room overlooked the street, and she could see men in long dark coats clutching their hats and bending into the wind.

One man drew her attention like a lodestone. Something about him—the shape of his shoulders, or his height, or the way he carried himself—reminded her of Mason. Her heart began beating slow and heavily. She forced herself to look away, but it still took several long moments before her pulse regained its steady rhythm.

Was she going to stay in Boston for the rest of her life, hoping that she'd somehow run into Mason on the street but knowing that she wouldn't? Or was she going to find him?

She looked at the small silver clock on the mantel, then down at the timetable again. A train traveling through Denver would leave Boston within the hour.

"Peter Cooperston asked about you at the Bacons' party last night," Annabelle told her. "He asks about *you* every time I see him." Annabelle's surprise and dismay was etched in each syllable. She was the beauty in the family, and having a gentleman ask her about one of her sisters happened so infrequently that Annabelle didn't quite know how to react. Lily smothered a smile.

"He's a nice boy," Lily said, injecting disinterest in her voice out of habit. *A puppy* was how she'd described him to Mason, but Peter had proven to be more stalwart than that, and she often eventually drifted to his side at any party they happened to be at together, where they talked of fossils and the West. But after a few moments she'd have to walk away, knowing that the eyes of her family were on her.

She had had to be so careful these last few months. If she suggested to her mother or aunt that she had taken even the slightest notice of a man, they would find ways for her to "happen" to run into him at the park or during a lecture.

She wasn't seeking a man to fall in love with. She had already found him. What she needed to do now was find him again.

"Peter wondered if you'd be at the Richards' party on Saturday," Annabelle continued, a pout in her voice. "I said that I thought you would."

Lily took a deep breath. Really, she'd made the decision to find Mason even before she'd returned to Boston. Now she must go through with it. "Actually, I won't be at the Richardses' party. I'm leaving for Denver this evening."

"What?" howled four feminine voices.

Dickon, his expression darkening, said, "Would you repeat that, please?"

"I'm leaving for Denver this evening." It was easier to say it the second time; maybe saying it twice unraveled a strange enchantment that had cloaked her these past few months, for energy surged through her arms and legs.

"But why leave at all, sweetheart?" Her mother's eyes dropped to the newspaper in Lily's lap, then rose again to Lily's face. "I thought you were happy here."

"I am." Lily folded the newspaper, got to her feet, and moved to the window. The man who had reminded her of Mason was gone. She turned to face her family and mentioned the name that had been banned from conversation in this house. "I'm going to try to find Mason, you know."

Emily paled. "What? But why? That man tried to destroy our family."

"No." It came out harsher than she had intended, but she wouldn't soften it. She was tired of Mason being blamed for her grandfather's wrongdoings. Their mother should have told Annabelle and Emily the truth instead of letting Grandfather fill their ears with excuses, half-truths, and a few outright lies. "Grandfather was the one who made the choices that led to the scandal. If he hadn't agreed to Cecil's mad scheme in the first place and then tried to hoodwink Mason into announcing the sapphire finds, we wouldn't be in this situation."

One of the worst things that her grandfather had privately admitted in the days following Cecil's death was that he had deliberately chosen Lily to convince Mason to leave, knowing that her attempts would only heighten Mason's suspicions that something big was happening at the expedition. "You never could lie worth a damn," her grandfather had said. "I knew he'd see right through you. And if we could get a good story from Mason Donnelly about our sapphire finds, then we'd get ten times as many investors as we'd first hoped. We had planned to wait until the very end of the dig season to seed the rubble piles with sapphires, but when Donnelly arrived, the opportunity for publicity was too great."

She and Mason had been manipulated from the very beginning.

She looked again at the mantel clock. On either side of the clock were framed sketches that she'd done of the strange horn she had discovered on the day Mason rode into the expedition's camp. "I must hurry. The train leaves in an hour."

"And what if you do find this Mason Donnelly?" Annabelle demanded. "What then?"

"Then I shall apologize for not believing him."

Annabelle's eyes rounded. "Apologize?"

Lily almost laughed at Annabelle's astonishment. "And if he accepts my apology, I shall tell him again that I love him."

That certainly fastened everyone's eyes on her, and silence enfolded the family for a brief, beautiful moment.

Then Emily—Emily, who was the quietest of the three sisters and rarely made a scene—leaped to her feet. "Lily, you can't leave us to join that . . . that *traitor*. You're a Highfill. And Highfills always stick together."

During the week Mason had been at the dig, he had stood by her side, first helping with her plans to entice Cecil and then simply wanting to be with her. And at the very end he had asked her to run away with him. In contrast, Grandfather had bartered her hand in marriage to Cecil over a gemstone swindle, had used her to keep Mason around the camp, and had then offered her as a bribe to Mason to keep him quiet.

Lily sighed. "No, Em. Not always."

Emily was about to protest again, but Evaline reached out and laid a hand on her arm. "Emily, when you fall in love, you'll understand."

Lily hoped so—and hoped that Emily wouldn't make as much of a muck of it as she had done.

But Emily wouldn't be appeased. "I'm going to tell Grandfather. He'll stop you." She dashed out of the room, presumably to send a servant to Highfill with a note.

"He won't be able to stop me," Lily told her remaining family. "There's no time."

"In that case, I'll help you with your packing," her mother told her.

She was so thrown by her mother's acceptance that she said the first thing that came into her mind. "Have you ever packed anything?" This house had twelve servants.

"No. So I'll just supervise." Then she took Lily's hand and led her out of the parlor and up the stairs.

"I'd appreciate it if you didn't try to talk me out of this," Lily said as soon as her mother shut the door behind them and sat on the plush chair near the entrance to Lily's dressing room.

"Lily darling, you have that stubborn set to your mouth that I know so well. If I couldn't make you put roses in your hair during my wedding to Mr. Grant, why would I think that I can make you give up a trip to Denver to find Mason Donnelly?"

"Thank you." Lily pulled from the dressing room the battered trunk she had hauled between Boston and Denver four times now. Pulling her warmest dresses and jackets off their hooks, she slanted a glance at her mother, who was making no pretense of helping. Longtime habit made Lily ask, "But do you think I'm doing the right thing?"

Letting out a short laugh, her mother said, "I hope

so. I don't know this Mason Donnelly, so I have no firsthand knowledge from which to form an opinion. I only know that Dickon esteems him and your grandfather hates him. But I never would have imagined your grandfather and Cecil concocting such a scheme to rob people, so you shouldn't rely on me as a good judge of character. You know Mr. Donnelly better than the rest of us, Lily."

It wasn't a wholehearted endorsement, but it was good enough. Lily shoved heavy petticoats into the trunk, then topped them with wool stockings. When she arrived in Denver, she'd be throwing herself into the teeth of winter.

"Lily . . ." Her mother paused. She seemed to be struggling for words. "I'd hoped that when you came home this time, you were coming home for good. You're not my daughter by birth, but you are the daughter of my heart. I was with Evaline when she had you, and you'll always be my firstborn." Her eyes began to shine with welling tears. "It nearly tore my heart out when Evaline suggested that I send you out to Denver to live with her for a while. But in all fairness I couldn't refuse. Also," she added, laughter replacing the tears in her eyes, "you were being an absolute brat."

The last jagged edge of Lily's doubts about her mother was finally smoothed away. Her mother hadn't wanted her to leave, hadn't wanted to exile her to Denver. And her mother didn't want her to leave now—Lily could see it in her still-watery eyes.

"I know I was a brat. I spent hours devising ways to drive Mr. Grant away. I'm glad it didn't work."

"I as well."

"When I went to Denver the first time, I didn't want to go. When I returned to Denver after your wedding, I thought I had no choice: I didn't fit in here any longer."

Her mother made a sound of protest. Lily shook her head and continued. "But this time I want to go to Denver. And not to Denver, really, but to wherever Mason is. Does that make sense?"

Her mother stood and hugged her. "Of course it does, darling. I would have followed Mr. Grant across the sea, had he tried to get away. But if you can't locate your Mr. Donnelly, remember that you always have a home here."

"I will."

Her mother stepped back and wiped her eyes. "I'll get one of the footmen to strap your trunk closed for the journey," she said, opening the door. She nearly ran into Dickon, who was standing outside, his hand raised to knock. "Oh!"

"Sorry, Mrs. Grant. I just wanted a quick word with Lily before she left."

Lily pulled the door open wider. "Come in. I was hoping you'd come to say good-bye."

God, he hated this cold. It wasn't much different from the cold that locked down over the plains or the cold that howled through the Rockies, but still, he hated it. Mason stamped his feet to get the blood moving through them and stared again at the house across the street.

Now that he thought of it, though, he also hated

the cold of the plains and the Rockies. But if he could live with the cold in those places, he could live with it here.

He was just stalling. He needed to cross the street and knock on that door.

But his feet remained rooted where they were. What if Lily refused to see him?

Well, then he'd at least know where he stood with her. And he could leave this damn cold city and return to San Francisco, where the fog could chill your bones but snow was a rarity.

He adjusted his hat, tugged at his coat. Then he stepped out of the doorway he had been sheltering in and walked across the street to the tall, elegant house on the other side.

He knocked on the huge door. Seconds crept by, each one longer than the last. Mason found himself shifting from foot to foot. Finally the door swung inward, revealing a man in livery. Behind him, setting her foot on the first step of a carpeted staircase, was a blond-haired young woman in a long dark blue dress. One of Lily's sisters, he would bet.

"Sir?" the butler said. "May I help you?"

Mason returned his attention to the man. "I'd like to speak with Miss Lily Highfill, if I may."

"And your name, sir?"

He swallowed. "Mason Donnelly."

The butler's eyes flickered, and Mason tensed. "Ah." But the butler made no immediate move to summon footmen to toss Mason down the front stairs. That was a good sign.

The door opened a few inches wider. "If you would—" the butler began to say, but a blue lightning bolt flashed past him, cutting off his words. Two feminine hands planted themselves on Mason's chest and pushed.

He stumbled backward, and one of his feet slid in the snow. Wonderful. He was going to topple over into a snowbank after being attacked by a girl. Very dignified. But he managed to right himself and took a determined stride toward the door.

"Stay *out!*" the girl shrieked at him. Her face twisted in fury, she slammed the door shut a mere two inches from his nose.

He waited a moment to see if the butler might reopen the door, but the only change was a tiny *snick* as the bolt was thrown, locking him out.

His knees suddenly unsteady, Mason turned and headed back to the street.

He glanced over his shoulder, and a curtain near the door twitched. Who was watching him? One of the servants? Lily's sister? Or Lily?

Not knowing what else to do, he resumed his spot in the doorway across from Lily's house.

All right. The direct approach hadn't worked. But his ejection from the doorstep could have been worse. Lily herself could have slammed the door in his face. And at least he now knew that there were no standing orders to keep him out—though that could be because no one had expected him to show up.

He blew on his hands, tucked them in his pockets, and studied the house through the thin gauze of snow swirling down from the sky. He wasn't going to give up after only one setback.

He could try again later and hope that Lily's sister wasn't lurking around the door.

He could wait here and hope that Lily left the house for a walk . . . in the snow. No, that didn't sound probable.

Or he could go to an inn, settle in and get his bearings after the endless cross-country train ride, and tomorrow morning write her a note asking if he could see her.

He hated waiting. But sending a note sounded like the smartest solution.

Dickon squared his shoulders and put on his bulldog face. "I'm coming with you to Denver."

Lily blinked. It was a nice offer—except it wasn't an offer; it was a command. "No, you're not. Dickon, I need to do this without my family's assistance, and that includes yours. I need to do this on my own."

"Why?" Dickon demanded.

"Because it was my belief in and loyalty to my family that made me push Mason away! So when I do find him"—*when*, not if—"I need to be on my own. I need to have already chosen him. Do you understand?"

Dickon's mouth flattened into a line and he sighed. "I understand enough to let you do it your way—and I understand you well enough that you'd put up a royal fight if I insisted on joining you. But why do you think he'll be in Denver? He's not a man who spends time in towns, even towns out west. He's a traveler. A wanderer."

She had been hoping that no one would ask her this, for her reason seemed puny. "We spoke once about meeting in Denver in early January. No promises were made . . . but it's the best chance I have now."

His expression looked faintly pitying as he asked, "And if he doesn't show?"

Oh, he was going to like this even less. "Then I'll go to San Francisco. Mason has a good friend who lives there. I think I can convince him to put me in contact with Mason." No need to mention that all she knew about this "good friend" was his first name, Joseph, and that he used to be a journalist.

But Dickon was shaking his head again anyway. "Going to Denver is one thing. You have a place to live there. You know people there. But San Francisco . . . that's madness."

Lily lifted her chin. "Anticipating that Mason might not show up next month, I've already hired someone who used to live in San Francisco to escort me out there and help me search the city for him." Devlin Hills had come highly recommended through Peter Cooperston's older brother, who had spent time in San Francisco building up his family's shipping business. "I'll be fine."

Billy, one of the footmen, entered the room, forestalling any further argument from Dickon. "Are you ready to go to the station, miss?" he asked Lily.

She would never be entirely ready to leave her family, but if she was going to pursue Mason, it had to be done. "Yes, Billy. Thank you."

He swung the trunk onto his shoulder and disappeared out the door, his footsteps soon ringing on the back stairs.

Lily stepped forward and gave Dickon a hug. "I'll write to you, of course."

He returned the hug awkwardly, patting her on the shoulder. "I'd appreciate that." Swiping one knuckle across his eyes, he abruptly left.

Alone finally, Lily pulled in a deep breath. Icy flakes tinkled on the glass panes, and a gust shook the window in its frame. The room had grown darker in the ten minutes she had been in here, the storm shutting out even the weak winter sunlight.

Her mother reappeared in the doorway, wearing a heavier dress. "I'm going to the station with you, Lily darling. I want to see you off properly."

Lily's throat tightened, and she had to swallow before she managed to say, "That would be lovely, Mama."

The wind slapped Mason's face as he left the shelter of the doorway, and the driving snow pricked his skin. Tugging his hat down to shield his eyes, he trudged down the street toward an inn at the corner, its heavy sign rocking in the knife-edged gusts.

The sound of hooves clip-clopping on cobblestones made him turn his head and peer down the alley that ran alongside Lily's house.

The end of the alley must open onto a rear courtyard, for he could see only half of the brilliant blue and white coach that stood there. A footman with a trunk on his shoulder walked past the mouth of the alley, vanishing almost as soon as he appeared.

Mason came to a dead stop. That was Lily's trunk. He'd seen it in her tent in Colorado.

A chill colder than the snow feathering onto his shoulders settled in his chest, making inhaling difficult. Several possible scenarios spiraled through his thoughts. The worst one broke away from the pack, demanding his attention: Perhaps Lily had been recently married, and her possessions were being moved to her new husband's home.

Damn it, if he'd left San Francisco only a few days earlier—

"I'm just so excited, Mama."

Lily.

He couldn't see her, but he could hear her voice ringing off the courtyard walls.

God, she was there, only twenty feet away. But his stupid feet wouldn't follow his brain's commands, and he stood there, frozen in place.

"I wish you all the best, darling," said another voice—probably her mother's. Her next words were lost as wind sang around his ears. Then: "—be a married woman the next time I see you."

So Lily wasn't married. Yet.

He had to talk to her.

His feet finally came unstuck from the ground, but only just in time for him to dodge the carriage charging out of the alley. As it passed, Mason glimpsed Lily's profile. The color was bright in her cheeks, and she was laughing.

Determination flooded him. Wherever she was going, he would follow. Ducking his head into the building snowstorm, Mason began to jog after the carriage.

He'd worked up a sweat by the time Lily's carriage finally stopped its rush through the narrow Boston streets. Mason blinked and tried to get his bearings.

They were at the train station.

The sea of people milling around the station thickened as he pushed closer to the carriage and the train platforms. Lily appeared in the doorway of the carriage, then stepped down and was swallowed from view.

Was she leaving, or was she saying good-bye to someone else? She must be leaving: That was her trunk on the carriage.

—be a married woman the next time I see you. Jesus, perhaps she was on her way to meet her husband-to-be.

But on which train? Four waited on rails alongside the mobbed platforms, and two, clouds of steam rising from their engines, looked ready to leave at any moment. Of course, those two were the trains farthest from each other. He'd have time to check only one of them.

Mason grabbed the coat sleeve of a uniformed train porter. "Excuse me, but where's that train going?" he shouted over the hubbub, and pointed at the nearest one.

"Newport," the porter answered.

Newport. The Highfills might have a house in Newport. They undoubtedly had friends there.

"What about that train?" Mason asked. He pointed

to a line of railroad cars three tracks away. Steam billowed out of the hissing locomotive at the head of the procession.

"New York, Pittsburgh, Cincinnati, and Denver."

Denver?

Denver.

Denver! Maybe—just maybe—she was traveling to Denver to meet him, as they had half planned so many months ago.

His pulse thumping in his ears, he turned and started shoving his way through the crowd that lay between him and the Denver train.

Her mother's curls tickled Lily's nose as they hugged one more time outside the first-class coach. Mick loaded her trunk inside, then popped open an umbrella to shelter the ladies from the worst of the thickening snow.

"I'll write," her mother said. "Just as I did before."

Lily laughed past the tears that were beginning to clog her throat. "Please write more about yourself and Mr. Grant and Emily and Annabelle, and less about the manners I still need to learn."

Her mother made a face at her. "All right, darling. I may throw in some advice here and there, just to stay in practice, but you can always disregard it."

"I'll consider everything you say very carefully." And disregard most anything related to wearing gloves or what times were most fashionable for walking. As soon as the train crossed the Mississippi, she would toss her gloves out the window.

Another hug, and then Lily climbed the iron steps of the car. She paused at the top to wave good-bye.

Then, taking a deep breath, she entered the comfortable coach and took a seat. Immediately she found herself squeezing her hands together in a knot and had to will herself to relax. Patience. She had to have patience. This might be only the first leg in a long journey. If Mason didn't show up in Denver this winter, she would have to continue to San Francisco to hunt for him there. Patience might be her only ally for a long, long time.

The floor beneath her feet trembled, and the view of the snowy city slid slowly sideways as the train started to move.

Mason saw Lily climbing the steps of the coach and turn to wave good-bye to someone in the crowd. "Lil—" he yelled, but the whistle's scream cut him off, and Lily turned to enter the car without looking in his direction.

Mason sprang up onto the snow-slick platform and pushed himself into a sprint. The still-open door to her car grew closer. Closer.

As the whistle screamed again, the long train shuddered, then began to roll.

No. He wasn't going to get within a few feet of her only to let her go.

Legs bunching beneath him, he sprang, launching himself into the carriage.

He didn't quite clear the doorway. His trailing boot caught the top step, and he plunged face-first onto the carriage's sodden carpet.

He lay there for a moment, trying to think past the jolt his brain had taken. Jesus Christ. That was probably the stupidest thing he had ever done in his life.

Unseen hands rolled him over. "Mason?"

Or perhaps it had been the smartest thing he had ever done. Lily was kneeling next to him, her big eyes wide.

He struggled up onto one elbow. "Oh, hello. I happened to see you at the station, and—"

Wait. He'd just thrown himself at a moving train. Why couldn't he get up the guts to be honest with her?

"What I meant to say was, I saw you and I couldn't let you go without telling you that I love you." The words sounded a little funny, perhaps because he'd never said them before, so he said them again, trying out the feel of them on his tongue. "Lily, I love you."

She stared at him, her mouth a perfect O. He waited a moment to see if she would respond, but he had apparently shocked her into muteness.

"I know it's unlikely, after the story I wrote about your grandfather"—the words were jamming in his throat in their rush to get out—"but do you think it's possible that you could love me again someday?" That sounded a little too open-ended. "Someday soon?" he added.

"Mason," she breathed, and launched herself at him. Before he could do more than put his arms around her, she was kissing him madly.

Thank God. He pulled her tight against him, letting a groan escape as he kissed her back. She felt and tasted so right. She tasted like forever.

A stifled gasp made him open his eyes and look

over her shoulder. Damn. There were six other people in this car, all staring at him and Lily tangled together on the wet carpet. He cleared his throat. "Um, maybe we should move to a seat."

Lily glanced behind her. "Oh. I'd forgotten we weren't alone." She didn't sound worried about it. This wasn't the same girl who had rattled on about "proper behavior" at inopportune moments—such as when he was trying to take her clothes off. He grinned for a moment as he remembered that.

Mason got to his feet, then helped Lily to hers. They slid into an empty seat far from the other passengers. He draped his arm over her shoulder and settled her against his side. Funny how something as simple as this half embrace with Lily was one of the things he had missed the most.

"Why are you in Boston?" she asked.

"To find you, of course. Why are you going to Denver?"

"To find *you*, of course." Her hands gripped in her skirt. "But I admit I did not expect that you would be there. I said terrible things to you. . . ." She gave herself a shake, as if casting off the memory. "So I was going to travel on to San Francisco, to find your friend Joseph. I hoped he might be able to help me locate you."

This woman had been ready to cross a continent to find him, armed with only a single friend's name? And not even his whole name?

"You—you—" Words wouldn't serve him, so he kissed her instead. She melted against his chest with a happy sigh.

Hours or years later, he came up for breath. "I don't think I can kiss you enough," he said. "I think it would be impossible."

"Well, we can spend a lot of time testing that theory, if you like." She snuggled closer to him, and his chest pocket made a crinkling noise. "What's that?" she asked, prodding the pocket.

"That letter you wrote your mother. The one that was a joke."

"It wasn't a joke," Lily said softly. "And we knew it, even if we couldn't admit it then."

Yes, he had known it, which was why he'd kept it after she had rejected him. And he had read the letter almost every day during these past months. On days when he believed his chances of winning Lily back were very slim, he would read it two or three times, trying to boost his spirits.

"So, who are you writing for these days?" she asked. "I searched for your name in all the likely magazines but couldn't find it."

"I'm writing for myself. A memoir of my travels, I guess is how you would describe it. I've been in San Francisco, writing the thing, for three months now."

"Three months straight?"

"Yes." He grinned at her. "I can now stay in one place for more than a week without breaking into a rash. I think you somehow yanked the wanderlust out of me."

That was as good a setup as he was going to get. "So, uh . . . Well, I do have a house in San Francisco that I now live in."

She nodded.

"And, um, while I don't want to entirely give up traveling, I'm happy enough to stay around. In the same place." He should have practiced this. He sounded like an idiot.

A smile started to quiver at the corners of her mouth, and she nodded again.

"So . . ." A deep breath. "Will you marry me?"

Her barely concealed smile broke out into the open. "Mason Donnelly, I'd be overjoyed to marry you. How soon?"

"As soon as possible." He felt he had to add: "You'll probably want to invite your family—"

"Oh, no. Some of them are still quite angry at you. I don't want yelling at our wedding."

He remembered the blond girl slamming the door in his face only an hour before. "Right."

"Also . . ." She wrinkled her nose. ". . . I should tell you a few things. I'm probably going to be disinherited by my grandfather for marrying you. And I'm illegitimate."

The first wasn't a surprise, but the second— "So you're not really a Highfill?" he asked hopefully.

"No, I'm still a Highfill. My aunt Evaline is my real mother. But you'll never believe who my father is. It's Dickon."

Dickon had known Lily's aunt—Mason recalled that. And he remembered Dickon's cautionary tale about his own youthful love for a woman not of his social class. Clearly it hadn't been merely a platonic love between them.

He couldn't resist the urge to tease her. "Penniless

and illegitimate? Hmm, I think I'm being taken advantage of."

She narrowed her eyes at him. "If you back out now, Mason Donnelly, you're in for a lot of trouble."

"I have a better idea." He dropped his voice. "Let's give our fellow passengers a kiss they'll talk about for days."

Laughing, she flung her arms around his neck and kissed him and kissed him and kissed him. . . .

"Mason!" Lily hollered from the bottom of the stairs, then flew up them. She had gotten into the habit of giving him a few seconds' warning before she rushed in so that he could jot down whatever idea was floating through his brain. They'd had an argument or two early on about her making him lose his train of thought and about him not giving her his full attention, but they had managed to find a good solution. She paused at the top of the stairs to give him another second of writing time, then swung left into his office.

He lay down his pen, capped his ink bottle, and grinned at her. "What's the excitement? Fire? Flood? Indians?"

"I just received a letter from my mother." She handed the sheet of expensive stationery to him. "Read the last section."

He scanned her mother's loopy handwriting, then glanced up. "Your grandfather plans to disinherit you, as you thought." He frowned. "I know we expected it, but that's hardly fair. It's not your fault that I wrote the article or that your grandfather got greedy—"

"No, not that part." She leaned over the desk and pointed. "That."

His eyes darted over the final paragraph. "Your mother's coming to visit for at least a month this summer." He pushed the letter back to her and smiled. "You must be happy."

"Delighted!" And still amazed. During her regular correspondence with her mother, Lily had issued several invitations to come visit, but she had not really expected her to accept: She never had when Lily was living in Denver all those years, and Evaline had teased her mother more than once while they were all in Boston about her deep fear of train travel.

Crossing to the window, Lily looked out over the bay. "She's going to have a wonderful time here, I just know it. How could she not? The whole city seems to vibrate day and night with excitement. And the view . . ." She crossed her arms and hugged herself, then sighed. She had never imagined that she'd fall in love so quickly with San Francisco. Of course, waking up every day beside her husband contributed to that. When you woke up with a smile, the world seemed lovely.

When she looked back at Mason, he was giving her a smoldering stare that made her pulse pound. "The view is spectacular," he agreed. He pushed his chair away from the desk and reached out to her. "Come over here so I can see it a little better."

She plunked herself down on his lap and threw her arms around his neck. After a half dozen long, hot kisses, she was ready to burst into flames right in his arms.

"Bed?" he murmured, his breath grazing the tops of her breasts, which he'd just exposed with a few flicks of her shirt buttons.

Bed was only across the hall, but it felt like a continent away. "Desk?" she countered.

He laughed, gripped her around the waist, and lifted her so she perched on the edge of the desktop. "You're a wild woman."

"You make me a wild woman."

"No, you always were one. I think I simply encouraged it."

She didn't want to slow down their rush to make love on the desk, but she had to ask. "And what do I encourage in you?"

"Confidence." He nipped her shoulder lightly. "Contentment." A few more buttons came undone, and he peeled her blouse down her arms. "And the overwhelming desire to procreate."

"Hmm, a wild woman and a man with procreation on his mind." She laughed and held her arms out to him. "Sounds like a perfect match."

Author's Note

One of the most exciting—and nasty—fossil-hunting competitions was the bitter battle between Othniel Charles Marsh and Edward Drinker Cope, who sent out survey teams into the West during the last few decades of the 1800s. The rivalry went beyond mere professional competitiveness, with Cope once caught trying to pry open some of Marsh's crates, and survey teams from both sides even engaging in a bout of stone throwing. Between the two, thousands of fossils were uncovered, named, and cataloged, but often done with such haste in order to gain the glory attached to each new discovery that the same type of fossil was "discovered" several times over, often by the same man, leading to cataloguing problems that linger today.

I've taken a few liberties with the times and places of fossil discoveries, and of course Highfill's expedition is a fictional one. However, in 1887 a U.S. government geologist named Charles Whitman Cross did discover fossilized horn cores in the general area where Highfill's camp was located. The horn cores were the first discovery of a new group of horned dinosaurs called ceratopsians, one of which is the triceratops.

Sapphires have been found in Chaffee County, Colorado, but few of gemstone quality. Gem collectors would have better luck, as Dickon says, in Montana and Idaho.

Believe me: Gem hunting can be addictive. Having spent hours sifting through gravel at a Montana sapphire mine during a recent summer vacation, giving myself high fives when I found even the smallest gemstone, I understand the excitement!

Turn the page for a sneak peek
at the next steamy Western by

Adrianne Wood

Available from Pocket Books in 2013

Really, it was almost too easy.

Skirt weighed down by the gold coins she'd sewn into the hem of her dress the night before, and moving awkwardly under two layers of coats, Emily Highfill Grant still managed to dodge the porters on the train platform and haul herself up into her grandfather's Pullman car without being seen—or at least stopped. She eased the door shut behind her with a puff of relief and exertion and then looked around.

Inside the car, one oil lamp was lit, allowing her to see enough to avoid bumping into the gilt-edged chairs and table. Not much had changed since she, her sister, her mother, and four servants had traveled to New York from Boston last week in the private rail-car. The interior looked neater now than when they'd stepped down onto the platform and into the hustle and noise of New York—somehow her sister Annabelle had managed to impose chaos in the single-day trip from metropolis to metropolis. But the luxurious arm-chairs, the paintings on the wall, and even the smell of the oil lamp were as familiar as Emily's favorite pair of walking shoes.

Good—they hadn't removed the tablecloth on the card table. Although card playing wasn't considered proper recreation for young ladies, Emily's elder sister Lily had taught the girls games such as euchre and pitch last winter, and they had played for several hours on the ride to New York.

The long tablecloth would hide her admirably.

A whistle outside blew a long blast, making Emily's heart jump, and the noise level on the platform ticked up. The train was at least two hours away from departure, but not everyone still trusted the timetables to be correct, and passengers began to put themselves and their belongings on the train.

Her mother could arrive at any moment.

Peeling off both coats first, Emily got onto her hands and knees and crawled under the card table. Ugh. Grit clung to her palms, and dust crept up her nostrils. Well, it would only be for a few hours. Once they were well under way, and after Emily revealed herself to her mother, she could go back to sitting in an armchair instead of hiding like a sneak thief.

The card table had been pushed up against a wall, so Emily tucked her coats behind her and leaned back against the wall. If it weren't dirty, and dark, and cramped, and a bit too warm, this nook would be a nice place to spend some time alone, thinking her own thoughts. . . .

Emily sat up straight, knocking her head on the table-top. Blinking didn't help her see more—it was black as midnight under the table. The cloth, like everything of her grandfather's, was top-notch quality and woven tight.

Beneath her bottom, the train shuddered like a hypothermia victim. They were moving, and at a fast clip, too. How long had she been asleep?

Outside the tablecloth, the car was silent.

Emily leaned forward, grimaced against the pins and needles that bit her stiffened limbs, pressed her cheek against the gritty carpet, and lifted the edge of the tablecloth.

The windows were black, and nighttime had fallen. She must've been dead asleep for hours, and they were clearly well outside New York City. The lamps had been turned down so low that shadows slept in the corners of the car. Perhaps everyone had already gone to bed in the small chambers off the salon.

Waking her mother from a sound sleep was not how she'd imagined revealing herself, but she couldn't wait until morning.

Emily's stomach rumbled. There was another good reason to announce her presence. She'd napped through at least two meals.

Flipping up the tablecloth, she scooted out into the open and took a deep breath of nondusty air.

A pair of bare feet thumped down inches from her left hand. Emily shrieked. She whipped her head around and looked up into a face she didn't recognize. Emily promptly upgraded her shriek into a full-blown scream.

Another scream—not her own but familiar nonetheless—tried to rupture her right eardrum.

Emily whipped her head around again, almost smashing her nose against her younger sister Annabelle's face. Where had Annabelle come from? Well, it didn't matter—not when they were under seige from some . . . some . . . *stranger*. Emily reached behind her, grabbed Annabelle's hand, and dragged the two of them across the length of the car, where she pulled Annabelle behind her and twisted to stare at the man. A man who should not have been there.

"Who are you?" Emily demanded. "You are in the wrong car, sir." He looked more like a ruffian than a gentleman, with his bare feet and his shirt unbuttoned and showing more male chest than she'd ever seen in her life, but her mother would be deeply disappointed if Emily couldn't retain her good manners even in a crisis.

A tiny part of her—the part of her that wasn't gibbering with a mixture of indignation and terror—pointed out that she had smuggled herself on the train to gain more adventure in her life, and she was already getting a nice large dose of it.

"Who are *you*?" he countered. "And I must disagree—I am very much in the right car. I hired it only thirty minutes before the train departed the station. *You* are in the wrong car, lady."

Somehow "lady" coming out of his mouth didn't sound nearly as respectful as "sir" had coming from hers.

"Did you think to steal a free ride in an empty car?" he asked.

Emily shook her head, more to unscramble the

muddle in her head than to reply to his question. She looked around frantically. Yes, this was the right Pullman car. Over the desk in the far corner hung an oil painting of her, her two sisters, and her parents that had been commissioned seventeen years ago, when Emily had been two and Annabelle a newborn, and beneath Emily's feet was an autumn-hued rug her grandfather had ordered specially only last summer.

More confident, she said, "Sir, I am afraid you are mistaken—"

"The lady who was going to take this car changed her mind at the last minute," he interrupted—rather rudely. "There was not enough time to decouple the car before the train was scheduled to depart, so it was rented to me."

"Oh." It made hideous sense. Her mother hated train travel with a passion. She'd been pale throughout the daylong trip from Boston to New York, and she'd spent most of the past week lying on her bed in the hotel, a cool cloth pressed to her eyes. Emily simply hadn't considered that her mother would refuse to continue her trip. Emily's sister Lily was expecting a baby in a month, and their mother had been adamant that she would travel to San Francisco to be there at the birth. Apparently that adamantiousness—was that a word?—had evaporated after a single day of train travel.

"Oh," Emily said again. And then she didn't know what else to say, so she looked at the stranger more closely.

The low lamplight concealed most details—for

instance, she found it difficult to judge his age precisely—but the way he stood with his hands propped on his hips, uncaring that his shirt was open, and the impatient manner in which his dark eyes drilled into her spoke volumes about his personality. If the meek were to inherit the earth, he'd be lucky to get a measly half acre in the deal.

"Emily," Annabelle said breathily from behind her, "introduce us, please."

She'd completely forgotten about Annabelle. It was an unusual thing to do—Annabelle loved being the center of attention and took pains to stake a claim on that spot—but apparently Annabelle had correctly deduced that being quiet for a change was the smart thing to do. At least until now.

Emily flicked a glance over her shoulder. Annabelle was looking at the inconvenient stranger like he was a French dessert.

When Emily turned back, the stranger was, finally, buttoning up his shirt.

Somehow that gesture, that minor attempt at decency in an awkward and bizarre situation, gave her the courage to say what she did next. "We are two young ladies escaping to a new destiny, and we throw ourselves on your mercy, sir."

Emily actually had no idea why Annabelle was there, but her declaration was true for herself. She'd seized her mother's trip west as her best opportunity to break away from her old life filled with boring expectations.

These first few waking moments of her new life had proven to be anything but boring.

He didn't look impressed by her speech. "Names?" he said, and buttoned the final top button of his shirt. Emily got the impression from his brief grimace that he rarely used that button, but she would have concealed as much skin as possible if Annabelle were ogling her so voraciously, too.

"Emily." She pointed at herself. "And my sister Anna." She pointed at Annabelle.

Annabelle, bless her heart, didn't blink at having to don a childhood nickname, though it must have been a blow to her dignity.

The stranger waited, clearly expecting Emily to supply her surname.

"And you are . . . ?" she asked quickly.

"Lucien." And he raised his eyebrows a fraction, daring her.

She took a step forward, closer to him. From the way his eyebrows popped up all the way, she knew she'd surprised him. "Mister Lucien, we are in the unfortunate position of needing to entrust our good reputations to a man we do not know. We must know more of you than your first name." She paused. "And at the same time, we must not tell you more than we already have."

For as soon as he knew their identities, he would put them off at the first train stop, send a telegram to their grandfather or their stepfather, and leave them there to be picked up and hauled back home like misplaced baggage.

She had gotten on this train. And she was going to stay on it until she reached San Francisco.

"Are you always so dramatic?" Lucien asked dryly. "Or is this a special performance just for me?"

Emily smiled at him. No one had ever accused her of being dramatic before. "Just you," she assured him.

He stared at her, and then the corner of his mouth quirked up. "All right. Have it your way, Miss Emily the Mysterious. I am Lucien Delatour."

The name was familiar, but Emily couldn't pinpoint why. "Are you a businessman?" Her stepfather and grandfather were well known among the most successful industrialists in the entire country. It would be quite unfortunate if Lucien Delatour traveled in the same circles as they did.

"Isn't everyone?"

"I'm not," Annabelle said coyly.

"Indeed," Lucien replied with a little bow.

Emily was going to press him for more details, but her stomach growled at that moment in an embarrassingly noisy fashion. Well, in for a penny . . . "Would you happen to have any food?" she asked.

"Your wish is my command." Lucien padded out of the salon on his bare feet and disappeared into the small compartment that held the pantry. Hopefully a well-stocked pantry that included many of her mother's favorite foods, such as biscuits and lemon curd. The thin door snicked shut behind him.

Emily rounded on Annabelle. "What are you doing here?" she hissed.

"I saw you sneak out of the hotel, and so I followed. I thought you might be meeting a man." Annabelle sniffed, and her lovely brunette curls bounced around her equally lovely face. It was a face that artists in the public parks chased after, begging Annabelle to sit for them. "I might have known better. And then once you do find yourself practically alone with a man, you ask him for *food*?"

Emily put her hand on her stomach. "I was hungry!"

"This is why you've remained unmarried, Emily."

Because she ate when she needed to? Surely a good husband would want an intelligent wife, not one who forgot to eat and fainted on a regular basis.

Annabelle settled into one of the plush seats. "Where are we going?" she asked, sounding completely unconcerned.

"*I* am going to San Francisco. Where are you going?"

"With you, I expect. We should not tell Mr. Delatour who we are, though. He'll send for Mother or Grandfather to come get us."

"Precisely!" Emily heaved a sigh of relief and suffered another furious stomach growl.

The door to the salon swung open, and Lucien appeared, balancing a tray practically overflowing with bread, butter, and cheese.

"Let me handle him," Annabelle whispered, and then flowed gracefully to her feet. "My, what a feast!" she gushed. "You did a wonderful job choosing the food."

Emily was fairly sure she managed to not obviously roll her eyes. Well, if Annabelle could wrap Lucien Delatour around her little finger, it would make the whole journey much easier, she supposed.

Lucien stepped all the way into the room and placed

the tray on the card table. "I'm sorry, Miss Anna. This is for your emaciated sister. Did you want some victuals as well?"

The food he'd brought in could have fed four people. Had her stomach truly growled that loudly?

"Thank you," Emily said, and took a slice of bread and cheese. Then she proceeded to eat as much as she could, while her sister babbled away. Lucien watched both of them with an expression on his face that she couldn't quite identify but thought might be amusement from the way his eyes occasionally crinkled in the corners.

Lucien Delatour. A French name, of course, which loosely translated to "Light of the Tower." He was not light in any way, with walnut-brown hair trimmed fashionably short, dark eyes, and brows that she thought could be mightily intimidating, and skin that had spent a fair amount of time in the summer sun. Only his feet, still bare and bright against the dark-hued carpet, were light in any way. Presumably he didn't frolic with his boots off very often.

The "tower" part of his name suited him. While he was not alarmingly tall, he held himself in a way that added several imaginary inches to his height. A most effective tool to convey superiority, or at the very least confidence.

Her grandfather Charles Bertrand Highfill held himself the exact same way.

Emily swallowed the last bit of bread she could fit inside her happily full stomach, waited for Annabelle to finish her monologue on how tedious she found all the horse manure on the New York streets to be, and asked, "Are you a self-made man, Mr. Delatour?"

He nodded, then drawled, "My mother and father had an early hand in the process as well, I understand."

Humph. He was either making fun of her or trying to embarrass her. Well, Highfills were made of sterner stuff than that. She blinked at him innocently. "Oh, no, Mr. Delatour; you must have been misinformed. *I* understand that hands are rarely essential to that process."

Again, his eyes crinkled. "Not essential, no—but certainly helpful."

Annabelle was staring at Emily like she'd decided to douse her head with kerosene and light her hair on fire. *"What?"* Emily mouthed at her when Lucien turned away to snag a piece of cheese for himself, but Annabelle shook her head.

Fo[...]
Tem[...]
Ad[...]

**Visit Poc[...]
an all-new v[...]
Fantasy and [...]**

DISCARD

- Exclusive access to the hottest urban fantasy and romance titles!

- Read and share reviews on the latest books!

- Live chats with your favorite romance authors!

- Vote in online polls!

 www.PocketAfterDark.com

26119